THE KINSELLA CHRONICLES
BOOK ONE

A FATEFUL PROMISE

THE KINSELLA CHRONICLES
BOOK ONE

A FATEFUL PROMISE

GERALD WARNER

Marble Hill
London

First published in 2025 by
Marble Hill Publishers
Flat 58 Macready House
75 Crawford Street
London W1H 5LP
www.marblehillpublishers.co.uk

A CIP catalogue record for this book is available
from the British Library.

ISBN: 9781068360817
E-book ISBN: 9781068360824

Typeset in Abobe Janson Pro
Printed and bound by IngramSpark
Text design by Paul Harpin

To Iain Burns,
in gratitude

CHAPTER I

THE boy walked slowly up the boreen, avoiding the wet grass in the centre and stepping on the large, smooth stones in the ruts on either side that were drying out after the brief summer shower. A wisp of steam rose from them as the rainwater evaporated in the hot sun, distilling a rank, metallic smell from the vegetation. He tried, out of whimsy, to set his foot on the dry centre of each stone and slashed desultorily at the high grass verge with a hazel switch. The solitary cloud that had emptied itself so suddenly had gone and the sky was blue and untroubled again. All evidence of the downpour was fast disappearing. Teardrops of rain hung from each red bell of the early blooming fuchsia that hedged the steep lane; soon they would fall from the drooping blossom and be absorbed by the thirsty soil. Ancient cowpats that littered the ground had temporarily been saturated to the appearance of grotesque toadstools, but already they were being baked back into their former desiccated state. The crooked, crumbling boreen grew steeper as he neared its summit. Its twin ruts that had been made by rude carts long ago were kept bald by the passage of pedestrians and cattle: there was no other traffic on this road now.

At the crest of the hill the way was barred by a wooden gate, fringed by dense clumps of nettles. These posed no threat to the boy today, for he was still wearing jodhpurs – an old pair outgrown by an elder brother, skilfully cut down to his size by Bridie Byrne who was a wonder-worker with needle and thread, as everyone agreed. He knew he should have changed back into his short trousers after he had returned his pony to the stables, but negotiating this bed of nettles would have been more hazardous if he had obeyed the rules. He clambered over the five-barred gate (it was a point of honour to

1

climb it like an adventurer, rather than open it like a girl) and into the field beyond. Now it was only a matter of skirting a cluster of stunted hawthorns on his left and he knew the vista that would open before him – the view he had been looking forward to savouring, the special landscape that, in the marrow of his being, meant home. He walked round the bushes that were an outcrop of the vegetation hedging the boreen, looked across the fields and woods – and there it was.

The castle had never looked more beautiful. The late afternoon sun bathed it in a warm glow that seemed to radiate from its stonework. The square keep and ancillary parts of the older building gleamed golden, as the sunlight glistened on the yellow sandstone, still moist from the recent rain; to the right, the granite of the great round tower and the other slightly later additions glinted silver. Fusing this alloy of stone was the emerald sheen of the now wet ivy that straggled over half the surface area of the castle, like an unfinished coat of paint. Lesser turrets protruded haphazardly from the confusion of crenellations and machicolations (as Uncle Dermod had taught him to call them) which embellished the gothic extravagance that was his home. The declining sun was reflected on arched windows, so that they shone opaquely like cheval glasses tilted to the light; the walls were studded with cross-shaped loopholes, some framing smaller windows, others blind ornamentation in the stonework. It was the scale and proportions of the castle that gave it dignity: they were of a mediæval vastness that lent the structure credibility. He knew (again, from Uncle Dermod) that the main part of the house had been built from sandstone quarried in the west of the county, whereas the drum tower and adjoining wing added a generation later was of granite from a quarry some miles to the east. It was the original stone that had given the castle its name, which some claimed had belonged to an older building on the same site:

Lissanore – the Fort of Gold. Although the crested writing paper in the house bore the official address 'Castle Kinsella', to everyone in the county – and even the family – it remained familiarly and affectionately Lissanore.

He was accustomed, when he reached this place, to sit down on the grass for a while and gaze at the house and surrounding scenery; but the ground was still wet and Uncle Ulick (another of his father's brothers – the quartet whose combined admonitions and prejudices comprised much of his education) had often impressed on him the dangers of sitting on damp grass. So, he contented himself with standing there on the crest of the hill and contemplating his favourite view. This was the only point within accessible range of the castle from which one could look down on Lissanore. Even then, being built on an eminence where the ground rose gradually from the river, the house was just slightly lower than his vantage point: it was like gazing across a shallow valley for a distance of a quarter of a mile.

When he had looked his fill, he began the slow, convoluted descent by small ridges in the pasture made originally by cattle and rabbits. From a distance, some cows looked uninterestedly in his direction; a few that had sat down to preserve a dry place for themselves when the shower erupted remained recumbent, as if acknowledging that nothing of further significance would occur that day. When he reached the lower ground, he struck out at a more robust pace until, after crossing two more fences, he arrived at a trim lane that would lead him into the Lissanore demesne. Diverging from that path at the usual place, he took a well-worn short cut through the rhododendrons that brought him onto the avenue, a few hundred yards from the gate lodge. The curve of the drive at first hid the house from view, but gradually glimpses of its great castellated walls appeared through the rhododendrons and towering oaks and beeches that lined the avenue. Then the trees abruptly ended, while the rhododendrons petered out into a tamer shrubbery, and the castle, which had appeared to be hemmed in by foliage, was suddenly revealed as being fronted by a generous open space.

The area before the front door, to which a flight of half a dozen steps gave access, was occupied by a broad sweep of gravel, large enough to allow a number of carriages or, more recently, motor vehicles to manoeuvre. It was bordered by a broad grass verge, well trimmed and interspersed with shrubs and flowerbeds, separated by a post-and-rail fence from a large paddock that provided a vista of open ground stretching towards distant woodland. This expansive view dispelled the claustrophobic impression given to visitors approaching Lissanore for the first time via the heavily wooded avenue.

The boy stopped in his tracks and stared at an intruding feature in this familiar landscape. A large, highly polished motor car was parked in front of the castle door; its engine was running and the late afternoon sun reduced to silhouette the figure of a uniformed chauffeur at the wheel. It was much grander than any vehicle belonging to regular visitors. Feeling the urge to reconnoitre, he decided to make a detour past the front of the house, on his way to the rear where his illicit destination was the kitchen. So, swinging his hazel switch with studied nonchalance (he was, after all, a member of the household), he strolled across the gravel on a course that would bring him close to the imposing vehicle, while affecting indifference to its presence. He hoped to be able to examine it out of the corner of his eye and to take in further details with one swift, unobtrusive glance.

Unfortunately, as he approached the car he realized this reconnaissance strategy was doomed to failure since the sun, still bright and warm though now low in the sky, was blinding him. When he drew level with the burnished coachwork, however, the shadow cast by the house momentarily dimmed the glare of the sunlight so that he caught a glimpse of someone seated in the back. He was startled to see it was a girl, apparently about his own age, who turned to look at him as he passed. Her eyes met his in the solemn scrutiny peculiar to children. He gained only a blurred impression of her – generally, that she was pretty; specifically, that there was something very striking about her eyes. Then he blushed to realize he had stopped and was staring at her – gawking like a boor. An instant later, this guilty sensation intensified when the chauffeur threw open his door and began to climb out.

The boy hurried on across the gravel, ashamed to be warned off – as he thought was happening – by a strange servant in front of his own home. Yet almost immediately he knew, by the crunch of heavy footsteps receding rather than approaching, that the chauffeur was not pursuing him. By now he was walking close to the wall of the house and had reached a point where a large square tower jutted out. From the cover provided by the base of the tower, he peered back to see what was happening. The driver who, he now saw, wore a mulberry livery and high boots had walked round the front of the motor car to the passenger side, facing the house, and was holding open the rear door. It was evident that the door of the castle had also been opened, for voices raised in polite farewells could now be heard and his mother and father appeared on the front steps, escorting an elaborately dressed lady. Behind them shambled the shabby, black-coated figure of Corristeen the butler, making a rare excursion into the open air. His parents accompanied the visitor to her car, so that scraps of conversation floated on the air.

'…Very pleasant surprise… Delightful to see you…' This from his father.

'…That's right – in Grafton Street, you can't miss it… I don't get up to town often enough… You won't forget – luncheon on the fifteenth… Look forward to that…' His mother was either full of enthusiasm for the visitor or was going through the social ritual that she described as 'making an effort'.

The frustrating thing was, although these bursts of chatter in his parents' familiar voices were interspersed with deep-toned responses from the departing guest, not one word she said was intelligible from the distance at which he lurked. Finally there sounded a slamming of doors, a crescendo of goodbyes and the large vehicle, gleaming in the sunlight, lurched into motion across the gravel and slowly disappeared behind a screen of laurels and rhododendrons, down the avenue. His parents made their way back into the house, followed arthritically by Corristeen, wearing his most officious air of senior retainer. Then came the heavy sound of the front door closing.

What had been happening? Who was the exotic visitor? Immobilized by thought in the recess of the wall, he pondered the scene he had just witnessed. The lady had been someone important; he knew that, not just because she had an enormous motor car and a chauffeur in a mulberry uniform and high boots, but from his parents' demeanour. Papa had seemed more – well, alert – than usual and Mummie had really been making a terrific effort. It was all quite exciting. He felt an urgent need to know who the visitor was. The obvious solution was to go immediately to his parents and ask them; but he had an intuition they would be in an inaccessible mood, discussing the visitor between themselves – 'holding a post-mortem', as Mummie called it – and would reply to his questions with bantering evasions. Grown-ups could be quite rotten that way. No: a moment's consideration persuaded him he would get the best results by going directly to the intelligence centre of the household – they would already be discussing the matter knowledgeably in the kitchen.

So, he cut round by the side of the house and skirted the rear of the building until he arrived at the corner diametrically distant from his starting point. Here was the cluttered yard, where a couple of dim-looking youths were making heavy weather of some simple task. A gated path led off to the stables, where the horses' heads protruded from their loose-boxes, tossing irritably to rid themselves of the tormenting flies, impatient to be let out, as they knew they soon would be, now that the heat of the day had passed. Nearby, in the ivy-screened wall of the house, was a door that led into a long, stone-flagged passage lined with a scullery and small rooms stacked with disused domestic implements – an old mangle, rusty buckets, a hip-bath with a large hole in it – the discreet route he favoured for illicit visits to the kitchen.

When he cautiously opened the kitchen door and peered round it, he knew at once his surmise had been correct. Although the kitchen was empty, in the servants' hall that lay just beyond, through a large open archway, the entire indoors staff was assembled round the table at which they took their meals, gossiped and aired their grievances. Corristeen the butler sat in state at the head of the table. His tousled grey hair surrounded a tonsure of baldness, like a bird's nest with an egg in the centre; his face was unevenly shaven, leaving patches of white stubble, especially around his chin, and his black tailcoat was stained with specimens of past menus and flecked on the shoulders with a powdering of scurf. He was flanked by the cook, with the housemaids, kitchen maids and Liam, the jack-of-all-trades who claimed the honorary title of footman, dispersed around the board according to seniority. Bridie Byrne, whose status within the domestic hierarchy defied definition, was circulating, pouring the indispensable tea from an outsize pot.

'Fo'c'sle council,' the boy thought, the phrase from *Treasure Island* coming into his head at this sight. No one had noticed him, so he slipped into the cathedral-like kitchen, closing the door behind him as silently as possible, tiptoed into the next room and stood stock-still in the shadow of a large dresser festooned with plates.

'Are you sure of that, Mr Corristeen?' the cook was asking, in a tone that posed no real challenge to the butler, but was intended to flatter with incredulity.

'Sure, is it? As sure as my name is Calasanctius Corristeen. A real viva voce duchess, no less!' (Corristeen was a man of weighty learning who punctuated his conversation with Latin and other impressive foreign phrases.) 'Wasn't it meself announced her at the drawing-room door?'

'What did you say, Mr Corristeen?' Liam expressed professional interest.

'I felt it recumbent upon me to do the ould house credit,' the butler said in solemn tones, 'seein' the grand lady that was in it. So, I held meself as upright as a man a martyr to the arthuritis can hope to stand and shouted so loud ye could have heard me in Burras town: "Her Honour the Duchess of Shaladavicky!" Himself knocked over an ashtray and Herself nearly lepped out of her skin.'

An admiring murmur went round the table.

'Was that lady a duchess?' asked the boy breathlessly, abandoning discretion.

'Master Philip! What are you doing here?' The cook, who privately encouraged his visits, was not in the least surprised to see him, but she was anxious to convey the opposite impression to the butler.

'I saw her motor car at the door,' said Philip.

'I seen it too.' Liam spoke excitedly. 'That yoke was a Hispano-Suiza, Mr Corristeen.'

'One o' them filt'y, evil-smellin' machines is much like another,' said Corristeen sourly. He was displeased at the conversation being diverted from his own narrative to technicalities beyond his ken.

'What was the Duchess wearing, Mr Corristeen?' asked Bridie Byrne, anxious to restore the butler's authority and good humour.

'Just what ye'd expect a lady of the Quality out of Spain to be wearin','Corristeen replied evasively, his knowledge of female apparel being equal to his motoring expertise.

'Was she wearing diamonds and jewels?' Philip was anxious to determine this important point.

'She was, o' course.'

'How many?'

'Just as many as made clear she belonged to the high polloi, without smotherin' herself like somethin' out of the front row of the chorus.' Corristeen gave his authoritative verdict then addressed the cup of tea that the cook had just discreetly flavoured for him with something out of a small bottle whose label was obscured by her beefy hand. Between slurps, he yielded to his feelings of triumph. 'A real, live duchess, be the hokey. That'll show them beggars on horseback at Nowlanstown an' Ballymore. Heh, heh.'

A moment's silence, laced with dismay, greeted this claim.

'But, Mr Corristeen,' said Liam, 'aren't the boys after burnin' out Nowlanstown five years ago?'

'And Ballymore's shut up like a parson's strongbox,' said Bridie Byrne, 'with never a soul to be seen.'

Corristeen looked nonplussed for a moment, but made a speedy recovery.

'O' course I know that – what kind of an eejit d'ye take me for? I'm just sayin' it would have been a poke in the eye for all them black Protestants to see a grand Spanish duchess in the drawing room of Castle Kinsella.' (It was a matter of punctilio with Corristeen always to refer to the house by its official title.)

This view was endorsed with general gratification.

'They're real holy Catholics, the Spaniards, aren't they, Mr Corristeen?' asked Angela, the junior housemaid, who was rumoured to have a vocation to be a nun.

'So I have always heard tell,' said the butler gravely.

'I don't understand.' Philip voiced his frustration. 'What was a Spanish duchess doing here? How does she know Mummie and Papa?'

'That's not for us to conjecturize about, Master Philip,' said Corristeen with exaggerated humility. 'You'll have to ask Himself – I mean, ask your father. You could do it now,' he added slyly, calculating that the sooner the boy gleaned this information, the more promptly it could be extracted from him.

'Yes, I think I will.' Philip understood he had been entrusted with a commission.

Clearly there was nothing further to be discovered from the kitchen community. He would have to try a frontal attack on his parents. His preoccupation with the distinguished visitor had distracted him from the scones and newly baked sponge cake that sat on the table, as he now realized.

'May I have a piece of cake? Oh, thank you, it's delicious…'

His voice grew muffled as he crammed the cake into his mouth and hurried out through the kitchen, up the service stairs, past the holy of holies – Corristeen's pantry – then through a green baize-covered door, along a carpeted passage and into the front hall of the castle. A murmur of voices came from behind the drawing-room door, ending with a light laugh which he recognized as his mother's. He knocked on the door and heard a summons to enter. His parents were standing in front of the french windows that were open onto the terrace at the rear of the house. His mother was wearing a light summer frock that made few concessions to fashion; it was more redolent of the style of ten years earlier, apart from its shorter length. His father had forsaken his all-seasons tweeds, in deference to the hot weather, and was sporting a light linen suit that somehow made him look younger.

'Hello, Philip.' He stroked his well-trimmed moustache absently. 'What have you been up to?'

'Oh, nothing much, Papa.'

'Philip,' said his mother, as he had known she would, 'please go and change into your short trousers. I do not want you sprawling on the furniture in those filthy jodhpurs.' (Balzac, her extravagantly privileged terrier, was at that moment reclining luxuriously on a nearby sofa.)

'Yes, Mummie. Just in a moment.'

'Not in a moment – right now.'

'But, Mummie, I want to hear about the visitor. Was she really a duchess?'

'She was a *duquesa*, in fact,' said his father.

'Oh.' He felt crestfallen. 'I heard she was a duchess.'

'A *duquesa* is a Spanish duchess, Philip,' explained his mother, darting a reproachful smile at her husband.

'Gosh! I wish I had met her.'

'You may still meet her,' his father said. 'She is coming to luncheon in a fortnight's time.'

'She only called in, on impulse, on her way to Cork.' His mother enlarged on the theme. 'She had tea with us, very briefly, and left. She seemed to be in rather a hurry. So, I invited her to stop here on the way back and stay to luncheon. If she keeps her word – though I gather she leads a very busy life (there was just a glimmer of good-natured malice in her voice) – you should meet her then.'

'Is she a friend of yours?'

'Until today,' said his father, taking out his pipe and beginning the long ritual of lighting it, 'we had never set eyes on her.' He paused to concentrate on his tobacco pouch. 'But there is a connexion, of course. Her late husband was one of the directors of the Bank.' The note of reverence with which all Kinsellas referred to the Mexican and South American bank that, for generations, had sustained their stylish existence entered his voice. As if stimulated by this allusion to life-giving wealth, a flame flared up in the bowl of Count Kinsella's pipe.

'She wasn't very forthcoming about the state of affairs at the Bank,' his wife observed.

'She probably knows very little about it,' said Philip's father, expelling smoke contentedly. 'Since her husband's death, all she will have done is collect dividends, or whatever. She never had any role in the Bank's affairs: he was the one who inherited an interest in it.'

'You would know if there was any problem, wouldn't you?' his wife pressed him.

'To be honest, not necessarily. Not unless it was a real crisis.'

'Last year –'

'Last year was a hiccough – nothing more. It was all sorted out quite satisfactorily. As you know, I have always said we must learn to regard the Bank as no more than a minor asset, with the uncertain state of world affairs since the War. We need to be independent of our income – such as it now is – from the Bank. Anyhow,' his tone became rallying, 'did the *Duquesa* strike you as a woman on the verge of penury?'

Mummie laughed outright at that. Philip had prudently remained silent, from the first mention of the Bank: he knew that, on the rare occasions when grown-ups discussed anything relating to money in front of him, it was fatal to intervene or ask questions. Now he took advantage of the lighter atmosphere created by his father's last remark to re-enter the conversation.

'I saw a girl in the motor car.'

'Did you?' His father, uninterested, was poking inside the bowl of his pipe, which was not functioning to his satisfaction. 'Must have been her maid, I suppose.'

'No, I mean a little girl, about my own age.' He hated identify-

12

ing himself so emphatically as a child, but the desire for information was paramount.

'Oh,' said Countess Kinsella, 'that must have been her daughter – now that I think about it, I noticed a child in the motor car. Her mother only mentioned her just as she was leaving, otherwise I should have brought her in and given her some tea. I'm afraid I can't remember her name.' She turned to her husband with the same mildly malicious smile she had worn a moment earlier. 'There was certainly no maid with her. Do you remember the tirade we endured, because her maid had a migraine and had to be left behind?'

'I do indeed.' Papa gestured with his pipe. 'She clearly thought it indecently presumptuous of the woman to fall ill.'

'But you can't remember her daughter's name?'

'No, my dear, but since you are clearly smitten, I shall make a point of finding out when – *if* –' his mother qualified the promise, 'they come back in two weeks' time.'

Philip's cheeks turned beetroot at this teasing remark. How could Mummie be so cruel? He wanted to rush out of the room and her next words gave him a welcome cue to do so.

'What I do very clearly remember,' she said in her normal, no-nonsense voice, 'is telling you to go and change out of those britches.'

'Yes, Mummie.'

'And be quick now. Rosary in twenty minutes.'

As he hurried towards the door he heard Papa, who had been ruminating on another aspect of the visit, say with a chuckle: 'Wait till Dermod hears about this. He will be sick as a dog at missing her.'

Philip instantly understood what his father meant. Gosh, that was right. Uncle Dermod, who so seldom left home, was up in Dublin for a week. If there was one thing he would have relished, above anything else, it was meeting a duchess – especially a Spanish one.

Momentarily, a mean triumph of self-importance sang in his heart: *he* had seen the Duchess, while Uncle Dermod had not. He knew that would provoke hours, probably days, of relentless cross-examination, with himself in the unaccustomed role of dispensing information and his favourite uncle as the recipient. That would be a revolution in their relationship. He could not think of a single previous occasion when he had been in a position to impart any intelligence to the erudite Uncle Dermod – apart from trivial items, such as whether the post had gone yet, or that Slattery had fallen off a ladder in the hay-loft, which hardly counted.

This development was so momentous that, after he had closed the drawing-room door behind him, he stood in the hall, lost in thought. Uncle Dermod's chagrin at having missed the visitor was so certain that he felt a surge of sympathy for his disappointment. Yet it was short-lived, inevitably displaced by the thought of the importance that would attach to himself in Uncle Dermod's eyes. It was true, he reflected, that he had not actually spoken to the Duchess; but he had seen her and her imposing motor car, her chauffeur and her daughter. At that last thought he felt a tiny kindling of warmth in his cheeks again: the prospect of a momentary ascendancy over Uncle Dermod had until then banished the memory of his mother's teasing comment. Now it flared up again briefly, but was quickly extinguished by the larger consideration.

As he went up the broad, oak-bannistered staircase, he mentally rehearsed the exchanges during which he would slowly release information about the Duchess to Uncle Dermod, spinning out the process to prolong his power. Yes, she was beautiful (he had not really seen her face, shadowed as it had been by a broad-brimmed hat, but assuredly duchesses always were). She had been wearing diamonds and other jewels (he had Corristeen's authority for that), but not as many as ladies who sang in choruses (that would lend a pleasing touch of sophistication). Her motor car had been a – a – what had Liam called it? He would have to get the name from him before Uncle Dermod's return. By now, he had reached the first landing, where the staircase forked to left and right, beneath high mullioned windows aflame with the declining sun. He turned right, up past a large ancestral portrait of Lieutenant General Felix, Count Kinsella von Carlow, in powdered hair and white Austrian uniform, with the Grand Cross of the Order of Maria Theresia, the Empress-Queen who had made the fortune of the exiled Kinsellas.

For a boy of nine, Philip had a prodigious knowledge of his family history, thanks to Uncle Dermod, for whom the genealogy of the Kinsellas and allied houses was the consuming passion of his life. Philip could think of no greater enjoyment than to sit listening to his uncle's stories about the dispossessed Catholic nobility of Ireland and its exotic diaspora among the now similarly displaced Bourbon and Habsburg courts of Europe. From Uncle Dermod he had learned all about the career of the warrior on the wall above him, from his entry into the Habsburg forces as a humble cadet to his participation in the cavalry charge at the Battle of Kolín (Philip had memorized the name so that it tripped off his tongue, surprising the occasional adults whom he engaged in conversation on the topic) that had shattered the forces of Frederick the Great and won Count Felix the favour of the Empress and his title of nobility. There were two more Austrian generals downstairs, on the dining-room wall, illustrating the continued rise of the family in the Imperial service and exhibiting the broad brow and long nose of the Kinsellas; their biographies too were familiar to him. Then there was one other, more modern, Austrian military portrait in the house: a silver-framed photograph on the grand piano in the drawing room that had provoked a fierce controversy, when he had been too young to know about it. It remained defiantly there still.

Mummie and Papa made him proud, the way they had behaved about that.

After the lieutenant general, the upper wall was largely covered by a huge painting of some obscure biblical event ('A bad copy, out of a Bavarian convent,' Papa had once observed of it). Philip reached the top of the second flight of stairs, where corridors led off to numerous bedrooms. He was in dangerous territory now. Along the passage to his right lay the suite of rooms from which a dormant, but looming, presence diffused its menace throughout the house. Grandma lived there.

CHAPTER II

GRANDMA lived mostly in the seclusion of her gloomy brown rooms; but she was also dying, in a very slow and incomprehensible way. She had been dying all his life, for all the years Philip could remember. Bridie Byrne had once remarked cheerfully that Grandma had been dying for thirty years 'and never a feather out of her'. Bridie was the only person who could exercise any kind of restraint on Grandma, sometimes persuading her to change her mind or modify her behaviour – probably because she seemed to be the only one who was not afraid of her. Grandma had nothing to do with the noble Austrian generals on the walls: she was Mummie's mother, the daughter of a solicitor and the widow of a modest gentleman farmer in County Galway. Although she had formerly rejoiced in the style of Mrs Skerrett of Castle Skerrett, that imposing-sounding fortalice had in no way resembled Castle Kinsella, being a glorified farmhouse embellished with an outsize pillared portico by a Victorian owner who had come into some money and hankered to play the squire. Philip knew all this, as he did most of the information he acquired, by a process of meticulously piecing together scraps of knowledge imparted, often accidentally, by his parents, his uncles, the servants in the kitchen and – as regarded the more specious claims – Grandma herself.

Philip loved Grandma, or supposed he did, because she was part of the family and it was his duty to do so; but he did not like her. Nobody did, except perhaps Bridie, who would talk of her almost as of a child, when she had succeeded in damping down one of her tantrums ('She's herself again – the soul!'). Philip felt that the process of Grandma's dying, which she was the first to proclaim ('I'm not long for this world... You'll be glad when I'm gone and not a burden any more…'), was becoming unreasonably protracted. Why could she not just die like Father Phelan, who had suddenly collapsed in the sacristy after Mass? Even old Mrs Halloran who had gone into a slow decline shortly before Christmas had been buried just after Easter. Why could Grandma not either die and be done with it, or get better? In fact, she often did get better: better enough to pay a call upon another old lady in the next county; better enough to join a party visiting a house about which she was curious; even, on one notable occasion, better enough to go to a race meeting. Her health fluctuated as much as Uncle Ulick's, but his was a different case because, although he kept thinking he was falling ill, he hardly ever actually was.

Philip had also detected a peculiar equation between Grandma's health and her relations with Mummie, whom she treated dreadfully. Sometimes she even made her cry, but those occasions had grown rare since Papa had begun to intervene. It was noticeable, however, that Grandma seemed to draw strength from these scenes. Although they mostly took place behind closed doors, Philip knew they usually began with Grandma taking umbrage at some supposed affront and berating her daughter with heavily barbed recriminations, her rage mounting until she announced the onset of a probable heart attack. If Mummie became upset and rushed away, crying, to her room, Grandma would appear half an hour later looking reinvigorated and dressed for an expedition out of doors, either on foot or in the dogcart retained for her use. Once, in her early days at Lissanore, she had met the hastily summoned doctor on the gravel sweep in front of the house and reacted as if her family had been deranged to send for him, while qualifying this reassurance with the pregnant remark: 'There is nothing wrong with me that a little kindness and consideration would not cure.'

Uncertain of the state of Grandma's health today, beyond the fact that she had gone to her bedroom to lie down due to the heat, Philip skirted the entrance to the passage that led to her lair and darted along towards his own room in the west wing, adjoining the schoolroom and nursery. Mindful of his mother's orders, he hurriedly changed out of his stained riding breeches into short trousers. He glanced longingly at the book that lay on his bed – *The Triumph of the Scarlet Pimpernel* – but realized he had no time to spare if he wanted to reach the chapel punctually for family rosary. Sure enough, no sooner was he making his way back towards the stairs than he heard the gong for chapel. It was a device that had often confused non-Catholic guests staying in the house, sending them to dress half an hour early; then there was a further dislocation when they appeared prematurely in the drawing room, so that their host and hostess had to rush downstairs, with clothing barely fastened securely, to entertain them.

The chapel was the heart of Lissanore. The life of the house radiated from its gothic solemnity. It protruded from the western end of the north-facing front of the castle, in the protective shadow of the great drum tower that stood immediately behind and beyond it. Its fortunes had varied throughout the years – almost a century – that it had served the spiritual needs of the Kinsellas. Intermittently there had been resident chaplains, usually elderly priests who were glad to retire to the comfort and security of the castle in their declining years. There had also been periods of interregnum when, for one reason or another, no chaplain was available and it was difficult even to find a priest to say Mass there on Sundays. That had provoked problems with the local bishop over reservation of the Blessed Sacrament. Recently, however, the chapel had experienced something of a renaissance, since a French Dominican had taken up residence indefinitely. Father Yves was not half-senile like so many of his predecessors, but a man of middle age who had suffered some kind of theological crisis, provoking a conflict with his superiors who had given him indefinite leave to recoup his health, both physical and doctrinal. This had been a great convenience to Count Kinsella, who had opportunistically engaged Father Yves as both household chaplain and tutor to his youngest son Philip, whom he did not wish either to continue being taught by a mediocre governess or to send away to school.

Philip knew that Father Yves, whom he liked very much, would not be leading the rosary in the chapel that evening, since he had gone with Uncle Dermod to Dublin where the two men were spending a week immersed in libraries that catered for their respective interests. After hurrying downstairs, Philip made his way to the chapel by the long passage that ran like an artery through the west wing of the castle, slackening his pace when he saw there were people both ahead and behind him, so he must be in time.

Most of the household assembled for family rosary, which had been substituted for night prayers years previously so that even the youngest children could attend. The cook, who was always at the most sensitive stage of her labours at this preprandial hour, was permanently exempt. Bridie Byrne's presence was dependent on whatever duties she was performing, on her usual *ad hoc* basis; she was there more often than she missed. The rest of the indoor servants were routine attenders, especially Angela, the pious junior housemaid, who felt that working at Lissanore with its religious amenities was half-way to being in a convent, so that she sometimes had to be shooed out of the chapel at inappropriate hours by Countess Kinsella, to attend to her duties of state. Corristeen was an invariable member of the congregation, deeming it his responsibility as head of the domestic household to kneel immediately behind the members of the family. On these occasions he assumed the role of beadle, ushering visitors to their seats as solemnly as any *suisse*. 'I swear he would dearly love to take up a collection,' Philip had heard Papa say laughingly.

This evening the family had an unusually meagre representation. Uncle Dermod was away; Philip's elder brothers Edmund and Dominick were not due home from school for some weeks yet; his sister Maria Theresia's term at her Belgian convent would end about the same time, but she had been invited to stay with a school friend for the first part of the holidays. Uncle Arthur and Aunt Clara, who lived in the dower house, only came to chapel when they were dining at the castle and not always even then. Uncle Ulick's presence would depend on the state of his health which, in this hot weather, was likely to be poorly. Grandma, whose relationship with God was gracious but not overindulgent, never came. Apart from Philip's parents and his little sister Deirdre with her nanny, only Uncle Eanna could be relied upon to attend.

Sure enough, the first sight that met Philip's eye after he entered under the gothic stone archway, went down the four steps into the chapel and blessed himself at the holy-water stoup was Uncle Eanna's curly reddish hair and heavy shoulders hunched in the front pew. Philip was fond of Uncle Eanna, but always felt embarrassed by him. His flamboyant nationalist politics and his clumsy, uncoordinated movements were equal sources of social unease. He did not even look like a Kinsella, with his round face and bulbous frog's eyes. Philip knew that his thick voice, with its deliberately cultivated brogue, would dominate the responses to the rosary in that small congregation.

Corristeen, still in a state of exaltation from his recent contact with ducal rank, gestured Philip forward with an air of self-importance. Philip went to the second row of pews, genuflected and sat down. Usually he sat in the front row with his parents, but he had just realized he had left his rosary beads in his room; if he sat beside his mother she would notice this, so he thought it better to slip into the seat behind. Most of the servants were already in their places, dispersed randomly around the middle rows. When Count and Countess Kinsella came into the chapel, Mummie wearing her black lace mantilla and holding little Deirdre by the hand, everybody stood up, as they would normally have done for Father Yves. In his absence, Philip's father would lead the prayers. There was a creaking of benches, rustling of clothes and jingle of rosary beads as the congregation sank onto the kneelers. Papa intoned in his calm, clear voice: 'In the name of the Father and of the Son and of the Holy Ghost, amen.' He recited the Apostles' Creed and the other preliminary prayers then launched into the main part of the rosary: 'The First Joyful Mystery, the Annunciation. Hail Mary, full of grace…'

When Papa led the rosary the good thing was that he restricted himself to the basic prayers, leaving out the frightening bit between each decade about 'save us from the fires of Hell' that Canon Roche bellowed with such relish in the parish church; nor did he attempt to substitute any version of his own for the additional pieties that Father Yves always inserted, lapsing absent-mindedly into French. When Papa had said half of the first 'Hail Mary' he fell silent and the congregation took up the response in a Babel of voices, ranging from Deirdre's childish piping to Corristeen's gravelly wheeze.

'Holy Mary, Mother of God, pray for us sinners now and at the hour of our death, amen.'

In front of him Philip heard Uncle Eanna's deep, accented voice, with the slobbery intonation that his thick lips seemed to impose on him. He noticed the patch of baldness nestling at the back of his uncle's tousled ginger hair and the grubbiness of his old linen coat. Eanna was very devout and was completely immersed in the prayers he was saying. So was little Dee-Dee, kneeling beside her mother and clutching the child's rosary, with each decade strung in beads of a different colour, that was a cherished possession, but with no hope of keeping tally of the prayers with her small fingers. Although she could say the rosary, she continually fell behind the adults so that the last part of each response came like a diminutive echo after everyone else had finished. Aware of this, Papa waited for her before starting the next 'Hail Mary', a concession that Father Yves had never made.

Philip made a conscientious effort to concentrate on the prayers. It was easy enough for the first decade and he maintained a sketchy attentiveness for the next two; but by the time they came to the Presentation of the Child Jesus in the Temple, his thoughts had wandered, as they always did, to the contemplation of his surroundings. The chapel fascinated him, as did everything about his home. He would salve his conscience with the excuse that thinking about the chapel and its furnishings was still a religious topic and therefore permissible. 'It's by Pugin, no doubt about it,' his father had often said. 'All the correspondence and accounts were destroyed a long time ago, but the family tradition is unambiguous and he did quite a bit of work in this part of the country.' To which Uncle Dermod would add his testimony as family historian: 'He certainly worked for our Talbot and Redmond cousins, so it was quite natural that he should have come here too.' Then Papa would indulge his own keen pride. 'Look at that scissors beam roof – quite unmistakable – and the reredos is classic Pugin.' He was not particularly well informed about church architecture, but he had once heard a visiting enthusiast voice these opinions and regarded them as authoritative. Philip, in turn, had carefully memorized the phrases for repetition when the opportunity offered. It was possible to make a considerable impression on adults by employing erudite terminology they would not have expected one to know.

Behind the altar the reredos portrayed the Crucifixion in its central panel, with Our Lady and Saint John kneeling on either side.

This lifelike representation eclipsed the ornate crucifix with fleur-de-lisé terminals that stood above the tabernacle. Higher still, in a niche in the wall above the reredos, just beneath the three arched windows of stained glass that illuminated the sanctuary, was a white marble statue of Saint Michael the Archangel, to whom the chapel was dedicated. Philip knew this had been sculpted by a man called John Hogan, which apparently made it significant. His gaze wandered up the height of the chapel, occupying two storeys of the castle, to where the oak-framed panels of the ceiling were painted blue, studded with gold stars. If he narrowed his eyes, he could imagine he was looking up through a fretwork of beams open to the sky.

With a guilty start, he realized his father had just begun to recite 'Hail, Holy Queen…' which signalled the rosary was coming to an end. The congregation joined in '…Mother of Mercy, hail our life, our sweetness and our hope…' for the whole of the concluding prayer, their combined voices sounding suddenly thunderous, their fervency intensified by the approaching end of their devotions and the prospect of dinner or recreation. In the silence that followed, Count Kinsella crossed himself, kissed the crucifix on his rosary and sat up. After a moment's pause, he patted his youngest child absently on her head, covered in a white lace mantilla, then stood up and led his family out of the front pew, each genuflecting in the aisle and glancing with mild surprise at Philip in the row behind. He followed immediately after them and caught up with his mother as she helped Dee-Dee to bless herself at the holy-water stoup.

'So, you forgot your beads again,' said Mummie in tones of casual reproof, without even looking in his direction. 'You really are a scatterbrain.'

'Scattabain!' echoed Dee-Dee delightedly, spraying holy water like a wet retriever.

Philip could only stare speechlessly at Mummie's retreating

back. It really was quite uncanny how she always knew when he had committed some fault, saw through every subterfuge. He crossed himself indignantly and left the chapel, empty by now of all but Angela the housemaid, still rapt in devotion. Ahead of him in the broad passage he saw his mother return Dee-Dee to the custody of Nanny, take off her mantilla then turn in his direction and wait for him with a purposeful air that boded no good. He walked as slowly as he reasonably could, in the faint hope she would be distracted by something else, but of course that did not happen.

'Philip, you had better look in on Grandma before you have your supper.'

'Oh, Mummie, please, no.'

'What on earth do you mean?'

'Just that – I don't want to disturb her. I think the heat may have made her ill.'

'All the more reason to visit her.'

'But I'm feeling terribly tired. I think I may be ill myself.'

'Stop that nonsense. You sound like your Uncle Ulick – one hypochondriac in the house is quite enough.'

In happier circumstances he would have enquired about the exact meaning of that sinister-sounding word, but now was not a propitious moment. Instead he asked:

'Is Uncle Ulick ill?'

'Have you ever known him to be well?'

'Then perhaps I had better visit Uncle Ulick instead of Grandma.'

'You may visit Uncle Ulick, to find out if he will be down to dinner. Immediately after that, you will visit Grandma. Understood?'

'Yes, Mummie.'

'Hurry along then.'

To avoid the dispersing congregation he took the back stairs, his feet echoing on bare wood as he pounded up each narrow flight, then hurried along a passage and through a door where carpet replaced linoleum as he re-entered the public thoroughfares of the castle. He knocked on the door of Uncle Ulick's room, eliciting a strangled sound which he took for permission to enter. Uncle Ulick was crouched in an armchair, his face contorted around a thermometer protruding from his mouth; his eyes, which had been fixed on the pocket-watch in his hand, swivelled to confront Philip and he uttered a smothered gasp of frustration. He plucked the thermometer from his mouth and squinted at it distractedly.

'Just what I was afraid of – the timing was completely upset when I called out to you just now. The mercury has hardly moved. I shall have to take it again.'

He shook the thermometer vigorously, preparatory to reinserting it in his mouth.

'I'm sorry, Uncle Ulick. Mummie asked me to find out if you would be down to dinner. She hopes you are well,' he added, diplomatically inventing the last part of the message.

'That is very thoughtful of her,' said Uncle Ulick, touched by a concern for his notoriously volatile health that was unusual among his family. 'I felt very hot and flushed about half an hour ago and wondered if I was a little feverish. I was just taking my temperature. If you wouldn't mind waiting, I can give you an answer in a couple of minutes.'

Philip lowered himself into an armchair and watched the familiar routine with interest. Uncle Ulick peered again at the thermometer, to make sure the mercury was at the starting point. Then he scrutinized the second hand on his watch with the quivering intensity of a greyhound in the slips, while he held the clinical instrument poised near his half-open mouth, ready to thrust it under his tongue the instant the watch-hand reached the minute mark. Seconds later it did so and swiftly, but carefully, he slid the thermometer into place, holding it secure by setting his jaw into a taut rigidity that gave his features an unfortunately deranged expression. Philip knew better than to speak while his uncle was engaged in this meticulous exercise. He sat and studied Uncle Ulick, taking in his premature baldness, features deeply lined from years of concern about his health, slumped shoulders and thin, inelegantly splayed legs in houndstooth trousers. He felt sorry for his uncle and the burden that weighed him down, though he did not entirely understand its cause, since Uncle Ulick was not actually an invalid, but lived in the apprehension of imminently becoming one. His dressing-table and every other available surface were cluttered with bottles of medicine and boxes of pills, sufficient to supply a hospital. After a carefully timed interval, his uncle drew the thermometer out of his mouth with a practised movement and held it towards the light from the window to read it.

'Three points below normal,' he announced grudgingly.

'That means your temperature is really normal,' Philip informed him. 'If it says normal, it's a little too high.'

'Who told you that?'

'Either Mummie or Dr Dixon, I think. Or it might have been you.'

'Well, that is quite right, Philip. If the mercury had been directly on the arrow I should have known my temperature was on the way up. As it is, it is exactly where it ought to be.'

'That's good news, isn't it?'

'Up to a point; but there are many illnesses that do not involve a fever.'

'So you may still be ill?'

'It is always possible, but on this occasion I think not. It must just have been the heat affecting me. I must warn you, however,' he added, loth to allow a tinge of optimism to dominate the conversation, 'that what you did just now was very dangerous.'

'What did I do?' Philip's voice expressed hurt and dismay. He was still smarting from his mother's strictures. The grown-ups were being really horrid today – perhaps it was the hot weather making them bad-tempered.

'It is hazardous in the extreme to burst in on someone when he has a thermometer in his mouth. Suppose, for example, between being startled by your knock and my natural impulse to call out to you, I had involuntarily clenched my teeth on the thermometer and snapped it –'

'Gosh, yes, the broken glass might have cut your mouth.'

'No, no – I mean, yes – that too. But the fatal consequence would have been that the mercury from the instrument would have poisoned me.'

'Oh.' Philip was startled by the notion. 'I never thought of that.'

'Neither, apparently, have the manufacturers of medical instruments. I have often thought of writing to them to point out this hazard to patients. Imagine someone having convulsions. What are they thinking of? I understand some thermometers used for scientific purposes contain alcohol, which works just as well. Why not use it in clinical thermometers too?'

'Then, if it broke, you would only get drunk.'

'Precisely. Eh? Not at all – I hope you are not being impertinent?' He peered suspiciously at his nephew.

'No, honestly, Uncle Ulick!' His evident sincerity and the flush rising to his face reassured the hypochondriac.

'Well, since I am not shuffling off this mortal coil just yet,' said his uncle, trying to inject a tone of geniality into his words to compensate for his unjust suspicions and rising from his chair, 'I had better dress for dinner. Thank your mother for her kind enquiry and tell her I shall be down.'

'Yes, Uncle Ulick. I am glad you aren't ill.' Interpreting his uncle's words as his dismissal, he made his way reluctantly to the door. He had just remembered where his next port of call must be, but there seemed no hope of postponing it.

'Good night, Philip,' said his uncle absently, holding up a collar to the light to assess whether it was one he had discarded or was freshly laundered for use.

That 'good night' further depressed Philip: it was a reminder that his uncle did not expect to see him until tomorrow, an intimation of the remorseless approach of bedtime. Once adults started to employ that phrase, the day began to die, even with bright sunshine streaming in the windows and birdsong raucous outside. He had not even had supper yet, but already he was being bade goodnight. It had been a pleasant day, but in the past hour it had progressively soured; and now he had to visit Grandma.

Her response to his knock was the usual muffled shriek that expressed a mixture of astonishment and outrage even before she had identified her visitor. As he entered the room Grandma stared at him with an exaggerated expression of surprise, as if she did not know him. She received everyone in this way, making them feel like intruders under her baleful glare which seemed to say: 'Who is this coming to trouble me?'

'Hello, Grandma.'

She craned her neck at him with a continuing interrogatory air. When Mrs Blackwell, the Church of Ireland rector's wife, looked around in that way it was an elegant, swanlike movement; but Grandma's scrawny neck reminded him of a tortoise peering out of its shell. This was a pity, as even Philip realized, because Grandma had once been much more attractive than Mrs Blackwell – very beautiful indeed. This was evidenced by an old photograph in a silver frame that stood on an occasional table in the cluttered room.

Even the bright sunlight of early evening on a matchless summer day lost its power in that brown-varnished room, becoming diluted to the pallid amber of weak tea, highlighting the dust-specks that danced in the subdued sunbeams from the arched windows. Everything seemed brown, from Grandma's pre-War style of dress to the tasselled mats under the pots of aspidistras on tall, columnar stands. Through the open door to the adjoining room could be seen Grandma's bed and the bedside table, littered with accessories such as hairpins, a burned-down candle in a night candlestick, liver pills, a bottle of Cascara, a tumbler and teaspoon – the medical components forming a very modest collection compared to Uncle Ulick's vast pharmacy, but contributing to Grandma's feeble and self-confessedly reluctant hold on life.

Since his grandmother continued to stare at him as if seeing a ghost, or at least something very startling and distasteful, Philip tried again to break the uncomfortable silence.

'Mummie wondered if you were quite well.'

Grandma's stare grew even more intense. Her lips seemed to repeat his words silently, as if struggling to divine their meaning, while her brow furrowed up to the hairline from which a geometrically accurate centre parting ran back across the crown of her head. Then the parchment-coloured face rearranged its wrinkles into an expression of theatrical astonishment.

'What? Your mother was concerned about *me*? Why would she give me a second thought? I am only her broken-down old mother – a burden to her, running this great house. I can hardly expect her to spare me much attention, busy as she is. Too busy to visit me, obviously, so she sends you.'

'She has been very busy, actually,' said Philip, in what he hoped was a placatory tone.

'Oh, you don't have to tell me that.' Grandma's acerbity melted into self-pity as she assumed her martyred demeanour. This entailed supporting her cheek on one hand and staring at the ornamental screen in front of the empty grate in melancholy reflection. Philip was desperately anxious to change the mood, so he gambled on employing shock tactics.

'A duchess came to tea today.'

This was a dangerous expedient, proclaiming as it did that a woman whose social significance might be expected to eclipse Grandma had been in the house; but he hoped curiosity would get the better of her, so that they could have a more civil conversation for a few minutes, after which he would be at liberty to leave with a clear conscience.

'Don't!' With an anguished expression Grandma raised a hand to her brow. 'My poor head. That gossip Bridie Byrne has brought on my neuritis, chattering on and on about some grand visitor today – some great lady. What use is that to me? Oh, yes, the world is full of great people – but I don't see them doing anything great for me.'

She resumed her gloomy contemplation of the fire screen, where a brace of embroidered parrots was eternally imprisoned behind glass.

'She was a Spanish duchess,' said Philip, conscious that this additional detail represented the end of his conversational resources.

'What a world.' Grandma spoke as if some outrage against all the decencies had been reported to her. This remark did, however, throw Philip a lifeline, since it could be linked to her favourite aphorism regarding her place – or lack of it – in human society.

'You don't really like the world, do you, Grandma?' he prompted her hopefully.

Grandma sat up rigidly in her chair, disposed her hands on its arms, raised her head to an assertive angle and spoke with emphasis, delivering herself of an *ex cathedra* pronouncement:

'I am in this world, but not of it.'

Philip always enjoyed hearing her say that. He did not know anyone else who spoke in that way, so it was something between a distinction and a diversion. He knew that if he repeated it to Mummie, along with similar maxims that Grandma was prone to utter, it would provoke a reaction combining irritation and derision that she would instantly suppress in the interests of adult solidarity; but if he listened at the door afterwards he would hear her telling Papa about it in disrespectful tones. Recognizing that anything Grandma now said could only be anticlimactic – since she was in an uncommunicative mood and he had really manipulated her into rehearsing this classic dictum – he decided to make his excuses.

'Grandma, I must go now. While Father Yves is away I have to have supper early, with Deirdre. Thank you very much for having me,' he concluded, unable on the spur of the moment to think of a more suitable formula for leave-taking.

Philip delivered the message that Uncle Ulick would be down to dinner to Corristeen, whom he met at the foot of the staircase. He paused to stroke Conn, the elderly wolfhound, who was lying in the hall watching passers-by with his sad eyes. His mood matched Philip's. Supper with his baby sister was an engagement to which he was not looking forward. Dee-Dee's command of cutlery and table etiquette was still at a rudimentary stage, making her as undesirable a neighbour at mealtimes as Uncle Eanna; and her nanny was insipid and boring, a sad contrast to Father Yves who, although he dined with the family, often sat and drank coffee while Philip had supper in the schoolroom, in the Gallic conviction that one should not eat alone, discoursing on interesting topics.

With a grunt of acknowledgement, Conn the wolfhound rolled back onto the hall floor, rested his head on his front paws and resumed his surveillance. Philip found his attention drawn, as often before, to a small and undistinguished painting that hung near the front door, on the wall between the premises that served as a cloakroom for visitors and a former boot room that his father had converted into a cramped and chaotic office. The artist was unknown, but he had achieved a striking authenticity in this depiction of a skein of geese flying over a riverbank – the landscape was too anonymous to determine whether it represented the nearby river that marked the southern boundary of the Lissanore demesne. What had always drawn Philip to this painting were the eerie light effects the artist had contrived, capturing what must have been a very brief moment between evening and sunset – that and its evocative title: *Wild Geese Observed at Twilight*. Philip's family, as Uncle Dermod had frequently been at pains to school him, had been Wild Geese of a different sort: the eighteenth-century Irish Jacobite exiles who carried their swords into the service of European Catholic monarchs. This thought now caused him to fall into a romantic reverie in front of the dingy canvas.

'Ah, there you are, old man,' said his father affably, coming downstairs at that moment. 'Tell me, are you utterly exhausted after such a hot day?'

'Not utterly,' Philip answered guardedly, sensing some impending proposal.

'Glad to hear it, because your mother and I have just challenged Uncle Eanna to a croquet match after dinner and he is looking for a partner, if you feel up to it.'

'Ooh, yes, I do! Thank you, Papa.' If there was one treat Philip loved it was such occasional games of croquet on light summer evenings, which usually carried on past his bedtime.

'Good. Well, we shall see you first thing after dinner. We shan't be long – there are no guests and we are just having cold cuts; this weather kills the appetite.'

He clapped Conn around the ears and passed on into the drawing room, leaving Philip thinking it was a splendid day after all.

CHAPTER III

'THIS has all been most regrettable – an unhappy coincidence of events that could not have been foreseen. I am extremely disappointed – really, more than I can say. It is not as if I were a frequent traveller and yet, when I leave home for a very short time, this happens. I can only call it singularly unfortunate.'

Uncle Dermod's distress was palpable. The news that the Duchess of Saladavieja (for that was her title, pronounced with great gusto by Uncle Dermod) had visited Lissanore during his absence had deeply dismayed him. 'And to think, while she was here, I was in the Kildare Street Club, listening to Pierce Donabate prosing on about his problems with his pheasants.'

They were in Uncle Dermod's study, which was Philip's favourite room in the castle: the second storey from the top in the great drum tower (the floor above was his uncle's bedroom). The room was round and light due to the arched windows that opened it – literally, on this hot day when most of them had been raised high on their sashes – to every point of the compass. Beneath those that faced north, at the front of the castle, was a desk covered with papers. Uncle Dermod had a voluminous correspondence with deposed monarchs and their adherents across Europe, invariably supporting the senior, legitimist line of those dynasties in which the succession was disputed.

On the wall hung photographs of the Emperor Franz Joseph, several other sovereigns or claimants to thrones and Uncle Dermod himself, in the uniform of the Order of Malta, heavily decorated with the stars and crosses of other distinguished orders of knighthood. These portraits were complemented by military pictures, some illustrating the ornate regimentals of extinct foreign units, others featuring famous actions, the largest depicting the Battle of Fontenoy. Part of the circular wall was book-lined, the estate carpenter having risen creditably to the challenge of accommodating the shelves to its gradual curvature. Their contents reflected Uncle Dermod's passion for genealogy and heraldry. A dozen red-bound editions of *Burke's Peerage* and *Landed Gentry* ('I cannot, for the life of me, understand the popularity of Debrett, when it omits the pedigrees,' he was fond of saying) had pride of place, alongside the green-covered volumes of *Cokayne's Complete Peerage*. More books were piled on a table in the centre of the room, at which Philip and his uncle were seated facing each other. These represented their owner's closest interests and had many pages marked with slips of paper: O'Hart's *Irish Pedigrees*; D'Alton, *King James's Irish Army List*; O'Callaghan, *History of the Irish Brigades in the service of France*…

None of these compilations of genealogical lore was of service to Uncle Dermod in his present quandary. Just one volume lay open on the table: *Guía de la Nobleza Española*, by Felipe López-Valdemoro de Aranda, Conde de Cazalla del Rio. Uncle Dermod consoled himself by murmuring the author's sonorous name aloud, to Philip's admiration. His uncle had by now extracted all the available information from this and miscellaneous other authorities ('Unfortunately, the *Almanach de Gotha* excludes the Spanish dukes') regarding the Duchess of Saladavieja and her family.

'I am afraid I have culpably neglected the Spanish nobility,' said Uncle Dermod ruefully, as if apologizing for having snubbed the entire body of grandees and hidalgos. 'It is one of the greatest aristocracies of Europe. I shall write to Hatchards today and enquire if they have some more up-to-date reference works. Let me see, Ruvigny might be helpful about dates of creation.'

From a shelf he took a heavy tome, *The Titled Nobility of Europe*, and began leafing through it until he found the relevant entry.

Philip looked on with the same respect as when he watched Canon Roche in the sacristy marking the places in the big altar missal with ribbons before Mass.

'Here we are,' muttered Uncle Dermod. 'Created Conde de Vivar by John I, King of Castile, 24 April, 1385... Marquisate in 1563... Another in 1678... The dukedom inherited from an heiress in 1754... The entry for our recent visitor, of course, is still in the name of her late husband. She is Doña Maria de la Concepción de San Martín y Borbón, *Duquesa viuda* de Saladavieja. Her husband was three times a Grandee of the First Class.'

'Gosh,' said Philip, feeling it was time he contributed to the conversation. He had already been exhaustively interrogated by his uncle on the subject of the Duchess and, although he had inflated his brief glimpse of her into a circumstantial account of considerable inventiveness, his information had clearly been less than satisfactory.

'Did you notice a coat of arms on her motor car?' asked Uncle Dermod, looking up from the book he was consulting.

Philip racked his memory. He would dearly have liked to be able to confirm he had done so. Had there been any insignia? He thought not.

'It would have been on the door panels.'

'No – I – I don't think so.'

'Oh dear,' said his uncle fretfully. 'My small library is proving singularly inadequate today. I simply do not understand how I can have neglected Spain so badly, for so long.'

He spoke in the tone of a general who had allowed himself to be surprised on an unprotected flank. Philip felt sorry for his favourite uncle; any pleasure in having trumped him had evaporated in the face of his disappointment. Among the Kinsella brothers Uncle Dermod was closest in age and looks to Philip's father. He had the same high forehead, long nose and dark hair: except that he was clean-shaven while his elder brother had a military-style moustache, such was the similarity in their handsome, thoroughbred looks – so different from their siblings Ulick, Arthur and (especially) Eanna – they might almost have passed for twins. Philip tried to console his uncle by reminding him that the Duchess had promised to call again at Lissanore on her return journey, in little more than a week's time.

'Perhaps she will, perhaps she won't,' was the sceptical reply, accompanied by a look that said plainly: put not your trust in duchesses.

Philip resorted to the one distraction guaranteed to kindle Uncle Dermod's enthusiasm.

'Are we related to the Duchess? Is she a cousin several times removed?'

He wanted to display his knowledge of this terminology and show his uncle he had paid attention to his many lectures on genealogy.

'No,' said Uncle Dermod decisively. 'The connexion is purely commercial – involving a longstanding friendship as well, of course, over several generations. The dukes of Saladavieja have been directors of the Bank for almost as long as it has existed. There has been little contact in recent times, but our common interest in the Bank (he spoke of this institution with less reverence than any other member of the family, but still with a scintilla of respect) has always been an enduring bond between us. Have I told you the story of the Bank?'

He had, once, a long time ago; but Philip had forgotten the details, since they did not involve cavalry charges against heavy odds or the taking of enemy colours and laying them at the feet of the Empress-Queen, as most of the Kinsella chronicles related by Uncle Dermod tended to do. So, he asked his uncle to retell it.

'Well, you know our ancestor Bonaventure Kinsella served as an officer in the army of James II –'

'In Cavenagh's Regiment of Foot,' said Philip knowledgeably.

'That's right.' His uncle smiled, pleased that the information he had imparted had not fallen on stony ground. 'Anyway, after the Treaty of Limerick he went to France and entered military service there.'

'He was one of the Wild Geese.'

'Exactly; as I have often told you. Bonaventure had three sons, who all followed him in the profession of soldiering – the only living available to impoverished Irish gentlemen at that time. The two elder boys joined the French army: one was killed at Fontenoy and the sons of the other went to Austria where, as you know, the Kinsellas attained high military rank. Bonaventure Kinsella's third son, however, entered the service of Spain. He married a Spanish lady and distinguished himself in the forces of His Catholic Majesty – that is the traditional title of the King of Spain – and his son did likewise. It was the grandson of that junior line whose fortunes, by pure accident, took an unexpected turn.'

He paused, to create suspense, and glanced at Philip to see if he was paying attention. The boy had his elbows on the table and his chin cupped in his hands, staring with a rapt concentration that reassured his uncle, who resumed his narrative.

'In the early nineteenth century, when Spain's colonies in South America declared independence, Don Arturo Kinsella went with the royal army to Peru, to put down the rebels, but the King's men were defeated by superior forces that invaded from the other revolted colonies. By 1825 all of South America, including Peru, had been lost to the Spanish crown.'

Philip's face registered dismay: why were kings always on the losing side?

'Refusing to serve the republican regime, Arturo Kinsella resigned his commission and made his way north, to Mexico, where he met an old friend who was setting up a financial venture. They became partners and eventually established a banking house that developed vast interests in mining – gold and silver, as well as quicksilver – in Mexico and California. Then they branched out into railroads and other enterprises, in various South American countries and in North America. Arturo became very rich indeed. Unfortunately, his only son was killed in an accident, so he returned to his ancestral home, Ireland, after an absence of three generations. As you know, the senior line of the family – ourselves – had also by then resettled here, after gaining great distinction in the Austrian service. Arturo sought out his cousins – they had maintained a sporadic correspondence – and made them his heirs, bequeathing them large shares in his bank and associated enterprises. That is how our fortune was enlarged, dividends from South America supplementing the estates we had been granted in Hungary and Bohemia by the Habsburgs. We deserved no less, of course,' he added loftily, 'having contributed three generals to the Imperial and Royal Army.'

'Are we very rich, then, Uncle Dermod?'

'I am afraid not.' His uncle chuckled at the notion. 'We certainly were, half a century ago, but our interests in the Bank have been greatly reduced, as has its prosperity. It has been overtaken by larger and more enterprising rivals. The returns have been dwindling year by year. If it were not for what has been securely invested over decades, we could not afford to live at Lissanore in the style we do – though it is nothing to the great establishment your grandfather had here, in his day.'

'Did he have footmen with powdered hair?' Philip's preferred reading matter had led him to regard this as the touchstone of aristocratic splendour.

'An army of them.'

'Gosh. It must have been like *The Count of Monte-Cristo*.'

'Your grandfather simultaneously maintained an estate in Austria and a *palazzo* in Italy,' said Uncle Dermod proudly, intensifying his nephew's sense of romantic grandeur. 'He also renewed the family's connexion with Spain, making a campaign there with Don Carlos VII during the Carlist War of the 1870s.'

Philip knew all about that; he thought of his grandfather's portrait downstairs – the most exotic of the Kinsella military icons and the one that most excited his imagination.

'That was after he had fought for the Pope, wasn't it?' he asked, purely for form since he had his grandfather's biography by heart.

'Yes, indeed. He served in the Pontifical Zouaves against the Piedmontese and Garibaldi who robbed Pius IX of the Papal States. It was in their ranks that he became friendly with the Infante Alfonso Carlos, the brother of Carlos VII, and when the Carlist uprising began in Spain in 1873 he went there with some other former Zouaves and they were formed into a bodyguard for their recent comrade-in-arms the Infante. He was an enterprising commander whose forces swept through Catalonia and Aragón, into Castile. They came to within eighty miles of Madrid.'

'What happened then?' Again, it was a purely formal question. He already knew the answer: the good cause always lost.

'They were driven back and eventually defeated. Don Carlos had to leave Spain. Just before he crossed the bridge at the frontier, into France, after the trumpets had sounded the royal anthem for the last time, he promised his followers: "I will return." But he never did.'

Both lapsed into a melancholy silence after this account of royal defeat and exile. Some blackbirds in the trees outside had been inspired by the brilliance of the day to raise a chorus, only to be humbled by the more mellifluous song of a distant, airborne lark.

A bee that had been reconnoitring the ivy around one of the open windows drifted into the room, humming loudly, but finding its new surroundings uncongenial, made a disgruntled exit by another window.

Uncle Dermod observed its flight with an abstracted air then said: 'I have often thought a book should be written about the nomadic legitimists of the last century, who fought for a variety of *de jure* kings. It was a time of exceptional struggle for Catholics and royalists, beginning in the 1820s with the cause of Dom Miguel I, the rightful King of Portugal, who was forced off his throne by a handful of liberals backed by the British government, despite enjoying the support of most of the nation.'

'The British interfered a lot in other countries, didn't they?'

'Indeed they did,' said his uncle; but he was not to be diverted from his thesis. 'Then, in 1832, there was the last Legitimist rising in France, led by the Duchesse de Berry. The following year, the first Carlist War broke out in Spain; the subsequent Carlist Wars and the international crusade to preserve the Papal States for Pius IX kept Catholic legitimists occupied for most of the century. It was a noble coalition of selfless idealists, often fighting for the rightful sovereign of a country that was not their own – a sort of White International.'

'What's that, Uncle Dermod?'

'Well, you see, the Reds – the Communists and revolutionaries – have what they call "the International", to spread socialism in different countries. Now, White is the commonly accepted opposite of Red, in political terms. The people who fought against Lenin and the Reds in Russia were called Whites. So, you might call the Catholics who fought against liberalism in France, Spain and Italy in the nineteenth century a White International.'

'The White Russians – I remember now, Father Yves said

something about them once. So grandfather, when he fought for the Pope and then in Spain, was part of the White International?'

'Yes. If you choose to use my somewhat fanciful term for it, he certainly was – both as a Papal Zouave and a Carlist volunteer.'

'Did grandfather come back to Ireland after that?'

'Yes, after living for a year or so with our kinsmen in Vienna. Although his father, Field Marshal Count Gabriel Kinsella, had returned here and built Lissanore, Gabriel's brother had stayed on in Austria. One of his sons enlisted alongside your grandfather in both the Papal and Carlist armies. He distinguished himself by frustrating a conspiracy to abduct or murder the Pope. For that he was rewarded by Pius IX with a Roman dukedom, which is still held by the Austrian branch of the family – though, of course, they remain junior to us, despite having the higher title. Your grandfather returned to Lissanore, but his Austrian cousins and their descendants continued to serve the Habsburgs right up to the fall of the Empire – in your own lifetime, Philip, just think of it, though you were only an infant. Your cousin Nicholas, whom you have met, served in the Imperial and Royal Army. We always kept in close touch with the remaining Kinsellas in Austria and they visited here quite regularly. As you know, your father is the head of the whole family. That is why he is Bonaventure, Count Kinsella von Carlow, while the rest of us simply bear the title followed by our Christian name, like myself – Count Dermod Kinsella.'

'And me.' Philip asserted his claim proudly. He had never forgotten the thrill of being told by his uncle – his parents, typically, had never mentioned it – that he was a count of the Holy Roman Empire, since that title descended to all male and female heirs. Even little Dee-Dee was Countess Deirdre Kinsella von Carlow – or 'de Carlow', the style that had discreetly been adopted on the eve of the War, when feeling ran high against all Germanic affiliations and it had been thought prudent to substitute the French *particule* for the Austrian *prädikat*. It was the greatest satisfaction of Philip's life that he had inherited this distinction – in law, if not in usage, since no one ever had cause to address him by it – for it gave him fellowship with so many characters in the works of Alexandre Dumas, Anthony Hope or Baroness Orczy and it had always seemed to him the most romantic of all titles of nobility – far more so than any run-of-the-mill lord or baronet.

'Yes,' said his uncle, 'including you, of course. We belong to what I have termed, in a recent article for a genealogical publication, "Ireland's Black Nobility".'

'Black, Uncle Dermod?'

'Yes. You see, the Roman nobles who remained loyal to the Pope in 1870 and have refused to be reconciled to the usurping Savoyard dynasty are known as the Black, or Papal, nobility to distinguish them from the liberal aristocracy of the Kingdom of Italy. They continue to serve the Pope in his present constrained circumstances.'

'The Prisoner in the Vatican,' said Philip reverently.

'Precisely. Well, my point – and I think it was well made, as some correspondents have been generous enough to agree – was that those exiled Irish Catholic families that served in European armies during the penal days and were ennobled are analogous to the Black nobility of Rome. I think it quite possible that, among those who interest themselves in such matters, the phrase could gain currency and it may become common parlance to refer to the Irish Blacks.'

Philip had an ill-defined, but strong, premonition that it would not. Between a White International and a Black Nobility, he was finding his uncle's chequer-board image of history difficult to assimilate.

'Obviously,' said Uncle Dermod, 'I particularly had in mind those families like ours which entered the Austrian service and with whom we are allied by marriage – Count O'Donell von Tyr-connel, Prince Nugent von Westmeath, Count MacCaffry of Kean More, to name just a few. Those are what I have categorized as our Black nobility. The parallel is even closer,' he warmed to his theme, 'if you include Irish families with Roman titles, such as the Duke de Stacpoole or the Marquis MacSwiney of Mashanaglass.'

He rolled these rococo names around his tongue, like a fine vintage.

'We have a Papal title too. You said the Pope made somebody Kinsella a duke.'

'Well, yes, but that was one of our cousins in Austria. However, you are quite right: by extension, we are a ducal house.'

'So, we are just as important as the Spanish duchess who came here last week?'

His uncle hesitated, pride contending with punctilio.

'Not quite.' He made the admission reluctantly. 'The dukedom of Saladavieja is an ancient title which also carries with it the gran-deeship. I think one would have to concede it is senior to a nine-teenth-century Papal creation.'

Philip was disappointed, but consoled himself with the thought that Uncle Dermod was being over-scrupulous and that, in the pub-lic perception, one duke was as good as another.

'In any case,' said his uncle, 'the question of our ducal status is academic, considering we are a royal house.'

This was the cue for him to launch into the familiar account of the Kinsellas' kingly origins. Reaching for his much-thumbed copy of O'Hart's *Irish Pedigrees*, he opened it at the relevant page and turned it round on the table for Philip to scrutinize, though the boy could have recited it almost word-perfectly.

'See here, Dermod MacMorough, the fifty-eighth Christian King of Leinster – unfortunately known as Dermod of the Strangers because of his ill-judged decision to invite Norman warlords into Ireland to help him in his quarrel with O'Rourke – had three sons. The youngest was Eanna *Ceannsalach*, or "Unclean Head", from which our name Kinsella derives.'

Philip winced: that 'unclean head' epithet never failed to dismay him. It created an incongruous association between the royal, ducal and comital house of Kinsella and an unsavoury family in the village named Finnegan, whose heads had required to be shaved and varnished with a potent chemical to eliminate some distressing infestation. He wished that Uncle Dermod had never disclosed this information. His uncle, noting his discomfiture, offered a modicum of consolation.

'Other accounts suggest the name may mean "proud" or "masterful". At any rate, we descend from Eanna. His sister Aoife, or Eva, married Strongbow – Richard de Clare, second Earl of Pembroke, who brought the Normans to Ireland – and all kings of England since Henry IV, as well as many continental royal families, descend from her. You will note that Eanna's father King Dermod is numbered one hundred and thirteen on the MacMorough pedigree. If you trace his ancestry back from there, through the O'Toole and O'Connor Faley genealogies to the line of Heremon, you eventually come to Milesius of Spain, after whom the ancient Gaelic races of Ireland are called the Milesians. He is numbered thirty-six, signifying the thirty-sixth generation from Adam. Such a descent, going back through the Book of Genesis to our first parents, is of course mythological; but that is not to say it does not contain a great deal of sound tradition in the later generations. If you look at the Kinsella pedigree – and I really think O'Hart might have treated it more comprehensively – you will see that the last chief he records, Dermod Dubh, reigning in 1580, represented the one hundred and twenty-fifth generation from Adam. In fact, the author has made an obvious error and it should read one hundred and twenty-fourth. From that, I have calculated that Bonaventure Kinsella, who fought at the Battle of Aughrim and was the first of our family to migrate abroad, was the one hundred and thirtieth generation from Adam.'

He paused to gauge Philip's reaction; it was not entirely satisfactory.

'That's terribly interesting, Uncle Dermod, but...'

'What?'

'Well, if you trace your ancestry back to Adam...' Philip floundered, trying to express his misgivings coherently. 'I mean... everyone is descended from Adam.'

'Of course.' His uncle looked perplexed by this line of reasoning.

'Well, it just proves we are descended from the same ancestor as Slattery – or – or Bridie Byrne... So, it makes us seem less noble, doesn't it?'

Dermod regarded his nephew with some consternation. Really, the things that children came out with.

'Not at all.' He tried to suppress a note of irritation. 'It goes without saying, all humanity has a common ancestor; but a great house will have recorded its precise descent over many generations – such an unbroken tradition is unknown among those of lowly birth.'

'Would it not be better,' Philip's mind was revolving the implications of this new insight into genealogy, 'to trace a pedigree only a few centuries back? Then it wouldn't get mixed up with common people's ancestors.'

'It is a genealogist's responsibility to accumulate as much information as he can,' said his uncle mildly. 'However, there is something in what you say. Douglas Hyde, a considerable Gaelic scholar, believes the Irish genealogies are historically accurate, back to the third or fourth century A.D. Beyond that, they have become attached to fanciful mythological pedigrees, which arguably discredit the authentic material. He maintains, though, that one bloodline is more ancient than all the others, going back to 300 B.C. before it merges with the mythical inventions, and that is the line of the Kings of Leinster – the *Uí Cinnsealaigh* dynasty – in other words, ourselves. That antiquity may be why our surname, alone among Gaelic patronymics, is not preceded by "O" or "Mac". I have often remonstrated with Eanna for putting an "O" in front of his name in Irish – "Ó Cinnsealaigh" instead of the original *Ceannsalach* – which is incorrect and deprives us of an historical distinction. We are, on sound historical evidence, the oldest family in Ireland.'

'Gosh, Uncle Dermod, that's terrific. So, we really were a royal family?'

'Undoubtedly, though our power was greatly reduced after losing the Battle of Áth Senaig, or Ballyshannon, in 738. Nevertheless, one Kinsella, also named Dermod, became High King of Ireland, with opposition, in the eleventh century. The Kings of Leinster were inaugurated at Knockavoe, with their high officers in attendance: O'Nolan, the King's marshal; O'Doran, chief Brehon; and MacKeogh, chief bard. There are very few civilizations that can compete with the antiquity of Irish pedigrees, though I understand the Chinese have preserved remarkably ancient records, presumably because of their cult of ancestor worship.'

He could not disguise his sympathy with this pagan practice.

'How far back do the Chinese records go?'

'A very considerable time,' said Uncle Dermod evasively. 'But you distracted me from the point I was about to make which was that, by calculating forward from Bonaventure in the late seventeenth century, I have been able to arrive at a precise estimate of the number of generations separating *you*, Philip, from our first ancestor, Adam. In mythological terms, of course.'

'Golly.' Philip was touched by his uncle's research on his behalf. 'How many did it come to?'

'Well, work it out for yourself. As I have just told you, Bonaventure Kinsella was the one hundred and thirtieth generation. So, his grandson Felix, first Count Kinsella von Carlow in the Austrian service, was one hundred and thirty-second. That means *his* grandson, the great Count Gabriel – the only member of the family to become a full field marshal, as distinct from a general – was one hundred and thirty-fourth. Remembering that he was your great-grandfather, where does that place you?'

He smiled encouragingly while Philip did a quick calculation on his fingers.

'One hundred and thirty-seventh!' He beamed back triumphantly at his uncle.

'Correct. Well done, old chap. You are the one hundred and thirty-seventh generation from Adam, which is to say Adam was your one hundred and thirty-four greats-grandfather. Of course, it is all a legend got up by the ancient chroniclers; but, nevertheless, it is an imposing tradition.'

'Thank you very much for explaining it, Uncle Dermod. Wait till I tell Tom Dixon. I bet he doesn't know all his ancestors back to Adam.'

'Ah, don't brag about it now, Philip. A gentleman should be proud of his lineage, but also unassuming. Tom is a very nice lad and I don't want you putting on snobbish airs with him. His father is a fine doctor – and a real killer with the mayfly in the season. I must try investigating his pedigree,' he murmured, thinking aloud. 'I wonder, would his name be a straightforward Anglicization of O'Discin… or might he belong to the Dixons that come off the line of Burke of Clanricarde…? Of course, there could be a Huguenot origin…'

'Uncle Dermod,' his nephew interrupted this chain of thought, 'why have you pulled the furniture away from the wall on that side of the room?'

'Good heavens, I nearly forgot to tell you about my project.' His grey Kinsella eyes sparkled with enthusiasm.

'What project?'

'A project relating directly to what we have just been discussing. I intend to paint our extended pedigree, with heraldic illustrations, on the wall of this room, showing as many generations as the wall space will allow and displaying our numerous marriage alliances and collateral lines. The interruption of the surface area by so many windows does present some difficulties, but I am persuaded a coherent genealogy can be accommodated. I have already explained the scheme to your father,' he added hastily, 'and secured his consent.'

'Gosh, Uncle Dermod, that sounds a wonderful idea. May I help?'

'Certainly. Under strict supervision, of course. The one condition Bonaventure has imposed is that the work must be presentable, enhancing the decoration of the house, and not some amateurish daub. With that in mind, I have arranged for a professional artist to assist – a charming young man whom Father Yves and I met in Dublin last week. He has agreed to help out with any technical problems and should be able to determine the precise measurements necessary to accommodate so much detail. Both Father Yves and I were most impressed by him. He is a penniless artist,' Dermod admitted in a burst of candour, 'who is prepared to work for a nominal fee – not much more than bed and board.'

'When is he coming?' Philip's voice vibrated with enthusiasm. Visitors were always a welcome diversion and this one sounded particularly interesting.

'Next week. He is as keen as I am to get started – a pleasant and, I am sure, conscientious young man. As I say, Father Yves and I were greatly impressed.'

The mention of his tutor reminded Philip he ought at that moment to be practising French conversation with him.

'I must go now, Uncle Dermod. Father Yves is expecting me. Thank you for saying I can help with your painting.'

'Wait a moment,' said his uncle, smiling. 'Here is something else I nearly forgot: a small present I brought for you from Dublin.'

He took a package from his desk and handed it to his nephew. Stammering his thanks, Philip impatiently ripped off the wrapping-paper and gazed delightedly at the book in his hand, its cover proclaiming it belonged to his favourite, swashbuckling genre, though the title and author were excitingly unfamiliar: *Scaramouche*, by Rafael Sabatini.

'Oh, Uncle Dermod, this looks terrific! Thank you. It's terribly kind of you. Thank you very much.'

'You had better run along now to Father Yves,' said his uncle, his eyes twinkling with pleasure at the success of his present. 'Let me know if you enjoy it. If you do, I can get you other books by Sabatini.'

'I'm sure I shall. Thank you so much.'

Hurrying towards the schoolroom, Philip glanced out of a window in time to glimpse the flutter of Father Yves' black-and-white Dominican habit as it disappeared into a grassy alleyway running between high fuchsia hedges, known as the Priest's Walk, where he was accustomed to read his breviary. The secluded avenue had borne this name immemorially, presumably in allusion to some long-forgotten priest; it gave the Kinsellas satisfaction to see this tradition revived by a cleric regularly saying his Office there. Evidently Father Yves had either forgotten his appointed lesson or had given up on his pupil's attendance. Philip made a quick calculation of his options.

Since the priest was obviously going to say his Office, he would not thank him for interrupting his devotions. There remained the danger that his father might detect his truancy; in that event he would plead – plausibly, in the circumstances – that he had been unable to find Father Yves.

The schoolroom adjoined the nursery, which would be infested at this time of day by Dee-Dee and her nurse, so it was best avoided if he wanted peace and quiet to read the book that urgently demanded his attention. So, he stopped short of the schoolroom and took a detour to his bedroom. Curled up in the comfort of a chair at the open window, refreshed by the sweet summer air, he turned to the first page of Uncle Dermod's present with a quickening anticipation of the curtain rising on a new and enthralling world, as he read the opening sentence: 'He was born with a gift of laughter and a sense that the world was mad.'

CHAPTER IV

'DID ye read Yeats's drivel in the Senate, for God's sake?' demand-ed Eanna Kinsella, his brogue thickening in reaction to the offending parliamentary speech as he crumpled the newspaper in his ham-like hands and glared round at his brothers for support. They stared un-comprehendingly back at him across the débris of the breakfast table.

'I understood you to be an admirer of the poet Yeats,' said his eldest brother, raising his eyes from an article in *Horse and Hound* that offered a possible clue to the ailment he had detected in his much-loved hunter. 'Does he not belong to the artistic coterie that gave us incomprehensible dramas at the Abbey Theatre and pyro-technics at the General Post Office, to the great improvement of our lives? Surely he is part of the New Ireland you so heartily espouse?'

'Don't you go blackguarding the patriots now, Bonaventure.' Eanna reproved him with a scowl. 'If it wasn't for our dead heroes we'd still be under the English yoke.'

The last word struck an ominous chord with his brother Ulick.

'I thought my egg might have been slightly off,' he said anxious-ly. 'Did anyone notice a suspicious taste? You can get some very nasty upsets from bad eggs.'

'Ah, true for you, sir.' Corristeen endorsed this claim from his place at the sideboard where he was pottering ineffectually among the dishes, spilling kedgeree with reckless prodigality. 'An uncle of mine it was died in agony and he after eatin' an ould egg – in agony he died.' He repeated this detail with relish.

'What kind of an egg was it?' asked Ulick, turning even paler than usual.

'That, sir, I could not be precisely definite about, with regard to its provenience. But it was powerful bad. I did hear tell that some gurriers had stole it from the museum, for a wager. But the aunt said that was all mauryah and 'twas laid by one of Biddy Brogan's hens that never harmed a soul yet. It took the uncle eight months to die.'

'Eight months!' Ulick was appalled. 'Good heavens. What a dreadful end.'

'It was that, sir,' said Corristeen, picking up a tray to choreograph a well-timed exit at the conclusion of his narrative. 'They put tabercallosis on the death certificate, but sure he'd had that for years an' divil a harm it did him – 'twas the egg that kilt him.'

Eanna Kinsella, who knew the futility of interrupting Corristeen in full flow, stared resentfully at the door swinging shut behind the butler and returned to his grievance.

'Yeats has gone too far.' His round frog-face was flushed with indignation. 'That speech was an insult to Ireland. A worse example of Ascendancy arrogance I never heard.'

'What did he say? What was the debate about?' asked his brother Dermod, a slice of toast poised interrogatively in mid-air.

'Divorce,' Eanna told him shortly. 'Ireland not five years free from British rule and he wants us to fester in English degeneracy, as if we were still under the Union Jack.'

'So Yeats's grand remonstrance – I heard someone mention it yesterday – was about divorce,' said Dermod with a slow smile. 'Well, well, well. Is that what Irish Protestantism has come down to – the right to jettison an inconvenient spouse?'

'Heaven forbid we should speak ill of our non-Catholic neighbours and friends,' said Count Kinsella from the head of the table, 'but it is hardly reasonable of them to play the oppressed minority.'

'Especially when they retain both cathedrals in Dublin – stolen from the Catholic Church – with us condemned to worship in that miserable pro-cathedral.'

'By any standards, they have been treated generously,' agreed his elder brother. 'Particularly when one recalls how ruthlessly they imposed the penal laws in their day.'

'Five pounds for the head of a wolf or a priest!' Eanna recalled a bounty tariff from penal times.

'Myrtle Blackwell said something last week about the *Ne temere* decree,' Countess Kinsella remarked absently, looking up from a heavily scored-out and revised menu she was compiling. 'I gather the Protestants are very resentful about it.'

'I cannot think why,' said her husband. 'They have never before shown any inclination to marry Catholics – cutting off with a shilling was the usual response – so why restrictions on mixed marriages should trouble them now is beyond my comprehension.'

'It seems they want to marry Catholics and then divorce them,' said Dermod. 'The object, in fact, is to present themselves as the victims of a closed, priest-ridden society, which in the light of Irish history I can only regard as an affront to reason. They are trying to pretend the Free State's refusal to countenance divorce – its insistence on regarding marriage as sacred and binding – somehow outweighs centuries of persecution of Catholics and a murderous attempt to extirpate our religion.'

Eanna Kinsella had listened to his brothers' remarks with keen satisfaction, his nostrils flared with pleasure: it was a rare experience for his views to win their endorsement. Now he raised his newspaper and scanned it aggressively, searching for the most offensive passage to share with his siblings.

'Listen to Yeats's nonsense, will ye.' He began to read in his thick, slobbery accents from the closely printed page in his hand: ' "*We against whom you have done this thing, are no petty people. We are one of the great stocks of Europe. We are the people of Burke; we are the people of Grattan; we are the people of Swift, the people of Emmet, the people of Parnell –*" '

'Unfortunately,' Dermod interrupted him, 'they are also the people of Henry VIII, of Cromwell and of William of Orange.'

His brother acknowledged this intervention with a grimace of assent and resumed: ' "*We have created the most of the modern literature of this country*" – and burned the most of the ancient,' he added in parenthesis. ' "*We have created the best of its political intelligence. Yet I do not altogether regret what has happened. I shall be able to find out, if not I, my children will be able to find out whether we have lost our stamina or not. You have defined our position and have given us a popular following. If we have not lost our stamina then your victory will be brief, and your defeat final, and when it comes this nation may be transformed.*" What an eejit!'

Eanna ended his reading and crumpled the newspaper more forcefully as he laid it on the table and looked around.

'Very foolish,' said Bonaventure. 'As for their creating most of our modern literature, I should have thought Yeats was an admirer of James Joyce and, while I would hardly categorize Joyce as a daily communicant, he surely has his roots in the Catholic tradition.'

'Joyce is a worse blackguard than Yeats!' Eanna salivated with rage. 'A queer name he gave Clongowes in that book of his – what d'ye call it – *Picture of a Painter*. I threw it away when I got to the bit with some fella wettin' the bed.'

'If memory serves, that was on the first page,' said Dermod.

'Is that the report of the Senate debate? May I see it?' asked Bonaventure, reaching for the newspaper.

'What is this "popular following" that Yeats claims?' asked his wife. 'Are there hordes of malcontents marching round Stephen's Green, demanding divorce?'

'The fact of the matter,' Dermod put down a cup of lukewarm tea, 'is that Yeats is enslaved to his rhetoric. It would help his case if he had a popular following, so he claims one, out of wishful thinking. A poet should be a master of language, a craftsman in full command of his materials; instead, Yeats is carried away on a tide of verbiage. His poetry is beautiful and, at first hearing, deeply moving. It has a kind of mysticism that strikes a resonance within all of us; but it is not a true spirituality, because it is not inspired by any coherent religious belief. His mysticism is a mélange of old myth and new-fangled table-turning that the most superstitious old crone would balk at; but he clothes his absurd fancies in such emotive language.'

Dermod Kinsella's didactic propensities were not confined to genealogy.

'In contrast,' he enlarged on his theme, 'a much less significant poet such as Joseph Mary Plunkett could write about Christ's passion and the redemption of mankind – "*I see His blood upon the rose*" – with far more spiritual integrity. Yet the same man then compromised that integrity by putting on a republican uniform and joining the leaders of an uprising that caused terrible bloodshed – and all in supposed pursuit of a home rule that had already been conceded.'

'Ah, wait now, Dermod!' Eanna uttered an exclamation of outrage. 'I'll not hear a word –'

'Neither will I,' his sister-in-law said firmly. 'I will not have squabbling at the breakfast table. I cannot remember when we had such a disagreeable conversation, thanks to Senator Yeats.'

'I agree, my dear.' Her husband looked up from studying the report of the debate. 'I am sorry that Yeats should have spoken in such unbridled sectarian terms. It was thoroughly irresponsible – much more of this and we shall have the gunmen and arsonists back. When it was first set up, I thought the Senate would be a useful forum, composed of steady men of intellect and property, who would calm the passions that agitated the rawer politicians in the Dáil. Now, the most provocative speech since independence has come from the upper house. What is most repellent is his disingenuous attempt to represent himself as the spokesman for a persecuted minority.'

'Utterly disgraceful.' Dermod nodded in agreement. 'Have the Protestants forgotten how they forbade our worship, would not allow a Catholic to own a horse worth more than five pounds, denied us education at home or abroad, excluded Catholics from the professions –'

'Including medicine,' said Ulick indignantly.

'Five pounds for the head of a wolf or a priest!' repeated Eanna, who relished this slogan.

'The other distasteful element,' said their eldest brother, 'is the explicit blackmail regarding the North. Yeats says: "*If you show that this country, Southern Ireland, is going to be governed by Catholic ideas and by Catholic ideas alone, you will never get the North.*" Well, so be it. I am afraid my nostalgia for all those blue-jowled men in bowler hats is not so strong as Yeats imagines.'

'You will never defend Partition?' Eanna gaped, open-mouthed with dismay.

'Indeed I will. When one's neighbours are odious, a high demesne wall is the greatest comfort.'

Eanna uttered a strangled sound that caused Ulick to stare at him anxiously, fearing the onset of apoplexy.

'Yeats's thesis is straightforward.' Dermod summarized the case. 'When we were ruled by Britain we were, for centuries, denied the expression of our Catholic faith and principles. Now that we govern ourselves, we are to suppress those same principles in deference to our erstwhile rulers. He does not ask much. And for this demand he has a popular following.'

'Perhaps the heat affected him,' said Ulick, who was feeling poorly.

'Very possibly,' said his brother Bonaventure. 'Apparently he

57

was melting like a tallow candle while he spoke – Maurice Moore commented upon it in the chamber, though not in those words. I must say, Yeats has done this country a signal disservice. He has got us all thinking along sectarian lines, just when we should be forgetting our historical differences.'

'It is difficult for this family to forget historical differences,' said Dermod. 'The whole object of the penal laws was to decapitate Irish society by depriving it of its Catholic nobility. And in that they succeeded: we are among the very few survivors of an aristocratic Catholic diaspora that either met with extinction on foreign battlefields or was absorbed into the nobility of other countries. For two centuries Irish Catholics were deprived of leadership, except for the clergy. So, now we have a priesthood that, for all its undoubted virtues, has grown arrogant with power, having lost the habit of a proper subordination, in temporal matters, to a lay aristocracy.'

'Careful, Dermod, the Bishop would probably excommunicate you for voicing opinions like that.' His elder brother chuckled at the notion.

'The Bishop is a prime example of the phenomenon I am describing: remember the disobliging difficulties he has often raised over reservation of the Blessed Sacrament in our chapel.'

'That is precisely why I do not want to antagonize him in any way. I should be grateful if you would guard your tongue, Dermod, when next he dines with us.'

'I hope I am incapable of discourtesy to a guest,' said his brother stiffly.

'Anyway, you will be pleased to know the Church of Ireland Bishop of Meath is opposed to divorce.'

'So one would hope. But I must take issue –'

'Watercress soup!' His sister-in-law, who had no intention of allowing him to take issue with anyone, voiced a sudden inspiration. 'Of course – why did I not think of it before?'

She scribbled triumphantly on her much-erased menu card and stood up, followed immediately by her husband and brothers-in-law.

'I must take this down to Mrs Ennis. I suggest you move through to the morning room and let Kitty clear away in here,' she added, to indicate that all discussion of contentious matters was now at an end, with a servant in the room. Kitty, the senior of the two housemaids, a handsome dark-eyed girl, had come in and was hovering by the sideboard in readiness to remove the breakfast dishes.

As the men strolled through to the morning room Dermod briefly excused himself.

'There is something I must fetch – something that just occurred to me. I shall get the book from my room.'

Minutes after his brothers had sprawled themselves around the chintzy comfort of the morning room, Dermod reappeared, his finger marking a place in the book he carried. He cleared his throat self-consciously.

'If you will bear with me, I should just like to read you a short passage from this. It struck me as peculiarly apposite, since it is the perfect response to Yeats's "no petty people", with regard to the Anglo-Irish Protestants.'

'Very well,' said Count Kinsella cautiously. 'And then I hope we can abandon this unattractive topic.'

'Listen to this.' Dermod, standing before the empty hearth to command his audience, began to read aloud in his rich and musical voice: ' *"There were indeed Irish Roman Catholics of great ability, energy and ambition; but they were to be found every where except in Ireland, at Versailles and at Saint Ildefonso, in the armies of Frederic and in the armies of Maria Theresa. One exile became a Marshal of*

France. Another became Prime Minister of Spain. If he had staid in
his native land he would have been regarded as an inferior by all the
ignorant and worthless squireens who drank the glorious and immortal
memory. In his palace at Madrid he had the pleasure of being assidu-
ously courted by the ambassador of George the Second, and of bidding
defiance in high terms to the ambassador of George the Third. Scattered
over all Europe were to be found brave Irish generals, dexterous Irish di-
plomatists, Irish Counts, Irish Barons, Irish Knights of Saint Lewis and
of Saint Leopold, of the White Eagle and of the Golden Fleece, who, if
they had remained in the house of bondage, could not have been ensigns
of marching regiments or freemen of petty corporations. These men, the
natural chiefs of their race, having been withdrawn, what remained was
utterly helpless and passive." '

For some moments after he had finished reading, his three brothers remained sunk in reflection. None of them was unaffected by this passage that so accurately described the historical experience of their family. Presently Count Kinsella broke the silence.

'What is that from? It seems to me I have read it once, a long time ago.'

'You might think this ironic, but it is by one of the most bigoted of English Whig historians: it is from Macaulay's *History of England,* chapter XVII. The words are generous, but I suppose he felt he could afford such a tribute to those who had been dispossessed by the political system he championed.'

'You were right,' said Eanna in an unusually subdued tone. ''Tis the complete answer to Yeats's blathering about "no petty people". Those ignorant squireens were his people, after all.'

'If you will excuse me,' said Ulick weakly, one half of his mind depressed by revived atavistic antagonisms, the other still tormented by fears of a noxious egg, 'I think I shall go and lie down for a while.'

'I must go and look at Desertserges,' said Count Kinsella,

who was concerned for the health of his hunter. 'If I cannot work out what is the problem, I shall have to send for Dempsey, and be damned to the expense.'

'There is just one thing I am not sure about.' Dermod, thinking aloud, murmured ruminatively to himself. 'What Irish Knight of the White Eagle did Macaulay have in mind? I cannot think of one. The Golden Fleece, yes – Browne, Lacy, Nugent and, of course, Taaffe all received it; and O'Donell was awarded the Order of St Leopold for saving the Emperor's life. But what Irishman was given the White Eagle? Was Macaulay simply naming an order at random, to lend colour to his prose? I must find out...' His steps turned mechanically towards his tower-room study and the research materials that might satisfy his curiosity.

In the schoolroom, Father Yves had signally failed that morning to excite Philip's curiosity about the arcana surrounding the Latin ablative absolute. He sat at the heavily scored table, dressed in the habit of his Order, his arms folded beneath its scapular, seeking inspiration. The Dominican had an olive complexion and pronouncedly aquiline nose that gave him a hawk-like, predatory appearance, frequently softened by a kindly smile. He raised his hands and ran them through his coarse hair, black-and-silver in harmony with his habit, then gave a grunt of satisfaction as the solution came to him.

'You see, *mon enfant*, it is of the greatest assistance to analyse the words literally,' he told Philip in his Gallic-flavoured, but fluent English. 'For a long time I was myself baffled by the English idiom "me" and "I". I was asking myself, do I say correctly "He told Philip and I" or should it be "Philip and me"? So what do I do? Inside here,' he tapped his head and smiled, 'I am saying the sentence entirely: "He told Philip and he told me." Thinking it out that way, I would never say "He told Philip and he told I," so soon I have mastered the problem. *Compris?'*

'Yes, Father,' said Philip, truthfully, though he could not see how this practical expedient, which he resolved to adopt in future, unravelled the mysteries of the ablative absolute.

'So, with the ablative absolute, we must take the route of the literal. Think basically – think inelegantly. Say in your head,' he pointed towards Philip's furrowed brow, 'say "with Troy having been captured" – hideously ugly because you are looking at the skeleton, not the perfected body – then translate into Latin. What is it in Latin? "With Troy"…'

'Er – *Troia*…' It was difficult to get that familiar name wrong.

'*Ah, oui!*' Father Yves nodded encouragingly. 'Continue. What is "having been captured", ablative case, feminine singular?'

'*Capta*,' supplied Philip cautiously, more by instinct than syntactic skill. Then, more confidently as he saw the approving expression on his tutor's face: '*Troia capta.*'

'Excellent. Now let us, before leaving this captivating subject of the ablative absolute, (he cast a longing eye in the direction of a theological journal that had arrived from France by that morning's post and which he was eager to peruse) consider the more sophisticated instance where we venture beyond the perfect participle passive.'

Philip politely feigned an enthusiasm for this adventure he was far from feeling. The multifarious sounds of summer drifting in through the open window were as great a distraction for him as the unopened periodical was for the priest. Normally he quite enjoyed Latin, but today his heart was not in it. He longed to resume his greedy devouring of *Scaramouche*. He had reached the point where André-Louis Moreau, after swearing to avenge the death of his friend Philippe de Vilmorin, killed in an unfair duel by the Marquis de La Tour d'Azyr to silence his 'very dangerous gift of eloquence', had discovered his own powers of oratory by rousing the populace of Rennes. He was caught up in the story and urgently wanted to read on.

'Take, now, the situation,' said Father Yves, 'where we employ the future participle, meaning that someone is about to do something. Then we say *"Nuntius rege exituro advenit"*: "the messenger arrived as the king was about to depart." *Compris?* And finally, remembering always there is no present participle for the verb *esse*, it is silently understood in the Latin: *"Caesare duce Roma praevalebit."* Again, speak the whole words inside your head: *"with* Caesar *being* leader, Rome will prevail".'

'I see, Father.' And, in fact, he did. Philip was quick at Latin and quicker still at French. Father Yves suspected he had an aptitude for modern languages and recognized he was ahead of most boys of his age in certain subjects, including history and English. At the same time, his tutor was uneasily aware that Philip was badly behind in mathematics and that he himself lacked the ability to repair that deficiency, since this was his own academic blind spot. Concerned that the damage might be irreparable by the time his pupil eventually went to school, he had frankly broached the subject with Philip's father.

'No need for concern,' the Count had assured him with his customary calm. 'There is plenty of time yet.'

'He will gain no benefit from my teaching in mathematics,' Father Yves had confessed ruefully. 'We tried a simple algebraic equation this morning; by the time I had finished, without reaching a solution, it looked like a book of the *Iliad.*'

'Thank you for your candour, Father.' Count Kinsella had laughingly dismissed the problem. 'If the situation becomes really serious, in your view, we can always employ a mathematics tutor. Meantime, I hope you will continue to give my son the benefit of your scholarship in other subjects, which I greatly value.'

There the matter rested. Yet it offended the priest's sense of responsibility that he had failed his pupil, if only in one academic discipline. It reminded him of another failure, one perhaps more perceived than real, but which had made him an object of controversy and even vilification, leading to his present temporary detachment from his Order.

'Are you all right, Father?' Philip was disturbed by the black look that had darkened his tutor's face.

'Yes, I am quite well. I was just thinking of the injustice I have suffered at the hands of idiots, clowns, *scélérats*! You are too young to understand, *mon enfant*, the malice of the stupid, directed against one who has expounded a great truth.'

'The *filioque* clause.'

The words, uttered in muted tones almost of hieratic incantation, escaped Philip before he could stop himself. For months he had longed to discover what this esoteric formula meant. He knew it was the cause of Father Yves' rustication from his brother Dominicans, that it involved some kind of disgrace. Father Yves had 'blotted his copybook over the *filioque* clause', according to a casually dropped remark by Uncle Dermod. It sounded sinister. Now, Philip was horrified by his own indiscretion in uttering the phrase, as if he had called up some demon, and was afraid he might have offended Father Yves dreadfully. This did not appear to be the case.

'*Exactement, mon fils!*' The priest repeated the term, in something resembling exultation. 'The *filioque* clause. Never has there been a better instrument for distinguishing men of intellect from… *des sots*. I see you have heard of my situation. *Eh bien*, who has not? It is the celebrated cause. In effect, I am the Savonarola, the Jansen of our times. And why? Because I have written the treatise on the *filioque* clause, a fine work of scholarship as everyone has agreed, which leaves the Orthodox, as you would say, high and dry. But then comes the great Père Boscher, that ornament of our Order, who claims to find in it the heretical propositions. He says I have gone too far in favour of the Orthodox. And on what does he base this ridiculous claim? Only that I have examined the preference of Aquinas for *"per filium"*, even while I have repeated his unconditional acceptance of *"filioque"*. In effect, it is not me he accuses of heresy – this *bouffon* who could not with any confidence state how many persons there are in the Trinity – it is the Angelic Doctor himself.'

Father Yves paused and stared out of the window, his face registering bitter reflections. Philip preserved a scared silence, alarmed by the word 'heresy'.

'As for the Orthodox, have I not reproached them with their pretence that the *filioque* was forced on them at the Council of Chalcedon, when an eastern council in Persia – yes, Persia! – had already inserted it into the Creed forty years earlier? All are in agreement – my colleagues and superiors, men of learning who know I have written good doctrine. All except Boscher, who knows as much about the *pneumatologie* as I do about the engine of the automobile. Do you know what accusation he has made against me, this monument to ignorance? He has called me Photian heretic!'

'Ooh. When did he do that?'

'Last year, at a conference in Spain.'

'Gosh, Father Yves, you might have been burned at the stake.'

Philip's notion of Spanish jurisprudence derived from his addiction to historical novels.

'I do not think that sanction has been contemplated, though I am certain Boscher would approve. But that was not the worst of the matter. Boscher has made so much noise before he is silenced by our superiors that something very unfortunate has happened. The controversy, which until then has been a storm in a cup of tea, has reached the attention of the Jesuits. Like the sharks, they smell the blood in the water. Three of them – you will note that it takes three

Jesuits to attack the thesis of a single Dominican – have published objections to my work. One of them has gone further – he has denunciated me to the Holy Office. The Jesuits, in effect, cannot resist the opportunity to embarrass the Dominicans and this they now do, courtesy of Boscher – *quel crétin!* He has put our Order at the disadvantage to those black crows of Jesuits.'

Philip's eyes were wide with wonder and alarm. He had never before heard the Society of Jesus referred to in disparaging terms. His father and uncles had all been educated by the Jesuits – his brothers were currently at a Jesuit public school in England which was also his intended destination in a few years' time. Yet Father Yves' authority in religious matters could not be gainsaid. Perhaps (he tried to rationalize the situation) it was only French Jesuits who were malevolent. Nevertheless, there crept into the back of his mind a vague recollection of certain disrespectful remarks about 'the Js' made by his eldest brother Edmund, who was suspected of subversive attitudes, on many issues, that were beginning to concern his parents.

'And yet,' a note of renewed optimism entered Father Yves' voice, 'it may all be for the best. The entire Order is with me now, in this war with the Jesuits. My superiors have given me leave to retire here and prepare my *apologia*. I am composing the further commentary on my writings that will justify my opinions – a fourth volume explicating the previous three. I have the confidence of my brothers. The esteemed Père Garrigou-Lagrange, at the Angelicum, has expressed his approval of my work. Boscher will soon regret to have subjected me to the persecutions of this Jesuit *canaille*.'

Philip drew in his breath excitedly at that last word. It was regularly employed as a term of contempt in the works of Baroness Orczy and in *Scaramouche*, the book that currently preoccupied his waking hours; but he had not realized it was still in currency. To hear it applied to the Jesuits conveyed an even greater *frisson*, of taboos breached and totems overthrown. Seeing Father Yves was in so outspoken a mood, he was emboldened to ask the question that had been perplexing him.

'Please, Father, what is the *filioque* clause?'

'Why, Philip, you hear it every day. When you serve Mass for me in the morning, do I not say in the *Credo* the words *"qui ex Patre, Filioque procedit"*?'

'Oh, yes, of course.' He recognized the familiar formula.

'Well, there you have it: the Holy Ghost proceeds from the Father and the Son – *c'est ça.*'

'But, Father, I don't understand.'

'*Ni moi non plus, mon fils!* It is not given to us to understand – not even Our Holy Father the Pope, not even the great Saint Thomas. We can only conjecture on the basis of the deposit of faith. And now it is time, I think, for you to ride your small pony.'

Through Father Yves' memory raced recollections of crowded lecture theatres, of tiers of intent faces, of fierce disputation without resolution. From all of this remembered conflict one clear conclusion emerged: he had no intention of spending the remainder of the day attempting to explain the Procession of the Holy Ghost to a nine-year-old boy.

'Yes, Father.' Philip accepted the implicit bargain: refraining from further enquiry on the topic of the *filioque* clause, in return for his manumission from the servitude of Latin grammar. 'Thank you.'

'I hope your little horse is well. Through the window I have just seen Monsieur Dempsey, *le vétérinaire*, who goes with your parents to the stables.'

'Oh, dear. That must be to do with Desertserges – Papa was worried about him. I must go and find out how he is.'

Father Yves saw off his pupil with a valedictory smile. Then, while Philip pounded downstairs to the stable yard, the priest gave a sigh of pleasurable anticipation and reached for his copy of the *Revue thomiste*, on a morning when the Kinsella household had pre-occupied itself to an unusual degree with matters controversial and metaphysical.

CHAPTER V

DEMPSEY the vet opened the lower half of the door of the loose box and stroked the muzzle of the hunter inside. Desertserges gave a snort of acknowledgement and nuzzled the visitor's shoulder. He knew and liked Dempsey, and listened gravely to his social small talk.

'There's the boyo! Grand fella yeh are. Now then, let's have a look at the ould legs...'

The Kinsellas, husband and wife, watched anxiously, as at the bedside of a sickly infant. Dempsey was a thickset man in his forties with a toothbrush moustache, eight children and a sceptical view of the world. Still muttering the occasional endearment for the horse's benefit, the vet ran his expert hands down the near foreleg, travelling via knee, fetlock and pastern to the hoof, where he paused intently. His face preserved the non-committal expression of a physician making a diagnosis; his two spectators waited on tenterhooks. Desertserges submitted docilely to the examination, nuzzling Dempsey once more. When the vet released the hoof and looked up, the Kinsellas caught the expression of anger that momentarily crossed his face.

'Might I ask who put this shoe on the boy?' His voice was controlled, but the tone was unmistakable. 'Would it be little Miss Deirdre, for example, I wonder?'

'It was Bartie Lawlor, as usual, of course,' said Count Kinsella defensively.

'It's sorry I am to contradict you, Count, but Bartie Lawlor, drunk or sober, never did the like of that to a beast in his natural life.'

'Actually,' Countess Kinsella fingered her pearls nervously, 'now that I come to think of it, it might have been that young man he has working for him recently.'

'I knew it – and a right hames he's made of it. The clenches are too high.' He lifted the hoof again to exhibit the problem. 'No wonder the poor brute was unhappy. Now, here's what you must do. Put him in the trailer – don't try to walk or ride him – and take him below to the forge and have these shoes taken off. I'll stop by on my way back and give Lawlor a piece of my mind – tell him to get rid of that useless blackguard before he cripples half the horses in the county. And stand over him until the new shoes are on. Your splendid hunter, Count – I can imagine,' he added with a grim smile, 'what you must have been thinking. Laminitis, the ould navicular capers, every category of disaster, was it?'

'Certainly, I had him foundered at least. This is a great relief, Mr Dempsey.'

'Ah, I'm glad for him. Sure, he's a great lad.' He stroked Desertserges affectionately. 'And when he comes back from the forge, would you ever get him out to grass – we don't want a colic, do we?'

'I thought the heat of the sun –'

'Never trouble yourself about that. This boy has the sense to find himself a bit of shade if he feels the need. Hullo, here's someone with an enquiring mind…'

He gazed quizzically across the stable yard as Philip came running in under the arch beneath the clock tower where the time had stopped forever at twenty past ten, long years before.

'Is Desertserges all right?' Philip asked breathlessly. Then, feeling that this question had perhaps been too peremptory for social decency, he held out his hand and said: 'I hope you are well, Mr Dempsey?'

'Never better,' the vet assured him, shaking hands with proper solemnity. 'And the same goes for himself (nodding at the hunter), as soon as he patronizes a better class of shoemaker. How's Pegasus?' He posed this question out of sociability, though he already knew the answer since he had just looked Philip's pony over, in passing.

'Very well, thank you. I'm just taking him out.'

'That's the ticket.'

'And you can definitely confirm,' asked Philip's mother as they began to stroll towards the house, 'that both Calpurnia and Pompadour are in foal?'

'Carrying Derby winners, for sure, the both of them.'

'Thank you, I'm so glad. Do come into the house and have a cup of tea.'

'Or something stronger,' said Count Kinsella, who knew his man.

'Ah, that's very kind of you. Perhaps just a quick tincture, on a hot day like this.'

'Philip,' said his mother, who knew his propensity to attach himself to adult company, 'I thought you said you were going out on Pegasus?'

'Yes, I am, Mummie.'

'Well, off you go. If you come back in time – *and change into your short trousers* – you may join us for luncheon, since we are eating on the terrace, it's such a lovely day.'

'Oh, good! Thanks, Mummie, I shan't be late.'

He scampered back to the stables, fetched the necessary impedimenta from the tack room and saddled up Pegasus, watched by a stable boy seated on the wall, chewing a wisp of straw.

'Them irons is too low for you, Master Philip,' he observed critically.

'That's the way I like them.' Philip squinted appraisingly. 'Actually, I think you may be right, though.'

He shortened the leathers minimally (no harm in being diplomatic), mounted and rode out of the yard, under the dead clock in its weed-grown turret. As he walked the pony round to the front of the castle, Conn the wolfhound rose from where he was crouched in the shade, stretched himself and wagged his tail for a couple of lazy pendulum swings in greeting, then began to follow him. By the time Philip was trotting down the avenue, its grass verges overgrown with encroaching rhododendrons blooming pink, red and purple, the big dog had accelerated to a long, easy lope to keep pace. He would not escort him much further, Philip knew: the wolfhound would stop just before the curve of the drive revealed the entrance gates, the scene of tragedy for Conn some years previously, which his canine instinct told him to avoid. Sure enough, at precisely the predicted spot, the dog stopped dead; his shaggy face suddenly seemed haggard in the sun, as he stared after Philip with his great sad eyes.

The boy was no longer thinking of Conn: this was a moment, a prospect that he relished. Mostly, when he went out by himself on Pegasus, he took the back way, following familiar paths through rough pasture, or down towards the river; but today he was leaving the demesne by its most imposing route, out through the massive gatehouse. This was much grander than the modest south lodge. The northern entrance to Castle Kinsella was more like a fortalice in itself – a huge crenellated structure incorporating a sizeable house, ornamented with mullioned windows, blind cross-shaped loopholes and every elaboration of gothic military architecture. It was a relic of the days when Irish gentry competed to build gatehouses of extravagant grandeur, sometimes beggaring themselves in the process. Now it loomed ahead of him, three storeys high, its arched entrance framing the countryside beyond. The heavy wrought-iron gates were fastened back, as they always were, to afford open access. There was no sign of the family that lived in the lodge, but with the gates permanently open to all comers there was little need for a keeper.

Philip loved passing out this way on horseback. Now, with brilliant sunshine dappling the oaks and beeches above the rhododendrons on either side, as he approached the gates it pleased him to imagine he was D'Artagnan, riding forth to seek his fortune. He wished he had a sword at his side; its absence seemed a deficiency. When he had passed under the sudden shadow of the gatehouse and instantly out into the sunlight again, he paused on the broad expanse of gravel bordered with cut grass that separated the towering edifice from the road and looked back at it appreciatively. Although he had lived there all his short life and could not imagine calling anywhere else home, he was conscious of his good fortune in being brought up in a place that so perfectly suited his romantic temperament. Or had his surroundings moulded his imagination? It was a question that had never occurred to him. What was on his mind was the naked look of the empty flagstaff on the highest point of the gatehouse. There ought to be a flag flying there; and another over the castle itself. He had raised this issue with his father, who had replied dismissively: 'There's been enough trouble over flags in this country – I think we'd be well advised to fly no colours.'

Uncle Dermod had reacted more favourably. 'I'm sure we have a house flag somewhere, displaying our arms. That couldn't be politically controversial. I shall ask Corristeen if he remembers where it is. Yes, it would be good to see the family flag flying again. I remember it in my father's time.'

Still, no action had been taken. Philip tried to envisage what the flag would look like. He gazed at the large coat of arms carved in relief over the entrance. The one disadvantage suffered by gentlemen who had chosen the gothic style of architecture and fashioned their homes as castles, rather than classical mansions, with complementary gatehouses, was that they denied themselves the entrance pillars on top of which they could display their heraldic beasts and accessories. The compensatory alternative was to carve their arms on the front of the gatehouse in as ostentatious a style as possible. Few had indulged in greater ostentation than Field Marshal Gabriel, Count Kinsella, the builder of Lissanore, the confidence bred of his high rank and estates in the Austrian Empire reinforced by a generous income from South American banking interests. He had caused his full achievement of arms, surmounted by the coronet of a count of the Holy Roman Empire and his crest of ostrich plumes, supported on either side by rampant lions snarling in a lifelike manner, to be engraved in a large panel. The shield in the centre displayed the Kinsella arms, whose heraldic blazon Uncle Dermod had taught Philip to recite by heart: *Argent, a fess gules between in chief two garbs of the second, and in base a lion passant sable.* So, the house flag, he calculated, would be white with a broad red horizontal stripe, above it two red sheaves of barley, below it a black lion. Yes, he thought, that would look impressive.

Studying the huge heraldic carving, what particularly appealed to his aesthetic sense was the family motto on a scroll beneath the coat of arms. He liked the stylized diphthong in the first syllable of the final word, complemented by the letter 'u' rendered in Roman style as 'v' in the last: *ZONA DOMINI PRÆCINCTVS.* These two archaic conventions lent a pleasing air of antiquity to the motto. Uncle Dermod had told him it came from an old Latin poem in honour of Saint Patrick, each line of which began with a successive letter of the alphabet, this being the last. Enthused by this communing with his heritage, Philip turned Pegasus's head onto the road, flanked on his left by the high battlemented demesne wall built by grateful labour in the Famine years. His father had said this part of the country had not suffered starvation in those dreadful times, but there had been many deaths as a result of the cholera that spread from the afflicted areas.

Philip's intention was to ride over to his friend Tom Dixon's house and leave a message that he should meet him that evening.

On the road he encountered only a few vehicles, motor or horse-drawn, whose drivers raised a leisurely hand in greeting. While the demesne wall still bordered the road, he passed three small, dirty children with a donkey. They nodded at him gravely, staring at Pegasus with the informed interest of tinkers; but he noticed the donkey was splatter-footed, its untrimmed hoofs curling up, which reminded him of Desertserges, relieved of his discomfort by Dempsey's professional acumen. Soon after, an old woman at the door of a cottage smiled and returned his wave with some inaudible benediction, calling to heel a collie that threatened to harass Pegasus. Then he was taken by surprise, as a pony and trap came trotting round the corner towards him; it belonged to old McConkey, a morose character who provided a sporadic service as carrier and poor man's taxicab. He had a passenger, a young man who lolled back indolently in the primitive conveyance, one elbow resting on a battered suitcase standing on end in the trap behind him. He was smiling even before he saw Philip, but his smile widened in greeting. He wore a disreputable hat tilted far back on his head, as if displaced by the thick crop of curly brown hair on which it nestled.

'Grand day,' he said genially.

'It is.' Philip responded politely. 'Hello, Mr McConkey.'

The driver raised his whip about six inches in greeting, a gesture that, with him, corresponded to gleeful animation in other mortals. The trap passed by, the young man still smiling, though he was no longer looking at Philip, just gazing idly at the landscape. Philip wondered if he smiled all the time. He had only ridden a hundred yards when a more unsettling question struck him: where was McConkey's passenger going? He was definitely a stranger to these parts; the most obvious destination on that road was Lissanore, but he did not look like a potential house guest. So, where was he bound? The question was still unresolved when Pegasus turned unbidden into the short driveway that led to Tom Dixon's home.

Tom lived in a small, elegant, creeper-covered Georgian house that would have accorded his father the status of gentleman farmer if it had had a farm attached, instead of a few acres of woodland, thinning into the formality of a garden in its immediate environs and with a moderate-sized paddock occupied by the family's horses. As Philip rode up to the front door, Tom's father, Dr Dixon, emerged carrying a Gladstone bag which he deposited on the passenger seat of his motor car before turning to greet him.

'Hello, Philip. I'm afraid I'm off on my rounds, so it's hail and farewell.'

'Hello, Dr Dixon. I know Tom will have gone into Burras, but I just wanted to leave a message for him to meet me tonight, if he can.'

'Tell his mother.' He nodded in the direction of his wife, who had just appeared at the front door, got into his car and drove off with a cheerful wave.

'Come and have a glass of lemonade, Philip,' said Mrs Dixon hospitably.

Philip dismounted and a boy took charge of Pegasus while Tom's mother conducted him into the house, through a cluttered hall and out through a back door to the spacious lawn at the rear, where a table and chairs were positioned under the shade of a large willow. Philip waited until Mrs Dixon had sat down then followed suit.

'Another lovely day, thank God,' she said, looking around appreciatively.

Philip liked Tom's mother. He particularly enjoyed the calm, unruffled demeanour with which she went through life: it had a soothing, reassuring effect on everybody around her and was the ideal temperament for a doctor's wife. Philip always felt relaxed in her company. Her indestructible calm discredited the claim that people with red hair had fiery natures to match. Mrs Dixon's hair was only faintly red, really just a coppery-tinged brunette, and her freckles were sparse and faint, barely noticeable – unlike two girls in the village, sisters, who had flaming red hair in long ringlets and such heavy freckles they permanently looked as if they had measles. Philip thought them repulsive. Tom's mother, on the other hand, was quite nice-looking, almost pretty. Her housekeeper, a woman of unpredictable temper, brought a tray laden with a jug of lemonade and two glasses which she arranged on the table, greeting Philip civilly as she did so. Apparently it was one of her better days.

'So, Philip, are you enjoying the holidays?' asked Tom's mother, taking a sip of lemonade.

'I'm not on holiday yet – not until Edmund and Dominick come home from school. Then Father Yves will stop most of my lessons.'

'It must be very convenient having your tutor in the house.'

'Yes, it is. He's a very nice man and I am learning French amazingly quickly because I have somebody French to talk to.'

'That must be a tremendous advantage. I'm afraid Tom still doesn't know a word of French, apart from a few phrases he learned from you. Rather odd ones, at that. I'm not too sure about *"sacre bleu"*, for example.'

She looked significantly at Philip, who found himself blushing faintly.

'I'm sorry, Mrs Dixon, I hope it isn't something rude. But the musketeers are always shouting it when they are attacked by the Cardinal's guards.'

'All the same,' Mrs Dixon smiled, to take any sting out of her rebuke, 'I should prefer not to have Tom shouting it. Are you meeting him this evening?' She moved deftly to a more comfortable subject. 'I think he said something about going out to see you.'

'Yes, I was hoping he could come.'

'If you want him to bring back the book you lent him, I shall mention it, though I'm afraid he hasn't finished it yet. He left off *Ivanhoe* when he got his hands on another *Just William* book. I'm not saying he won't go back to it when he has finished the lighter one, but I think he was finding *Ivanhoe* rather heavy going – too much gadzooks and thee-ing and thou-ing for his taste. You know Tom – he's not greatly gifted with concentration.'

She smiled as she made this frank avowal of her son's short-comings and drank some lemonade. Philip recognized the truth of what she said: Tom was quite fond of reading, but did not share his avid interest in historical fiction.

'I think, in fact, *Ivanhoe* was the worst book I could have given him,' he said ruefully. 'It *is* heavy going if you don't like all the mediæval language, though actually I loved it. I should have lent him a Scarlet Pimpernel book instead.'

Mrs Dixon was amused by Philip's missionary zeal to convert her son to a proper appreciation of the past.

'That might have been better. Though he did enjoy the villain of the piece – Sir Brian – what was his name?'

'Sir Brian de Bois-Guilbert.' Philip pronounced the Norman name with great gusto and accuracy, thanks to his regular conversations with Father Yves.

'Yes, well, Tom is hoping he will come to a bad end – I think he might carry on reading the book just to find out. He loves when villains meet their just deserts. It's years since I read *Ivanhoe*, so I can't remember exactly what happens to him, but I think he was killed.'

'That's right. He was killed in the lists –'

'The lists?' To Mrs Dixon the term was associated with shopping or laundry.

'The jousting lists, at the Preceptory of Templestowe, in front of the Grand Master and the other Knights Templar. He was fighting Ivanhoe and they both fell from their horses, but the Templar was dead.'

'I see. So, Ivanhoe killed him with his lance?' She took a drink of lemonade.

'No, not exactly. He died a victim to the violence of his own contending passions.'

Mrs Dixon gave a convulsive shudder and choked on her mouthful of lemonade. Tears welled in her eyes and she groped urgently for a handkerchief. Philip watched her anxiously; he would have liked to help, but could think of nothing to do, except perhaps slapping her on the back, which might have been considered an impertinence.

'What – What did you say?' she finally asked weakly.

Philip was relieved to see her recovering. For a moment he had been afraid that his words, quoted verbatim from the novel because of his uncertainty over their precise interpretation, held some offensive meaning for adults – like *sacre bleu* – but this was clearly not the case, since Mrs Dixon had asked him to repeat them.

'He died a victim to the violence of his own contending passions.' He intoned the quotation solemnly.

'That's what I thought you said. Oh dear. I'm afraid the lemonade went down the wrong way. Do forgive me, Philip.'

'Of course, Mrs Dixon. It wasn't your fault – it was an accident. Deirdre keeps doing the same thing at tea in the nursery. I mean...' The infelicity of comparing his hostess's mishap with the clumsiness of his baby sister suddenly came home to him and he felt the blood rising to his face.

'Good, so I am forgiven, then,' said Mrs Dixon brightly. She was practised in glossing over the gaucheries of young boys.

Philip murmured something grateful and incoherent. To cover

his embarrassment he drank some of his own lemonade, realizing at the last moment he must do so very carefully: if he spluttered over it, it might look as if he were parodying Tom's mother. Life was full of social pitfalls. He was relieved to hear the welcome distraction of the Angelus tolling distantly from the church tower. Mrs Dixon crossed herself with the measured serenity of all her movements; Philip made the sign of the cross more hurriedly and inclined his head to say the prayer mentally.

'The angel of the Lord declared unto Mary…'

By the time he reached the end of the first verse he realized that Mrs Dixon was not praying the Angelus through, but had contented herself with the reverential gesture. To avoid keeping her waiting, instead of saying the full 'Hail Mary' between each verse he simply said the two words, an abbreviation he thought justified in the circumstances; and so to the closing payer: 'Pour forth, we beseech Thee, O Lord, thy grace into our hearts, that we to whom the Incarnation of Christ Thy Son was made known by the message of an angel, may by His Passion and Cross be brought to the glory of His Resurrection. Through the same Christ Our Lord. Amen.'

It took him less than two minutes and he felt guilty that, even though praying silently in his head, he had gabbled the words. What made it worse was that Mrs Dixon, respecting his piety, had given no sign of irritation at his withdrawal from the conversation. In fact, she was the least likely person to do so he could think of: her invincible serenity cast a stillness over their surroundings and, even after he had finished, she made no attempt to resume the conversation, instead placing her hand on the broad brim of her straw hat to shield her eyes from the sun while she gazed absently around. Philip sighed. He should have said the full 'Hail Mary' all three times.

'How is your mother's garden?' his hostess asked at last. 'Is she still having trouble with those calceolaria? I told her she should cut her losses and get rid of them. It's like having an invalid permanently on one's hands. I wouldn't have the patience.'

'I think Mummie is getting pretty impatient too. I heard her talking about it to Wilson.'

'I don't blame her.'

Philip drained his glass of lemonade. The Angelus had reminded him of the time.

'If you will excuse me, please, I must go now, Mrs Dixon, or I shall be late – we're lunching outside on the terrace today.'

He stood up slowly, to avoid giving the impression of a precipitate departure.

'What a good idea. I think we might lunch alfresco too. Please give my regards to your mother.'

'Yes, I will. Thank you very much for having me. And thanks for the lemonade. I'll go and fetch Pegasus myself, I know the way. Please tell Tom I'll meet him on the bridge tonight, as usual.'

'I shan't forget. Goodbye, Philip. Come again soon.' She smiled a farewell.

Philip retrieved Pegasus and rode back towards Lissanore, pleased to have arranged a rendezvous with his friend. Since they had not seen each other for a week, they would have a lot to talk about. Just how much, Philip did not realize until he arrived home and found a startling new development had occurred in his absence.

A long table, sheltered from the sun by a gaily-striped awning, had been set for luncheon on the broad, battlemented terrace at the rear of the house, which overlooked a lawn and informal gardens below, accessible by sets of stone steps at either end. Creeper and climbing roses straggled up the castellated front of the terrace, its military aspect unconvincingly asserted by two cannon positioned near the top of each flight of steps. (It was Philip's long-cherished ambition to fire those guns one day.) Golden laburnum cascaded like a fountain from the garden below, while the purple and white-blossomed crests of lilac trees reared as high as the embrasures of the wall, wafting their fragrance onto the terrace where groups of adults stood chatting, with drinks in their hands. It was to create this secluded haven at the rear of the castle on sunny afternoons and evenings that Count Gabriel Kinsella, the builder of Lissanore, had chosen a north-facing orientation for his house. Corristeen, whose ancient black coat made no concession to the climate, was officiously distracting the two housemaids as they finished setting the table.

Philip stared, instinctively aware of some novelty, though he could not immediately identify it. His parents were there and all three of his resident uncles; Father Yves, as was to be expected; Mrs Blackwell, the rector's attractive wife, he noted with pleasure – she was a frequent luncheon guest; with less pleasure he saw his sister Dee-Dee and her nurse hovering, by some exceptional dispensation, on the outskirts of the throng. His little sister was clasping a vessel made from some unbreakable, child-proof material, containing lemonade or orange juice, in both hands; but instead of slurping greedily at its contents, she was staring in shy wonderment at someone obscured from view by the black-and-white-robed figure of Father Yves. Philip had just begun to make a detour across the flagstones to see who it might be when his mother intercepted him.

'Ah, there you are – just in time. Say hello to Mrs Blackwell.'

'Hello, Mrs Blackwell.'

'Hello, Philip.' The rector's wife was dark and striking-looking, very fashionably dressed – excessively so for a clergyman's spouse in a rural parish, her critics claimed – and smoking a cigarette in a short amber holder, another indulgence for which she was condemned as 'fast' by the more conservative women in her husband's congregation. She favoured him with a dazzling smile. 'I see you were out on Pegasus.'

'Yes, I –' He lapsed into confused silence, realizing it was the sight of his jodhpurs that had provoked this observation. He had forgotten to change into his shorts.

'It doesn't matter,' said his mother with unusual leniency, reading his mind, 'since we are lunching out of doors. Come and meet our new house guest.'

She led him across the terrace, threading her way through family members and bustling housemaids. Uncle Dermod looked round at his sister-in-law's approach then caught sight of Philip.

'Hah! Just the man. Here is someone I want you to meet. This is my nephew Philip, who will be helping us in our project. Philip, this is Declan.'

He was startled to find himself confronted by the young man he had passed in McConkey's trap that morning. His mop of curly brown hair, he now saw, was complemented by eyes of the same colour. The smile was still in place; Philip wondered if it had been extinguished at any point during the time since he had last seen him.

'Hullo again.' The smile broadened.

'How do you do?'

'Very well, thank you, Philip.'

'What's this I hear about him helping in your project?' asked Philip's mother. 'I thought it was a highly artistic task, requiring great skill and aptitude.'

'And so it is,' said Uncle Dermod, 'which is why we have brought Declan down from Dublin to help with the draughtsmanship; but there is room for a keen helper, on the less technical side – under strict supervision, as I have already emphasized.'

Philip suddenly grasped the situation: the young man, Declan, had come to help Uncle Dermod paint the Kinsella armorial pedigree on the wall of his room in the drum tower. His uncle had told him about it, but he had forgotten until now.

'You're an artist!'

'Guilty, as charged.' The young man answered him good-humouredly. 'Though you might have difficulty persuading some of my teachers – those that used to teach me, that is – to agree.'

'I have seen some of Declan's work,' said Dermod Kinsella firmly, 'as has Father Yves, and we both agree it displays a high standard of professionalism.' He glanced at the Dominican for confirmation and Father Yves, who had momentarily turned away to talk to Eanna, immediately complied.

'Eh, bien – formidable!' He gestured appreciatively.

'That,' said Countess Kinsella, 'makes me all the more apprehensive about Philip's role in the project.' She was laughing, but he grew suddenly concerned that she might jeopardize his right to participate.

Further discussion was cut short by Corristeen's wheezy but stentorian announcement: 'Luncheon is served, if yeh please, madam!'

As the company milled around the table, seeking their places under their hostess's direction, the butler took his stance behind Countess Kinsella's chair which, the instant she sat down, he propelled so vigorously towards the table that she put out a protective hand to ward off the likely impact. Corristeen was impervious to her indignant glance as he shook open a crisp linen napkin with a flourish and held it for her to dispose on her lap, remarking conversationally as he did so: 'Wasn't it the grand idea, on a day like this, to be dinin' andante in God's fresh air?'

CHAPTER VI

CALASANCTIUS Corristeen, the idiosyncratic butler of Lissa-nore, had not been fully sober since some time before the War; but neither had he been drunk, within the meaning of the act. Rather, he had maintained an equilibrium between the two states by con-stantly fortifying himself with alcohol, seldom to evident excess, but sufficiently regularly to fend off indefinitely a return to sobriety. The main base for his campaign against intrusive reality was the but-ler's pantry, which was always well stocked with a variety of wines and spirits salvaged from the dining room and drawing room; it was supported by a chain of supply depots around the house, hidden caches where the butler had secreted small deposits of drink to be consumed as required. The library was particularly suited to this purpose: Father Yves, seizing with satisfaction on a rare edition of a Papal *Bullarium*, had been nonplussed to discover a half bottle of whiskey concealed behind it. Newly engaged housemaids, on mak-ing similar discoveries in unexpected places and carrying their finds to Mrs Ennis the cook, or to Bridie Byrne, had been quietly instruct-ed to 'Put that yoke back where you found it.' If they reported it to Corristeen himself, he would engage in an elaborate pantomime of mystification ('Well, isn't that a quare thing! And yeh came across it in the game larder, begob? 'Twas used for dowsin' the maggots, maybe. Give it here and I'll see to it…').

These discoveries were not necessarily unwelcome to Cor-risteen: sometimes, squirrel-like, he had forgotten the location of a cache until its contents were recovered in this way. He did not realize his employers knew about his network of '*apéritifs*', as Count Kinsella called them – though not its full scale – having sometimes stumbled across a concealed bottle and diplomatically ignored it, since the butler's alcoholic foibles did not impede the performance of his duties, albeit in a highly individual style. They suspected, with good reason, that Corristeen's comportment, if he could have been restored to full sobriety, would not have been discernibly different. So, the butler had continued to inhabit his half-world, limited to the confines of the Lissanore demesne and mostly to the house itself, detached from the realities outside. In this way, the Great War, the Troubles between Ireland and its English suzerain, and the civil war resulting from the partition Treaty had made little impact on Corristeen, even though the survival of Lissanore had at one point hung in the balance, subject to the whim of a guerrilla 'commandant'. He was not unaware of these events; they had simply impinged on his consciousness at a muted level. One discipline he imposed upon himself: except on the rare occasions when he left the confines of the property – for that was what a drinking flask was designed to accommodate – he never carried alcohol on his person. That he would have regarded as degenerate.

Although his intake of drink had not shaped his personality, already established in its eccentricity long before he fell into the habit, the varying quantity and character of what he had consumed (dependent on the household's leftovers) did dictate Corristeen's mood at any given moment, ranging from the darkly taciturn to the volubly loquacious. The latter generally predominated. Today, as he presided over luncheon on the terrace, glowing internally from a fortifying libation poured for him by the cook and externally from the warmth of the sun and the unaccustomed stimulus of the open air, the butler was feeling, as he himself expressed it, 'as frisky as one of them yearlings Himself has in the field below'.

Countess Kinsella had already noted this phenomenon with some concern. She tried to watch the butler unobtrusively, though aware of her almost certain inability to avert any catastrophe that might threaten, while fulfilling her responsibilities as hostess. She felt grateful there were only two guests – Mrs Blackwell and the new arrival Declan – since any excess Corristeen might commit would provoke little surprise or consternation within the family circle.

'So, Declan,' she was saying (no one ever used the artist's surname, so that most people – perhaps everybody – remained in ignorance of it), 'you and Dermod are going to paint the tower room?'

'We are that.' The painter grinned, laying down the spoon with which he had just eaten a plateful of soup with gratifying enthusiasm.

'I am going to help,' said Philip, anxious after his mother's disparaging remark to establish publicly the compact made with his uncle. 'Isn't that right, Uncle Dermod?'

'It is. As I said – under strict supervision. This is not a job for amateurs, that is why I have called in a professional.'

'Is this the kind of work you normally do?' Philip's mother asked Declan, strongly suspecting it was not.

'Well, you know, I do a bit of this and that. I'm no Michelangelo, but I can turn my hand to most things. In my line of work you have to be versatile, you see. So, when Count Dermod asked me to help with his mural I jumped at the opportunity. The fact is, I hadn't any other work on offer.'

'Were you starving in a garret?' asked Philip interestedly.

'*Phil-lip!*' His mother pronounced his name in two drawn-out syllables, as she did when administering a rebuke.

'Well, were you?' Mrs Blackwell mischievously pursued the question, to the discomfiture of her hostess, turning to regard the young man directly for the first time.

'You were right and you were wrong,' said Declan, addressing himself to Philip. 'I was starving in a basement.'

This adroit response sent a ripple of laughter down the length of the table. Count and Countess Kinsella sat at opposite ends. On the inside, with their backs to the windows of the house, sat Declan on his hostess's left, with Uncle Dermod next to him, in the role of sponsor. Then came Mrs Blackwell and Uncle Ulick who was taciturn at mealtimes, being preoccupied in inspecting his food for any hazard to his health. Beyond him was Eanna, at the end of the table where Philip's father presided. Facing them, with their backs to the parapet of the terrace, sat Dee-Dee on her mother's right, with her nurse, then Philip (who thus had Mrs Blackwell and his Uncle Ulick opposite him), with Father Yves on his right. Philip had carefully appropriated this seat, midway down the table, since it meant there was no conversation that might take place from which he would be excluded.

He was still baffled as to what unusual indulgence had permitted Dee-Dee to join the company, but was relieved to have her nurse on his left, acting as a buffer between his little sister and himself. Deirdre's nanny, busily supervising her charge and slightly overwhelmed by the occasion, contributed nothing to the conversation apart from muted exhortations and a commentary on evolving disasters ('Careful now, childie... Watch out for that sauce boat... Ah, no! That stain will never come out... Would you be able for her!').

Much of Dee-Dee's clumsiness was due to her preoccupation with Declan, at whom she stared up, shyly but persistently. For the first few minutes of the meal she had done so from barely above the level of the table, since her chair was too low for her diminutive person, until Corristeen shuffled up with unusual vigour, carrying some cushions which he piled beneath her.

'Somethin' for the smallest little child... There y'are – monarch of all yeh survey.' He chuckled hoarsely while her nurse hoisted the giggling little girl onto the heaped cushions. 'Sure, Nelson hasn't as good a view from his pillar… Don't I always say it – the elevation is yer man every time.'

'Thank you,' said Countess Kinsella, discreetly removing two layers of cushion from the towering edifice on top of which her daughter was now precariously perched. Attracted by signs of activity, Conn the wolfhound appeared at the far end of the terrace. Diffidently rejecting invitations to join the company, he settled in the shade of a cannon, the juxtaposition of the dog of ancient breed and the obsolete artillery piece creating an image reminiscent of a sculpture on a military monument. Conn's advent was interpreted as an affront by Balzac, Countess Kinsella's terrier, who rose from his place under her chair and ran forward, barking fiercely, to confront the wolfhound. The much larger dog raised his head from his paws and, brows knitted in puzzlement, stared at the terrier with an expression of mystification and concern. This was his invariable response to Balzac's routine challenge and the family ignored the incident until the terrier, presumably claiming some kind of moral victory, returned to his place and lay there panting, his tongue lolling out, but too lazy to visit the bowl of water that had been placed on the flagstones for his refreshment.

Mrs Blackwell who, Philip thought, was looking particularly pretty that day had engaged him in conversation across the table. He was flattered by the attention and strove to retain it by responding in an adult fashion. She dismayed him, however, by asking what he wanted to be when he grew up. Apart from the implicit, unwelcome acknowledgement of his present status as a child, this question demanded careful handling. Philip knew the conventional cliché was to say a train driver, or something equally banal. There was no question of fobbing off Mrs Blackwell with nonsense like that. On the other hand, he was not sure he could bring himself to answer with complete frankness. He could, with near veracity, claim his intention was to become a soldier. And yet…

'Well?' Mrs Blackwell's curiosity was sharpened by his hesitation. She smiled encouragingly, showing white, pearly teeth. 'Do tell – what do you want to be?'

Philip discarded caution. Mrs Blackwell was a woman of the world and deserved to hear his decided ambition, even if less imaginative people might be unreceptive. In fervent tones, he told her:

'The greatest swordsman in France.'

For the second time that day he reduced a woman to struggling incoherence. Mrs Blackwell's hand sprang to her mouth as if to suppress a gasp or, Philip momentarily suspected, a laugh. She recovered more quickly than had Mrs Dixon (possibly because she was not drinking anything at the time) and, with her now very wide-open eyes fixed on him, began to interrogate Philip.

'Why, may I ask, in France?'

He was disappointed by the lack of sophistication this question betrayed.

'Because that is where the finest swordsmen are. All the books make that clear – not just D'Artagnan and the musketeers, but lots of others too.' He had not yet reached the chapters in *Scaramouche* where the hero transformed himself into a deadly duellist, but he knew from the description on the dust jacket that this would happen. Naturally, the action took place in France. He wondered if Mrs Blackwell was as well-read as he had supposed her to be.

'I see.' She smiled apologetically. 'Of course. I should have realized – silly me. And how will you set about equipping yourself for this – er – vocation?'

Philip furrowed his brow. This question had been exercising him lately.

'Well, I thought I could take up fencing as soon as I go to school.'

'Like father, like son,' said Philip's mother, overhearing this last remark.

'What do you mean, Mummie?' He sensed some potentially exciting revelation lurking behind her words.

'Your father was a very good fencer in his day – I think he got a Blue or something for it. Isn't that right, Bonaventure?' She raised her voice to attract her husband's attention at the far end of the table.

'What?' He looked up from his conversation with Eanna and Ulick.

'I was just saying you were a very good fencer in your university days.'

'Is that right, Papa?' asked Philip excitedly. 'Were you?'

'I believe I was thought reasonably proficient, but I probably spent more time on the river.'

'Did you win cups and medals?'

'Very few, if any. I really cannot recall.'

'I thought you were awarded a Blue,' his wife reminded him.

'It's really of no consequence,' the Count said with elaborate casualness, telegraphing to his wife with his eyes that the topic should not be pursued. '*Mauvais sujet*,' he added significantly, if unidiomatically.

'Why is it a bad subject?' Philip sounded indignant. 'I think it's terrific.'

His parents exchanged rueful smiles: they had forgotten about their son's precocious progress in French. Then came the request Philip's father had long dreaded and to avoid which he had concealed his past prowess with the foil.

'Will you teach me? Please, Papa, will you? *Please* say you will!'

'Well, Philip, I really don't know. It's a bit early for you to be learning to fence.'

'Oh, please!' His face was contorted in pleading.

'Very well, I tell you what: some day soon, we might go through the basic principles – the rudiments as it were – without actually using weapons, of course.'

'Ooh, yes! Thank you, Papa. When? This afternoon?' He was ecstatic at this concession, though he did not like the soul-destroying restriction imposed in the final clause. He would have to talk his father round that later.

'Certainly not this afternoon. Some day soon – either this week or next.'

With that he had to be content.

'Are you planning to fight a duel?' Declan asked him, with a broad grin.

'Not at the moment.' Philip responded vaguely, annoyed by the painter's patronizing tone, especially in front of Mrs Blackwell.

'Not ever, I hope.' Father Yves spoke gravely, from his place on Philip's right. '*Jamais!* The duel is the ritual murder. It is forbidden by the Church and the participants may not be buried in consecrated ground, even if they repent.'

Philip, who had just been thinking he would like to fight a duel in defence of Mrs Blackwell's honour (a concept of which he had an ill-defined notion), found this anathema depressing. Occasionally, when he was expounding the laws of the Church, Father Yves could be a dispiriting influence, as when he had told Philip that *The Three Musketeers* was on the Index of forbidden books – fortunately after he had already read it. A sudden alarming thought occurred to him.

'Father,' he asked in a low voice, 'is *Scaramouche* on the Index?'

'No, *mon fils,* not to my knowledge.' He turned away to re-engage Count Kinsella and his brothers in conversation.

Mrs Blackwell had listened discreetly to Philip's exchange with Father Yves. Her reaction to this manifestation of the authority of Rome was half resentful, half fascinated. She enjoyed the society of the French priest, dressed in his mediæval habit with the uncompromisingly large rosary that hung from the cincture around his waist rattling whenever he moved; she felt he imparted a degree of *chic* to life at Lissanore, like some gothic minor character in grand opera. As she expressed it to herself, when she visited Castle Kinsella, with its canvases of foreign generals, its air of belonging to an earlier century and the exotic ecclesiasticism personified by Father Yves, she felt as if she were *abroad*. That, to a woman whose private demon was the constant menace of ennui, represented a significant amenity.

Corristeen now processed solemnly along the terrace, carrying a salmon on a large salver and attended by Kitty and Angela bearing ancillary dishes. Conversation around the table was disrupted while the food was served, the seated guests leaning away from one another, like parted hedgerows, through which the white-capped and aproned girls leaned to dispense vegetables. Kitty, the dark, attractive senior housemaid, moved behind the members of the party who sat with their backs to the house, eager to serve Declan, whose arrival had caused a flutter in the kitchen; this arrangement was satisfactory to the pious Angela, on the outside of the table, since she liked to wait upon Father Yves. Corristeen circulated, pouring Count Kinsella's distinguished Meursault with a gracious air that suggested it was his personal gift. When he reached Philip he paused and glanced at Countess Kinsella; she nodded and made a sign with her thumb and forefinger to authorize a small amount. The butler filled one third of the boy's glass. Philip hoped Mrs Blackwell had noticed this adult treatment and he tried to look as if it were an everyday occurrence. The meal was perfectly judged to tempt appetites despite the hot weather, so that the murmur of conversation grew muted as the company appreciatively addressed their plates. Corristeen retired to the end of the terrace to replace a bottle of wine in the ice-bucket he had positioned in the shade. There he was brought up short by a sudden apparition.

'Merciful hour!' The butler croaked in alarm. At the same moment Conn the wolfhound rose from where he lay beside the cannon and slunk away with an intimidated air, as if retreating from some malign presence.

Grandma Skerrett had emerged from a french window and stood like an avenging angel, leaning on a long-handled parasol, a symphony in brown, staring with ostentatious disdain at the luncheon party ingesting its food. She expressed her distaste forcefully.

'Just like the animals.'

Corristeen gaped at her, shading his eyes since the sun was blinding him, making the indistinct silhouette confronting him more menacing.

'Ah, now, ma'am,' he was feverishly trying to calculate whether the objects of her disgust could have heard the comment, 'there's no call for talk like that. Can I give yeh a hand down them stairs?' he added coaxingly, trying to steer her towards the steps that led down from the terrace.

This was a fatal miscalculation. Mrs Skerrett's original intention had been to descend to the garden, snubbing the luncheon party by ignoring it after her disparaging comment; but the butler's anxiety to shepherd her off the terrace provoked her resistance, due to the perversity of her nature, followed by the realization that she might more thoroughly abash the ingrates seated there by seeking an encounter with them, rather than by neglecting them. She began to advance along the terrace, Corristeen keeping pace while desperately trying to deflect her purpose.

'We've the rector's wife today,' he said, hoping this information would at least prevent a recurrence of the kind of remark she had already passed. In some measure this caution was effective. Mrs Skerrett faltered in her stride, appraising the company around the table, until she caught sight of Mrs Blackwell. At the same time the luncheon party became aware of her presence, the men clutching napkins as they rose to acknowledge her.

'I hope you're not getting up for *me*,' she chided them, though the only alternative hypothesis – that the courtesy was directed at Corristeen – was hardly sustainable.

'Will you join us?' Her son-in-law gestured towards the table.

'I will not. I'm sure nobody wants the company of a poor, broken-down old woman.'

There was a polite, dispirited murmur of dissent. Philip cringed, shoulders hunched, over his plate as Grandma moved up to stand directly behind him, her quarry now being Mrs Blackwell, seated opposite. She was singled out for favourable treatment because she was a Protestant. Mrs Skerrett had lately begun to express sympathetic sentiments towards the Church of Ireland. There was no theological basis to this change of heart, it simply reflected the fact that the household at Lissanore, which had never accorded her sufficient consideration, was uniformly Catholic. From this she had concluded, on no empirical evidence, that she might have met with greater appreciation in a Protestant milieu. This theory was reinforced by an alteration in her political views. For most of her life Mrs Skerrett had professed a pallid nationalism, of a vaguely Redmondite hue. It was innocent of ideology and made no demand on her energies beyond sporting a shamrock on Saint Patrick's Day. On her first visit to Dublin after the Troubles, however, she had been shocked by the spectacle of Sackville Street in ruins, by the prevailing air of disorder and the evidently low social origins of those who now constituted authority. Reacting to these symptoms of revolution, she had announced herself as 'dying for the sight of a Union Jack'. It was this recently adopted Unionist identity – which had caused Eanna Kinsella to denounce her scornfully as a 'West Brit' – that now impelled her to salute the rector's wife with unusual warmth.

'Mrs Blackwell, how are you? I am pleased to see you.'

'Very well, thank you. Are you keeping well, Mrs Skerrett?'

Grandma assumed the expression of one who bravely endures adversity without wishing to advertise the fact.

'As well as could be expected.' She cast a meaning glance around at her assembled persecutors. 'The world has not been kind to me; but I don't think I'm long for this vale of tears, thank God. I shall be glad to go. You may see me in your church some day soon, Mrs Blackwell,' she added insinuatingly.

The rector's wife gave a non-committal smile. Privately she thought the Church of Ireland had suffered many reverses lately: the adherence of Mrs Skerrett might well prove the *coup de grâce*.

'All I have ever asked for is a little Christian kindness,' said Grandma plaintively.

'Would you like some watercress soup?' asked Countess Kinsella, as if responding practically to this appeal. 'I think there is some left.'

'I would not.' Grandma brusquely declined the offer, accompanying this rebuff with the savage glare she reserved for intercourse with her daughter.

'Something to drink...' the beleaguered hostess struggled, 'a glass of lemonade?'

Her mother's malevolent eye, however, had just detected a fresh outrage.

'Lemonade! Is that what you call lemonade?'

She pointed accusingly at Philip's glass.

'A very little wine will do him no harm, as a special treat, once in a while,' said his mother, her tone acquiring authority now that her conduct as a parent was being challenged.

'Absolutely.' Her husband voiced his support from the end of the table. 'He should learn to appreciate wine, like children on the continent. In fact, I insist upon it.'

Such unexpectedly firm resistance from Philip's parents and the united front they presented forced Grandma onto the defensive.

'Well,' she said, with the air of one who has dutifully tried to avert catastrophe, but has been frustrated by purblind opposition, 'don't blame me if he turns into a dipsomaniac (she cast a sidelong glance at Corristeen) by the age of twelve.'

'I hardly think that is likely.' Her daughter contradicted her with a forced laugh.

'He looks liverish to me.' Grandma leaned over and made a pantomime of examining Philip's features, while he squirmed beneath her scrutiny. Then she posed the indelicate question with which she had persistently harassed her grandchildren from their earliest years. 'Have his bowels moved?'

Philip blushed beetroot. At that moment he would have liked to kill Grandma for shaming him in front of Mrs Blackwell and the rest of the company. Only Uncle Ulick welcomed this turn in the conversation, which he found interesting.

'He is perfectly healthy,' said Philip's mother curtly, sympathizing with her son's predicament.

'A dose of Cascara –'

'Quite unnecessary.' Countess Kinsella peremptorily dismissed the subject. 'You haven't met our new house guest: this is Declan.'

'How d'you do, ma'am?' said the young painter politely, broadening his smile to an unprecedented intensity.

Mrs Skerrett treated him to the expression of querulous, outraged astonishment with which she greeted newcomers. She disliked all young people; but young men were less objectionable than young women – her ultimate aversion. She had noted from her daughter's introduction that this young man was going to be resident at Lissanore. It occurred to her that his membership of the household, however temporary or humble, made him a potential pawn in domestic *realpolitik* and therefore deserving of assessment and, if appropriate, subornation. So, she assumed a more gracious aspect and unbent sufficiently to ask what brought him to Castle Kinsella. When he told her, she could not conceal her distaste for the project.

'Painting the wall of the tower – whatever next! I suppose you are going to cover it with the horrid German names of my son-in-law's relations. I was always in favour of hanging the Kaiser. What a lot of damage he caused.'

She made it sound as if the former Emperor of Germany had indulged in some kind of hooligan spree that had resulted in much broken glass.

'Sure, the War was a terrible thing,' said Declan. 'Fifty thousand Irishmen dead – God rest them. And millions more in other countries.'

'Man's inhumanity to man,' Mrs Skerrett's voice assumed a sententious, quasi-liturgical tone, 'makes countless thousands mourn.' It was one of her favourite clichés, second only to her claim to be in this world but not of it, and Declan had gained favour by innocently affording her an opportunity to rehearse it.

Countess Kinsella had signalled to the company to continue with luncheon and Mrs Skerrett's exchange with Declan had allowed general conversation to resume around the table, if initially slightly constrained. Sensing she had lost command of the stage, Grandma decided to make her exit.

'Come and visit me some time,' she said to Declan, 'if it's not too much trouble to talk to a poor old woman who has lost interest in the world as much as the world has lost interest in her.'

'I will, so.' Declan cheerfully accepted this seductive invitation.

To Philip's relief, Grandma withdrew along the terrace, attended nervously by Corristeen and energetically waved goodbye by Dee-Dee, who had little attachment to her or appreciation of their relationship, but greatly enjoyed this ritual of farewell. Tactfully, Mrs Blackwell avoided speaking to Philip until he had had time to recover from the crippling embarrassment his grandmother had inflicted upon him. She turned to her hostess.

'That watercress soup was divine.'

'It turned out quite well. Actually, it was rather an afterthought.'

'Well, it was scrumptious. So is the salmon. I wish our cook could make mayonnaise like this.'

Around the table conviviality was reasserting itself after the blight cast on the proceedings by Mrs Skerrett.

'She really ought to carry a scythe and an hourglass.' Count Kinsella glanced jocularly at his wife as he made this irreverent observation about his mother-in-law.

'She's turned into a terrible Castle Catholic,' said Eanna, scowling.

'She may not be any kind of Catholic for much longer.' Father Yves accompanied this forecast with a smile that would have seemed inappropriate when canvassing the potential apostasy of any other member of the household of the faith. 'You have heard what she has said to Madame Blackwell…' He drew the rector's wife into the conversation with mischievously raised eyebrows.

Mrs Blackwell raised her hands in disclaimer.

'Honestly, I haven't been proselytizing, I do assure you.'

'Please feel free to engage in some missionary work,' said Count Kinsella. 'You have our wholehearted approval.'

Philip's mother laughed out loud at this exchange: her filial piety had been strained to breaking point.

'Is there any more wine?' asked her husband. 'Where is Corristeen…? Ah, good man.'

The butler approached with a bottle in each hand. He started to pour indiscriminately from both, to disguise the fact he had just abstracted a glass of Meursault from one of them, to restore himself after the ordeal of Mrs Skerrett's visitation.

'Clink glasses with me, Philip,' commanded Mrs Blackwell.

He obeyed then felt obliged to imitate her example by cautiously drinking some of his wine. It did not taste as horrible as the red wine he had had at Christmas, but it seemed a little bitter – he had expected it to be sweeter. Nevertheless, the important thing was that he felt able to meet Mrs Blackwell's eye again; he had sloughed off the embarrassment that had engulfed him since Grandma's dreadful intervention. He ventured another sip of Meursault. It seemed to have improved slightly. Around him, the mounting crescendo of conversation demonstrated that the world was an interesting and lively place after all.

'Not that it affects us, but the farmers are pretty concerned about all the Canadian cattle flooding the English market...'

'No, I missed the meeting, but they have formed a Leinster branch of the National Game Protection Association...'

'She is playing in the Croquet Championships next week at Carrickmines, believe it or not...'

'Of course, it's Ascot next week too – amazing how quickly the year goes round...'

'Don't remind me – I lost a packet on that horse...'

Philip's thoughts had drifted, by a sequence of random associations, to an expression he had occasionally heard employed, the precise meaning of which he was anxious to establish. With disconcerting abruptness, he asked loudly:

'Papa, are we the Ascendancy?'

This question, resonant with embarrassing echoes of historical antagonisms, provoked a sudden silence, apart from Uncle Eanna spluttering with incoherent outrage at the suggestion. Count

Kinsella, with admirable tact, instantly dispelled any awkwardness by responding good-humouredly:

'No, I'm afraid we can only be described as the *Descendancy*.'

A burst of relieved laughter greeted this deprecatory remark. Philip understood that the topic was not to be pursued: apparently this was another *mauvais sujet*. Uncle Eanna recovered and began telling Father Yves about some Celtic congress that was due to open in Dublin in a few weeks' time. Philip's father resumed discoursing on matters of the turf, Uncle Ulick obliquely participating by recalling various racing accidents that had resulted in gruesome injuries or death. Uncle Dermod and Declan were earnestly discussing their project and what preliminary steps they should take that afternoon.

'May I come and help?' Philip spoke urgently.

'There is nothing for you to do,' his uncle told him. 'We shan't even be in the tower room. We have to go over some large sheets of paper onto which I have transferred the relevant pedigrees and the only place to do that is the library, where we can spread them out fully on a table. I promise,' he added in a conciliatory tone, 'as soon as we start work properly I shall conscript you. Right, Declan?'

'Right.' The painter grinned broadly at Philip. 'Your man here is an indispensable part of the team – no mistake about it.'

'In fact, I think we should make a start. Thank you for a delicious luncheon,' Dermod said to his sister-in-law, rising from the table as he spoke.

'Absolutely.' Mrs Blackwell also began making preparations for departure. 'That was too heavenly.'

'Must you go?' her hostess asked.

'I'm afraid so: *parishioners coming to tea*.' She mouthed the words in a stage whisper, with a pantomime pout, as if reporting some malady it would be indecent to mention aloud. As she stood up, the rest of the company rose with her, in one of those movements that so often signalled to Philip the end of proceedings he was enjoying. He found such moments depressing: when things were pleasant, why could they not continue? There was nothing he could do about it; but adults, who had the power to order their lives, never seemed content with their circumstances, but constantly preferred to move on to some new venue or activity. This sensation of the world insistently progressing from the happy and familiar to the uncongenial frequently oppressed him.

'God almighty.' Corristeen groaned, breaking in on his thoughts as he stood beside the luncheon table abandoned by the company. 'Not a drop left in them bottles – ye'd think the Quality would have more lessie faire than to drink themselves legless at this hour of the day. Yeh'll have to excuse me, Master Philip,' he added in a confessional tone, 'but the ould one there scared the bejayzus out o' me, and she makin' a holy show of us all in front of the Protestant rector's wife. Sure, if the ould Biddy had four legs instead of two, yer man Dempsey would have put her down years ago.'

CHAPTER VII

THAT evening Philip went to meet his friend Tom Dixon at their usual rendezvous on the bridge that spanned the river where it flowed closest to Lissanore, a little to the south-west of the Kinsella demesne. He rode his battered, but much prized, bicycle, a veteran machine that had successively been the property of his brothers Edmund and Dominick before him. He took the opposite direction from his journey that morning, passing out of the demesne by the gate at the south lodge, a much humbler building than the imposing gatehouse that guarded the main entrance to Castle Kinsella. He had not pedalled far when he saw a familiar figure advancing towards him: Uncle Arthur, the only one of his father's brothers who had married and who lived with Aunt Clara at Ardmullen, the dower house of Lissanore, half a mile to the north. Philip slowed to a halt beside his uncle, who smiled a shy greeting.

'Hello, Uncle Arthur.'

'Hello, Philip. Where might you be bound for?'

'To the bridge, to meet Tom.'

'Good man.' His uncle nodded approvingly. 'You'll be in time for the evening rise.'

To Uncle Arthur, a fanatical devotee of fishing, the river and some neighbouring loughs supplied the gravitational pull of his existence. Nothing seemed more natural to him than that his nephew – and the rest of humanity, for that matter – should repair to the river at the time of the evening rise, as monks regulate their lives by the liturgical hours. Making no concessions to the hot weather of the past two weeks, he wore his customary tweeds, much stained with grass and mud; his calves were encased in a kind of gaiters that ensured his readiness to resume the offensive against the finny foe at a moment's notice. On this occasion he carried no rod, but a canvas bag slung from his shoulder still lent him a piscatorial character. In looks he favoured his brothers Eanna and Ulick, rather than Philip's father and Uncle Dermod. He had something of Eanna's thickset build and Ulick's drab, sandy-coloured hair, presently concealed by a battered tweed hat resembling an inverted flowerpot, ornamented with fishing flies, but evident in the well-trimmed moustache that bisected his weather-beaten face. Although the youngest Kinsella, he had married before Bonaventure and his only son was as old as Dominick, the second of Philip's brothers; like his cousins, he was away at school, but at Clongowes rather than in England. It was rumoured some complications resulting from his birth had prevented Arthur's wife Clara from having any more children.

'Have you been fishing, Uncle Arthur?'

'No,' his uncle said, with the apologetic air of one admitting to having neglected an important duty. 'I had to do one or two things for your Aunt Clara – haven't been on the river all day. I might just manage a cast or two in an hour's time,' he added hopefully, as if pledging a purpose of amendment.

'I hope you catch something.'

'Well, as to that, one never knows, at all.' His uncle spoke cautiously, as though afraid of provoking fate through hubris. 'You might tell young Tom to pass this on to his father – it's to do with a chat we had last week. I changed that fly I wasn't satisfied with. It was one of those times when you know you have nearly got it right, but there is just something that doesn't quite fit. I'd used hare's ear fur and I had a suspicion it would have been more suited to the spring, but wouldn't do much good this far into the season. It needed something to give it a bit of extra weight and allure. Well, on a sudden inspiration, I took a clipping from Pecksniff – you know, your aunt's spaniel – and used it for the tail – on the fly, I mean. Then,'

104

his features glowed with rekindled excitement, 'it was down to the river, with all the spirit of inquiry of Isaac Newton – or was it Isaac Walton? – and I tried it out. You know what? It barely kissed the water before the handsomest trout this side of the Blackstairs leapt up and committed suicide. Two and a half pounds – or thereabouts,' he added hastily, showing a respect for the Eighth Commandment unusual among fishermen.

'I wish I'd seen that. I never seem to catch anything worthwhile.'

'Have you been practising your casting the way I taught you?'

'Yes, Uncle Arthur.'

'In the pools I showed you?'

'Yes.'

'Then you must be putting up the wrong flies.' His assessment was as analytical and decisive as Tom Dixon's father diagnosing a patient's ailment. 'You know, a young chap like you could easily get discouraged by a long bout of failure, perhaps even lose interest in the sport. (His expression momentarily became as anguished as if he were addressing the putative loss of religious faith.) What you need to do is stick to a reliable fly for a while and catch a few fish, gain some confidence. You couldn't do better than put up a Green-well's Glory – old reliable. I'll bring a box of them with me next time we come up to the house. That should be pretty soon: I gather your mother telephoned to invite us to dinner next week – very kind of her. We have the telephone now at Ardmullen,' he added, with modest pride.

'Thank you for your advice, Uncle Arthur. Greenwell's Glory – I'll remember that.' He began to remount his bicycle.

'Please don't mention what I told you – about Pecksniff – to your Aunt Clara when you run into her,' said his uncle urgently. 'Just in case the experiment proved a success – which it has – I took a rather generous clipping from his coat and unfortunately it shows.

In fact, she noticed it this morning. I have been trying to divert suspicion onto Lucifer the cat, with whom he has a fractious relationship, but I saw her looking at me very thoughtfully when I was leaving the house. I fear trouble in the offing – she dotes on that dog.'

'That's all right, Uncle Arthur, I promise I won't say anything. Except to Tom, of course, so he can tell his father.'

They parted cordially and Philip pedalled energetically towards the bridge, where he found Tom Dixon waiting for him. He was the same age as Philip and of similar build, perhaps an inch less in height; his hair had a coppery tinge to it, inherited from his mother, along with the freckles that were more pronounced on his cheeks than on hers. His habitual expression was of quizzical good humour, with a hint of mischief in his eyes. He was chewing a blade of grass ruminatively as he watched Philip approach.

'Hello there.'

'Hello, Tom. Any exciting news?'

'Exciting? Around here? Don't be an eejit.'

'Eejit yourself.' Philip grinned, aiming a mock punch at his friend. 'Anyway, I'm sorry you live such a dull life, but, as it happens, I have some interesting news.'

'Don't tell me – Dizzycourse Slattery fell into the septic?'

'No. Something rather more interesting than that.'

'Holy Angela's been caught stealing the teaspoons?'

Philip was afraid that if he allowed Tom to construct any more fanciful hypotheses he would come up with a scenario so dramatic it would reduce his news to anticlimax, so he cut short further speculation with the announcement:

'We have someone new staying at the house.'

'Aw, jeepers! It's not that Spanish duchess again – I couldn't stand any more of that. I thought you'd never shut up about her.'

'No, no, it's not her. It's a man called Declan. He's a painter and he's going to paint Uncle Dermod's study.'

'What was wrong with Mattie Brennan? My mother says he's quite good – though you have to keep the whiskey under lock and key when he's in the house.'

'No, you don't understand! He's not that kind of painter – he's an artist. He's going to paint coats of arms on the wall and he says I can help. Uncle Dermod sent for him and he arrived today. From Dublin,' he added, to emphasize the metropolitan credentials of Lissanore's new resident.

'An artist?' To Philip's gratification, it was evident Tom was impressed. 'What's he like?'

'Quite young. He smiles a lot.'

'Maybe he's a bit simple,' said Tom maliciously. He was conscious he had conceded too much interest in his friend's news and was anxious to recover his pose of sceptical detachment.

'You can't be an artist and be simple.' Philip was shocked by the suggestion.

'Yes, you can. Wasn't the nun telling us only last week about this fella that cut off his ear and him a famous artist.'

'Why did he do that?'

'Because he was soft in the head.'

Philip received this information with incredulity: it seemed farfetched, but he had insufficient knowledge to contradict it. He made a mental note to question Father Yves on the subject. During these exchanges the boys had taken up their bicycles, which had been propped against the parapet, and started to wheel them across the bridge. At the far end they exchanged civilities with a group of about half a dozen men of varied ages, leaning with their elbows on the stonework and gazing out over the river, smoking and talking quietly. A few yards after Philip and Tom had crossed the bridge they turned off the road, onto a steep footpath that led down to the riverbank. By unwritten law, at the solemn observance of the evening rise, the bridge was the preserve of the men from the vicinity. If the boys had joined them they would have been received in a friendly way and indulged with conversation; but they would have known they were interlopers. So, their custom was to make their way down to the water's edge and watch for the first telltale ripples from close at hand – in any case a more immediate and exciting experience – while conversing on whatever issues and enigmas of existence were currently preoccupying them.

'I asked the nun.' Tom spoke suddenly, as they laid their bicycles on the grass beside the track that ran along the riverbank.

'About the artist that cut off his ear?' Philip's mind was still revolving this dubious proposition.

'No. About the Ten Commandments – remember what we were talking about last week?'

'Oh, yes.' Philip's interest was instantly kindled. 'What did you say?'

'I said: "Please, Sister, what is adultery?"'

'And what did she say?'

'She said: "It is a very serious sin that you will learn about when you grow up" – fat lot of help that was.'

'Was that all?'

'No. I said: "But, Sister, if I don't know what it is, how can I be sure I'm not committing it every day?"'

'That was good.' Philip was impressed by the forensic logic of his friend's argument. 'What did she say to that?'

'She just gave me one of those looks – like I was something the cat brought in – and said (he assumed a high-pitched, genteel voice in mimicry): "I think you can be confident that is not one of your vices – regardless of how many others you may have." And all the teacher's pets in the class laughed like she'd made a funny joke.'

Philip, who had imagined he was about to penetrate the mystery of what constituted adultery, was disappointed by this report, though admiring of Tom's tenacity in pursuing his enquiry in the face of adult obtuseness.

'I thought they were supposed to educate us,' he said resentfully, 'not hide things from us.'

'Maybe they haven't had much luck this time.'

Tom's tone was elaborately nonchalant as he selected a fresh blade of grass to chew. Philip stared at him. His friend's offhand demeanour could not mask an underlying smugness.

'What do you mean?'

'Only that I've found out all about adultery – in spite of Sister Eejit.'

'Have you? How? Are you sure?'

'Of course I'm sure. Tim Hackett's brother told him and Tim told me.'

'Well, what is it?'

'It's when you…' Tom hesitated and glanced up at the bridge. The voices of the men talking there carried across the water, though not distinctly enough for their conversation to be followed; but there was a clarity of tone that made them sound closer than they were. 'I don't want those old codgers to hear.'

'They can't. Anyway, at their age, they must know about adultery already.'

Not entirely reassured, Tom leaned close to Philip's ear and began to relay the information he had gleaned. He had barely started, when Philip recoiled with an expression of utter disbelief.

'Don't be stupid! Everybody does that – they have to – it can't possibly be a sin.'

'No, no! Would you just wait a minute, I haven't finished.' Tom shouted in frustration, his earlier caution abandoned. 'It's only adultery when you do it where you shouldn't,' his voice grew quieter again, 'behind people's houses and barns, and suchlike.'

Philip stared unseeingly at the river, his mind churning this thesis. He found it difficult to believe. Living largely in the open air and going for long rambles or hacking across the countryside on Pegasus, he had often found the need to relieve himself in some se-cluded spot. Being extremely modest by nature, he had always gone to elaborate lengths to ensure strict privacy. Perhaps that was the theological nub of it: such conduct was only sinful if observed. He put this point to Tom, who considered it earnestly.

'Maybe that's it.' He was beginning to feel uneasy about de-fending the proposition, especially if he was required to do so in any detail. 'Maybe it's not a sin everywhere outside the jacks. It may be all right on your own land – like you doing it in the woods around the castle.'

Philip winced at this example.

'I'll ask Tim Hackett to find out more from his brother,' said Tom. 'I don't want to have to tell Canon Roche about it in confes-sion, if I haven't committed a sin.'

'You can't have committed a sin.' Philip, fortified by the firm grounding in catechism he owed to Father Yves, spoke authorita-tively. 'Neither of us can – at least not a mortal sin, because we didn't know and nobody would tell us. So it's not our fault.'

'True for you.'

'It may all be nonsense, after all.'

'I think it must be.' Tom was no longer concerned to insist on the accuracy of his information, now that he had considered its im-plications for his next confession. 'Tim Hackett is a bit of an eejit, his brother was probably codding him.'

At that moment a splash in the water made both boys swing round to stare at the river. Sure enough, concentric circles of ripples were spreading across the surface. The sound made by a rising fish was distinctive, unlike any other; it piqued them to have missed seeing the first rise of the evening. Up on the bridge, thin spirals of blue smoke rose on the still air, as the men removed pipes and cigarettes from their mouths to comment on the sight, a couple of arms extended to point at the spot. Amplified by the water, a solitary comment could be distinguished:

'Only a tiddler, that fella.'

'That's Patsy Foley,' said Tom dismissively. 'He'd be hard put to it to catch a minnow himself.'

The men on the bridge fell silent, as did the two boys. The splendour of the evening exacted reverence. The glass-smooth river glided imperceptibly on its course; wherever its surface was rippled by reeds or eddies, the sunlight caused it to sparkle like diamonds. The sun, though low in the western sky, was still brilliant, turning the mountains that screened the eastern horizon to mauve, streaked with gold. Although the trees on the side of the river where they stood were mostly ash and sycamore, the opposite bank was fringed with willows, drooping delicately to the water's edge. Far downstream, a small, overgrown island protruded from the current; it was connected to the far bank by a submerged causeway and a tumble of rubble smothered beneath its foliage was said to be the remains of a fishing-house belonging to ancient monks before the Normans came to Ireland. Swans could be seen skirting the island, their plumage an ethereal white in the nearly horizontal sunlight.

Several furtive disturbances on the surface of the water signalled the evening rise was getting properly under way. From somewhere, the call of a cuckoo sounded, absent-minded and monotonous. As if in competition, a skylark rose almost vertically into the heavens, until it was a distant speck, and began to circle, sending back the warbling notes of its song with liquid clarity. A curlew, looking ungainly at the water's edge on the opposite bank, emitted a brief cry then desisted from further dialogue. The birdsong at this time in the evening, unlike the raucous intensity of the dawn chorus, sounded contented, fulfilled. To the east, the green pasture, broken up by hedgerows and clumps of trees, extended towards the distant mountains at whose base it coarsened into scrub and gorse. It was a moment of total tranquillity, savoured by the boys, as if they realized this experience would nurture their spirits, in some way fortify them against the disenchantments life might visit upon them in future years.

After a few minutes' silent absorption, a new bird call from close at hand arrested their attention.

'Look – a yella yite.' Tom pointed to a bush on top of which the yellow-headed and billed bird was reciting its well-known song. 'D'you hear him? "A little bit of bread and no chee–ee–se!" ' He mimicked the yellowhammer's refrain.

'That's nonsense,' said Philip. 'He never seems to get as far as the "cheese" bit. None of them do, at least none that I've heard.'

'Well, all I can say is you haven't heard much. Lookit,' Tom said solemnly, 'that yella fella is my top favourite of all birds. He'd be yours too, if you knew enough about it – Sacre bleu!'

He started as an almighty splash erupted downstream. They looked just in time to see the sun gleam on the silver arc of the leaping salmon and its body thrash the water as it returned to its element, a second tide of turbulence erasing the spreading ripples it had already created. The boys exchanged admiring glances. A murmur of appreciation floated down from the connoisseurs on the bridge.

'Your mother wants you to stop saying "sacre bleu",' Philip told Tom after a few moments' awed silence.

'Don't I know it? She told me off for saying "lookit" too. There's no freedom of speech.'

'It's my fault for telling you about *"sacre bleu"*.'

'That's all right,' said Tom graciously. 'I wanted to learn French. You're lucky you have the priest to teach you so easily.'

'Yes, I've learned a lot from Father Yves. From Uncle Dermod too. Do you know what I found out from him the other day?'

'The earth is round?'

'Very funny. No, Uncle Dermod has worked out that I am the one hundred and thirty-seventh generation in descent from Adam.'

'Adam who?'

'*Adam*, you clown! In the Garden of Eden – our first parents, you know.'

'You're telling me your uncle has discovered you're descended from Adam and Eve?'

'Yes, but –' Philip's misgivings about Uncle Dermod's genealogical coup returned, in the face of Tom's sceptical tone.

'Well, aren't we all descended from Adam?'

'Yes, of course; but, you see, Uncle Dermod has worked out the exact number of people between Adam and me.'

'That means the number of people that have lived since Adam's time?'

'That's right.'

'Well, then, I must be one hundred and – what was it you said? – in descent from him too. If that's the number of people that were born and died since the Garden of Eden.'

'Not necessarily.' Philip's protest sounded limp; he was conscious that Uncle Dermod's thesis was turning into a dialectical liability. 'Some of your ancestors might have lived longer than mine, or died younger.'

'What difference does that make, so?'

'Er – not very much, but it is interesting to know. In fact,' he added, regaining confidence as a thought struck him, 'you wouldn't have known how many people there had been since Adam if it wasn't on our pedigree.'

Tom's silence grudgingly conceded the justice of that claim.

'I found out something else amazing today,' said Philip, anxious to move onto safer ground. 'My father was the greatest swordsman in England.'

Even as he uttered the phrase, it sounded unsatisfactory. It ought to have been in France: as he had explained to Mrs Blackwell, that was the home of true swordsmanship.

'In England? What was he doing there?'

Tom's uncanny knack of subverting every self-aggrandizing claim that Philip came out with guaranteed a healthy equilibrium in their relationship; but it did not make moments like this any less irritating for the more romantically minded of the two boys.

'He was at university.'

'Which one?'

'Oxford.'

'Did he row in the boat race?'

'No – yes – I think he may have.' He had just remembered his father saying something about spending more time on the river than on the fencing *piste*.

'Great! I'd really like to do that. Mind you,' Tom added deflatingly, 'the Oxford boat sank this year. My father was angry because he had a bet on it.'

'You'd be hopeless at rowing, Tom. Remember the time you lost an oar when we were out in Feeney's boat?'

'Aw, rats! That was just an accident. Did your father ever kill anyone with a sword?' It was Tom's turn to divert the conversation.

'He didn't say. Probably not. I don't think it's allowed in England – they take life very seriously there. Now, in France...'

Philip launched into a lecture on the congenially murderous

traditions of French aristocratic society, leading inevitably to a ré-sumé of the plot of *Scaramouche*, so far as he had read. Tom listened attentively: a less voracious reader than Philip, he found his friend's narratives, for which he had rather a gift, a painless way of acquiring literary knowledge. When Philip had finished, he brought his critical faculties to bear on the story.

'That markee sounds a right blackguard. I hope he gets – *Janey Mac!*' He broke off in alarm. 'What was that?'

For an instant, they thought another fish had jumped, very close at hand. Almost immediately, however, they realized a stone had been thrown, striking the path with great violence a few feet away and raising a plume of dust, like a bullet. Its source was betrayed by a low snigger, followed by more audible laughter, coming from a group of youths standing up on the road. They were in shirtsleeves; one, who seemed several years older than the others, in his early twenties, wore a flat cap that did not entirely cover his unruly black, curly hair. His mouth was twisted in a cruel grin; his eyes, a startling blue, burned with a disquieting intensity that might have been hatred, or fanaticism, or the recklessness of the mentally deranged.

'Simmie Toal!' Tom's voice sounded urgent, tremulous. 'With those gurriers from the village.'

'Why did he do that?' Philip's pulse had quickened and his cheeks were slightly flushed.

'Simmie Toal doesn't need a reason. He's a bad article, that one. I hope to God some big-gob hasn't said I called him "Slimy Toad".'

Philip nearly laughed, despite his state of alarm. This was, in any case, diminishing as he appraised the situation. Toal and his gang – there appeared to be four of them – showed no sign of coming down to the riverbank. The men on the bridge continued impassively to smoke and talk among themselves. They made no acknowledgement of the presence of Simmie Toal, who was known to have contacts with the I.R.A., the black market and criminal elements that made him an undesirable man to cross; but they would see fair play, if any harm threatened the two boys below. In fact, there was no such threat. The stone had been thrown deliberately wide, designed not to injure but to express hostility. It was unlikely youths of their age would descend to violence against two nine-year-old boys, one of them the son of Count Kinsella, the other of the popular local doctor. This the men knew: there was little prospect of their intervention being required.

Toal's grin had receded, to be replaced by the sneer that was as permanent a fixture on his face as the smile on that of Declan the painter. For several minutes he and his cronies muttered among themselves, making much play of lighting cigarettes; once the name 'Kinsella', pronounced in a deliberately loud voice and derogatory tone, rose above the sullen murmur, followed by more contrived sniggering. Finally, tiring of their surroundings, the gang of youths slouched off down the road, Simmie Toal pausing to expectorate into a clump of nettles, as he looked back down towards the riverbank, in a parting gesture of contempt.

'Good riddance to bad rubbish.' Tom's voice sounded more relaxed.

'You can say that again.'

'Good riddance –'

Philip acknowledged the feeble joke with a pretended swipe at his friend. Yet he was shaken by this encounter, had felt himself trembling for some moments, accompanied by a hollow sensation in the pit of his stomach. This was not because of any imagined danger that evening: it was provoked by the memory of a dreadful experience four years previously, of which Simmie Toal had been the instigator and with which he was forever associated in Philip's mind, rendering him a creature of nightmare. The boys resumed their conversation, trying to recapture the atmosphere of ten minutes earlier, of comfortable intimacy lulled by the tranquil beauty of the evening. They did not succeed. Unconsciously, their voices had sunk to a conspiratorial murmur, betraying their recent state of apprehension: there was a serpent now in Eden.

'I'd better be getting home,' said Tom, glancing at the sky, though he had stayed out much later on other occasions.

'Me too.' Philip accepted this capitulation to an enforced change of mood with something approaching relief.

They wheeled their bicycles up to the road, mounted them and said goodnight to the idlers on the bridge. Fortunately, both their homeward routes lay in a different direction from that taken by Toal and his hangers-on. He was always surrounded by youths a few years below him in age, whom he presumably found easier to dominate than contemporaries. Philip and Tom bicycled side by side until they reached the crossroads where their paths diverged, when they parted with lively pledges to meet again soon.

Philip's journey home was haunted by Simmie Toal. He remembered, through the haze of early childhood, the day when Toal had come with the Volunteers to burn Lissanore – to destroy his beautiful home. Philip had been too young – about five at the time – to retain much coherent recollection of that nearly tragic occasion. He remembered the men in trench coats, carrying revolvers; Nanny grasping his hand so tightly it hurt, while repeatedly ejaculating, 'Jesus, Mary and Joseph!'; his family helping the servants to carry furniture and paintings out of the house and stack them in the paddock at a safe distance from the impending conflagration; some of the Volunteers lending a hand, perspiring under the weight of heavy items, shouting contradictory instructions; one of them, with apparent sincerity, remarking it was fortunate it was a dry day. He recalled their conspicuous courtesy to his mother ('I'm truly sorry for your trouble, ma'am...'), their demeanour suggesting they themselves had no agency in an event that was an act of God.

Two other things he remembered, or rather two men. One was his father: calm, civil, insistent on the injustice of the proposed action and the need for the arsonists to consult their superiors as to whether a grave error was being committed. The other was Simmie Toal, sneering on the sidelines, biting his nails over the slow progress of events, impatiently carrying cans of petrol into the hall. Of Corristeen there was no sign: he had collapsed in an alcoholic stupor in his pantry, to the amusement of the raiders. The remainder of the picture had been supplied to Philip during the intervening years by fragments of reminiscence – though it was a forbidden topic in the house – from family members and servants. Uncle Eanna confusing matters by waving a tricolour flag from the battlements and shouting rebel slogans; Uncle Dermod carrying out boxes of family papers; and his father reasoning indefatigably with the leader of the irregulars ('Do those portraits look like British army uniforms? We were Catholic, Jacobite exiles... Yes, I was in the British army, briefly, at the start of the War – when Redmond urged us all to go – were none of your people in the same situation? I thought so... We have never been involved in politics... What about the chapel, for God's sake?'); all this had happened, like a dream, around him. Finally had come the breakthrough, the harassed guerrilla leader telling his men: 'I'm not entirely happy about this, boys. This is a Catholic house, with a chapel – that's a serious matter, I think ye'd all agree. I'm going to call Brigade. D'you mind if I use your instrument? Many thanks...'

Then, after a bizarre interlude, while tea was being served to the intruders, a motorcyclist had ridden noisily up the avenue: the

Commandant. He was an old-young man with sunken eyes, unshaven, his clothes much slept in and the imminent smell of death – others' and his own – about him. As he listened to the preliminary details from his subordinate, a car arrived: Father Roche (as he then was), the parish priest, summoned by bush telegraph. Brusquely, he led the Commandant to the chapel. While the rebel officer stood, startled, on the threshold, the priest demanded brutally: 'Would you burn Our Lord Himself in the tabernacle?'

'Mother of God!' The Commandant, appalled, had turned rigid with shock. Killing had distracted him from religious practice; but he had a brother in a seminary and an ordained uncle, secretary to a bishop. (In fact, Father Roche had told a white lie: the Blessed Sacrament was not at that time reserved at Lissanore.) 'Our intelligence has been badly misled about this household. Where is Toal?' he had asked grimly.

The informant was nowhere to be found, having prudently made himself scarce. Under the Commandant's direction, the Volunteers carried the furniture back inside the reprieved castle in a more disciplined manner than they had brought it out. Father Roche then completed his ascendancy over the irregulars by saying to the Commandant: 'I imagine your men don't get the chance to fulfil their religious duties as regularly as they might like. I am going into the chapel now; tell the boys I'll hear their confessions before they leave.'

That was how it had ended: a docile queue of penitents lined up outside the chapel, to be shriven one by one. Then they had disappeared, as suddenly as they had arrived. Father Roche had remained, at Count Kinsella's request, to lead the family rosary, a fervent prayer of thanksgiving for the preservation of the house. Nevertheless, Lissanore was not fated to escape the Troubles completely free of casualties. The Republican raid provoked intensive military activity in the neighbourhood. Next day, a lorryload of Black and Tans roared past the gatehouse, where Conn the wolfhound's mate Orla, who had had a litter of pups not long before, stood gazing out curiously.

The Tans shot her for sport. Conn, running to the spot, whining with grief, had desperately licked her face in a pathetic attempt to restore life. Thereafter, he could not be induced to go anywhere near the main gatehouse, the scene of his bereavement; he had almost pined to death, but the determined kindness of the entire household had coaxed him back to subdued, melancholy existence.

All these half-memories and second-hand reports ran chaotically through Philip's mind as he bicycled home. Yet they were quickly exorcized by his mother's casual remark, as he passed through the hall, where she was finishing a conversation on the telephone. His father came out of the drawing room just after she had hung up and looked enquiringly at his wife, who laughed as she explained:

'Well, it seems I misjudged her. That was the *Duquesa* – telephoning to confirm she is coming to luncheon on Monday.'

CHAPTER VIII

MONDAY was another hot, sunny day in this glorious early summer. Only a quarter of an hour later than the appointed time, the large motor car belonging to the Duchess of Saladavieja emerged from the screen of rhododendrons at the head of the avenue, purred across the gravel sweep and drew up in front of the house. Corristeen watched its arrival through a narrow window in the porch, where he was lurking in ambush. As soon as the vehicle came to a halt, he hissed at Liam, arrayed for the occasion in the red Kinsella livery with silver buttons that he assumed when performing the role of footman:

'Would yeh ever stop gawpin' like a half-wit at that filt'y great monster and go and open the door for Her Honour!'

Liam rushed obediently down the steps, only to find himself forestalled by the chauffeur, who slid agilely out of his seat and held open the rear door with practised aplomb. Momentarily checked, Liam quickly recovered and, displaying commendable initiative, made his way round the back of the car and opened the door on the far side. The woman who emerged was a considerable disappointment to the expectant footman. Wearing a nondescript dress and drab grey cloche hat, she could not have looked less like a duchess. The reason immediately became apparent, even to Liam: this was not the Duchess, but her maid, who now hung back sheepishly, effacing herself behind the vehicle, while an infinitely more impressive personage debouched from the opposite door of the car.

The Duchess of Saladavieja, a vision in lilac silk, her eyes shaded by tinted lenses and the broad brim of a hat elegantly disposed upon her fashionably styled blonde hair, advanced with a languid stride to the steps leading up to the front door. She was followed, a pace behind, by a girl of about nine, evidently her daughter. At the top of the steps Corristeen bowed extravagantly from the waist, to the grave prejudice of his arthritic condition, and ushered the Duchess and her daughter into the house, leaving Liam to conduct the lady's maid and chauffeur to the servants' hall. The butler threw open the door of the drawing room and stood aside to let the guests enter as he uttered a stentorian bellow.

'Her Honour the Duchess of Shaladdieveckie!'

Startled by this explosion of sound and disoriented by the change from bright sunlight to interior shade, it momentarily seemed to the Duchess that the room was empty. Then she saw Count and Countess Kinsella standing in the wide-open french windows with welcoming smiles; on the terrace beyond, she glimpsed a table set for luncheon.

'I am so sorry to be late,' she said in flawless English, her origins hinted at only in the Hispanic huskiness of her intonation, as she crossed the room.

'You are hardly late at all.' Her hostess graciously dismissed the notion. 'Considering our remote situation and the state of the roads, you did very well.'

'Better than we should have done,' said Count Kinsella, gallantly bowing over the Duchess's hand, to the delighted approval of Philip who was standing behind his parents.

'This is my daughter Constanza,' said the Duchess, introducing the girl as she emerged from the french windows onto the terrace. 'My darling, this is Count and Countess Kinsella.'

The girl bobbed a curtsey to her host and hostess, with a polite smile, then glanced round as Countess Kinsella, in turn, said: 'This is my youngest son, Philip.'

Philip stepped forward and held out his hand to the Duchess, who shook it very civilly. He would dearly have liked to raise her hand close to his lips, in the chivalrous style of his father, but feared such a gesture would have been thought presumptuous.

'What a fine-looking boy,' said the Duchess in her throaty voice. 'You have a very pretty daughter.' Philip's mother smiled in reciprocal courtesy, though the compliment was well deserved, as her son noted with a sensation of amazed excitement while he exchanged a shy greeting with Constanza.

He had never seen such a beautiful girl. Her hair was light brown, slightly streaked with blonde, held in place by a tortoiseshell comb and she was wearing a yellow frock, patterned with tiny blue flowers; but it was her eyes that fascinated Philip – as they had done when he had glimpsed her indistinctly through the car window on her previous visit. Now he understood why: they were a startling green – large and brilliant. The effect of those green eyes was overwhelming; they added to her lovely, delicate features an extraordinary and vivid distinction. Yet, despite their striking impact, the emerald depths reflected calm and gentleness, as if revealing something of their owner's soul. All this Philip dimly apprehended, with a precocious insight that elevated his admiration of this girl beyond an incipient schoolboy crush to an intuition that here was someone touched with a special grace. He reminded himself, with an effort, that it was rude to stare.

'Constanza is a dreamer,' said her mother deprecatingly. 'I try to make her live in the everyday world, but it is a losing battle. What a wonderful view you have here,' she added, gazing out over the crenellated wall of the terrace to the informal gardens below and the wooded prospect beyond.

'It is a constant challenge to prevent it turning into a jungle,' said Countess Kinsella.

Corristeen, who was hovering nearby, as if joined by some invisible link to the Duchess, now interposed.

'Shall I dispense a soupsong of champagne to the company, madam?' He indicated an ice-bucket from which protruded a magnum bearing a majestic label of a renowned year, which he had extracted unbidden from the cellar.

'Yes, please, if you would,' said Philip's mother, accepting the *fait accompli* with a good grace.

Uncle Dermod appeared at that moment, having left Declan to continue their work on the wall of the tower room. He greeted the Duchess in a courtly manner then proceeded to interrogate her about genealogical matters, without receiving entirely satisfactory replies. Ulick and Eanna joined the company a few minutes later and the conversation became eclectic. By now they were seated on chairs at one end of the terrace, leaving the housemaids freedom of access to the luncheon table, to which they were adding some finishing touches. Corristeen stood to attention, keeping a watchful eye on the glasses of champagne: he had calculated he would eventually be justified in opening a second magnum, which would then leave a gratifying amount of wine undrunk.

Philip and the Duchess's daughter were seated together on smaller, more Spartan chairs than the deep, cane-bottomed ones in which the adults reclined; they were on the outer circumference of the straggling circle formed by their elders, silently listening to the conversation, which was dominated by the Duchess. Soon, however, a diversion occurred which broke the social ice between the two children and drew them into animated discussion. Conn the wolfhound came loping along the terrace and warily edged close to the company. His distinguished appearance attracted the attention of the Duchess.

'What a splendid dog. My husband kept a pack of Alanos for boar hunting, but that hound looks much more impressive. Will he come to me...? No, apparently not.'

She laughed, accepting the snub from a fellow thoroughbred in good part. The flow of conversation resumed. Disregarded, Conn made a half-circuit of the group and slowly approached to where the children sat. Diffidently swaying his tail, he crouched down beside Constanza then rested his head on her lap, gazing up at her with affectionate, submissive eyes. She smiled delightedly and began to stroke the big dog. The babble of talk died down again as the adults noticed what was happening and turned to observe.

'You are singularly honoured,' Count Kinsella told the girl. 'He is very shy and seldom goes near anyone he doesn't know.'

'He is lovely,' she said, cupping Conn's head in her hands.

Philip was fascinated by this spectacle – and impressed that the wolfhound had reacted so favourably to Constanza. Animals were said to have very reliable instincts. When they sat down to luncheon, Conn followed them over to the table and settled on the flagstones beside the girl's chair. By this time, she and Philip had exchanged so much conversation about the wolfhound, jointly stroking and making much of him, that all constraint had evaporated and they chatted easily. At intervals, they preserved a polite silence while the adults talked. Philip could not quite decide whether Constanza's mother (as, in a significant shift of perception, he now thought of her) was enormously sophisticated, or frivolous to the point of silliness, but it was entertaining to let the waves of cosmopolitan *chic* sweep over him. He sensed that his mother was savouring the visitor in the same spirit.

'The Saint-Arnouls gave a marvellous party – they always do – but it was completely ruined by Geneviève's coming down with mumps…

'We had an utterly heavenly week on the Van Rensselaers' yacht and then – out of the blue – a positive hurricane hit us. My dear, I was completely prostrate…

'So, I said to Prince Paul, "Take care, *monseigneur*, or that monkey will steal more than your grapes" – everyone was convulsed...'

When they had risen from the table and returned to their chairs at the end of the terrace, to Philip's keen satisfaction the Duchess produced an enormously long cigarette-holder – about three times the length of Mrs Blackwell's, a disparity which he attributed to her ducal rank – and proceeded to fit into it an exotic cigarette with a gold tip. His father hastened to light it for her, then took out his pipe and embarked on the ritual of kindling it. Uncle Dermod resumed his efforts to draw out the Duchess on the topic of various Spanish grandees and other European nobles with whom she was on familiar terms. This was an unproductive exercise, since people whom Uncle Dermod esteemed as the inheritors of thirty-two quarterings, or Knights of the Golden Fleece, or privileged to wear a hat in the presence of their sovereign, figured in the Duchess's scheme of things as the hosts of amusing parties, or implicated in some stimulating scandal, or married to women whom she detested. So, there was little meeting of minds and Dermod had to console himself with scraps of information that were purely incidental to their guest's voluble accounts of cosmopolitan society.

Uncle Ulick had at first been gratified to hear the Duchess refer to a famous doctor who attended her; but it emerged she seldom suffered from any malady and valued the physician chiefly as a source of gossip – a shocking trivialization of medicine, in the eyes of a hypochondriac. Uncle Eanna had enjoyed a brief, but surprisingly successful, conversation with their guest, since he had been able to give her an authoritative account of the history and mythology of the Irish wolfhound breed. Father Yves, who had excused himself from luncheon on the grounds of a voluminous correspondence, joined the company for coffee. Philip was struck by the grace with which Constanza kissed the priest's hand – a reverential custom that was dying out in Ireland, but which subsisted among devout Spaniards.

'Philip,' said his mother, 'why don't you show Constanza around the grounds?'

'Good idea.' His father nodded agreement. 'You can take her to see the yearlings.'

'Make sure you come back in time for tea,' his mother instructed him, as the children rose with alacrity, followed instantly by Conn who signalled his intention of accompanying them.

'Yes, Mummie. I'll show you the horses first,' Philip told the girl eagerly. 'They are in a field out at the front. Then we can go to the farm.'

The children walked round to the front of the house, Conn keeping station at the girl's heels as if she, rather than Philip, had been familiar to him for years. They followed a path that skirted the paddock, running parallel to the avenue but separated from it by the oaks, beeches and rhododendrons that lined the main approach to the castle. The trampled grass track led past the expanse of empty paddock to distant fields, in the most remote of which could be glimpsed the indolently browsing horses. Philip plucked a hazel switch and gallantly used it to point out treacherous clumps of nettles that might have stung Constanza's legs. He was vulnerable himself, since he was wearing his grey flannel suit in honour of the visitors and his short trousers left his legs exposed. The sun was hot, so that he was feeling uncomfortably warm by the time they reached the fence bordering the field where the horses were, but he felt it would be a social solecism to take off his coat while escorting this grave and dignified Spanish girl. Philip ordered Conn to 'Sit!' in case his presence alarmed the foals he hoped to attract to the fence for Constanza's inspection.

'Good dog,' she told the wolfhound in soothing tones, in case his feelings had been hurt by Philip's peremptory command.

Conn, obediently prone, swayed his tail appreciatively.

'Look,' said Philip. 'He's coming over – the one I specially wanted to show you.'

He pointed to where a chestnut colt, his curiosity aroused, was prancing across the field towards them. He strode arrogantly between two other foals whose ears moved back at his approach; but his ears remained confidently forward.

'O-o-oh,' breathed Constanza, when the foal came up to them, entranced by his beauty. She stroked his velvet muzzle, the colt submitting to her caresses for a short time until, realizing no edible reward would be forthcoming, he withdrew in disdain and retreated haughtily across the field. Philip had contented himself with a perfunctory stroking of the foal's flank: he had been preoccupied in watching his companion. Her slim limbs and delicate frame lent her an affinity with the highly bred horses they were admiring. The visibly soft texture of her skin and the long lashes that fringed her green eyes confronted him, in a way he had not experienced before, with the mystique of femininity.

'We should introduce ourselves,' she said suddenly, with an underlying intonation in her voice that had already puzzled him several times. 'We do not know each other's full names.'

'Yes, I suppose so. If you like.'

She assumed a solemn expression. 'I am María Immaculada Constanza Eulalia Victoria de Vivar y San Martín, Fernández de Fuenterrabía y Borbón.'

Impressed, Philip absorbed this fanfare of aristocratic names.

'And you, now?' she enquired, with a suddenly roguish smile.

Thanks to the tutelage of Uncle Dermod, Philip felt capable of rising to this challenge. He cleared his throat determinedly.

'I am Philip Dominick Ignatius Kinsella de Carlow, Count of the Holy Roman Empire and one hundred and thirty-seven in descent from Adam.'

He felt he had acquitted himself well. The girl considered this information.

'That is a very noble name,' she told him gravely. 'I am descended from the Cid, but it is complicated in some way. I have heard my uncle speak of it. I do not know if I am descended from Adam.'

'I think you must be.' Philip refrained from elaborating; he had become wary of this topic. 'Who was that you said you were descended from? You mentioned someone Spanish...'

'*El Cid*. You have heard of him? No?' She looked scandalized by his ignorance. 'He was the greatest *caballero*, the greatest hero of all time. Don Rodrigo Díaz de Vivar – the *Cid Campeador* of King Alfonso – he conquered Valencia from the Moors. He had a famous sword. My uncle has seen it.'

This was a thrilling intimation. He noted that Constanza, like himself, relied on the authority of an uncle.

'Is your father dead?' he asked, then wondered, too late, if the question might be insensitive.

'Yes. He was killed by the Moors.'

Philip was confused. His mind, still running on the legend of the Cid, conjured an image of the late Duke of Saladavieja, clad in armour, cut down by Saracens.

'Are there still Moors in Spain?' he asked uncertainly.

'No, they were all driven out many years ago, stupid – I am sorry,' she added contritely. 'I must not say that, it is very rude. Miss Sullivan has told me often.'

'Who is Miss Sullivan?'

'My governess.'

'She's not Spanish?'

'No, she is Irish. And my mother's maid is English. She and Miss Sullivan do not like each other.'

'Yes,' said Philip, with an authoritative air. 'Irish and English people often dislike one another.'

'Perhaps you are right. I think it is because Miss Sullivan is pretty and the other is ugly.'

Since the foals had retreated to a distant corner of their field, Philip suggested visiting the farm. Deep in conversation, they turned onto a path that cut through the rhododendrons until they reached the avenue and began to saunter down it.

'You speak very good English.'

'I have been speaking it almost as long as I have been speaking Spanish.'

'How long have you been in Ireland?'

'For about two weeks.'

'Have you ever been here before?'

'No, this is the first time.'

'That's funny.'

'What do you mean?'

'Well... It's just that you sometimes sound quite Irish – the way you speak English. You don't speak with a foreign accent, more like a... well, actually, an Irish accent. It's a bit strange...'

His voice tailed off into startled silence. Coming from the direction of the castle, but still out of sight, he heard the clop of a horse's hoofs and the rumble of wheels. Calling Conn to heel, he led Constanza off the driveway onto the grass verge. Moments later, round the corner at a brisk trot came Grandma's dogcart, driven by the still gorgeously liveried Liam. Grandma sat back-to-back with him, bolt upright in the small carriage, holding her open parasol like a ceremonial *ombrellino*. For an instant her basilisk stare swept over the two children, without any sign of recognition. Then this chariot of the furies disappeared in a cloud of dust round another bend in the avenue, the sound of its progress dying away as if it had never been. Constanza glanced in wide-eyed enquiry at Philip.

'That was my grandmother,' he explained. 'She is in this world, but not of it.'

The cause of this apparition was that Mrs Skerrett, piqued by the attention devoted to the Duchess of Saladavieja, had ordered her dogcart and driven off in a deliberately ambiguous fashion, calculated to alarm her daughter that she might have taken permanent leave, thus disrupting the entertainment of the guest. In fact, Countess Kinsella remained ignorant of her mother's departure, so the stratagem failed.

The children resumed their progress down the avenue, until they noticed Conn was lagging behind.

'Is he tired?' asked Constanza.

'No, I forgot: he won't go near the main gate. It's where his wife was killed.' Philip employed this anthropomorphic terminology to explain the wolfhound's behaviour. He recounted how the Black and Tans had shot Conn's mate.

'Oh, *poor dog!*' Constanza, deeply affected, crouched down and hugged the wolfhound tightly. He wagged his tail mournfully in response.

'I suppose this means we can't go to the farm after all,' said Philip. 'He likes you so much, it would be cruel to leave him behind.'

'Can we go to that funny little house instead?' The girl pointed towards the rising ground behind the trees that fringed the drive. Many years before, some attempt had been made to create informal gardens there, now run wild, so that a mixture of cultivated plants and encroaching ferns covered the slopes.

'You mean the summerhouse? Yes, that's one of my favourite places. Let's go there.'

131

He unlatched a gate leading off the avenue and held it open for her. Conn, delighted at his reprieve, bustled through in her wake. A path led up the slope towards the summerhouse, a small pavilion like a Greek temple, its classical style contrasting with the gothic appearance of every other structure around Lissanore. There was a dreamlike quality to the afternoon, walking up the hillside beside this golden girl, that made Philip feel light-headed. He supposed he must be falling in love with her; that this was what that mysterious emotion, featured in so many books, was like when actually experienced. He thought of Rudolf and Princess Flavia in *The Prisoner of Zenda*. He had wept at the end when, in deference to duty, they both nobly renounced their love, its only enduring expression the yearly exchange of a rose, with the message: 'Rudolf – Flavia – always'. In love, such tokens were very important.

Like timeless figures in a tapestry, among the ferns and late bluebells, the two young dreamers and the ageing wolfhound made their way to the miniature temple. As they strolled in the warm sunshine, Philip told Constanza of all the noble deeds of his house: Bonaventure Kinsella at Aughrim; Felix, Count Kinsella charging with the cavalry at the Battle of Kolín; his own grandfather fighting for the Pope and the Carlist King of Spain.

'¡Ah, sí, muy bueno!' She was suddenly fired with enthusiasm. 'Los carlistas – they were great soldiers. I have often heard about them. It is good that your grandfather fought for Don Carlos.'

By now they had reached the summerhouse. Originally designed as a folly, it had degenerated into a garden shed. Twin pillars supported a classical pediment shading a veranda where a stone ledge running along the wall was covered with worn leather cushions to provide seating. The door was ajar and the atmosphere inside stifling. Philip let his companion glimpse the jumble of garden implements, deck-chairs, a lawnmower and a long wooden box containing croquet mallets, then suggested they sit on the veranda. With Conn stretched at their feet, they resumed a conversation that revolved around epic adventures, mythical and real, of past ages. Constanza told him tales of the Cid and other Spanish heroes; he was surprised and delighted that a girl should possess such knowledge. He told her so.

'I have many books,' she said in explanation, 'some with beautiful pictures. My favourite, after the Cid, is the story of Amadís and Oriana.'

She began to relate it, but it was complicated, so that she had to retrace her steps several times, finally giving up and dissolving into apologetic laughter. Yet she had fortuitously given Philip the opportunity to broach the proposal he had nervously been formulating.

'Constanza, you understand – I mean, about knights and their ladies… Not many people do, nowadays… Would you… I mean, would it be all right… Would you let me be your knight?' he ended in a breathless rush, his cheeks blazing with embarrassment at his own audacity.

The girl considered this with a grave expression. When she looked up after a moment, her green eyes were alight.

'I think I should like that. I would be very happy for you to be my knight, Philip.'

It was the first time she had spoken his name. A surge of joy ran through him.

'Thank you very much. I promise always to be a faithful and true knight, Constanza.'

There was silence between them for a minute. Then, emboldened by his success so far, Philip tremulously ventured to make the further request for which he had been steeling himself.

'Would you let me have a token? You know, something to prove I am your knight. Like at tournaments, when they wore a lady's favour.'

'I don't know… I suppose so. What should I give you?'

'Oh, any small thing of yours. A ribbon – something like that.'

'I haven't got a ribbon. Not at the moment, I mean. I was wearing one yesterday,' she added regretfully.

'Of course,' said Philip with assumed casualness, though his heart threatened to burst from his ribs, 'the best token would be a lock of your hair.'

'Oh, yes.' She responded with unexpected enthusiasm. 'I know. My father always wore a lock of my mother's hair, in a little silver case hung round his neck.'

'You see – that proves it's a good thing to do. So, may I have a lock of your hair?'

'Yes, but how can I cut it off? I don't have scissors.'

Philip was so exultant he felt that no obstacle was insurmountable. Inspired, he dived inside the summerhouse, from which his triumphant cry rang out moments later. He emerged carrying a pair of secateurs his mother used for pruning roses. He inspected them critically. They were quite new and rust-free; they looked sharp, but he could not risk hurting the girl if they turned out to be blunt. He tested them on a nearby plant and the result was reassuring.

'Are these all right?' he asked shyly.

'I think so.'

Wearing a doubtful expression, she took the secateurs and held a strand of hair away from her head. The secateurs were rather stiff and, after several unsuccessful contortions, she handed them back, saying:

'It's too difficult. You had better do it yourself.'

With trembling hands, Philip very gingerly took hold of a small tress of light brown hair, streaked with gold.

'Be careful,' she said. 'You mustn't leave a space my mother will notice.'

For an instant, an image of Uncle Arthur taking a clipping from Pecksniff, his aunt's spaniel, invaded Philip's mind; ashamedly he banished the ignoble comparison.

'It's all right. I'll cut it just here, where it hangs back from the comb. No one will notice.'

With a supreme effort of concentration, holding the strand of hair loose so that he could not hurt Constanza, he closed the secateurs on the silken tress: it parted cleanly. Holding his prize tightly, he beckoned the girl to follow him inside the summerhouse. There he knelt down in the nearest corner and, single-handed because of the precious lock of hair he was clutching, began to prise a stone out of the wall, close to the floor. While she watched, he slid the stone out, reached into the exposed aperture and brought out a tin box.

'Look. This is my top-secret hiding place. Nobody else knows about it except me – and now you.'

He carried his secret cache outside, laid it on the seat and opened it with his free hand. Constanza, with feminine curiosity, craned forward to see the contents. They consisted of several ancient foreign coins, one prized exhibit bearing the image of Louis XVI; a medal of unknown origin with some unidentifiable heraldry on it; a miniature penknife; and a round metal box. Philip unscrewed the lid of this smaller container. Inside was a brooch, discarded by his mother, which he had persuaded himself must be made of gold. This he presented to Constanza, then replaced it with the lock of her hair, which he coiled inside the little circular box before closing it tightly. He put it back inside the tin and returned it to its hiding place in the summerhouse, carefully reinstating the stone that concealed it.

'Thank you for my present,' said the girl. 'Is it very valuable?'

'It may be.' Philip answered noncommittally.

'Well, it is valuable to me because it is a present from my knight.'

Philip felt his heart would burst with the pride swelling within him. He took her hand very gently, lifted it and brushed it with his lips, marvelling at the softness of her skin. He hoped she would not be offended by so intimate a gesture, but she lived in a society where hand kissing was conventional and she responded with calm acceptance.

'It's a sign that I am your knight,' he told her, 'and you are my lady.'

'I am glad to have a knight. My father used to be my knight – he was a true *caballero*, everybody said so – until the Moors killed him.'

'But you said there were no Moors in Spain now.'

'He was killed in Morocco, at a place called Annual. Many Spanish soldiers died.' A wistful expression came over her face as she gazed into the distance, recalling her father. 'I was quite a little girl when he died, but I remember him very well. He used to pick me up and carry me in his arms. He had a nice smell. There was a song he used to sing to me, to make me go to sleep.'

In a childish, but beautiful, liquid voice she began to sing:

'Ay, ay, ay, ay,
Canta y no llores,
Porque cantando se alegran,
Cielito lindo, los corazones.'

The lilting melody died away, followed by a profound silence. Philip wondered what the words meant, but decided not to ask: sometimes things were more affecting when their meaning remained obscure.

'That's all I know,' Constanza said at last. 'I don't remember the rest of the song.'

'It was lovely. You sang it very well. I suppose,' he added reluctantly, yielding to returning normality after this dreamlike interlude, 'we had better be getting back or we shall be late for tea.'

On their walk to the house, Philip returned to the topic of the Cid and his celebrated sword, which Constanza had described to him.

'We have a famous sword too. My ancestor carried it at the Battle of Aughrim and my grandfather took it with him when he went to fight for the Pope and afterwards in Spain, for Don Carlos.'

He led her into the castle through the front door and up the staircase, to where pride of place was given to the relic that embodied for Philip all the romance of his family – the sword of Bonaventure Kinsella. It hung high on the wall: a plain, straight-bladed sword with a hand-guard around its hilt, of a pattern that had broadly remained in use among soldiers throughout the centuries since it was forged. This ancient weapon spoke to Philip more eloquently than all Uncle Dermod's lectures. It moved him so deeply that he rationed his visits to it, for fear it might ever become commonplace; often he even averted his eyes when passing it on the stairs.

After Constanza had admired it, he took her back downstairs and showed her the portrait of his grandfather Dominick, Count Kinsella, dressed in his baggy blue-grey uniform of a Carlist Zou-ave. Philip pointed to where the sword they had just inspected was accurately represented in the painting, his grandfather's hands rest-ing on its pommel, his head crowned with a red beret ornamented with a gold-threaded tassel.

'See. He fought for Spain too.'

'Like my father.'

'Yes. They were both heroes.'

With a depressing awareness of mundane reality flooding in to inundate the fairy tale that had been that sun-drenched afternoon, he led the girl back out onto the terrace, where the adults had al-ready risen from the tea table.

'You are late,' his mother told him reproachfully, while greeting

Constanza with a smile, to indicate she was not in any way to blame. 'You will just have time for a cup of tea and a slice of cake.'

They consumed this viaticum in silence, the intimacy between them dissolved by the presence of the grown-ups, chattering and laughing, insensitively as it seemed to Philip while Constanza's departure loomed so imminently. When everybody trooped round to the front door to see off the guests – the proceedings being protracted by the excessively ceremonious conduct of Corristeen – the *Duquesa* said something to her maid, who hurried to the waiting motor car and returned carrying a small leather case from which her mistress extracted a camera, ordering the company to close ranks, remain quite still and smile. This they did while she took three photographs, slightly rearranging the composition on each occasion. Finally she said:

'And one just of the children. Constanza, stand beside Philip… No, over there… That's right… Not a move, now… Smile… Very good. At least, I hope so.'

Philip had the presence of mind to ask:

'May I please have a photograph?'

'Of course. I shall send it to you.' She turned to her hostess. 'Thank you so much for an utterly lovely luncheon… So kind…'

She exchanged valedictory kisses with Countess Kinsella and a brief volley of Spanish with the polyglot Father Yves, then entered the car, in which Constanza was already seated. The chauffeur slammed the door, took his place behind the wheel then began to turn the heavy vehicle, spewing up spurts of gravel.

'Did you hear the brogue on the child?' Uncle Dermod's voice rose from among the group standing on the steps to wave farewell. 'It's not uncommon, since so many of the Spanish nobility have Irish governesses. I remember a high-ranking grandee in London years ago – spoke purest Castilian, but when he broke into English he sounded like a Moore Street stall-holder.'

Philip waved to Constanza, who shyly reciprocated as the car purred off towards the head of the avenue.

'What a beautiful child,' said Countess Kinsella.

'She will break hearts,' agreed her husband.

Philip, with the disconsolate Conn at his side, watching the large motor car disappear from sight, thought that this was true and that he was possibly the first victim.

CHAPTER IX

JULY arrived, bringing with it Philip's brothers, Edmund and Dominick, home from school three weeks before the end of term. This was due to Dominick, the younger, having succumbed to appendicitis. After being operated on and returned to the school infirmary, where he had malingered convincingly, a genially complicit doctor had prescribed the country air and comforts of home as the best aid to recovery. He had therefore been grudgingly released by the Jesuits, to be conveyed back to Ireland under the care of his elder brother. Dominick had tried to sustain the role of invalid during his first day at home by lolling around, looking pale and interesting, as his mother sceptically described it.

This, however, had attracted the solicitous attentions of Uncle Ulick, who had manfully overcome his jealousy of someone with claims to be in worse health than himself to dig deep into the resources of his extensive pharmacy and produce vile-smelling draughts, pills and other remedies which he pressed upon his nephew. The medication worked with disconcerting speed. This harassment, combined with the glorious weather and the realization there was no danger of his being sent back to school, restored Dominick to robust good health within twenty-four hours. He dismayed his uncle, who had strongly recommended a month's confinement to bed, by immediately resuming his normal vigorous activities. Only the scar from his operation bore testimony to his recent illness. This he proudly exhibited to all comers – including Angela the housemaid, whom he surprised in the servants' hall, engrossed in *The Irish Messenger of the Sacred Heart*. She uttered a shriek of terror ('Saint Joseph tonight!'), dropped her devotional periodical and nearly fainted.

After the first excitement of his brothers' homecoming had

subsided, Philip recognized that things were falling into a familiar pattern. At first he looked forward to his brothers' company; then there was a short interlude during which he listened eagerly to their tales from school and was treated affably by them (if rather offhandedly by Edmund, the elder); finally, after a day or so, they were reclaimed by their respective interests and Philip was again left to his own devices. It was the same at the end of every school term.

Within days he had resumed his normal routine, though time hung more heavily on his hands since he had been released from classes, his lessons with Father Yves reduced to a short catechism instruction each day and some informal conversation in French. During one of these sessions he took the opportunity to make a request he had been gestating since the Duchess's visit.

'Father,' he asked shyly, 'you were talking to the Duchess in Spanish, weren't you?'

'Ah, oui, mon fils – comme une vache espagnole. Or rather,' he added, acknowledging the inappropriateness of this simile, 'like someone who has not the great command of that noble language.'

'But she understood everything you said. She talked to you as if you were Spanish. You speak Spanish quite well, don't you?'

'Hélas, it is greatly inferior to my Italian, which I was able to perfect while living in Rome. You make me think I must work hard to improve it.'

Philip could not have asked for a better opening.

'Will you teach me Spanish, Father? I'd love to learn.'

'Quoi? Eh bien, I really do not know if that is wise. It might confuse you, learning both French and Spanish at the same time. On the other hand,' he mused aloud, 'you have a good knowledge of Latin and that is very helpful with the Spanish tongue...'

It had just occurred to Father Yves that adding a further language to Philip's curriculum, at little extra effort to himself, might compensate for his deficiency in teaching mathematics; it would be an honourable *quid pro quo* to present to Count Kinsella. It would also give him an incentive to improve his command of Spanish.

'I promise I will try very hard.' Philip pressed him anxiously.

'Very well. I shall speak to your father and ask his opinion. I promise nothing, but if it is agreeable to him, I see no reason why we should not start with a few lessons. However, if your French suffers in consequence we shall have to abandon the project.'

'Oh, it won't, Father. I promise. Thank you very, very much.'

Philip felt an urge, amounting to a need, to learn the native tongue of the girl Constanza who had made so deep an impression on him. Her tales of the Cid and other Iberian heroes had convinced him that Spain was home to all that was most romantic. He still cherished, in his inner ear, the remembrance of her singing that in-comprehensible but haunting song. The cadences of the language had captured his imagination. By learning Spanish, he thought he would somehow bring himself closer to Constanza, even though he was unsure whether he would ever see her again. Like all infatu-ated hearts, he longed to talk about her, but realized the hazards of attempting to do so. When Tom Dixon had enquired sardoni-cally about the visit of 'that Duchess of yours', he had omitted any mention of her daughter from his brief, affectedly casual, account of the occasion. Uncle Dermod, on the other hand, was himself ea-ger to reminisce about their noble visitor, so Philip could engage in conversations with him about the topic that most preoccupied him, without provoking questions or derision. He found his uncle surrounded by books and papers in the library, to which he had re-treated, displaced by the painting work being carried on by Declan in his tower-room study.

'It was a great pity the *Duquesa* could not stay overnight,' said Uncle Dermod, 'then I might have got more information from her about her family connexions; but she was going over for Ascot and then to Esher, to visit the Infanta Beatrice. She herself is a Bourbon – of a very minor cadet branch – on her mother's side, which is interesting.'

'You mean the royal family?'

'Yes – though it is a fairly distant relationship.'

Philip received this information with deep satisfaction. So, Constanza was of royal blood, as well as being descended from the Cid. It seemed wholly appropriate.

'That's right, I remember now. One of the names she said sounded like "Bourbon", but she pronounced it in a funny way, so I didn't realize.'

'The *Duquesa?*'

'No, Constanza... her daughter.' He hoped his uncle had not noticed he was blushing.

'Ah, yes, the pretty little infanta with the Irish brogue,' said Uncle Dermod, smiling.

'She told me she was descended from the Cid as well.' Philip urgently sought to introduce a distraction into the conversation.

'Yes, well, so she is; but not in the male line. They descend from one of the Cid's daughters, Cristina. Centuries later, an ancestor of the Duke of Saladavieja assumed the designation "de Vivar", with royal approval, having acquired a fief of that name; but they are not the heirs male, which is why they do not bear the Cid's surname, Díaz. Their motto *"Buen vassallo, buen señor"* celebrates their descent from the famous hero, being taken from the *Song of the Cid*, an epic composed in his honour.'

Uncle Dermod, with the aid of reference works dispatched to him from Hatchards, had been repairing his ignorance of the Spanish nobility and was glad of an opportunity to parade his newly imbibed knowledge.

'What does that motto mean?' Philip was anxious to begin penetrating the mysteries of the Spanish language.

'Er... I would say, "Worthy vassal, worthy lord", meaning they fulfil their responsibilities both to those above them and those below. That, after all, is the essence of the feudal principle: *noblesse oblige.*'

'Father Yves is going to teach me Spanish.'

'An excellent idea. I am glad to hear it. As you see, I have just acquired a few books in Spanish. Feel at liberty to browse through them whenever you want. It might help.'

'Thank you, Uncle Dermod.'

'Now I really must go along and see how Declan is getting on. I am afraid the project is progressing more slowly than I had hoped; but that, of course, is because it has become more ambitious than I originally envisaged.'

'May I come too?'

'Of course.'

They found Dominick talking to Declan in the tower room, where he had come to inspect the work in progress. Aged twelve, Dominick had the classic Kinsella features, grey eyes, a longish nose and dark hair, so that he resembled Philip much more than their elder brother Edmund. He also had an easy-going manner and a ready smile second only to Declan's in spontaneity and frequency.

Philip had already paid several visits to the tower room and had been awed by the scale on which the genealogical mural was now projected. Declan had conceived the ingenious notion of replacing the conventional tree with festoons of ivy, to mimic the dense growth on the outside wall which clustered intrusively around the windows. The estate carpenter had been set to removing all bookshelves and other fixtures more than four feet above the floor. No paint had yet been applied, but Declan had painstakingly drawn in outline almost as many ivy tendrils as grew on the outer wall, each bearing scrolls for individual names, accompanied by shields that as yet displayed no heraldry but only pencilled numbers, allocated from a master-plan drawn up by himself and Uncle Dermod, to indicate which coat of arms was to be painted onto them. Although the pedigree was still only an austere outline in black and white, its eventual scope was already evident, as well as its potential grandeur, if well executed.

'Do you see there, now,' the painter was explaining to Dominick, 'that scroll is a bit larger than its neighbours because I checked its number against the key and found it's going to have to display more information. That's your man – the famous Field Marshal Count Gabriel Kinsella who built this place – so he gets a bigger notice.'

'But, Declan,' said Uncle Dermod urgently, 'those shields are different sizes. That can't be right, surely?'

Declan's grin broadened.

'Ah, you're a hard man to fool, Count Dermod. You're quite right, they are different sizes.'

'I don't understand – surely that will spoil the uniformity?'

'Not at all. The larger size of shield only occurs about half a dozen times, as you can see. They're reserved for the big potatoes, the fellows who really matter. There's the Field Marshal… and over there the other one you were telling me about – Count O'Donell, is that right? Well, when you told me how he saved the Emperor's life and all – and was given the right to add the imperial arms to his own – I thought we should create a big enough space to display it.'

'Yes, yes.' Dermod nodded vigorously.

'So, what we'll do is fiddle with the perspective around the half-dozen large shields, so they seem nearer and therefore bigger.

You might call it *trompe l'oeil* – which the painted ivy leaves are anyway. Trust me.' His grin expanded to dimensions of irresistible reassurance.

'I certainly do.' Dermod clapped him on the shoulder.

'Terrific!' Dominick exchanged delighted smirks with Philip who, greatly impressed by this confident exposition, was convinced Declan was a painter of genius; certainly one who could be relied on not to cut off his own ear. He confided this opinion to his brother as they made their way to the stables, Dominick having graciously consented to go for a hack with Philip, since no more appealing entertainment was on offer.

'I shouldn't be surprised,' Philip said with a judicial air, 'if this painting turns out to be very valuable, once it's finished. It might save us if we fell on hard times – the sort of thing Papa is always worrying about.'

'You mean we could sell it?'

'Yes.'

'In that case,' Dominick displayed the superior smile he adopted when exposing his younger brother's naïvety, 'hadn't you better go back to Declan and suggest he paints it on canvas, instead of on the wall? Otherwise, we'll have to sell the house along with it.'

He rumpled Philip's hair playfully to show he was only teasing. Philip refrained from any further essays in art criticism for the duration of their ride. Anyway, he reflected, he would soon be ten, an age whose double figures surely conferred authority, when he hoped he would be treated less patronizingly by his older brothers.

The more intensely supercilious of these by far, the thirteen-year-old Edmund (who, as he liked to emphasize, was Dominick's senior by more than a year), was at that moment reclining in a deckchair on the terrace beside his parents and Mrs Blackwell, whose visits had grown more frequent during the brilliant weather. The two women were discussing books.

'Have you seen St John Ervine's new biography of Parnell?' asked Mrs Blackwell.

'No,' said Countess Kinsella. 'I'm afraid I have fallen woefully behind in my reading. Is it good?'

'I can't say, as I haven't read it myself, but the reviews make me want to.'

'Good heavens!' Count Kinsella swivelled round in his chair, holding out his open copy of *The Irish Times*. 'Look at this.'

'What?' His son and heir stared uninterestedly, without troubling to lean out of his deckchair to look at the proffered newspaper.

'This photograph: someone has presented the Royal Dublin Society with an equestrian portrait of the Empress Elisabeth. See, she is riding Merry Andrew, her Irish hunter.'

Edmund received this information with indifference; but it aroused the interest of his mother and the rector's wife.

'Wasn't she a great beauty?' Mrs Blackwell craned forward to study the photograph.

'The most beautiful woman in Europe, of her generation,' said Count Kinsella with enthusiasm. 'My father once saw her out with the Meath, from Summerhill, when she took the place during the seasons of 1879 and 1880 – though, come to think of it, he must have seen her in Vienna too – and he always said the reports of her beauty were, if anything, understated.'

'We have her room in the house here,' his wife told Mrs Blackwell, with a sideways smile at her husband.

'Did she stay here too?'

The Kinsellas both laughed.

'No,' said the Count emphatically, 'to my father's great chagrin, she did not. She was invited and accepted, so special apartments were prepared for her. No expense was spared. A great four-poster bed was made specially, with draperies that incorporated the Imperial arms. In the event, the Empress changed her plans and sent apologies. My father was furiously disappointed: he thought, as the son of one of her husband's field marshals, he had more right than anybody in Ireland to offer her hospitality. The interesting thing is, though, he never held it against her. As a strict upholder of monarchy, he believed the whims of royalty must always be accommodated by their subjects.'

'More fool he,' said Edmund ungraciously.

'Whatever your grandfather was,' Count Kinsella spoke in an even tone, 'he most certainly was not a fool.'

'Since then,' his wife explained to Mrs Blackwell, 'the bedroom has been kept exactly as it was, prepared for the Empress. I have to oversee the cleaning of it every month, some of the things are quite delicate. Otherwise, the Empress's Room is kept locked. Would you like to see it sometime?'

'I should love to.'

'What a senseless waste,' said Edmund, 'keeping a room reserved for a woman who has been dead for ages.'

'Nobody is sleeping on the floor as a consequence.' His father looked at him coolly. 'We are hardly short of accommodation. Anyway, it is a family tradition.'

'Tradition!' Edmund uttered a snort of impatience. 'Was there ever a family, anywhere on earth, more hidebound by tradition than ours?'

'We have strong roots and a distinctive identity, that's true,' said Count Kinsella, rising from his chair. 'If you will excuse me,' he smiled at Mrs Blackwell, 'I must go and speak to Slattery about one or two things.'

'You should speak to him about doing an honest day's work for a change,' Edmund told him from the depths of his deckchair. 'Old Dizzycourse treats this place like a rest home.'

'Edmund, I will thank you not to refer to the staff by possibly hurtful nicknames. They may call one another what they like, but it is an abuse of authority for us to join in. I should have thought someone who professes the kind of radical principles you claim to have espoused would have been conscious of that.'

His heir, momentarily abashed, made no reply. Countess Kinsella, who had never heard her husband, in private conversation, refer to Slattery other than as 'Dizzycourse', kept her features carefully composed. Mrs Blackwell studied Edmund appraisingly through her sunglasses, taking in his sandy-red hair, thin mouth and supercilious expression, and thought he was turning into a singularly unattractive youth. Although there was no physical resemblance, he reminded her of his grandmother Skerrett.

In the yard, Count Kinsella advanced upon Slattery, who emerged from the outhouse that served as his office prepared to give battle. Word of the impending confrontation had drawn an interested group of spectators – stable boys, under-gardeners and odd-job men, with whom Lissanore abounded – disposed around the yard at favourable vantage points, in a mood of enjoyable anticipation. Only Moriarty, the disreputable ginger tomcat whose prolific progeny was dispersed across the county, regarded this disturbance with displeasure from the roof of the turf shed where he had been dozing. Dizzycourse Slattery wore his greasy brown trilby rakishly tilted on the back of his head. He sported a two-day growth of pepper-and-salt beard, his nose was heavily veined, and his eyes were small and set closer together than was decent. He was coatless, his waistcoat – which belonged to a different suit from his trousers – unbuttoned for relief from the heat; a racing newspaper protruded from his pocket, in testimony to the business on which he had been engaged until interrupted by his employer. Despite his resentment, he was willing to exhaust every negotiating tactic to preserve peace, if that should prove possible.

'Good day to Your Honour,' he said unctuously, touching his hat.

Count Kinsella's heart sank at this anachronistic salutation, which he rightly interpreted as the formal prelude to a battle *à l'outrance*.

'Good day to you, Slattery. I was just wondering why the fences on the plantation up at Donnelly's Hill have not been mended. You assured me a week ago they would be seen to the next day.'

Slattery removed his hat to facilitate the scratching of his head, glanced inside the battered trilby as if expecting to find some cue there to prompt his reply, replaced it on his balding pate and stared at his employer with an air of concern.

'Finces?'

'Yes.'

'Up by Donnelly's Hill?'

'That's right.'

'Finces up by Donnelly's Hill, is it?' Slattery pieced this information together with forensic acuity.

'It is.' Count Kinsella fixed him with what he hoped was an implacable stare. The consequence was to unleash the full torrent of Slattery's notorious volubility when defending his actions or, almost invariably, inaction.

'Ah, well now, d'ye see o' course (he employed the phrase that constantly punctuated his speech and had earned him his nickname), there was some terrible complications with regard to them finces – terrible problems that has me near diminted! Wasn't it Barney Heffernan let me down entirely – bad cess to him – after promisin' a load of timber for fince poles an' neither hide nor hair of him to be seen this past week, d'ye see o' course.'

'Surely we have plenty of wood still in store? We only used half of the last load for the paddock.'

'Ah, true for you, sir, but d'ye see o' course, there was terrible problems too with the men.'

'The men? What's wrong with the men?'

'Ah, yeh might well ask, sir. Hasn't it been like the twelve plagues of Egypt in this yard? I never knew the like. Didn't Patsy Grogan sprain the ould ankle on Tuesday and isn't Peter Heenan in his bed with the Eyetalian influenza, d'ye see o' course?'

'Influenza – nonsense. At this time of year – in this heat? If I know Heenan, his influenza came out of a bottle.'

'Ah, God forgive yeh, Count. That's monstrous un-Christian to his widow an' seven childer.'

'What? He's not dead, is he?'

'As good as, sir, if what I heard in Flanagan's last night is even half true.'

He doffed his hat out of respect for a colleague *in extremis*. A ripple of appreciation ran through his audience at this virtuoso performance. It increased Count Kinsella's exasperation.

'So, you are telling me you don't have enough men to repair the fences on Donnelly's Hill?'

'Not if the Lord Mayor o' Dublin himself went down on his bended knees an' begged me. Sure, we're barely keepin' our heads above water as it is, we're that short-handed, d'ye see o' course.'

A note of impatience entered Dizzycourse Slattery's voice. He had just remembered one of the stable lads was waiting to take his betting slip into Burras and he had not written it out yet, though he fancied a sure thing in the three-thirty. Verbal duelling with Count Kinsella always provided a welcome relief from boredom, but he must not let it interfere with business. He had indulged his employer long enough.

'What about Richards?' asked the Count. 'Surely he is available to work on Donnelly's Hill?'

'Billy Richards is workin' out by Nowlanstown today.' Slattery tersely dismissed the notion.

'Or Fogarty?'

'Fogarty is below.'

'Boylan?'

'Boylan is beyant.'

Count Kinsella's palate registered the bitter taste of defeat. All he could hope for now was to withdraw in good order, salvaging his dignity and preparing the ground for a future engagement on more favourable terms.

'Now look here, Slattery, I am not at all pleased about this. Nor do I accept your excuses about a shortage of timber or manpower. I shall ride up to Donnelly's Hill on Monday afternoon and I expect to find the work well under way. Do I make myself clear?'

'Ah, yeh do that, sir. I'm truly sorry to have disobliged yeh, but 'twas act of God, as they say, d'ye see o' course.'

'Monday it is, then. Unless, of course,' he added with heavy sarcasm, 'you all have to take the day off to attend Heenan's funeral.'

'Ah, sir, there's no call –'

'Monday,' repeated Slattery's frustrated employer, turning away, ruefully conscious he was leaving his opponent master of the field. For a moment he was tempted to remind the sinecurist who affected the title of land steward of Castle Kinsella that there had been ten plagues of Egypt, not twelve; but common sense dissuaded him from so puerile a riposte.

He strode back to the terrace in a mood of considerable disgruntlement and dropped heavily into a chair, after ordering Corristeen to bring him a glass of whiskey – a departure from his normal pre-luncheon abstemiousness. His wife, who knew perfectly well what had occurred – had foreseen it before he left on his futile errand – diplomatically ignored the atmosphere, as did Mrs Blackwell who shared her insight. Tact, however, was foreign to Edmund Kinsella, who asked his father:

'Well, did you sort Slattery out?'

'That,' said his father, 'is a matter of opinion.'

'The men are completely insubordinate now,' said his brother Dermod, who had joined the company in his absence. 'I suppose that is what comes of having a revolution and a Free State.'

'It has nothing to do with the Free State.' Count Kinsella sighed resignedly. 'It was the same in our father's time and, I imagine, our grandfather's. The people have always manipulated us as they pleased – it is how things work in Ireland. In a way, it is a reassuring sign of continuity. However, Edmund, I spoke too severely to you earlier. From now on, you may call Slattery by any name you like.'

That afternoon Philip met his mother on her way to the walled garden, with a basket over her arm. He saw at once that she was in a radiantly good mood, which caused his own spirits to rise.

'Hello.' She smiled warmly. 'Where have you been?'

'Talking French with Father Yves – I still do it for an hour every day.'

'Ah, très bien. Veux-tu m'accompagner dans le jardin, mon chéri?'

'Mais oui, Maman. Permettez-moi de vous ouvrir la porte.'

He took the key to the garden from her basket and turned it in the lock, then swung open the door. It was like stepping into an enchanted world beyond, as he followed his mother inside and closed the door behind them to exclude Conn, Balzac, Moriarty and other marauders who might wreak havoc in this fragile, carefully ordered domain. The scent hit them at once, like a wall of fragrance engulf-ing them. The exceptionally warm weather had turned the enclosed garden into an open-air hothouse, riotous with colour. His mother inhaled luxuriously then gave a little skip of joy.

'Ah! C'est la vie, c'est la vie!'

Philip smiled up at her, enjoying her skittish mood. In a quick movement of her free arm she drew him against her in a quick hug, uttering an unaccustomed endearment.

'My little Phillie-love.'

Philip was delighted by this spontaneous demonstration of af-fection, though he glanced round quickly to make sure Wilson the head gardener or, worse still, the boys who worked under him were nowhere in the vicinity. The garden was quite deserted. He felt a surge of pure happiness at his mother's loving gesture: it was the sort of thing that had sometimes occurred in the nursery, but had become rare in recent years. Mummie walked over to a tumultuously blooming rose bed and inhaled deeply again.

'This hot weather brought my roses out early this year... On the other hand,' she frowned and moved across to another cluster of flowers, 'it seems to be turning my hydrangeas green. I can think of no other reason. Look at them – ugh!'

They wandered down the paved paths, walled with brilliant co-lours on either side. Lupins hemmed them in like sentinels, spears of blue and white, purple and yellow. Foxgloves tall as Philip's head framed his mother in violet, their bell-like blossoms industrious with the hum of bees. The garden assailed all the senses simulta-neously: besides the spectacle of the multi-coloured blooms and the heady scents they gave off, nature also provided an orchestra in which the droning bees played the strings and fluting songbirds sup-plied the woodwind.

'See,' said his mother, pointing towards a carpet of orange, red and yellow flowers sweeping up against the wall in one corner, 'those nasturtiums have taken charge – they don't need cultivation. I shall have to watch, though, that things don't get out of hand. Pick some for the salad, Philip… Not all the same colour, silly. Oh, I wish my freesias weren't long past their season, they have a wonderful scent. I do love flowers. Did you know, we nearly gave Edmund the name Hyacinth?'

This was startling information. Philip looked up from his task of gathering nasturtiums to see if she was joking.

'After a flower? Surely that would be a girl's name?'

'No, after a saint. Apparently it was a traditional name among your father's Talbot cousins. We decided against it. Just as well, really.' She giggled girlishly. 'Poor Edmund – what a lucky escape.'

Philip filed away this indiscretion at the back of his mind and they continued their tour of the garden. This was his mother's private Eden, where she alone reigned. She moved familiarly about, inspecting plants with an expert eye, sometimes deadheading a spent bloom.

'I don't think Wilson is giving those arum lilies enough water.' She deposited a couple of decapitated heads in her basket. 'I must speak to him about it.'

By now they had reached the area close to the greenhouse around which stood the remnant of the kitchen garden that had once predominated within the walled enclosure, but had gradually been reduced in favour of more ornamental cultivation. Philip absently pulled a leaf from a mint bush and rolled it between his fingers and thumb to smell the aroma. The sight of the greenhouse reminded him of something.

'Mrs Dixon said you should get rid of your calceolaria.'

His real motive in relaying the message was to demonstrate his ability to pronounce this name, which he had spent some time mastering. It enabled him to talk about horticulture with his mother on terms of some sophistication.

'She is absolutely right. I ought to burn it, but I don't like the thought of being beaten. I am not even going into the greenhouse today – it would simply put me in a bad mood.'

To banish this thought she gazed around, inhaling now with her eyes. Philip sensed she would like to be alone to commune with burgeoning nature in the sanctuary she had created.

'Excuse me, Mummie, I think I should go and find Dominick.'

'Off you go, then. He is playing croquet with the others. If you join them, I'm sure they will let you play too.'

He left his mother in happy contemplation of her flowers. His parting sight was of her slim figure standing beside the sundial in the centre of the garden, enveloped in a sea of colour and a haze of sweet scents; a picture he would always remember. When he closed the door in the wall behind him he felt a momentary pang, as if he had lost her to some other time or place, like Alice through the looking-glass; yet he also had a feeling he was not just protecting the plants from intruders, but his mother from the world outside.

The loud thwack of a mallet on a ball as he neared the lawn told him the croquet match was still in progress; but there was only one game still to be played. Dominick sportingly surrendered his place to Philip, who partnered Declan against Uncle Dermod and Mrs Blackwell. Philip's usual partner Uncle Eanna was in Dublin, attending a Celtic congress. At the fourth hoop Declan managed to roquet Mrs Blackwell's ball. He moved in to take the croquet stroke, placing his foot on his own ball to steady it as it rested against his opponent's. Then he struck it hard, without dislodging it, sending Mrs Blackwell's yellow ball across the lawn at high speed, into a shrubbery.

'Sorry about that.' He grinned cruelly at the rector's wife.

'He has sent you well and truly up the country,' said Uncle Dermod sympathetically to his partner.

'So it would seem.' Mrs Blackwell went to retrieve her ball.

Philip had watched Declan's performance with admiration. He had often tried to execute this manoeuvre, but more often than not had hit his foot with the mallet. Despite his poor play, Declan's skill enabled them to win. When they retired to the terrace for tea, Declan and Uncle Dermod drank a cup quickly, then excused themselves to return to their labours in the tower.

'No hard feelings, now, about that croquet shot?' Declan asked Mrs Blackwell in a rallying tone, pausing on his way into the house.

'None whatsoever.'

'Grand, so.' Declan smiled and passed in through the french windows.

Mrs Blackwell was sitting in a wicker chair. Some ash fell from her cigarette onto her lap and she shook it off irritably, flapping her skirt in a movement that sounded like sails coming to life in a sudden gale. She stubbed out her cigarette, which she had hardly smoked, and stood up.

'I must be off, Philip. I shall just go and find your mother – Oh, here she comes.'

Countess Kinsella was approaching from the direction of the walled garden, a now laden basket over her arm. Mrs Blackwell went to meet her and the two women, their voices in indistinct conversation floating behind them, moved out of sight on their way round to the front of the house, leaving Philip to ponder a question that had just occurred to him.

Why does Mrs Blackwell dislike Declan?

CHAPTER X

DESPITE enjoying the amenity of a private chapel and a priest to serve it, Count Kinsella was at pains to ensure his family played a full part in the life of the surrounding parish. So, Philip, like his brothers before him, had enlisted as an altar server in the parish church and performed that duty for one week in every month. He and Tom Dixon had arranged to serve together, so that they met at the church every morning and spent a short time idling together after Mass, until the pangs of the communion fast sent them speeding home to breakfast.

Sundays had a different routine. Almost the entire household of Castle Kinsella repaired to eleven o'clock Mass, in a motley variety of conveyances. Count and Countess Kinsella, with Deirdre and her nanny, drove to church in their car. Uncles Eanna and Dermod travelled in a decrepit vehicle belonging to the former, who drove so erratically as to terrify even the local people, who were inured to most motoring excesses; this Sunday the additional passenger was a white-faced Edmund, whose laziness had unwisely prompted him to beg a lift (Dominick had opted to bicycle to church). Uncle Ulick, out of consideration for his health, heard Mass at home, as did the reclusive Corristeen. Bridie Byrne, Mrs Ennis the cook and a couple of other domestics were transported in the side-car (or 'jaunting-car', as Grandma always called it), driven by Liam, unless Mrs Skerrett had decided to make one of her rare forays into the parish, in which case he would be detailed to drive her in the dogcart. The housemaids and youths employed about the place preferred to bicycle to church, since independent transport gave them an opportunity to loiter afterwards, exchanging gossip or flirtatious banter with their contemporaries. Declan, who had acquired a barely roadworthy bicycle, took to pedalling companionably with them to Mass, although, as he phrased it, he was not gospel-greedy. During the sermon he was to be seen smoking outside the church door with a knot of male kindred spirits who shared his lack of appetite for evangelization.

'It's my fault, I suppose, if my sermons aren't worth listening to,' Canon Roche would say humbly. 'Anyhow, the sermon is the least important part of the proceedings, what matters is the holy sacrifice itself.'

The sprawling caravanserai from Lissanore, shortly after straggling out from the castle gates, passed the Protestant church. Its proximity reflected the fact that when it had been built in the eighteenth century it depended on the patronage of the family whose house had occupied the site of Castle Kinsella, before the Austrian general returned from exile, bought the property and demolished it. The Kinsella family vault was situated on ground adjoining the old Church of Ireland graveyard, but within the demesne: a separate fiefdom of mortality, consecrated by Roman rites. A relic of the former relationship between the rectory and the castle was the path connecting the two, which Mrs Blackwell used on her frequent visits. The Church of Ireland service began half an hour earlier than the Mass the Kinsellas attended; as they drove past the Reverend Mr Blackwell's church this sultry Sunday morning, the members of his congregation could be heard petitioning the dear Lord and Father of mankind to forgive their foolish ways.

'Parson's Pleasure today, isn't it?' Count Kinsella asked his wife, glancing sideways at her before concentrating again on negotiating his way through the thickening traffic of bicycles and traps as they neared the parish church. He raised his hand to acknowledge greetings through the car window.

'Yes,' said Countess Kinsella. 'Parson's Pleasure it is.'

This was their facetious name for the Sunday in every month

when both Canon Roche and the Blackwells came to luncheon, by established custom.

'I'd better tell Corristeen to bring up a couple of extra bottles,' said the Count dryly, manoeuvring into a parking place beside the presbytery garden wall.

Philip had left home earlier than the rest of the household; his duties required him to see that everything in the sanctuary was prepared for Mass, that the wine and water cruets were filled and the vestments laid out for Canon Roche in the sacristy. It was an easy task at this fallow season of the liturgical year, when a green chasuble was invariably worn during the long procession of Sundays after Pentecost; but weekdays could still be treacherous, with feasts of saints and martyrs, demanding white or red vestments, lurking in ambush. Since he was effectively the sacristan in the chapel at Lissanore, Philip was well qualified to handle the responsibilities at the parish church which his colleague Tom Dixon was content to leave largely to him. Both boys would serve Mass together every morning for the remainder of the week, but since it was Sunday, when six altar boys traditionally thronged the sanctuary, they were joined by four underlings. To his distaste, Philip saw that one of them was Simmie Toal's youngest brother, Finbar, a sly seven-year-old of a naturally criminal bent. Although the Toal family, like Declan, was far from gospel-greedy, its matriarch had insisted on enrolling her youngest son among the altar staff as a token of respectability, though her social ambition had not extended to washing or ironing his cotta, which was disreputably grubby and crumpled. Philip's own red cassock and white cotta had been immaculately laundered by Bridie Byrne. Over it he carefully arranged the medallion that testified to his length of service as an altar boy, suspended round his neck on a red ribbon; he relished this distinction, since it reminded him of the decorations displayed in his ancestors' portraits at home.

'Ah, there ye are, lads.' Canon Roche grunted in satisfaction as he entered the sacristy and glanced approvingly at the preparations made. 'Good man, Philip. Where's the maniple? Oh, I see it there.'

He went over to the altar missal which sat on its lectern on top of the cupboards holding racks of vestments, riffled through the pages to find the appropriate places, marked them with the broad ribbons and nodded to Philip, who picked up the lectern and carried the missal into the church. The building was almost full by now, but he was too experienced a hand to glance curiously at the congregation as he moved to the foot of the sanctuary, genuflected then walked up the red-carpeted steps and placed the missal carefully on the right-hand – the Epistle – side of the altar and returned to the sacristy.

Presently, Mr Prendergast, the head pass-keeper, opened the sacristy door and jangled the bell to alert the congregation. The altar boys filed into the sanctuary two by two, followed by Canon Roche, carrying the square-shaped object that was the chalice and burse draped in their green veil. At the foot of the altar he handed Philip his biretta; all of them, celebrant and servers, genuflected and Canon Roche went up and placed the chalice on the altar then opened the missal. He came back down to the bottom of the altar steps, made the sign of the cross and intoned the familiar formula:

'*In nomine Patris, et Filii, et Spiritus Sancti. Amen. Introibo ad altare Dei.*'

When it came to the servers' turn to repeat the prayer of the *Confiteor* after the priest, Philip strained his ears during the phrase '*mea culpa, mea culpa, mea maxima culpa*', to check that the young delinquent Toal was not reciting the parodic version 'me a cowboy, me a cowboy, me a Mexican cowboy' – a good, if hackneyed, joke in the sacristy or playground, but sacrilegious during the celebration of Mass. He had been punished for this once already and warned of instant dismissal if he repeated the offence; but his coarse voice and impenetrable accent, gabbling an impressionistic Latin that might have been Hebrew, baffled interpretation. During the sermon – an admonition against uncharitable talk and behaviour – Philip's attention drifted to the plaster pinnacles and niches behind and above the altar, an icing-cake structure of fretted gothic stalagmites rising against a blue sky sown with golden fleurs-de-lis, an outsized angel kneeling on either side. Uncle Dermod had said it was in very poor taste, but Philip liked it. He loved, too, the sanctuary smells of beeswax, starched linen, stale incense and the heady bouquet of the altar wine in its cruet; these, like the familiar brocade texture of the priest's chasuble when he held it up during the elevation, were part of the intimacy of serving at Mass, a sensory experience not shared by the rest of the congregation.

The choir, competent but with a limited repertoire, sang snatches of popular devotional pieces at intervals: *Panis Angelicus* during the distribution of communion. It was Philip's responsibility to accompany Canon Roche along the altar rails, keeping pace at his elbow, holding the paten under the chin of each kneeling communicant in case the host might fall – a catastrophe he dreaded – and he performed this duty with intense concentration. This meant he had no opportunity to make his own thanksgiving after Holy Communion. He would have to return to the church after Mass to say the Prayer Before a Crucifix and the prayers for the Pope's intentions, to gain a plenary indulgence which he would allocate to anyone he knew who had recently died; failing that, to the longest-serving Holy Soul in Purgatory. Every few weeks he kept the plenary indulgence for himself, to ensure his spiritual bank balance was in credit, though he always felt a slight qualm of selfishness on these occasions.

Back in the sacristy, after Canon Roche had said the usual prayers and taken off his vestments, while the altar boys bustled around with the various accoutrements, Mr Prendergast came in, carrying the canvas bags containing the collection. He was a thin, bony man with a permanent expression of disapproval.

'Is that me bound for Monte Carlo, then?' asked the parish priest.

'Ah, God help yer foolish wit, Canon,' said Prendergast sourly. 'Sure, yeh'd be hard put to take a bus to Dublin with what's in them bags. A tighter-fisted bunch o' Scrooges than this congregation I never seen.'

'I'm sure people give what they can,' said Canon Roche mildly. 'These are not easy times.'

This cut no ice with Prendergast.

''Tis easy enough times for some o' them gombeen men – they could buy an' sell the both of us. And look at the women – all paint-ed mouths an' skirts so short they might as well have left them at home.'

Prendergast's lapel bristled with the insignia of an impressive number of confraternities of a quasi-Jansenist orientation, whose members were dedicated to the improvement of other people's mor-als. He was mounting a well-schooled hobby-horse now.

'Hasn't the Pope told us this Holy Year he wants to stamp out immodest dress for women? Well, he's wastin' his sacred breath on the women and gerrills of Burras – a walkin' invitation to carnal de-pravity and licentious lascivity is what they are!' (The parish priest took a step back from the fine spray erupting from the pass-keeper's indignant mouth.) 'Did yeh see the state of the Gallagher gerrill – and her aunt a Poor Clare?'

'Ah, now, Mr Prendergast –'

'Not to mention Maura Donleavy – mark my words, she'll

come to a bad end, that one, the mother was no saint in her young days…'

'That's quite enough, Prendergast –'

'Ah, I don't envy the cross yeh bear, Canon, in a place that's more like Sodom an' Gomorrah than a decent Catholic parish. If the Vigilance Association came down here they'd have a conniption.'

'We can do very well, thank you, without the interference of those busybodies,' said Canon Roche testily. 'Don't let me detain you from your duties.'

To lend weight to the dismissal, he turned away and crossed to the far corner of the sacristy where Philip and his remaining colleagues from the altar staff had been covertly listening to the exchange, while folding cottas and soutanes. The parish priest was concerned they might repeat the scandal they had overheard, but knew boys well enough to realize that forbidding them to do so would be fatal: better to ignore the episode and let it evaporate from their memories.

Prendergast, while making his exit, turned in the doorway and called across the room in suddenly congratulatory tones: 'I forgot to say, Canon, that was a grand sermon today against backbitin' and blackguardin' yer neighbour. (His tone became emphatic.) *They needed that.*'

The parish priest glanced helplessly at a statue of Saint Anthony of Padua as he heard the door close behind the head pass-keeper and let out a controlled sigh. Canon Roche felt beleaguered by sex recently. The two hours he had spent in the confessional the previous day had been plagued by an epidemic of adultery among his seven-to-nine-year-old penitents. In his early days in the priesthood, fresh out of Maynooth, he would have taken pains to unravel the misunderstanding. Now, he had contented himself with saying in kindly tones through the grille: 'Well, son, you won't do that again, will you? Good boy. For your penance say three Hail Marys...' He considered that any attempt to elucidate the matter ran the risk of bruising innocence and he made a mental note to speak to his curate, in case his youthful zeal might lead him to intervene clumsily in what was best left alone. The sight of Philip, his cassock now discarded, returning to the church to make his thanksgiving reminded the priest he was lunching at Lissanore, where he could look forward to generous hospitality and good company, and the thought cheered him. He went outside in a more buoyant mood to chat with his parishioners at the church door.

On his return to the sacristy, Philip immediately became aware that a bitter altercation was taking place inside: raised voices could be heard through the door even before he opened it and entered the room. The only altar boys remaining were Tom Dixon and Finbar Toal, the two of them in a state of fierce confrontation. Tom was shouting angrily.

'Keep your slobbery gob off that bottle, you dirty article!' He held up a bottle of altar-wine for Philip's inspection. 'Lookit, we all take a sip now and then, but your man here has swilled down the half of it. We'll get blamed for it, you'll see. I've a good mind to tan his hide – and what was he up to over at that press? *Sacre bleu!*' Realization dawned, as he noticed the canvas bags Prendergast had deposited on top of a cupboard. 'He's been at the collection.'

With a rat-like scuttling movement the young Toal made a rush for the door, but Tom's foot shot out to trip him and sent him sprawling. Tom seized the thief by the ankles, hauled him upside-down and shook him; a cascade of coins tinkled out of the pockets of his shorts onto the floor.

'Janey Mac! Look at that.' Tom bent to retrieve the coins and counted them. 'One and threepence – you thieving little gurrier. Wait till the Canon hears about this. You're for the high jump, Toal, and no mistake.'

He placed the money on the mahogany surface where the vestments were customarily laid out before Mass. Finbar Toal scrambled to his feet, his face red with rage and dismay, and reached a hand out towards the coins, but Tom deftly intercepted him.

'One o' them's mine.' howled Toal. 'That's me Saturday panny! Gimme back me *panny*, Dixon!'

'Better give him back his pocket money,' Philip counselled his friend.

'How do we know it's really his?' asked Tom, though the urchin's indignant yells carried conviction. 'Oh, all right.'

He contemptuously tossed a copper coin in the direction of Finbar Toal, who dived, snivelling, to snatch it up. Clutching it in his grubby paw he darted to the door, turning on the threshold to snarl abuse at his tormentor.

'I'll tell the brother. I'm tellin' Simmie. The brother'll kill ya, Dixon – ya big gobshite!'

Then, with the practised agility of one well used to fleeing from the scene of a crime, he ran out of the sacristy.

'Simmie Toal – Slimy Toad!' Tom shouted after him derisively, to assert his unconcern at this threat, taking comfort in the thought that the young delinquent was probably beyond earshot.

'Are you really going to tell Canon Roche?' asked Philip.

'I suppose not.' Tom spoke regretfully, pouring the recovered coins back into their bag. 'I can hardly play stoolie, even on the likes of Toal. If the money had been missed and we, or the other lads, were being blamed, it might be different; but the way things are, I think we'd best forget it.'

'Do you think he'll tell his brother?'

'Probably not. Anyway, Simmie Toal will be keeping his head down. I hear the Guards are looking for him.'

'What for?'

'I don't know – could be anything, knowing him. Murder, most likely.'

'I wouldn't put it past him.'

'Come on.' Tom dismissed the topic. 'Let's go. You haven't forgotten I'm coming home with you today?'

Dr and Mrs Dixon were among the guests invited to luncheon at Lissanore that Sunday and Tom had been included, as a companion for Philip. When the boys pedalled up the avenue they could tell, by the vehicles parked in front of the castle, among them Dr Dixon's familiar motor car and Uncle Arthur's modest two-seater, that most of the guests had already arrived. They parked their bicycles in the yard and made their way into the house through the domestic quarters. In the kitchen, it was evident Canon Roche's sermon against uncharitable talk had fallen on stony ground.

'Did you ever see the like of Maeve Noonan in the chapel today?' Bridie Byrne was asking Mrs Ennis the cook, against a background pandemonium of pans and dishes as the preparation of the meal hastily proceeded. 'Hullo there, boys.'

'I did not. Was she wearin' that outfit for a bet, d'you think? And did you see the gazebo on her head? Mother of God…! Mind that bowl of cream now, Tom.'

'See it? Hadn't I the hankie stuffed in me mouth to stop laughin' out loud?'

'I was in the same state, at the sight of Philomena Scanlon – the skirt on her.'

'She wasn't doin' herself any favours, that's for sure – beef to the heel like a Mullingar heifer.'

' 'Tis them with the shoddiest goods puts their wares in the window, I always say.'

'Ah, true for you, Mrs Ennis. I thought the Canon would never get himself out of the clutches of Annie Synnott – poor man, she had the ears talked off him.'

'She's a fierce priest collector, that one.' The cook tentatively tasted a spoonful of gravy.

'Don't I know it. Had you heard, Maureen Daly is gettin' married?'

'Go to God!'

'After all these years – and to Tim Harkins. Sure, he's twenty years older than her, if he's a day.'

'The ould divil. Could she not find a husband with a full set of teeth?'

'He has a full set o' teeth – the trouble is, they'll be on the bedside table when poor Maureen's lookin' for some romance.'

The two women dissolved in cackles of laughter, brought to an abrupt halt by a thunderous crash as one of the harassed housemaids dropped a stack of plates on the stone-flagged floor.

'Sacred Heart!' The cook shrieked in dismay. 'Is it you again, Angela? The bone china too – Herself'll be fit to be tied.'

Philip and Tom judged it a suitable moment to make their exit from the kitchen, having absorbed with interest the information being freely traded there. Upstairs, a party mood already prevailed, due to the operation of generous amounts of drink on guests who had endured the communion fast since midnight. An earlier threat of thunder had caused Countess Kinsella to order luncheon in the dining room, rather than on the terrace, where the family had been eating many of its meals during this exceptional spell of brilliant weather; the storm had not materialized and the sky was now a radiant blue, but it was too late to change the arrangements. So, the guests were dispersed between the drawing room and the terrace, wandering in and out through the open french windows, drinks in hand, chatting and exchanging gossip. Tom politely went to greet his host and hostess, while Philip, after securing a glass of lemonade, began to scout around the company in search of diversion.

Father Yves, Canon Roche and Mr Blackwell had formed a clerical cabal in a corner of the drawing room. Philip hovered on the fringe and discovered they were discussing the Classics. Since he was making good progress in Latin, he hoped he might be able to distinguish himself by contributing, but the clergymen were talking about two writers of whom he had never heard: Catullus, who seemed to provoke a deal of laughter, and Horace – which he regarded as an incongruous name for a Latin poet.

'Salve, Philippe.' Father Yves, noticing his presence, greeted him with the salutation they employed in the schoolroom.

'Salve, magister.' Philip responded automatically, pleased at the opportunity to display his familiarity with the language of Catullus, whoever he might be.

'This is my pupil,' Father Yves told his two colleagues of the cloth, 'my very promising pupil.'

'What are you reading in Latin?' asked Canon Roche.

'De Bello Gallico.'

'Ah, old faithful,' said the Canon, in a tone that reminded Philip of Uncle Arthur recommending a Greenwell's Glory fly. 'Everyone cuts his teeth on Cæsar. "Gallia est omnis divisa in partes tres"...' he quoted.

This confirmed the view Philip had already formed, from occasional remarks of Father Yves, that Cæsar did not rank highly in the estimation of classicists, but represented the milk-and-rusk nursery stage of Latin. That was a pity, since he enjoyed the military flavour of his writing; for his own credit, he added: 'I am reading Cicero too.'

'Jolly good.' Mr Blackwell took his pipe from his mouth and, with the air of one coming out of the pavilion to bat for the Church of Ireland against Rome, recited in turn: ' *"Quo usque tandem abutere, Catilina, patientia nostra?"* That takes me back,' he said nostalgically. He was a slightly built man of medium height whose prematurely thinning hair made him look older than his age. The wistful expression with which he recalled his schooldays was little different from his everyday look of indefinable melancholy.

Father Yves listened in silence, marvelling at these islanders' pronunciation of Latin. As if reading his mind, Canon Roche said, glancing at his altar boy:

'I've often wondered how it is that lads learning both classical and Church Latin – with the *more romano* pronunciation, all Italianate soft consonants – don't get them confused. Yet it never seems to happen. Your man here serves Mass like an Italian, but I'll wager he reads Latin for you, Father, like a Roman?'

'*Ah, oui.*' Father Yves loyally endorsed this proposition. Then, thinking the conversation had perhaps taken too Catholic a turn, he politely inquired of the rector: 'Did I hear you say you have visited some monasteries in Greece?'

'Yes, years ago, during the long vac from Cambridge. A group of us set out to investigate…'

Philip discreetly withdrew, feeling disgruntled that he had not had an opportunity to utter a single Latin quotation while, as it seemed to him, the three clergymen had shown off to one another in a quite immature manner. Looking around for alternative company, he glimpsed Dominick through the open french windows, moving surreptitiously towards the steps leading from the terrace to the garden, in an evident attempt to evade Uncle Ulick. On the far side of the drawing room, Edmund was moving ponderously from group to group, leaving pockets of unease in his wake. Then Philip saw Tom on the terrace, talking to Uncle Arthur and Aunt Clara, so he went out and joined them.

'Hello, Philip, how are you?' asked his aunt, a thin, nervous woman with a permanent air of barely suppressed hysteria.

'Very well, thank you, Aunt Clara.'

'Tom has been telling us about the film you both went to see recently,' said Uncle Arthur. 'What was it called again?'

'*Claude Duval.*' Tom assumed a critical expression. 'It was quite good, but I've seen better.'

'I liked it,' said Philip. He had secretly enjoyed the scene where the highwayman danced a minuet in the moonlight with the girl he had rescued from her abductor – though he knew Tom was bored by it – since he had imagined himself doing something similar with Constanza. Previously, it would have bored him too.

'I don't like the cinema.' Aunt Clara spoke in her high-pitched, fragile voice. 'I always feel nervous in the dark and they won't let me take Pecksniff in with me. I couldn't bring him here today either,' she added in slightly aggrieved tones, 'because you know how your mother's terrier – that nasty Balzac – always attacks him.'

'How is Pecksniff?' asked Philip dutifully.

'I am rather worried about him – he seems to have a touch of mange, just in one place, but the bald patch is really deep.'

Uncle Arthur darted an alarmed glance at Philip, remembering he was privy to the secret of his canine rape of the lock, and hastened to create a diversion.

'Did I see your father here, Tom? I wanted a word with him… Oh, there he is. Excuse me for a moment.'

He hurried across the terrace to where Dr Dixon was a prisoner of Ulick Kinsella, who was consulting him at length about some alarming symptoms that had manifested themselves that morning. Even from a distance, the relief with which the doctor greeted his rescuer was obvious. This left Philip and Tom alone with Aunt Clara, a situation they found awkward; but they knew it would be rude to abandon her. Their embarrassment was ended almost immediately by the arrival of Philip's mother, who was circulating among her guests and engaged her sister-in-law in conversation. Shortly after, Eanna joined them and began to talk about the Celtic congress he had recently attended in Dublin. The two boys listened in polite silence, until Tom plucked at Philip's sleeve and urged him in a low voice:

'Come away out of this now – I want to look at those cannons. Do they still work?'

'I'm not sure.'

They went over to the nearer gun and crouched down to examine it. Philip was kneeling alongside the oak carriage when he heard Mr Blackwell's voice above him.

'Is this one spiked too? I have just been looking at its companion and there is something blocking the touch-hole.'

Philip stood up, surprised by the rector's interest in so military a matter. Mr Blackwell's habitual manner was mild even by the standards expected of a clergyman. He tended to hover protectively around his wife, fetching wraps for her when she had not asked for them, touching her elbow or shoulders at other times, for no practical purpose, as if to assure himself she was real. Mrs Blackwell gave no sign either of appreciating or resenting these attentions; she seemed unconscious of them. Women sometimes remarked that the rector doted on his wife and they would refer to the disparity in the couple's ages; in fact he was little more than a decade senior to her, though he seemed older than that. Now, here was Mr Blackwell inspecting a weapon of war with evident relish.

'I'm not sure, sir,' said Philip doubtfully. 'What was that word you used?'

'I asked if it was spiked. Has something been driven into the touch-hole to prevent its being fired? No, by golly, this one is undamaged.'

He squatted beside the cannon, squinting down the length of the barrel; the smoke of his pipe, curling up from the breech, created the pleasing illusion of a slow-burning fuse. The boys found the rector's unexpected enthusiasm infectious.

'Could you fire it, sir?' asked Tom.

'May be... may be...' Mr Blackwell leaned perilously out over the embrasure in the wall to peer into the muzzle of the cannon. He clambered back and stood up, brushing dust off his linen jacket. 'The danger would be of the gun bursting, but perhaps an experiment could be made with a very small charge.'

'Oh, yes!'

Philip was thrilled at the prospect, but further plans for an artillery demonstration were cut short by Corristeen summoning the company to luncheon.

In the afternoon most of the guests played croquet. The highlight of the match came when Mrs Blackwell, presumably seeking revenge for her previous defeat, managed to roquet Declan's ball with a difficult shot that drew applause from the spectators. Impassively she placed her foot on her own ball and vigorously dispatched her opponent's out of play, before glancing briefly at Declan who remained smiling as usual, apparently unperturbed by this setback. Philip was pleased to see Mrs Blackwell avenge herself on the self-confident artist. He assumed this levelling of the score between them would end hostilities; but he soon found he was mistaken.

After tea, while the guests were taking their leave, he strolled off along a path that led from the croquet lawn into the surrounding trees. Philip enjoyed wandering through the wooded demesne, where a rich variety of ivy cloaked the trunks of the trees and carpeted the ground, ranging from large leaves, which his historically driven imagination compared to squat halberd heads, to smaller foliage resembling green-and-gold starfish. Sometimes, beneath this shroud of ivy, tumbledown stonework of castellated design could be discovered, a relic of the days when a superabundance of labour had enabled Irish landowners to gothicize even the humblest outbuildings and walls on their properties. To Philip, these moss-grown, fragmentary monuments to past grandeur seemed intriguing and romantic.

He had not gone far when he heard voices, indistinct but unmistakably angry. Then he caught sight of Mrs Blackwell in the distance, walking away from a stationary figure he recognized as Declan. She looked back once at the painter, with an irate gesture, then strode on. Declan stood motionless beneath a tall beech. It was the first time Philip had seen him with a completely unsmiling expression and he was dismayed by this fresh evidence of discord. How could grown-ups take croquet so seriously? It was only a game, after all, not worth quarrelling over. Saddened by such silliness, he turned back along the path for fear of running into either of the belligerents.

His retreat also had another purpose: he had just remembered he had promised himself he would finish reading *Scaramouche* that evening. Although he had greatly enjoyed the book, he had taken weeks to read it, having put it aside for a time, following Constanza's visit, when things Spanish had monopolized his imagination. Eventually, however, he had returned to *Scaramouche*: the romantic interest between André-Louis Moreau and Aline de Kercadiou, which he might formerly have resented as a distraction, now appealed to him as much as the swordplay. He had three remaining chapters to read and sensed a dramatic resolution of the various strands of the plot was imminent. Philip quickened his pace towards the house.

CHAPTER XI

'*TOUCHÉ!*' Philip's triumphant shout, prompting his father to concede the point, echoed through the empty ballroom.

'That was a pretty unorthodox stroke, old man,' his father said mildly, stepping back from the menace of the slim bamboo cane his son was brandishing erratically.

'But I hit you.' Philip's voice was muffled by the outsize fencing-mask that shielded his face. 'If this was a real duel you would be dead.'

'Perhaps, but you can't invent new lunges before you have even learned the basic movements. Now, shall we get back to what we are supposed to be practising – the "on guard" position? Right… Feet apart… Yes, about that distance. Make sure you are standing with your weight equally balanced on both legs… Now, swivel your right foot round until it's at a right angle to your left…'

They were using the ballroom as a fencing *salle*. This was a long gallery on the ground floor, directly beneath the library. It was shut up for the summer – the only occasions when it was regularly used were Christmas and the hunt ball hosted by Lissanore every third year – and the majestic crystal chandeliers were bagged in white sheets. The polished floor made a serviceable *piste*. Since an adult foil would have been too large for Philip, they were armed with thin canes, appropriated under the grudging eye of Wilson, the head gardener, from his jealously guarded stock. Philip, who had looked forward to the clash of steel that was the prevailing motif in his favourite books, deplored this humiliating substitution and hoped it would prove temporary. Bridie Byrne was already engaged in running up a rough-and-ready fencer's *plastron* for him, made from canvas and stuffing out of an old mattress; perhaps when he was equipped with that protective clothing he would be allowed to use a proper blade.

'I think that will do for today,' said his father, after he had exactingly made him assume the "on guard" position a dozen more times. He picked up his coat.

'How am I coming on?' asked Philip, struggling out of his badly fitting mask.

'Oh, quite promisingly – but please refrain in future from improvising moves such as that very unconventional *balestra* from which you impaled me.'

'Is that what it was called?'

'Well, it is the nearest term I know in the vocabulary of fencing to describe your Dervish attack on me.'

His duty done for that day, his father was evidently in a good mood. Philip tried to take advantage of it.

'Papa, you know you said about the Cossacks –'

'No, Philip.' The good humour had evaporated on the introduction of this topic. '*You* know what I said about the Cossacks – it is out of the question. Please let me hear no more on the subject.'

'Oh, but, Papa –'

'I said no more.'

'Yes, Papa. I'm sorry.'

Chastened by his father's snub, he followed him in silence to the morning room where Uncle Eanna was already ensconced, reading a journal of Celtic studies. Count Kinsella picked up a newspaper and sank gratefully into an armchair; then, in an attempt to dispel the uncomfortable atmosphere his curt rejection of his son's overtures had created, he spoke in a kindlier tone.

'I don't think those cane foils will stand much punishment, once we begin to cross swords in earnest. If I were you, I should make up another half-dozen by tying some tape around the end to serve as a grip, like the two we have already. We don't want to have to stop in the middle of a bout to fiddle with something like that. If you can't get the knack of it, ask Uncle Eanna to help – he is good with his hands.'

'Certainly, I'd be glad to help.' Eanna looked up from his reading, gratified by this tribute.

'Thank you, Uncle Eanna. I'll just go and see if I can do the grips by myself. If not, I'll come and ask you.'

Philip left on this errand, passing his mother in the hall. She was carrying a bunch of flowers which she brought into the morning room.

'How is our young blade progressing?' she asked her husband smilingly.

'Oh, well enough. Of course, we are only at the most rudimentary stage, but at least he takes it seriously and listens to what I say.'

'Well, that's a good beginning.' Countess Kinsella took a couple of blooms and inserted them tentatively into a vase on the table, as the foundations of an arrangement. 'Helen McCalmont telephoned, incidentally. She is starting a new event at the Horse Show this year, a Ladies' Hunter Class, to be ridden side-saddle in hunting costume. Apparently she is presenting a cup for it and absolutely everybody is putting their name down. She asked me, so I said yes. I think Chatterbox could do reasonably well in it; he certainly won't disgrace himself. It sounds rather fun.'

'Which day is it?'

'The second day – the Wednesday – in the morning. She says she has more than forty ladies who have entered.'

'Sounds impressive. I just hope it doesn't clash with the sales I have to go to.'

'Well, if it does, I shall quite understand. Helen said she must have us for a Saturday to Monday at Mount Juliet, some time soon.'

'I hope she remembers the invitation,' said Count Kinsella wistfully. 'It's one of the few places one can get a game of cricket nowadays.'

'Pah!' Eanna expressed his feelings with a snort of contempt. 'I don't have any truck with garrison sports.'

'And yet, Eanna,' his brother said, with a smile not entirely free of malice, 'I seem to recall hearing you were regarded as a fairly formidable leg-spin bowler at Clongowes – a budding Jack Hearne, by all accounts.'

'Sure, I didn't know any better then. I was just a youngster, with no thought for my country's heritage.' Abashed by the memory, he reimmersed himself in his Celtic periodical.

'Speaking of the Horse Show,' said Countess Kinsella brightly, 'I thought we might take Dee-Dee up to Dublin with us.'

Count Kinsella's newspaper sagged; he stared at his wife with stricken features. Horse Show week was his annual holiday, hallowed by certain observances established over the years. These encompassed the serious transactions in the sales ring, spectating with keen enjoyment at the most important competitions and some decorous dissipation at parties in the evenings. Now his wife, who had evidently taken leave of her senses, was proposing to intrude his much-loved – but in this instance distinctly *de trop* – youngest child into that cherished routine. There was desolation in his eyes as he enquired weakly:

'What did you say?'

'I said we should take Dee-Dee with us, to show her Titania's Palace – I'm sure she would be absolutely thrilled.'

'Titania's...?' Her husband's voice faltered in bewilderment.

'Honestly, Bonaventure. Do you read nothing in the newspapers apart from the prices for yearlings and the racing columns? Clery's is putting on an exhibition of the Fairy Queen's miniature palace; apparently it is a terrifically detailed and impressive model, made by Sir Nevile Wilkinson. It sounds absolutely charming and I think Dee-Dee would love it. Things like that make an enormous impression on a child, you know, and it's good to stimulate her imagination.'

'You think Deirdre needs stimulation?'

'Of the right kind, yes. Titania's Palace is the sort of experience a young child will always remember. An occasional treat – especially if it is educational – is just as important as instilling good discipline.'

'A treat is all very well, at a suitable time, but not in Horse Show week. Does nobody understand that? I've just had Philip pestering me again about those damned Cossacks. I gave him a pretty dusty answer.'

'Yes, he spoke to me about it too. Frankly, I think it is a reasonable request. They say the Cossacks give a superb display of horsemanship and it might encourage Philip to be slightly less nervous about hunting – you know that concerns you. He could come up with us, as well as Dee-Dee and Nanny. Perhaps we could take Tom Dixon too, as company for him.'

Count Kinsella wore the expression of a man whose world is collapsing around him. It reminded his wife of an occasion when he had been kicked by an unruly gelding.

'Oh, absolutely,' he said with heavy sarcasm. 'Why not bring Edmund and Dominick too – and Corristeen and Bridie Byrne, for that matter? They can all camp in our suite at the Shelbourne. I'm sure you and I could accommodate ourselves on top of the wardrobe.'

'That is exactly what I was going to suggest,' said his wife imperturbably. 'Not Corristeen and Bridie, of course, but taking all the children. Mattie (she used the nursery nickname of her elder daughter Maria Theresia) should be home by then and she will need some new clothes, you know how fast she is growing. It would save me making a separate trip to Dublin.'

Count Kinsella, by now thoroughly alarmed, realized he was confronting a well-thought-out plan. Desperately he played his trump card.

'Yes, of course, I can see your point; but the problem is it's too late. I booked into the Shelbourne at the end of last year's Show, otherwise I doubt if we would have got in. The hotels are all full, there is nowhere for the children to stay.'

'The big hotels, yes; but there are plenty of decent commercial hotels where we could put them up. I took the precaution of telephoning a couple of places and there are still a few rooms available,' she added, delivering the *coup-de-grâce* to her husband's resistance. She followed this up with a conciliatory flurry of reassurances. 'You have nothing to worry about: the children's visit need not overlap with the Horse Show. We can take them up to Dublin on the Saturday morning and I shall do some shopping while you go to Ballsbridge to make your arrangements. I shall take Dee-Dee to see Titania's Palace on Monday and the boys could go to the Cossacks' show in the afternoon – there's a matinee performance. Then we can pack the whole tribe off on an early evening train back down here, before the Horse Show opens the next day. If you are busy with the horses you won't have to be with the children at all.'

Count Kinsella began to be persuaded.

'I suppose it might work,' he said grudgingly, 'if there is decent accommodation available.'

'Of course it will work, Bonnie,' said his wife cajolingly, laying her hand on his shoulder. 'I knew you would see reason.'

'You always manage to get round me.' He smiled up at her and placed his hand on hers.

Eanna, embarrassed by the suddenly uxorious atmosphere, cleared his throat and left the room with a muttered excuse.

Philip received the news that he was, after all, to be allowed to go to the Cossack equestrian circus with jubilation bordering on the ecstatic. After profusely thanking his mother, whom he rightly guessed was responsible for his father's change of mind, he hurried off to tell Tom Dixon about it. Tom, for once, could not maintain his pose of worldly indifference, but responded as gleefully as Philip.

'She is going to telephone your mother and sort out the arrangements,' Philip told him. 'We'll be in a different hotel from the grown-ups – apart from Deirdre's nanny, but she won't bother us. It's going to be the greatest fun ever.'

Tom turned a celebratory cartwheel, an athletic feat that Philip had never been able to master and which he had stopped attempting, deterred by the indignity of failure. Knowing Tom would exploit the situation by challenging him to follow suit, he created a diversion by producing an advertisement for the Cossack display, torn out of a newspaper, and reading it aloud.

' *"The Cossacks. The Show of a Thousand Thrills. The most romantic fighting figure of all time is surely the Cossack. Daring, dashing, irresistible Dogs of War, heroes and sons of heroes, born and bred to the use of arms and to deeds of daring horsemanship they have scored their name deep on the bloodstained pages of history."* See.' He held out the newspaper cutting to show Tom a drawing of a mounted Cossack flourishing an extravagantly long whip.

'Jeepers!' Tom was impressed. 'You wouldn't want to get on the wrong side of those fellas.'

'Uncle Dermod says some of their officers were generals in the Tsar's army, or in the Imperial Guard. They are White Russians who fought the Reds, but they were beaten.'

'They can't be such great fighters after all, then.' Tom's customary scepticism reasserted itself.

'That's not fair, Tom. I think there were a lot more of the Reds than the Whites, so they didn't have a chance. I'll tell you something else, too, if you promise to keep it to yourself...'

Tom, his curiosity aroused, gave the required pledge.

181

'Uncle Dermod thinks Edmund is turning into a Red. "That boy is little better than a Bolshevist" is what he said.'

This information did not satisfy Tom's expectations of some interesting secret to be divulged.

'Little better than an eejit,' he said contemptuously. 'Brothers are all like that – mine are the same. Desmond doesn't know what day of the week it is and Noel spends all his time running after that stupid girl. Tell you what, why don't we play at being Cossacks?'

'I don't think we can play at being Cossacks,' said Philip, piqued by his friend's abrupt dismissal of his revelation of Edmund's Bolshevik sympathies, 'until we've been to the show and seen what they do. Besides, we should need our ponies and yours has something wrong with him.'

'Dempsey says he'll be fine in a couple of days, but you're right, I suppose; we can't be Cossacks without horses.'

The boys were wandering aimlessly along a quiet road close to where Tom lived. The blazing sunshine of June had momentarily faltered in the closing days of that month, with a sprinkling of rain, but had resumed almost immediately, so that July was proving just as glorious, though the farmers were distraught at the continuous dry weather. The meadows were wan and scorched after the persistent heat, but from the fields around came the sweet smell of freshly saved hay and beyond the pallid green expanses of the stubble fields stood acres of ripening corn, heavy with promise.

'Look,' said Tom, as a startling figure appeared round a bend in the road. 'It's Petticoats Flaherty.'

Tom waved to the man who was striding towards them with a purposeful air. Despite the hot weather he wore a greasy high-necked woman's blouse of pre-War pattern and a stained, almost ankle-length, tweed skirt. This female attire sat incongruously on his angular frame and contrasted with his three-day growth of whiskers and thinning red hair. His eccentricity of always wearing women's clothes, even at Mass on Sundays – though he reserved a conventional suit of mildewed subfusc for funerals – was accepted with incurious tolerance by the local community. Tom and Philip, while conscious of this foible as the distinguishing characteristic of 'Petticoats' Flaherty, regarded it as part of the natural order of things. Flaherty eked a living partly from cultivation of an inhospitable patch of land behind his cottage and partly from a variety of commissions, carrying parcels and messages on foot across the countryside, a duty he performed with an air of self-importance.

'Another grand day,' said Tom civilly.

' 'Tis murderin' the spuds.' Petticoats Flaherty spoke severely. 'Six weeks now and nivver a spit of rain, God be good to us.'

'We're going to Dublin,' Tom told him, diverting the conversation from rural matters, 'to see the Cossacks.'

'Russian soldiers,' added Philip, seeing the look of mystification on Flaherty's face.

'Russian soldiers, is it? In Dublin? Mother of God – and the British soldiers not five minutes gone. Isn't ould Mrs Molloney after tellin' me there was somethin' divilish in the tea leaves – she does be readin' a power of them.'

'Do you know Dublin, Mr Flaherty?'

Flaherty fixed Philip with a withering gaze, as if he had suggested familiarity with Babylon.

'You foolish man! I was nivver more nor a day's walk from Burras in me natural life.'

Crestfallen at this rebuke, Philip fell silent.

'Where are you going?' asked Tom.

'That's for me to know, young fella-me-lad,' said Flaherty pompously. 'I am not at liberty to reveal clients' private business. It might be,' he continued in a more amenable tone, 'I am takin' a message to a couple of very black Protestants and the both of them widows that was nivver married.'

'The Misses ffreney-Donovan!' Philip risked another rebuff, in his elation at having decoded this paradox.

'Tush!' Flaherty raised a finger to his lips to enjoin discretion. 'I've said nothin', as the Man Above is witness. I'd best be on me way – I haven't time to be standin' here all day blatherin' with yiz.'

He resumed his journey with a determined gait, his tweed skirt flapping around his skinny loins in a most unfeminine way. Tom looked meaningly at Philip and gestured towards his head to indicate a mental defect on the part of Flaherty. Then curiosity overcame his instinct to deny Philip any credit for intellectual acumen.

'How did you know he meant those two women up at Glenmore?'

'That's easy,' said Philip off-handedly, enjoying his moment of ascendancy. 'He said they were widows, right?'

Tom nodded.

'But then he said they never got married.'

'You can't be a widow if you've never been married.'

'That's right. But the Misses ffreney-Donovan were engaged to be married, to officers who were killed in the War – Uncle Dermod told me all about it. After that, they started to wear mourning, as if they actually had been married, and they will never marry anybody else.'

'Why not?'

'Because they loved the men they were engaged to.' Philip was exasperated by his friend's lack of sensibility. He respected the two bereaved sisters for their fidelity to their dead fiancés. They lived as semi-recluses, receiving few visitors, though diligent in attendance at services and charitable functions of the Church of Ireland, outside which their carriage was a familiar sight.

'I think they're just a bit potty,' said Tom disrespectfully.

'You thought the same about Petticoats.'

'He's simple too.'

'I see. So, everyone is soft in the head except Tom Dixon. Well, that's funny, because most people think if there's anybody around here who's a bit simple – it's you.'

Tom duly rose to the challenge and an enjoyable scuffle ensued. Later, as they lay panting in recuperation on a fragrant stack of fresh hay, Philip observed blissfully:

'I can hardly believe we're actually going to see the Cossacks. I never thought my father would change his mind. That must have been Mummie, of course.'

'Your mother is a real topper,' said Tom appreciatively.

'So is yours.'

On that note of mutual tribute they decided it was time to go home. Philip suddenly realized that, in his excitement at the prospect of seeing the Cossacks, he had forgotten to give Tom an account of the dénouement of *Scaramouche*, which he had now finished. He shrugged off the thought: he could tell him all about it in Dublin.

Collecting his bicycle from Tom's house, Philip pedalled back to Lissanore punctually for tea. He was determined not to give the slightest grounds for reproach in the days leading up to his promised trip to Dublin: there was too much at stake. Tea was being served on the terrace, as had become routine during the endless weeks of hot weather. His mother was already seated under the awning, alone, with a bundle of mail in front of her.

'I have something here that will interest you, Philip.'

'What is it, Mummie?'

'The *Duquesa* has kept her promise. Do you remember she said she would send us copies of the photographs she took? Well, she has written to thank me for hospitality and has enclosed a couple of snapshots. I must say the pictures are much better than I expected. See, there we all are on the steps, seeing her off...'

Philip craned his neck to study the group. As his mother said, the photograph had come out well. Everybody was clearly identifiable and no one was blinking or grimacing. He saw himself and Constanza in the foreground; the sight brought back the emotions of that idyllic afternoon. He felt suddenly bereft: if only he could be back in that day; why did such moments pass so quickly, why was it not possible to relive them?

'And this,' his mother took another print out of the envelope, 'is one of the best photographs of you I have ever seen. Usually you have your eyes shut or a scowl on your face – you have always been a photographer's nightmare – but this is really good.'

Philip stared at the photograph his mother held out to him. It was the picture the Duchess had taken of him and her daughter together. His mother was right: though he normally disliked having his photograph taken and the results were correspondingly poor, on this occasion he looked natural and happy; at his side, Constanza smiled enchantingly, he thought. Even in the monochrome snapshot her eyes were arresting – he could almost see their green colouring.

'May I have it?'

'Well, Philip, I don't know... It is so extraordinarily good of you, I thought of framing it and putting it on the piano...'

'Oh, please, Mummie! Actually, I think the Duchess must have meant it for me – I asked for a copy and she said she would send one.'

'That's true. I remember you asking – Oh, very well. But take good care of it.'

'Yes, of course. I'll put it away carefully in my room right now.'

He took the precious photograph and hurried into the house, and upstairs, before his mother could change her mind. Sitting in the sunlight at his open bedroom window, he gloated over the small picture for a few minutes before crossing to the chest of drawers and carefully depositing it in the special drawer he reserved for his most prized belongings. He remembered how he had cut off a lock of Constanza's hair (he marvelled at his daring) and hidden it in the tin box behind the loose stone in the summerhouse. He wondered now if that was the safest hiding place. Should he retrieve it and put it in the drawer beside the photograph? No, he thought, after a moment's reflection: it might easily be discovered and the embarrassment would be dreadful. The cache in the summerhouse was absolutely secret, known only to him, and the lock of hair was in a metal container, safe from damage. Still, it would do no harm to go there and check that everything was secure. (In fact, the sight of Constanza in the photograph impelled him to revisit this more intimate souvenir.)

He returned to the terrace, where other members of the household had by now gathered around the table, and ate so perfunctory a tea that his mother wondered if he were sickening for something. Then he excused himself and made his way furtively to the summerhouse. He entered the little folly apprehensively and stooped to loosen the stone from the base of the wall. It was undisturbed, as was the tin which he carefully withdrew from its hiding-place and opened. The motley collection of objects he called his 'treasure trove' was intact. Philip lifted out the small, round metal box that contained the lock of Constanza's hair and gazed at it. His intention had been to open it and admire this token from his lady; but now something inhibited him from doing so. He suddenly wanted to postpone that pleasure until another time, to defer the gratification. Feeling self-conscious despite his total privacy (he sensed the colour rising in his cheeks), he brushed his lips against the cold lid of the box; then, with a decisive movement, he replaced it in the tin, put the lid back on and restored it to its place of concealment, which he closed up again with the stone, carefully removing any signs of its displacement.

He emerged from the stuffiness of the summerhouse and shut the door behind him. While inside, he had heard the distant sound of a motor vehicle driving up the avenue towards the castle, but a cautious survey of the landscape reassured him there was no one in the vicinity whose curiosity might have been aroused by his movements.

Philip walked back to the house in a reverie. He was perplexed by his own behaviour. Why, spurred by the sight of Constanza's photograph, had he taken the trouble to go to the summerhouse and retrieve the box containing the lock of her hair, only to deny himself the privilege of viewing the tiny silken tress belonging to his lady, whose sworn knight he was? He supposed it was like putting off eating a delicious cake until the end of tea... No, he quickly realized, that was not an apt comparison; but he had just thought of something that was. This act of self-denial resembled his habit of deliberately not looking at the sword of his ancestor Bonaventure Kinsella when he passed it on the staircase, to preserve its mystique and prevent it becoming commonplace. It was a gesture akin to that. He felt he had done something disciplined and ascetic, like persevering in whatever he had given up for Lent. It was with a sense of elevated conduct that he entered the house via the back door.

He found chaos reigning in the kitchen and extending into the dairy, as testified by the noises coming from that direction. He also found Grandma reigning in those regions – a phenomenon peculiar to the annual ritual of jam making. Although it was rare for Mrs Skerrett to descend to the domestic quarters, the one function she reserved to herself was superintendence of the making of jam. She possessed an expertise in this field which she believed was lacking in Mrs Ennis the cook and even the eclectically talented Bridie Byrne. Philip had taken a prominent part in the fruit picking and so regarded the operation with a proprietorial air. It was the gooseberries that took a heavy toll every year: the quantity he ate while picking them had once again given him such bad stomach cramps he had had to lie down in his room, his indisposition provoking derision rather than sympathy from his mother.

Today the kitchen was full of the sweet aroma of strawberry jam in the making. Bridie and the cook each tended an enormous copper basin swirling with steaming crimson liquid. Grandma presided, brandishing a large ladle like the conductor of an orchestra; but here was no harmony. The restraint that Mrs Skerrett's intimidating presence had at first imposed on the proceedings had dissolved in the face of conflicts, collisions and a mounting atmosphere of crisis. Kitty the housemaid was kneeling on the floor, her cheeks flaming from Mrs Skerrett's reproaches, mopping up a spilled bag of sugar.

'Mrs Ennis.' Grandma spoke peremptorily. 'I told you, no more sugar – you'll poison the jam with sweetness.'

' 'Tis a fault nobody will find with herself,' muttered the cook mutinously under her breath, 'the ould stag.'

'Angela!' Bridie Byrne's normally placid voice rose to a shriek. 'Is it blowin' the glass you're at for them jam jars? I want them in here ready before the jam sets.'

A crash, a squeal and the tinkle of shattering glass echoing from the dairy was the response.

'Mother of God.' The cook uttered a wail of despair. 'I'll swing for that gerrill... Ah, watch yerself there, Mr Corristeen...'

'Jayzus!'

Corristeen, who had just entered the kitchen, had stepped in a large basket of strawberries. He raised an arthritic leg inches from the floor to exhibit his foot and the bottom of his trousers saturated in squashed fruit, running red like a bloody wound. Mrs Skerrett, heedless of the butler's authority among his staff, banished him from the scene with an imperious gesture of her ladle. Corristeen, despite his injured dignity, was glad to retire; the cook hurried after him with a wet cloth to repair the damage. Grandma caught sight of Philip.

'Shoo!' she shouted, as if at an intrusive dog or cat.

He had not even had a chance to lick the warm, liquid jam off a spoon, as he had hoped – it never tasted so good after it had cooled and set – but he knew any appeal against Grandma's inflexible will was futile. Sheepishly he slunk out of the kitchen by the door through which Corristeen had already made his exit. Behind him he heard the clamour of the jam makers rising to that crescendo of hysteria which he had observed gave women great satisfaction. He also heard Grandma call after him:

'Roll on schooldays.'

This was her latest slogan, employed whenever Dominick or he engaged in some supposedly noisy or annoying activity, expressing the wish that they would soon return to school or, in Philip's case, repair there for the first time. It was never invoked against Edmund, who was well regarded by his grandmother and regularly visited her in her rooms, holding conversations on topics that could only be surmised. Grandma was jolly rude, really, Philip reflected.

When he reached what seemed, after the turmoil in the kitchen, the sepulchral quiet of the front hall he saw two trunks lying there, bearing the initials: M.-T. K. de C. His elder sister had returned from school in Belgium. He now understood the significance of the motor car whose arrival he had heard from the summerhouse. Taking a shortcut through the drawing room and out onto the terrace, he found Maria Theresia seated at the tea table, holding court to her parents, Uncle Ulick, Dominick and Edmund, who was pretending to read a book: he resented his sister's arrival, since her eighteen months' seniority undermined his status. The Kinsellas' elder daughter, aged fifteen, had the typical family looks and colouring: dark hair, grey eyes and straight nose, forming features that were comely rather than pretty. Philip greeted her with a carefully rehearsed speech in French.

'*Bonjour, ma soeur. Vous êtes bienvenue chez nous. J'espère que vous avez fait un voyage agréable.*'

His sister wrinkled her nose disdainfully.

'*Ah, qu'il a l'accent atroce.*'

'It's not atrocious at all.' Philip flushed with indignation. 'I'm being taught by Father Yves and he's a real Frenchman – not just someone at school in Belgium, like you.'

'Don't be silly,' said Maria Theresia. 'It's a French convent – the nuns only moved to Belgium twenty years ago when the beastly government threw them out of France.'

'Really, Mattie,' Countess Kinsella reproved her daughter, 'that was very ungracious, when Philip was welcoming you home so nicely. Anyway, I think his accent is quite good.'

She smiled placatingly at her youngest son.

'I thought it was pretty pathetic,' said Edmund.

'Did you?' His father raised his eyebrows. 'I find that encouraging, since your school reports had misled me into supposing you unqualified to comment on the French language.'

Countess Kinsella, in an effort to restore civility, asked Maria Theresia:

'How is that girl who is your best friend – you know the one I mean – Marie-Marguerite?'

'Marie-Marguerite de Grailly is *not* my best friend. She's not a friend at all – she's a traitor!'

'Oh dear. I am sorry. It's just that you talked about her all last holidays. I thought you were very close.'

'We were, *maman* – until she betrayed me with Gabrielle d'Espinay, the girl I hate most in the whole convent. Then the two of them pretended to be friendly with Yvette Dumont, even though they always despised her – she doesn't even have the *particule* and her father is some kind of businessman. He is filthy rich and she gets masses of pocket money. She spent it on chocolate and gave heaps of it to Gabrielle and Marie-Marguerite – I'm glad to say they came out in spots. They used to have their *goûter* together and ignore me.'

'That was very unkind of them,' said her mother absently. This chronicle of schoolgirl passions and hatreds had transported her back nostalgically to her own days in convent. Philip, still smarting from his sister's rebuff, thought her conversation extremely silly; she reminded him of the Duchess of Saladavieja. Edmund, more openly scornful, rose with a snort and departed. Count Kinsella sought solace in his pipe, which he kindled with concentration.

'Surely you still have friends, though?' her mother asked Maria Theresia.

'Oh, yes. I am best friends now with Blandine de Kersabiec – *c'est une ange.*'

'The Belgian climate is very unhealthy, is it not?' Uncle Ulick felt that this critical issue should be addressed.

'Is it?' His niece considered this suggestion uncertainly. 'I don't think so, though a few girls went down with *la grippe* last winter.'

Uncle Ulick, his worst fears confirmed, shook his head despondently.

'May I have a bath?' asked Maria Theresia. 'I'm feeling rather sticky after the journey.'

192

'Of course, darling.'

'Very unwise.' Uncle Ulick, wearing a dark expression, denounced this folly. Then, believing he had detected a breeze getting up, he hurried indoors.

'Bet I can beat you by at least three hoops at croquet.' Dominick challenged Philip.

'Come and try,' said his brother spiritedly, rising as he spoke.

The boys disappeared in the direction of the croquet lawn. Maria Theresia resumed her litany of grievance.

'What utterly infuriated me was that I had taught Marie-Marguerite the crossed backstitch – and how to crochet – she hadn't the least notion. Then she won the needlework prize and *Mère Prieure* praised her up to the skies, while that hag Gabrielle put out her tongue at me, with everyone congratulating Marie-Marguerite. That girl betrayed me…'

'I think you should have your bath right away,' her mother told her, 'or there may not be any hot water.'

Finally her parents were left alone.

'Well,' said Countess Kinsella contentedly, 'that's us all together again – the whole family under one roof.'

Her husband uttered a carefully modulated sound, inscrutable in tone and further encrypted by the stem of the pipe clenched in his mouth, which the most gifted philologist would have been at a loss to interpret.

CHAPTER XII

DUBLIN was recovering from the recent onslaught of history – was already fully restored in character and prosperity, according to the more optimistic civic patriots. There were even those who claimed that throughout the troubled times and the civil war the normal life of the city had continued, regardless of murder by day and curfew by night. In reality, though Dubliners' irrepressible spirit had preserved a heroic semblance of normality while the Crossley tenders carrying Black and Tans or Auxiliaries on deadly man-hunts careered along the thoroughfares, killing was done daily on street corners and the night was broken by gunfire and the thud of rifle butts on splintering doors, few could truthfully have maintained their lives had been unaffected. The subsequent civil war had left deeper scars, not only on the landscape of the city, where the Four Courts and similar burned-out buildings had added a second generation of ruin to the General Post Office and other strongholds of the 1916 rebels, but in embittered relations among Irishmen.

Yet there was a resilience and pulsating vitality about Dublin that reached a crescendo on the eve of Horse Show week. It was widely predicted this would be the best Show since the carefree days before the Great War. All that survived of pre-War society was converging on the capital, bringing with it a nostalgic reminder of departed *ton*, while the new rulers and the new rich would contribute their substance to an event that promised to foster a welcome climate of harmony, as recently conflicting factions and classes united in devotion to Ireland's secondary deity: the horse.

The young Kinsellas, with Deirdre's nanny and Tom Dixon, were billeted in a shabby but respectable hotel on the west side of Parnell Square. They had been deposited there by Countess Kinsella, after she had searchingly inspected the premises and staff, and awarded the bed linen a clean bill of health. The party had come up to Dublin by train, occupying an entire compartment; Count Kinsella travelled separately, with his horses and a couple of grooms. Edmund was annoyed by his mother's insistence that authority over him and his siblings was to be shared between Nanny and Maria Theresia. For the moment, that meant Nanny alone, since Countess Kinsella, after lunching with her offspring, had swept her elder daughter off on a shopping expedition. That did not leave Edmund master of the situation, for Nanny, who at Lissanore was mousey and deferential, was a Dubliner by birth and returning to her native city had made her uncharacteristically assertive.

'We'll go to Mass at Dominick Street tomorrow morning,' she said (it was Saturday). 'What are you boys doing this afternoon?'

Edmund disdained to answer. Philip and Tom exchanged uncertain glances. Dominick ventured a suggestion.

'I suppose we could go for a walk around town.' He hoped the proposal had a suitably boulevardier flavour.

'Oh, yes.' Philip reacted enthusiastically to this suggestion. 'May we?'

'You can, of course – so long as Edmund goes with you.'

Edmund, out of perversity, was on the point of scuttling the expedition by saying he intended to spend the afternoon reading in his room, when it occurred to him that a stroll around Dublin was what he wanted too, so he muttered a surly assent. They were in the hotel dining room, from which the other patrons had by now departed. It was a large room facing onto the square, the view obscured by long net curtains billowing inwards in the breeze from the open windows. On the wall was a gilt-framed painting of a rugged moonlit landscape with the silhouette of a castle in the foreground; nearby was a large print of a periwigged man in eighteenth-century dress leaning over a seated girl, with the inscription: *Dean Swift and Stella*. The period atmosphere of both pictures pleased Philip. Dee-Dee was being made much of by the girls clearing the tables, who were already on familiar terms with her.

'There you are, pet – isn't she lovely?'

'Ah, she's a real doatie.'

Away from the enclosed world of Lissanore, it was beginning to dawn on Philip that his little sister attracted popularity wherever she went. It was not just the ritual petting of an infant, in a country where children were traditionally cherished. Deirdre had a trusting, outgoing nature that made her loveable. She was such a sunny child, always smiling or laughing, that she seemed radiantly pretty although, on close scrutiny, like her elder sister she had no more than averagely good features, without promise of great beauty. Nanny took her charge upstairs for a nap and the waitresses transferred their attention to the boys.

'Your mammy is a lovely lady – isn't she, Dervla?'

'She is that. Are yous all brothers?'

'I'm not,' said Tom.

'No.' Dominick explained the situation in tones of deep sadness. 'He's a foundling who was left on our doorstep.'

'Oh, Jesus, did you hear that, Peggy? The creature!'

'God be good to him!'

'He's a bit simple too, you know. I think that's why he was abandoned.' Dominick warmed to his theme. 'You can tell by the vacant look on his face.'

'Ah, God, I see it now you come to mention it.'

'Jeepers!' Tom, who had listened to this exchange with mounting incredulity, finally exploded. 'I'll black your eye for that, Dominick Kinsella, big and all as you are.'

'He's prone to fits of rage, you see,' said Dominick, 'due to his affliction. But he's quite harmless really.'

'I'll harm you, you big eejit! Don't be paying any heed to him – there's nothing wrong with me at all. It's his idea of a joke – sure he's half English and they're all mad.'

'Jeez. Would you believe it? Your man was coddin' us!' Dervla burst out laughing.

'Would you be able for him?' said Peggy admiringly. 'Isn't that a lovely English accent he has, though?'

'It is. I could listen to him till the cows come home.'

'The town is full of the Quality for the Horse Show.'

'Just like the old days. Is it English you are, then?'

'Not at all.' Dominick was nettled in his turn. 'I'm only at school over there.'

'In London?'

'Quite near.'

'Did you ever see the King and Queen?'

'No.'

This seemed to lower him considerably in the girls' esteem.

'What's that building over there?' asked Tom. He was anxious to engage in rational conversation, to dispel any lingering doubts about his mental capacity.

'That's the Rotunda. You'd have to be a real culchie not to know that,' Peggy told him witheringly.

'What is it?'

'The Rotunda Hospital.' Edmund briefly entered the conversation, his tone curt. He disapproved of this fraternization with the hotel staff and felt that Tom's display of ignorance reflected on his companions. He detached himself from the group and went to look out of the window.

'A hospital,' said Tom in measured tones, determined to maintain a flow of small talk, in order not to appear put down. 'Well, I hope I never end up there.'

'Jesus,' Dervla uttered a choked gasp, 'there'll be somethin' far wrong if you do.'

She dissolved into helpless laughter, joined by Peggy. Between paroxysms, they provoked each other to fresh outbursts of hilarity.

'"I hope I never end up there," sez he. Holy Mother!'

'Well, now we know he's a bit soft in the head, right enough.'

They lifted their pristine white aprons (one of the signs that had reassured Countess Kinsella) to wipe the tears from their eyes. Philip felt obliged to come to the aid of Tom, who was his guest as well as his friend.

'What's so funny about what he said?'

'Only – only that the Rotunda,' Dervla spoke with difficulty between bursts of giggling, 'is a – a lyin'-in hospital.'

'But every hospital has people lying in beds.'

'It's a place where women go to have babies,' said Dominick dismissively. He felt the girls were taking undue advantage of the younger boys.

'Psst!' The hall porter put his head round the dining-room door at that moment and hissed urgently at the waitresses. 'Herself is comin' – and she lookin' like an avengin' angel.'

With noisy alacrity the girls began to pile crockery and cutlery onto trays and put them into the dumb-waiter (a device that had fascinated Dee-Dee throughout luncheon), which they were energetically lowering to the kitchen by the time the housekeeper appeared in the room.

'Are you girls asleep in here?'

'Ah, not at all, Miss Mullen. We have the tables nearly done.'

The housekeeper treated the guests to a frosty smile and retired.

'Come on, then,' said Dominick. 'Are we going for that walk?'

The following morning Nanny shepherded her charges, dressed in their Sunday best, to Mass at Dominick Street. The short walk exposed them to the startling contrasts of this city: just one block away from where they were living, some of the most squalid slums in Europe were to be found. These overcrowded dwellings were lent an added grotesquerie by the evidence they displayed of former grandeur. Through broken windows stuffed with rags could be glimpsed ceilings whose ravaged plasterwork rivalled that of any great country house. In derelict eighteenth-century drawing rooms that were now home to two families, Grattan and Flood had once warmed their coat-tails at marble fireplaces that would not have disgraced a Roman palace, declaiming the rights of the Irish parliament to patriotic listeners who later sold their allegiance for peerages and, shortly afterwards, their houses, when the Act of Union emptied Dublin of society. Famished dogs foraged for scraps in this street where, in its heyday, carriages and sedan chairs had deposited famous beauties and dandies, to be ushered by liveried servants through front doors above which the cracked fanlights now displayed cheap statues of Our Lady of Lourdes or the Infant of Prague.

Sighting the Kinsellas' well-dressed group, some grimy urchins began to caper mockingly, sketching rude gestures. Dee-Dee, who alone of the company had breakfasted that morning, since she had not yet made her First Communion, was in high spirits and saw this as an invitation to her favourite form of social intercourse. She waved back so vigorously and cheerfully that the two youngest slum children returned the greeting, purging the situation of any hostility.

'Gurriers,' said Deirdre's nanny. 'But there's no harm in them.'

Maria Theresia made a moue of distaste and walked on disdainfully.

'This street was named after me.' Dominick pointed at a street sign as he made this facetious claim.

'Very appropriate.' Edmund gave a supercilious sniff. 'Nice neighbourhood.'

'Sure, the poor can't be blamed for their condition,' said Nanny good-naturedly.

'Of course not. It is the fault of the ruling class.'

'I don't know about that.' The nurse nervously evaded this issue. 'The Saint Vincent de Paul does a lot of good, though.'

Philip enjoyed Mass. The church – Saint Saviour's – was a gothic pile like a mediaeval cathedral, though of nineteenth-century construction. Here the profusion of white plaster spires in the sanctuary was on a much grander scale than in the parish church at home. Three stained-glass windows, each a triple lancet blunted at its peak with tracery roundels, rose loftily heavenwards, a riot of colour resembling precious stones in the morning light, the dazzling figure of Our Lord at the moment of his Transfiguration high above the tabernacle. With an altar server's professional interest Philip noted that the Dominican priest who said Mass did so in the slightly abbreviated rite peculiar to his Order, like Father Yves in the chapel at Lissanore. His attention was sporadically distracted by the odours emanating from neighbouring members of the congregation, a discomfort he was spared at home through being isolated in the sanctuary. Maria Theresia, her head draped gracefully in the white Brussels lace mantilla that was regulation wear in her convent chapel, was more obviously distressed by this encounter with the great unwashed, wrinkling her nose in disgust. Before they left the church, Dee-Dee's nurse took her to light a candle. Crow-like old women cowled in black shawls, their eyes filled with a lifetime's sorrows, who knelt nearby did not pause in the telling of their beads or the rhythmic movement of their lips; but their parchment faces softened at the sight of the little girl kneeling in solemn concentration at her devotions, as if remembering a time when they had been like her, free of care and full of hope, before life took its toll.

Outside, Nanny steered a course down to the bottom of Dominick Street, left into Parnell Street, skirting the square where their hotel was, and into the main artery of Dublin. They were bound for the Shelbourne Hotel to lunch with their parents. Sackville Street, recently renamed O'Connell Street, was the broadest thoroughfare in Europe. Its grandeur was sadly reduced, however, by the ruined state of the buildings at its upper end, especially on the east side, from Parnell Square to Cathedral Street. The Kinsellas gazed wide-eyed at this detritus of war, which was less evident on the west side, down which they were walking, though even here some buildings were derelict. A line of plane trees along the centre of the street gave it a continental look. At the upper end Parnell was poised dramatically on his monument, proclaiming that no man had a right to fix the boundary to the march of a nation and pointing, so the Dublin wags claimed, at the Rotunda maternity hospital behind him to illustrate this claim. The focal point, halfway down, was Nelson's Pillar, the heart of the capital, where the famous admiral stood in stylite splendour, high above the mêlée of tramcars, motor cars, horse-drawn vehicles and bicyclists that congested the street below. Uncle Eanna had written a letter to several newspapers suggesting Nelson should be removed from the top of the pillar and replaced by Pádraig Pearse, the leader of the Easter Rising – or the Sacred Heart, he had added as a devout afterthought – but it had not been published.

The pavements were crowded with a rich variety of humanity, including dark-suited church-goers, women in shawls, working-men in flat caps, bearded Capuchin friars in brown habits and sandals, bare-foot urchins, tweeded ladies and gentlemen in town for the Horse Show – a scene to delight a painter, a mélange not just of classes and ages but, it seemed, of different centuries. All around, the

Sunday crowds chattered, argued, flirted and exchanged greetings or farewells. It was noisy, but unaggressive; even the church bells of the competing denominations somehow blended into a harmonious symphony. Against the background din of motor engines and horns, or the fizzing of tramcars' trolleys on their overhead wires, the steadfast clop of horses' hoofs on the cobbles asserted itself, as if to say: progress or no, we are still here. Philip had noticed, as they walked along Parnell Street, that the occasional breeze blew up chaff from between the cobblestones, a pulverized mixture of old straw and horse-droppings that stung the eyes. This city was still the capital of a rural nation.

It was the second day of August, bright but cool. The brilliant weather of June and July was now gone – a golden idyll to be recalled with wonder. They passed the columned portico of the ruined General Post Office, on which preliminary repairs had begun, and the press of trams around the base of Nelson's Pillar, to lower O'Connell Street. Here the damage was much less and had nearly all been repaired, though the Gresham Hotel was still out of commission. Clery's department store had been back in business for three years; its top storey was crowned by a row of flagpoles displaying the Irish tricolour flanked by the flags of other nations. The southern end of the street, approaching the River Liffey, was a medley of architectural styles in granite, limestone and red brick, with a variety of ornamentation surrounding the upper-storey windows. Coloured awnings, bleached to pastel by the recent weeks of relentless sun, shaded the shop windows at ground level. As they crossed the river by O'Connell Bridge, Philip stared at its ornate lamp standards.

'That looks like Paris.'

'Do you go to Paris a lot?' asked Dominick sardonically.

'Actually, he's right,' said Edmund, for whom snubbing Dominick was a higher priority than putting down his youngest brother and who welcomed this opportunity of reminding his siblings he had visited the French capital with a party of school friends. 'That wrought ironwork is reminiscent of Paris.'

'*Quel imbécile!*' Maria Theresia muttered contemptuously.

Philip and Tom exchanged complicit smirks. Dominick sketched a dismissive gesture at Edmund's back. In this state of armed neutrality they negotiated Westmoreland Street, where Philip ecstatically inhaled the aroma of freshly ground beans from Bewley's coffee shop, then walked on up to College Green, a destination that might have eluded them if they had followed Grandma's anachronistic instructions, imparted with authority: 'Bear left, past the redcoat sentry at the Bank of Ireland…' Here the city was at its most imposing, the stately pillared edifice of the former Parliament that was now the Bank facing the fortress-like gates of Trinity College, crowned by a blue-faced, gold-handed clock, with statues of Anglo-Irish luminaries standing guard before this intellectual barracks of the Ascendancy.

A discordant note was struck, amid so much sculpted patriotism, by the statue of William of Orange which stood on a massive plinth surrounded by railings with lamp posts at each corner, facing down Dame Street at the end of a rank of cabs. The Glorious and Immortal Memory was represented as a Roman general in classical armour, his bare legs straddling a bronze horse that dwarfed those harnessed to the cabs below, his hand grasping the sceptre he had wrested from James II, despite the best efforts of Lieutenant Bonaventure Kinsella, of Cavenagh's Regiment of Foot, and his luckless comrades. Uncle Dermod had said this monument was cast by Grinling Gibbons; its removal was currently being canvassed (Uncle Eanna had written to the newspapers about that too).

The Kinsella party strolled round past the railings of Trinity and up Grafton Street, where Nanny dawdled in front of the elegant shop windows. Finally they arrived in Stephen's Green and processed decorously up the steps at the entrance to the Shelbourne, where the smiling doorman made much ceremony of ushering Dee-Dee inside. Their waiting parents led them to the dining room, exchanging greetings with acquaintances as they crossed to the large table reserved for them beside the windows. The conversation at nearby tables was almost exclusively about horses, as was most of the talk in Dublin during this week of the year. While Count Kinsella gave instructions to the waiter, Philip tried to observe the other people in the room without craning round too obviously. His parents made some perfunctory enquiries about their children's wellbeing, but once the first course was served they talked mainly to each other, exchanging the gossip of the day.

'There are more than eight hundred horses being sold at Ballsbridge this week,' said Count Kinsella. 'That's including yearlings, horses in training and brood mares – things are really looking up.'

'Yes, somebody told me it's the largest entry since the year the War started.'

'Nearly a hundred thoroughbred yearlings – the competition will be pretty stiff.'

'I hear it's going to be a good season – that should help the sales of hunters.'

'Unfortunately I have only one hunter in the sales. Incidentally, Randall Ardgroom has invited me to join his party at Leopardstown tomorrow – you don't mind if I go?'

'Not in the least. Dermod has very kindly offered to go with the boys to the Cossacks' show and I am taking Dee-Dee to see Titania's Palace, so you would be *de trop* in any case.'

'Is Uncle Dermod staying here too?' asked Philip, glad to hear that his favourite uncle would be accompanying him to the Cossack display.

'No,' his father shook his head, 'he is round the corner, at the Kildare Street Club.'

'Mummie,' said Maria Theresia pleadingly, 'may I come and stay here with you and Papa? It's much nicer than that beastly place you have put us in.'

'There is nothing beastly about it at all,' said her mother sharply, 'it is a perfectly respectable hotel and spotlessly clean. I hope you are not becoming spoiled.'

'Spoiled?' Maria Theresia's voice rose indignantly. 'In convent? Oh, *maman*, if you could only taste –'

'That's quite enough, Mattie.' Her father closed the topic with an air of finality.

Philip, too, preferred the elegance of the Shelbourne, with its deep carpets and imposing chandeliers, to the hotel in Parnell Square, but refrained from saying so. He enjoyed the friendly, well-judged deference of the waiters; even when Dee-Dee had a nasty accident with the ice she was eating they behaved as if it was a pleasure to clean up the débris. When the meal was over, Countess Kinsella gave detailed instructions to Nanny about the arrangements for the following day, then saw off her brood from the steps of the hotel, as they crossed the road and went into the small park where Dee-Dee had been promised the treat of feeding the ducks on the pond with scraps of bread salvaged from the table. This ritual completed, they retraced their steps and crossed the Liffey back into O'Connell Street, before making a brief detour into Moore Street to savour the sights, sounds and smells of this boisterous open-air market. Dominick paid close attention to the women's cries and banter with potential customers; he fancied himself as a mimic and had mastered several Moore Street phrases to be used as occasional party pieces, delivered in a surprisingly good imitation of the oily, nasal accents of the traders.

'Panny for roipe pears!'

'Treepence a box, ma'am, sure I'm givin' them away – yeh'd best buy them quick, before I come to me senses.'

'Carmel! Take the babby out o' the pram and let the lady see the fish...'

They loitered for a while to allow Dominick to expand his repertoire then bought some cherries which they ate on the way home, a breach of etiquette that would not have been tolerated under parental supervision. Tom voiced the general feeling as they turned into Parnell Square and approached their hotel.

'This town is great gas.'

Philip woke on Monday morning with a sensation of keen excitement: this was the long-awaited day of the Cossack circus. The morning dragged by intolerably slowly; he and Tom passed part of it in surreptitious banter with Dervla and Peggy whenever they were able to evade the housekeeper's vigilance. After an early luncheon the whole party was marshalled by Nanny and marched down to Nelson's Pillar, where the boys boarded a tramcar for Lansdowne Road. Uncle Dermod, who eschewed mechanized forms of transport whenever possible and insisted on travelling by horse-drawn cab when in Dublin, was to make his own way to the stadium and meet them at the gates. Nanny, Dee-Dee and Maria Theresia were to rendezvous with Countess Kinsella at Clery's, where the miniature fairy queen's Palace was on display. Maria Theresia had little interest in this spectacle, but hoped to persuade her mother afterwards to indulge her with some shopping in Switzer's and other expensive Grafton Street emporia.

Uncle Dermod's tall, lean figure was easily spotted among the crowds pouring into the Lansdowne Road stadium. With his customary efficiency in such matters, he had obtained good seats for his party. Behind the ground could be seen the large tents in which the

Cossacks were encamped. When the show began, it exceeded even the boys' expectations. The Russians' horsemanship was spectacular, including a wild charge *ventre à terre*, with daredevil riders hanging from the stirrups to snatch up coloured handkerchiefs. When they rode through a blanket of roaring flame they used neither crop nor spurs to urge on their highly trained mounts. There was a choir too, that lent an appropriately Slavonic atmosphere by singing the *Volga Boat Song* and other ditties redolent of old Russia.

'I wish I could identify the officers,' said Uncle Dermod fretfully, his eyes darting between his programme and the arena. 'Some of them held very high rank in the Imperial army. Tolstoy's grandson is apparently among them, as well as a former minister of war, and according to the newspapers General Malichenko was Master of Horse to Nicholas II… Colonel Seydelev was chief of staff to Wrangel – or was it Denikin…? But I have no idea which they are.'

Philip was, for once, indifferent to his uncle's informative chatter. When seven riders formed a mounted pyramid with four in the saddle, two standing on their shoulders and another on top holding aloft a flag – and the whole ensemble then charged through belching black smoke and a wall of fire – he rose excitedly in his seat, cheering wildly with the rest of the audience.

'Jeepers!' Tom applauded ecstatically, rolling his eyes in wonderment at Philip.

'Bravo!' Dominick joined in and even Edmund uttered a grunt of approval.

For the thousands of spectating Dubliners it was the perfect prelude to the Horse Show and they were not backward in showing their appreciation with thunderous ovations. When the show reached its impressive finale it seemed to Philip it had lasted only a quarter of an hour. The Kinsella party was one of the last to drift out of the stadium, since Uncle Dermod insisted on importuning stray

Cossacks in an effort to make social contact with their officers. Unfortunately, the few men in the exotic crimson coats with cartouches and sheepskin hats he encountered were monoglot troopers who could only respond to the queries he directed at them in English and French with shrugs and vacant grins.

During the tramcar journey back into the city centre, on which Uncle Dermod deigned to accompany them, the boys animatedly discussed the spectacle they had just witnessed. Most of their fellow passengers were doing the same. When they arrived back at Parnell Square, they found their luggage stacked in the hall where Countess Kinsella, who had arrived just ahead of them with Dee-Dee and Maria Theresia, was exchanging polite small talk with the housekeeper.

'Ah, there you all are.' She turned to survey her offspring. 'Dermod, it was saintly of you to look after them. Was it a good show?'

A babble of excited reports assured her it had been.

'We have had a successful afternoon too,' she said, when she could finally make herself heard. 'Deirdre loved Titania's Palace, didn't you, sweetheart?'

Dee-Dee, whose eyes still sparkled with delight from the experience, confirmed this in piping tones.

'It really is the most amazing thing, you know,' her mother said in an aside to Dermod. 'So clever of Sir Nevile Wilkinson to make it.'

'Whatever his talent for building dolls' houses, Nevile Wilkinson is a thoroughly unsatisfactory Ulster King of Arms.' Dermod Kinsella spoke severely. 'He only got the job after poor Sir Arthur Vicars was disgraced when the crown jewels were stolen. He was appointed because his wife's family had influence at court; heraldically, he is quite unqualified. I can only describe his attitude to Irish holders of foreign titles as positively churlish.'

That anathema ended the discussion. The youngsters ate a

collation of cold meat to fortify them for the journey home, after which two taxi-cabs arrived to transport them to the station, waved off by Dervla and Peggy. Dee-Dee was still waving back vigorously as the cab rounded the corner. She indulged in a similar marathon when the train pulled out of Kingsbridge station, held tightly by Nanny at the open window, until her mother and uncle disappeared from sight. Soon after, she fell asleep on her nurse's shoulder, exhausted by the excitement of the day. For the first half of the journey the boys noisily recalled the highlights of the Cossack display then they too succumbed to drowsiness. Philip heard the sound of the train take on the rhythm of the *Volga Boat Song* as he dozed off; the same melody lulled him to sleep later that night, back in his own bed at Lissanore.

Dermod Kinsella, resplendent in morning coat, stiff high collar and stock with a pearl pin, glossy silk hat and dove-grey spats, descended the steps of the Kildare Street Club. For reasons of ceremony he carried a shooting stick rather than the umbrella that the overcast sky might have prescribed. He glanced absently at the arched windows of the club, where carved stone monkeys played an eternal, fossilized game of billiards, then walked the few paces to the bottom of the street and turned left. With measured, stately stride he passed the park of Trinity, scorched and yellowed like the rest of Ireland by two months of relentless heat, following the railings along Nassau Street and round into College Green where a row of horse-drawn cabs lined the centre of the road. He climbed into a bottle-green brougham, removing his top hat as a precaution, and settled himself as comfortably as he could against its ravaged upholstery. As the cab lurched into motion, it occurred to him he had forgotten to tell the jarvey his destination, then he realized it was unnecessary: his costume spoke for itself.

Above the showground at Ballsbridge flew the flag of the Royal Dublin Society: the red saltire of Saint Patrick on a white ground, with the helmeted figure of Hibernia holding a spear in the centre. It was the flag of pre-independence Ireland, modified by the inclusion of an allegorical personification of the nation. It accurately advertised the occasion. Dermod was bound for the enclosure, to watch his sister-in-law compete in a new event: Ladies' Hunter Class, to be ridden side-saddle with competitors dressed in hunting costume of habit and veil. At least he could rely on sartorial standards being maintained there, he thought, grimly noting the paucity of morning coats and proliferation of suits and soft hats among the male patrons. He intended to give his sister-in-law moral support, since her husband was attending the auction in the Bloodstock Sales Paddock, where he had three yearlings under the hammer. Dermod was disappointed to see Countess Kinsella's hunter fail to reach the final seven. He commiserated with her afterwards.

'Bad luck. The judges obviously had no eye for a good horse.'

'No, it was perfectly fair,' his sister-in-law gathered up the apron of her riding habit to increase her mobility, 'that brown gelding deserved to win. Chatterbox wasn't himself; competition nerves, I suppose.'

Dermod remained unconvinced. He had been further irritated by the latest innovation: a loudspeaker announcing the results, which he thought raucous and vulgar. It was now raining, which lowered his spirits. Then his worst fears were realized: he caught sight, in quick succession, of a pair of Oxford Bags and a girl sporting an Eton Crop. This further intimation of the collapse of civilization reduced him to a profound depression. He gained no reassurance from the sight of competitors in correct hunting attire passing to and fro in the throng. The colourful Summer Show of the Royal Horticultural Society of Ireland in the Sandymount

Hall, to which he escorted his sister-in-law, held no charms for him. The Irish Arts Industries Exhibition in the Main Hall bored him; the string orchestra that serenaded the public there did nothing to soothe his soul. The Garda Síochána Band playing in the Grand Band Enclosure deafened him. Upon all the diversions he had once enjoyed he now cast a baleful eye: this was Eden after the Fall.

When he met his brother later, as the day's proceedings were drawing to a close, he launched into a denunciation of the decline in standards of dress – rather tactlessly, since Bonaventure was among the offenders.

'I've just seen Powerscourt in a chalk-striped suit – and Holm-Patrick looking equally bounderish. I shouldn't be surprised to see the competitors in the championship tomorrow wearing ratcatcher. At least Bertram Barton is properly turned out.'

'He can afford to be; I hear he still has nearly twenty servants at Straffan. That shows the advantage of owning a famous French vineyard.'

'Well, we have the Bank to shore us up.' Dermod was determined to hold his brother to account for his slovenly dress.

'I think claret will always be a more reliable investment than any bank. Come along, Dermod,' he said cheerfully, as his wife, now wearing everyday tweeds, joined them. 'We are going back to the Shelbourne to drink champagne before dressing for the ball – I made rather a killing in the yearling sales. Quite above my expectations, in fact. That colt I pointed out to you fetched three hundred guineas. Join us for a drink.'

Having made his point, Dermod yielded graciously to this invitation. The Kinsellas followed the ebbing tide of humanity out of the showground, past barefoot newsboys hoarsely bawling their incantation – 'Herl-a-Mail!' – and a blowsy woman selling wilting

211

flowers, who enjoined her brats in a nasal whine to 'come away outta that an' don't be gettin' in the way of all them lovely Protestant people'.

Dermod arrived punctually at the ball that evening. He had no incentive to linger over dinner at the club during Horse Show week when his fellow members, who normally indulged his obsession with genealogy, were interested only in discussing equine pedigrees. Surveying the animated crowd, he noted with displeasure the intrusive black ties mingled with the white – cockle among the wheat – but consoled himself with the reflection that this was not some court function at the Castle, but a charity event in the Imperial Ballroom, Clery's Buildings, open to all who had purchased a ticket.

'Remind me – what is tonight in aid of, Randall?' he asked Lord Ardgroom, who hove into sight at that moment.

'The usual sort of thing – Mercer's Hospital – though most of the people here would have come if it had been in aid of white slavery.'

'Where is Bunty?'

'In a huddle with some other black and midnight hags, demolishing reputations. I'm on my way to the bar. I advise you to join me; there are some pretty dreary people here tonight.'

'There were some pretty dreary people at Ballsbridge today,' said Dermod, as they threaded their way with difficulty towards the bar. 'Hardly anybody had bothered to dress properly.'

'I know. At least the Governor General and his party were in morning dress.'

'It is coming to it,' said Dermod resentfully, 'when the Shinners are better turned out than we are.'

'I don't know that I'd describe Healy as a Shinner – he's here tonight, incidentally – but I take your point. The world has turned topsy-turvy. Bunty is beside herself because she has to bring out

Violet – that's our eldest – next year and that means London and a hellish amount of expense. Nothing else for it. There is nobody at the Castle now except a lot of grubby clerks in paper collars.'

There were other exchanges in the course of the evening that revealed the distaste for the new order felt by many of the company.

'Imagine calling it O'Connell Street – after that rabble-rouser,' said a woman wearing a crowned harp brooch. 'I shall continue to call it Sackville Street.'

She stared challengingly at Dermod Kinsella, whom she knew to be a fish-eater. He smiled urbanely.

'I'm afraid I cannot share your enthusiasm for such newfangled nomenclature. I shall continue to call it by its original name of Drogheda Street.'

He left grinning faces behind him after this riposte and went to join his brother and sister-in-law at their table.

'I thought Hazel Lavery looked lovely today,' Countess Kinsella said to Lady Ardgroom and the other women seated with her. This view did not find favour.

'She thinks she's the new Queen of Ireland.'

'She dyes her hair.'

'Bad luck about the Ladies' Hunter event this morning,' Lord Ardgroom said sympathetically to Countess Kinsella.

'Chatterbox had an off day, that's all. What was bad, though, was that forty-two ladies entered their names for it, but only twenty-three of us turned up. Helen McCalmont was not too pleased. You must excuse me,' she said, rising, 'I promised Dermod this waltz.'

Dermod danced only the waltz: he believed it incumbent on him, in deference to his family's Viennese associations.

'I don't think the McCalmonts will be upset for long,' said Count Kinsella. 'With sales going the way they did today, the Ballylinch Stud will be a bigger goldmine than ever.'

'Yes, yes,' said Ardgroom impatiently. 'We all know McCalmont's horses are marvels – nobody was a greater admirer of the Spotted Wonder in his 1913 season than I was – but they are all prodigies as two-year-olds, over distances up to six furlongs. How many three-year-olds has he produced that could lead the field over a mile and a half? Tell me that, eh?'

A lively debate ensued; but it petered out in shocked dismay when someone said abruptly:

'The future may not be so rosy as you think. The Land Commission is threatening to take over the Rathmoyle Stud.'

There were two phrases guaranteed to turn Bonaventure Kinsella's blood to ice: one was 'dry rot', the other was 'Land Commission'.

'What on earth for?' he asked agitatedly.

'To split it into smallholdings.'

'This country,' Lord Ardgroom, with an angry snarl, ground his half-smoked cigar into the base of a potted palm, 'is hurtling towards the hottest corner of Hell in a hundred-horsepower handcart.'

CHAPTER XIII

THE veil of mist that had curtained the castle since dawn was dispersing into an archipelago of isolated wreaths, like smoke from woodcutters' fires. Pegasus added his contribution every time he exhaled, the breath from the pony's nostrils clouding the cold air as Philip sat him anxiously, waiting for the hunt to move off from the paddock. For the moment, it showed no inclination to do so. A lawn meet at Castle Kinsella was traditionally a hospitable occasion and even though many of those who had been entertained inside the house had by now emerged and mounted, they were not disposed to refuse the stirrup cup being proffered by Corristeen and Liam as they weaved their way, bearing large silver trays, among the horsemen. The assembled field, a motley array of mostly dark-clad riders, with a smattering of scarlet, filled the area of the paddock closest to the house; the pack, a tumult of quivering tan coats, was with difficulty contained on the sidelines by repeated staccato commands. On the gravel in front of the house and for some distance down the avenue were parked the miscellaneous vehicles belonging to the hunt followers.

Although Philip could feel the familiar knot in his stomach that preceded every day's hunting – and this was his first outing of the season – he was also gripped by a grim resolution. Since he had become the sworn knight of the lovely Spanish girl during the summer that now seemed so long past, it behoved him to display the courage so high an honour demanded and conquer his shameful fears. This season he would ride to hounds as a Kinsella should, taking his fences and eschewing tame alternative routes via gates and lanes, in the straggling company of the timid and the poorly mounted. He had already discovered surprising reserves of will power: this morning, unlike the opening meet of the previous season, he had not had to retire to the rhododendron thickets verging the avenue to be sick in decent privacy. His mind was made up. As a precaution, however, after he had served Mass that morning for Father Yves he had applied the indulgence attached to the Prayer Before a Crucifix to himself, rather than to some deceased beneficiary, as he usually did.

Philip was burdened with a vivid imagination that tormented him with the image of every grizzly accident that could conceivably overtake him, aggravated by the recognition that it was all unnecessary. He found it difficult to accept it was worthwhile to risk his neck for sport; yet he was absolutely convinced he would not hesitate if he were taking part in some cavalry charge, under heavy fire, to serve the cause of a king or his religion, as so many of his ancestors had done. Now, that feeling of pointlessness had been superseded by the need to prove his worthiness of Constanza, to know that she would approve his conduct and not despise him as a coward. For that purpose, he could take fences he had previously shunned: he now had good reason. There was the further consideration that, since the summer, he had celebrated his tenth birthday and promotion to a double-figure age group also demanded more manly conduct.

He had adopted this resolution weeks earlier and it had given him the assurance to plan his campaign, using his lessons as a pretext to absent himself from cub hunting, in the measured determination to prove himself during the season proper. His father, who knew nothing about his new frame of mind, but was aware of his visits to the shrubbery during the previous season, had diplomatically colluded.

'Between ourselves, old man, cubbing bores me too – I only turn out occasionally, as you know, to keep the committee happy. I'm glad you realize your lessons are important and, in any case, I should never permit you to come out three days a week. Once a week is quite enough. If it should turn into an exceptional season and you feel really keen, we might run to two days every other week. Strictly speaking, you ought to be at school by now.'

That dispensation had reassured him. These thoughts, revolving in his mind as he sat Pegasus in the paddock, surrounded by the chatter of the assembled sportsmen, reinforced his resolution and his brittle calm – or would have done, if only the field had shown the longed-for signs of moving off. It was the waiting he found unnerving. Nearby, two farmers who had emptied their glasses at a gulp debated the arcana of scent.

'There's the fog lifted anyway.'

'Divil a fog – 'tis the blue mist and there's a quare difference. With the blue mist and the east wind, lookit, the scent will be burnin' through the gorse. There's herself now – isn't she the fine figure of a gerrill?'

Countess Kinsella emerged from the house, the veil of her bowler hat drawn down tautly over her face and under her chin, the apron of her indigo habit gathered over her arm, and hobbled across the gravel sweep to where a groom waited with Chatterbox, her veteran hunter. Philip's mother enjoyed a high status with the hunt: when Count Kinsella, who had been Master at the time, had gone off to the War she had carried the horn in his place for a season, until a wound – thought at the time to be incapacitating – had resulted in his being honourably invalided out of the army. Now, in a gallant gesture that was an established ritual between them, her husband, resplendent in scarlet swallow-tail coat and silk hat, stooped to help her mount and to remonstrate, as he invariably did, to no purpose.

'Really, my dear, I wish you would let me shorten this stirrup leather. You know I worry about you.'

'Stuff and nonsense, Bonaventure. I am actually quite tall, you know.'

'Even Myrtle Blackwell,' he lowered his voice confidentially, 'has hers higher than yours.'

'She is smaller than me,' said his wife dismissively, arranging her apron in a graceful drape as she settled herself on the heavy side-saddle.

'Well, no heroics – promise?'

'Oh, Bonnie, you are sweet.' She placed her hand briefly on his shoulder. 'I promise to be careful – I always am. Don't be such an old fusspot. Good morning, Mrs Rosseter.' She turned away to converse with an acquaintance.

Philip had affectionately watched this exchange between his parents. Although he was out of earshot he knew what had passed between them, since it was a familiar routine. His father's concern about his wife riding with such a long leather to the left stirrup – the badge of a lady thruster – always aroused a small anxiety in him about his mother's safety; she was an intrepid rider to hounds, though also disciplined and expert at calculating risks. Philip's apprehension on these occasions usually gave way quickly to concern for himself. He glanced impatiently around the paddock full of horses, jingling harness and lively conversation, punctuated with bursts of laughter from jovial riders whose insouciance he envied. Surely they must be ready to move off. Yes, here was the Master calling for attention before he delivered the 'sermon' that was an unvarying feature of the opening meet. Colonel Blennerhassett, a ruddy-faced warrior with a walrus moustache, had allowed a Master's pride in the work of his hounds to supplant every other consideration, to the point where he regarded the field as unwelcome intruders and made no secret of the fact.

'Ladies and gentlemen...' He began the lecture his hearers

knew so well that young Miss Malley, the most reckless and rebellious among the field, recited it ahead of him under her breath, to the amusement of her neighbours. 'Be so kind as to remember the purpose of today's sport. We are not taking part in a point-to-point – still less a cavalry charge. We are here to watch hounds work and, I confidently expect, work superbly. I will not have them overridden by irresponsible people looking for a reputation as *thrusters*. (He pronounced this word with deep disdain.) If your ambition is to break your neck, kindly do so in some other country.' He glanced sidelong at Miss Malley who dimpled demurely through her veil. 'You will at all times pay due heed and attention to the Field Master. Do I make myself clear?'

A low murmur of placatory assent came from the field. The Master, red-faced from his rhetorical effort, blew out his moustache, nodded to the Field Master and rode across to have a word with the huntsman and whippers-in, who were by now barely containing the excited pack who sensed the moment had come. Major Fenton, the Honorary Secretary of the hunt who also acted as Field Master, but who regarded himself in more military terms as adjutant to Colonel Blennerhassett, walked his horse forward to the place vacated by the Master and surveyed the field as he might have done a badly turned-out squadron on parade. In the manoeuvres that would follow he saw his role, uncomplicatedly, as seconding the Master in his attempt to keep the field as far away as possible from the pack and any fox it might flush from cover. He knew from experience this would prove a fruitless ambition, but duty demanded he make the effort.

'Ladies and gentlemen, please wait until hounds move off.'

The pack, sterns fluttering like banners, flooded out of the paddock in a tawny tide, escorted by the hunt servants with trailing whips. They were followed at a respectable distance by the field, casually forming by twos as they moved out of the grassy enclosure and across the sweep to the head of the avenue. Philip watched his uncles Dermod, elegant in scarlet tailcoat and top hat, and Eanna, in a costume that could scarcely be dignified as ratcatcher, ride past, the latter ambling comfortably on his lumbering cob. From a window above, Uncle Ulick, a shawl draped around his shoulders, gazed out with morbid interest at family, friends and neighbours he bleakly regarded as destined for imminent death or maiming. Mrs Blackwell favoured Philip with a smile as she passed and several other riders similarly acknowledged him. Today, instead of loitering to join the tail end of the procession, he moved forward when about one-third of the field had still not exited the paddock, faithful to his resolve.

The next few minutes were the part of a day's hunting he most enjoyed, even if his stomach was tremulous with butterflies: the exhilarating moment when the long cavalcade clattered down the avenue of Lissanore beneath an arcade of oaks stripped bare, in early November, of all but a vestigial gilding of foliage and beeches clad in a coppery winter coat, out under the vast gatehouse like an army riding to war. On the road outside they found those followers on bicycles who had swooped down the avenue like a flight of swallows ahead of the hunt, waiting for confirmation that the Master intended to draw the nearest covert. Among them Philip recognized Declan, taking a holiday from the now prodigious mural in the tower room on which he had been engaged for five months, so that he had become regarded as part of the Lissanore landscape, a native by adoption. The pack had turned left out of the gates of Castle Kinsella and the field followed.

'Browne's gorse.' The bicyclists pedalled off, expectations confirmed.

Nobody had seriously doubted this favourite covert would be the first port of call. Under Major Fenton's jealous eye, the field dispersed to strategic points to watch hounds drawing the vast expanse of gorse that was the hunt's most reliable resource.

'Untenanted,' opined a pessimist within earshot of Philip.

'Nonsense!' Miss Malley contradicted him. 'It was simply swarming during cubbing.'

'Well, it's not swarming now.'

At that moment there came a tentative yelp from a young bitch.

'There you are – she's found something.'

'Rabbit.' The sceptic was unmoved.

Another bitch ran to the first one's side and began to speak more strongly. The field tensed with excitement.

'Leu in!' from the huntsman gave place to a more urgent 'On! On!'

A large black-and-tan hound bounded with an air of authority to where the bitches were snuffling through the gorse, inhaled the scent and gave tongue rapturously. The rest of the pack joined in chorus as they found the line and plunged purposefully through the undergrowth, some visible, others displaying only the pennants of their sterns, many completely submerged in the heaving, snapping, gold-flecked greenery. For several minutes this struggle beneath the blanket of gorse continued in apparent confusion. Then a russet projectile catapulted out of the far side of the covert, saluted by a roared 'Holloa!' and the hunt was on.

'Ladies and gentlemen –' began the Field Master in his stentorian voice, but he was crying in the wilderness. The futility of attempting to dam a tide of Irish sportsmen in view of a fox, at the first meet of the season, was quickly borne in upon him. Unlike the Master, he was a foreigner, from the far side of St George's Channel: marriage had brought him to this disquieting country, the most difficult posting he had experienced. Major Fenton habitually wore the expression – part baffled, part appalled – which denotes that most pitiable of creatures, an Englishman cast adrift in Ireland.

'All on,' the First Whip reported to the huntsman, who grunted approval as they dug their heels into their horses' flanks and surged forward. Behind them Major Fenton, with a muttered curse, galloped grimly in the midst of the unruly field, determined to find an opportunity of regaining the initiative.

This came at the first check. For no apparent reason, the pack faltered and lost the scent. The field sat their horses while hounds cast around anxiously. The large black-and-tan hound asserted his individuality by working his way far ahead, exploring a blackthorn thicket and a distant ditch, to no more profit than his kennel mates. Philip, who was now feeling more at ease than he could ever remember at this stage of a hunt, studied the landscape with interest. They were still close to the Lissanore demesne. Not far away stood a large grassy tumulus crowned with three oak trees that was popularly known as Mount Calvary: to avoid blasphemy, no name was ever given to the largest oak, but the smaller ones on either side of it were called the Good Thief and the Bad Thief. A lightning strike some years previously had shrivelled half of the Bad Thief, reinforcing the metaphor. The mound was believed to be of considerable archaeological significance; but when a university department had asked permission to excavate it, the request had been rebuffed by the farmer ('No luck will come of disturbing the old king buried below'). Now, hounds ran around in increasingly erratic circles, snuffling disconsolately at the unresponsive scrub and pasture overlooked by this ancient barrow.

'I doubt we're out of business,' said the same defeatist voice as before, his pessimism confirmed.

'Don't you believe it.' Miss Malley remained defiant.

Her unfounded confidence was unexpectedly vindicated at that moment by the lone hound, who suddenly struck the line again and gave tongue triumphantly. The pack rushed to his cry, leaving the huntsman – who had gone on foot to investigate something – stranded, with the Second Whip riding to his rescue. The followers momentarily forgot their fox, gaping incredulously at the spectacle of the two scarlet-coated hunt servants galloping past on the same mount. A roar of laughter greeted this vision, Philip convulsed along with the rest of the field.

'Don Quixote and Sancho Panza.' Miss Malley's giggling sally provoked increased mirth.

The Master masked his embarrassment by turning his rein; Major Fenton covered his with harsh shouts of 'Hold hard!' directed at the field. His injunctions proved as ineffectual as before; again he found himself carried along by an impetuous flood of riders streaming closely in the wake of the tail hounds. This was easy ground that posed no challenge to Philip or anybody else. The field processed in an orderly fashion through gates held obligingly open, the more impatient scouting for cow gaps. Even the most reckless thought it pointless to look for fences that might delay them when the priority was to keep up with hounds. The Field Master began to be appeased. In this decorous, but brisk, style they passed familiar landmarks, ritually identified by veterans as they speculated on the fox's intentions.

'Rathconnell crossroads coming up – he's headed for Woodville, sure enough.'

'He's never going for Woodville – a snug cave on Knockraggett will be more to his liking.'

'Ye're wrong, the both of yiz. See – he's runnin' for Nowlanstown.'

This last assertion proved correct. Their quarry ran into the derelict demesne of Nowlanstown, the huntsman and the half-dozen leaders of the field catching a glimpse of his ruddy coat as he streaked up the grass-choked avenue and plunged into an overgrown laurel covert. There was another check, as hounds set about drawing this laureate jungle while more of the field trotted up the avenue every minute.

Over the stationary riders and questing hounds loomed the vast ruin of Nowlanstown, burned in the Troubles and by now so completely encased in ivy as to resemble a giant piece of topiary. Only the pillared portico and surmounting pediment revealed the dignified grey stonework that everywhere else was submerged beneath a dense layer of glossy green tendrils. Philip stared at the ruined house, which fascinated him, as fallen grandeur always did. He had visited it often before, when out hacking on Pegasus, haunted by the morbid reflection that this was how Lissanore might have looked if the caprice of a rebel commandant had inclined differently. In summertime, the abandoned gardens blossomed unexpectedly with an archipelago of flowers that punctuated the knee-high grass, betraying where formal beds had once been laid out. Heralded by a riot of renascent azaleas, tall foxgloves came into bloom, languidly overlooking the neighbouring nettles and joined soon after by a miscellany of lilies, all displaying the finery of fallen aristocrats amid the plebeian weeds. Now, in winter, the drab scene gave no hint of this dormant exoticism. Tumbled and broken garden ornaments lurked among the undergrowth and in one corner a rusted garden roller, whose weight and limited function made it unattractive to appropriate, rested half-concealed by the encroaching briars. Nobody but Philip paid any attention to the ruin: it was a reminder of past but recent discord, to acknowledge which might rekindle dangerous antipathies.

So, the hunt followers sat their horses with their backs to this ghost of a house in its ivy shroud and affected a more intense interest in the drawing of the laurel covert than some truly felt. For there were those among them who had dined and danced here, in its days of glory – had played tennis within a misdirected ball's range of those same laurels. Nowlanstown had been a hospitable house and therein had lain its downfall. Lively daughters of marriageable age had attracted young officers as tennis and dancing partners, sometimes as suitors; the avenue had become rutted by the tracks of armoured cars and Crossley tenders, delivering and collecting men in transit between social dalliance and war. Those with whom they were at war had observed and retaliated. This was by no means the only great house in Ireland that had been doomed as a consequence of its owners deferring to the demands of importunate young women for the diversion provided by the well-bred sprigs officering the local garrison. That was another reason why, despite its near-disastrous visit from the petroleurs, Philip's home had survived. No officers had danced at Lissanore: the family had no daughters of an age to partner them on the dance floor, nor sons to engage with them in sporting activities; the military, when they called on official business, had been civilly received, but not cultivated. The ruin of Nowlanstown was a melancholy monument to the fate of those who had pursued a more committed course during the last days of British rule in Ireland.

If such reflections were entertained by some of the hunt followers, they were abruptly cut short by hounds giving tongue from the far side of the covert, signalling they were again in ownership of the line. A whooped 'Holloa!' and a frantically waved cap informed the Master and the field that the fox had bolted, with his mask set towards the rougher country beyond the Nowlanstown demesne. The chase resumed, with Philip uncomfortably aware his resolution would shortly be tested. There would be a limit to his trial, however, dictated by how long Pegasus could keep up with the field. For the moment, the pony was running easily. He and his rider, following a procession of others, successfully negotiated a modest fence, no more demanding than the practice jumps they were used to in the paddock at home, with a competence verging on the stylish. Buoyed by that achievement, Philip took another, slightly more challenging fence and landed safely, glancing complacently over his shoulder at some less enterprising spirits queuing patiently at a gate in a corner of the field he had just left.

Soon he had caught up with the more thrusting elements – not that Pegasus was capable of keeping pace with their powerful hunters, but the going had worsened considerably for those in front. Three fields ahead he glimpsed his mother soaring effortlessly over a high bank, as if airborne. He noticed his father in the next field with a number of other riders, including Major Fenton in a state of near-apoplexy over some misdemeanour. Flushed with the success of his abnormally good run, Philip determined to cut a dash. Ahead lay a gorse-covered bank, more formidable than the two jumps he had already taken, but just within Pegasus's range. To leap it and land beside his father and the other adults in the field beyond would establish his character as a hard rider to hounds. Gritting his teeth, his face taut with determination, he set Pegasus at the bank and gave him the office. The pony responded obediently, gathering pace as he galloped towards the gorse-smothered barrier, snorting purposefully. Suddenly, without warning, he stopped dead in his tracks. Philip, in contrast, continued towards his destination: parting company with saddle and stirrups, he flew over the head of his abruptly stationary mount, catapulted through the air. His only emotion was intense surprise; for a couple of seconds he felt strangely peaceful in his airborne trajectory. Then, with sickening force, the earth fell on top of him with the weight of a mountain.

For a few moments he lay, winded, on ground still hardened from the overnight frost. Groggily he raised himself on one elbow; the effort made him feel giddy and he thought he was going to be sick, but after a single dry retch the sensation subsided. A few yards away he saw Pegasus regarding him impenitently, with the air of one who has made a considered decision and sees no reason to regret it. A farmer who had been riding nearest to Philip approached and dismounted solicitously.

'Are you in one piece there, young fella?'

Still breathless, Philip nodded his head uncertainly. He tried to scramble to his feet, but his movements were uncoordinated so that he stumbled onto his knees.

'Easy, now,' said the kindly farmer.

Several other riders who had come up sat their horses in a semi-circle around him, grateful for a respite from the chase. The farmer raised Philip carefully to his feet, enquiring about the condition of his limbs, and satisfied himself he was uninjured. Somebody took the reins of the unresisting Pegasus and led him over to his master.

'The boy is grand,' the farmer informed the company, 'not a bone of him out of place, thanks be to God.'

Philip, though still dazed, felt obliged to live up to this verdict by remounting his pony. He was preparatorily straightening a stirrup leather when a bellow, as of an angry bull, arrested him. Major Fenton had ridden back into the field with two companions, one of them Philip's father, who had been told of his son's accident.

'What do you mean by this, sir?' The Field Master's face was puce. 'Have you taken leave of your senses?'

Philip could only gape in incomprehension.

'Are you all right, old man?' His father rode forward to interpose himself between Philip and the irate major.

'Yes, I – I think so, Papa.'

'Have you seen that double ditch from the far side?' The Field Master's clipped moustache bristled with indignation. 'A Grand National winner couldn't take it. What possessed you, boy?'

'I'm sorry, sir, I – I didn't realize.'

'Didn't realize!' Major Fenton snorted incredulously. 'Fortunately, that pony of yours has more sense. He was right to refuse – saved both your necks.' He turned away, his mind already dismissing the delinquency of one small boy to focus on the probable anarchy being perpetrated by the remainder of the field in his absence. As a Parthian shot he called out to Philip's father: 'It's a pity that boy of yours has ten times more guts than brains.'

Even in his cowed state Philip thrilled to this backhanded compliment. Energized by the Field Master's comment, he swung himself up into the saddle. The onlookers were already filing out through the gate in the wake of Fenton.

'He's quite right, you know, Philip,' his father told him severely. 'That was an impossible jump; I doubt that I could have taken it. The trouble is, so early in the season, the fences are often blind. You must learn to gauge things better – if you don't know the country, don't take risks. I must admit,' he added, his features assuming an expression of mild perplexity, 'I never thought you would give me cause for concern by behaving recklessly. You always seemed rather – well – cautious, out hunting. I appear to have misjudged you.'

Philip jogged along in a daze that by now had little to do with his fall: his father's words, like the Field Master's moments earlier, amounted to an accolade. Yet he could not repress a shudder when Count Kinsella stopped in the next field to point out the formidable ditch into which he would have propelled himself, had his pony's instinct not saved him. His father was content to ride with him, behind most of the field now; no one enjoyed a good run with hounds more than Count Kinsella, when the occasion offered, but he was equally happy to potter along beside Philip for a while, in the well-founded expectation of soon rejoining the proceedings at the next check. So it proved. Within minutes they caught up with the field, watching dispiritedly while the pack cast around in a meagre spinney that should have carried the scent well, but for some reason left them baffled.

'We've had our fox,' said the Jeremiah who had predicted failure all morning.

This time there was no rebuttal from Miss Malley, who had suffered a tumble while taking a totally unnecessary fence, rather than queue at a gate; though unhurt, she had parted company with the apron of her habit and was carrying out repairs on it in the privacy of a hawthorn hedge, assisted by two other lady riders. The Master was coming to the same pessimistic conclusion.

'This is a wild-goose chase, I'm afraid. We'd best cut our losses and draw Kilgarvan.'

So, Major Fenton marshalled his forces and the hunt rode in good order through Burras town, attended by much questioning from well-wishers as to what kind of sport they were having. Taking the right-hand road, where the main street forked at a building with a large sign proclaiming 'Medical Hall', the cavalcade clattered out of the far side of town and made for the second draw of the day. The new covert also supplied a fox and they enjoyed a good run until he gave them the slip in a drain beside the railway line. By this time the hunt was close to the boundary of its country, so that a time-consuming hack was necessary to visit two more coverts, both of which proved blank. And that, as the increasingly unpopular commentator observed, was that. In fact, most of the field felt they had had a good day, flushing two foxes and enjoying several reasonably long runs during which the thrusters had had an opportunity to risk their necks and the faint-hearted had been able to conduct themselves with passable credit.

The anticlimax of ending the day with two tenantless coverts was compensated for by the happy proximity of Flanagan's, the hunt's favourite watering hole. This was a public house in an isolated situation on high ground overlooking the road to Burras, a location that betrayed its remote origins as an illicit shebeen. The thirsty hunters crowded into the long stone-flagged bar, cheered by a turf fire that blazed hospitably and clamorously interrogated about the day's sport by the patrons already on the premises. A babble of orders for drinks engulfed Flanagan, the fourth of his dynasty to preside behind the bar, mixed with loud and disputatious analysis of the recent proceedings. Already history was being rewritten.

'The run after that first fox must have been a three-mile point.'

'I'd say nearer four.'

'Two blank coverts – some blackguard must be trapping, same as last season.'

'There's no trapping – the farmers have seen to that.'

'Then we need to improve the coverts.'

'Somebody was telling me one of the Cork hunts put thirty mountain foxes down in their coverts and had record litters.'

'Try that one on the Master – I dare you.'

Several people made jocular references to Philip's mishap, including his uncles Dermod and Eanna who drifted into the pub shortly after. Since a boy tumbling off his pony while out hunting was such an everyday occurrence, of no significance whatever, it was obvious what had caused this buzz of interest was the formidable nature of the bank he had tried to jump. Although he conscientiously told everyone who raised the topic that he had not realized it was a massive double ditch, his honest disclaimers were met with smiling scepticism. Philip was encountering, for the first time in his young life, the irresistible power of myth, founded on oblique impressions and propagated by rumour. To the hunt followers exchanging gossip ('You should have heard Fenton rating him, poor little chap...') in a crescendo of conversation as the drink circulated and the cigarette smoke created a dense haze, he was now marked down as a daredevil, a young thruster over-keen to take his fences who would have to be watched; and nothing would thenceforth erase that reputation.

Philip emerged from Flanagan's with his father and mounted Pegasus, to whose quick-wittedness he owed his new status and possibly his survival. McConkey's trap stood outside the pub, opportunistically waiting to poach customers who might find the challenge of riding home beyond their capability, given another hour or so of conviviality. For the moment, only Petticoats Flaherty occupied the vehicle, using it as a resting place to break his journey, whatever mission he was engaged on, and repaying this hospitality by retailing local gossip to the taciturn McConkey. ('He drives a trap, so naturally he's a Trappist,' Count Kinsella had once remarked, indulging a fondness for bad puns.) In companionable silence, father and son rode home to Lissanore, where Philip's mother was already installed, bathed and changed.

'Myrtle Blackwell went home early,' she said. 'One can hardly blame her – not our best day's sport by any means – though it's not like her to pack it in just because we drew a blank.' She turned quizzically to Philip. 'I hear you made a fairly determined effort to break your neck, young man.'

'It was all right, Mummie. Pegasus refused – he must have known it was a bigger jump than I thought – and I fell off before we even reached it.'

'That pony is the best investment we ever made,' said his mother. 'He is worth his weight in gold – so different from the succession of beastly, bad-tempered horrors I had as a child, all with just one ambition: to kill me. Now, Philip, off you go. You just have time for a quick bath before family rosary.'

In the bathroom, Philip lowered into place the long metal cylinder that blocked the plughole and ran the hot, brackish water into the tub, his mind racing exultantly. He had overcome his fear of

231

hunting, the shame that had secretly oppressed him for so long. Of course he would still feel the familiar knot in the pit of his stomach every time he went out; but he would take his fences confidently, without overreaching himself. He now had no need to worry about people observing him and guessing at the apprehension that gripped him. If other members of the field watched him in future, it would be with a view to restraining his supposed recklessness. He felt a glorious sense of emancipation. He was a thruster.

CHAPTER XIV

CONN the wolfhound died in his sleep two weeks later, ending his days as unobtrusively as he had lived them. His burial was conducted under conditions of secrecy to avoid further upsetting Dee-Dee, whose extravagant grief was painful to see. The wolfhound was laid to rest beside his mate Orla, shot by the Black and Tans years before, in a small clearing in a rhododendron thicket close to the croquet lawn. Dizzycourse Slattery presided over the obsequies, having energetically supervised the digging of the grave ('Good an' deep now, boys – we don't want the foxes gettin' at that fine beast, d'ye see o' course...'). All the Kinsellas in residence attended the interment, even Uncle Ulick who had hesitated until the last minute, weighing the dangers to his health from the cold weather against loyalty to a faithful old retainer and – the deciding factor – his fascination with illness and mortality.

'Poor old dog,' said Count Kinsella, as they made their way back to the house, 'he didn't have much of a life after his mate was killed. With hindsight, I rather wish we had kept one of the pups. We had such a struggle rearing them after their mother's death we were only too glad to place them with good owners as soon as possible. Lissanore won't be the same without a wolfhound around the place.'

Philip was deeply affected by the death of Conn. He had been fond of the big, gentle dog whose unassertive presence was an intrinsic part of his childhood. Philip always dreaded the removal of anything familiar, finding it vaguely threatening. Now Conn's absence became more intrusive than his presence had ever been. There was, too, a further dimension to this particular loss. Conn had accompanied him and Constanza on their expedition to the summerhouse on that sun-drenched day when he had acquired a lock of her hair and pledged himself as her knight. He remembered how the normally shy wolfhound had gone immediately to the girl, cradled his head on her lap, followed her devotedly and looked as forlorn as Philip at her departure. That had made Conn a part of their romantic adventure: with its only witness gone, that golden afternoon somehow receded from reality; the wolfhound's death made Constanza seem more remote, as if Philip might have imagined her. The high spirits that had buoyed him in the days following his triumph in the hunting field (as the power of public opinion had by now persuaded even him to regard his tumble) gave place to melancholy.

'Never mind, old man.' His father, sensing his mood, clapped him encouragingly on the shoulder. 'Fetch the foils and we'll have another lesson.'

This was an offer that admitted of no hesitation. To avoid the mourners returning to the front and back doors of the castle, Philip took a shortcut via the entrance that gave public access to the chapel. In the dim passageway he glimpsed a female figure coming out of the chapel and walking ahead of him: the pious Angela, he thought, paying a surreptitious visit to the Blessed Sacrament. When they turned into the broad corridor leading to the rest of the house, however, he was surprised to recognize Kitty, the other housemaid, who was not noted for her religious devotion. He quickened his pace to overtake her and say hello. She returned his greeting absently and excused herself, rather abruptly he thought, to disappear through a door that would take her to the kitchen. Philip felt his depression return at this offhand treatment from Kitty, whom he liked. She had often smuggled pieces of cake or soda bread out of the kitchen as treats for him and kept him informed about the politics of the servants' hall. Even in the poor light of the passage it had seemed to him she looked less pretty, her face puffy as if she had been crying. Perhaps she was upset about Conn's death. No, come to think of it, she had been behaving oddly for the past couple of weeks, long before the wolfhound died.

He dismissed this conundrum and went to his room to fetch the foils for his fencing lesson. To his disgust, they still consisted of bamboo canes with taped handles, despite his progress in the noble art of swordsmanship. Philip was truly dedicated, so that his father had by now been converted into a willing instructor, impressed by his pupil's earnest application. His outsize fencing mask had been adapted by Bartie Lawlor, the blacksmith, so that it fitted him better. Since Bridie Byrne had also completed the crude fencing jacket she had made for him, Philip dutifully wore this, though the prospect of injury was slight: besides making him feel properly equipped, he hoped it would help persuade his father to substitute steel for bamboo. He collected his accoutrements and made his way downstairs. When he reached the bottom landing of the staircase, overlooking the hall, he saw that something unusual was happening which froze him in his tracks.

Bridie Byrne was steering someone across the hall – he saw now that it was Kitty – with her arm around her shoulders, as if the girl needed support. As Philip watched unseen, they passed into the drawing room, from which he heard his mother's voice issuing. Then the door closed behind them, leaving him perplexed. His instinct told him something strange was in train, but what it might be completely baffled him. There was one obvious recourse – to listen outside the door – but that presented certain moral issues. Philip had wrestled long and hard with the dilemma of eavesdropping. He was guiltily aware that he had practised this black art for much of his childhood; but he had rationalized it as the only means of acquiring information that grown-ups insisted on withholding, which it might be important for him to know. He had also noted, from his favourite reading matter, that D'Artagnan and the musketeers, with many similar heroes, were routinely to be found concealed behind every variety of arras, secret panel and other contrivance, eavesdropping on conversations – indeed, they relied on such intelligence to preserve the throne of France. So, it could not be completely dishonourable. Philip had resolved the matter by concluding that if adults were secretly deliberating about something that might have a bearing on himself, then he was justified in listening; otherwise he was not. A minute's reflection forced him to admit that, whatever the significance of the scene he had just witnessed, it was difficult to imagine it could concern him. Rather than do something he would feel obliged to recount at his next confession and conscious he must not keep his father waiting any longer, he reluctantly descended the stairs and made his way to the ballroom.

'Ah, there you are,' said his father. 'I had almost given you up.'

'I'm sorry, Papa. Just give me a moment to put my things on.'

'I thought today we might embark upon a rudimentary exploration of the art of the parry, in its various forms. We could start with the high-line parry, from *sixte* to *quarte* or vice-versa.'

Philip loved the sound of these French fencing terms, which he was beginning also to understand. He nodded enthusiastically.

'When you are ready, then. *En garde.*'

In the drawing room, Countess Kinsella said: 'I really am so terribly disappointed, Kitty. I would never have expected it of you. As for your poor parents...'

She left the sentence unfinished. The girl huddled on the sofa began to sob convulsively. Bridie Byrne drew her close to her ample bosom and thrust a handkerchief into her hands, at the same time turning on her mistress a look of appeal.

'It's all right, Kitty.' Countess Kinsella relented. 'Don't cry. We'll sort things out somehow.'

Kitty swallowed several times and tried to speak, her face distorted with tears. Her words came out as an indistinct croak.

'I'm so – so sorry! So – so – *ashamed!*' The last word distended into a keening wail.

'We are going to help you. I know you're very upset – and that's understandable – but we have to talk things over calmly and work out what is to be done. Bridie,' she added in a tone that struggled to sound normal, 'I think this might be a good time for you to demonstrate what a superb pot of tea you make.'

'Tea it is.' Bridie rose from the sofa, watched desolately by the distraught housemaid as she left the room.

'Now listen, Kitty,' said Countess Kinsella in a voice that was gentle, but firm. 'If I am to help you, there is one thing I must know straight away. Who is the father?'

The girl gave a strangled sob, hesitated for a moment, then blurted out an answer in which despair was mingled with a hint of defiance.

'Martie – Martin Farrell.' She buried her face in the handkerchief.

'Martin Farrell – the lad who sometimes helps out Slattery with the heavier jobs? He always struck me as a very decent young man.'

'Oh, he is that, ma'am.' Kitty, whimpering, grasped at this morsel of approval.

'Do you think he would be willing to marry you?'

'*Willin'*? Mother of God, he talks about nothin' else. He's mad keen to marry me.' Even in her predicament, the pride of conquest was discernible. 'But we've no money at all – no hope of settin' up home. We'll be a queer age by the time Martie comes into his father's farm – the old man's good for another twenty years – God forgive me if that sounds like wishin' him into his grave.'

237

'But the main thing is, the young man would marry you if he could? You're quite certain of that – even in your condition?'

For the first time, the ghost of a smile flitted across the girl's stricken features.

'I am that, ma'am – as sure as I live and breathe.'

'Then we must see what can be done. We need to talk to your young man. Where is he today?'

'Beyant with Mr Slattery.'

'Very well.'

Her mistress lapsed into deep thought, pondering the implications of the situation, while a silence descended upon the room in which the ticking of the clock on the chimneypiece sounded unnaturally loud. Countess Kinsella only came out of her reverie when Bridie Byrne returned, bearing a laden tea tray.

'Bridie, could you please go and find Slattery, and if young Martin Farrell is with him, bring the boy here. Discreetly, of course. There is no need to trouble Corristeen.'

'I'll do that this minute.' She hesitated, a trifle theatrically.

'What is it?' asked Countess Kinsella.

'Only that it crossed my mind – if I'm not too bold, ma'am – that we should maybe tell Himself about it.' She ignored an anguished gasp from Kitty. 'It might be that Himself would see some way to an arrangement, so to speak, that would sort it all out and no harm done.'

'Of course he must be told. I shall speak to him while you fetch the young man. No, Kitty,' she admonished the girl who, white-faced, was now writhing with apprehension, 'you know there is no alternative, if we are to do anything for you. Stay here and drink some of Bridie's excellent tea while I speak to the Count.'

The two women left the room. In the hall, Bridie looked significantly at Countess Kinsella.

'Again, ma'am, not wishin' to say anythin' out of place, when you speak to Himself you might see fit to remind him the ould cottage the Widow Halloran had that died is lyin' empty. 'Tisn't much of a place, but a young couple with no prospects could do worse.'

'Bridie Byrne, you are a conniving creature, always ready with the soft word – and I'm grateful for the suggestion. Now, bring that boy here as quickly as you can – but take care how you go about it. We want as few wagging tongues as possible.'

Countess Kinsella made her way to the ballroom, where she found her husband and son sprawled on a dust-sheeted sofa, resting from their exertions. After dutifully enquiring about Philip's progress, she said in a carefully measured tone that immediately alerted her spouse to a coded message:

'I'm sorry to break things up, but a piece of estate business has come up that you need to attend to right away.'

'Very well,' said Count Kinsella, putting on his coat, 'I shall see to it at once. Remember now, Philip, what I told you about the way you hold the foil – half the work should be done with your fingers.'

'Yes, Papa, I'll remember.' Philip was disappointed at the early ending of his lesson, but knew it would be futile to press for more time. He began to disengage himself from his cumbersome home-made fencing *plastron*. Sensitive to atmosphere and recalling the strange tableau he had witnessed at the drawing-room door, he was now more than ever convinced that something mysterious was afoot. Unfortunately, he was even more confident that it did not involve him – his mother's demeanour had confirmed that – so eavesdropping remained forbidden to him by his code of honour. It was all dreadfully frustrating. Faced with this impasse, he decided to exploit his time-honoured resource: the bush telegraph that operated so efficiently below stairs. Gathering up his fencing equipment, he headed for the kitchen in the hope of satisfying his curiosity.

In the morning room, to which Countess Kinsella steered her

husband in order to brief him on the latest domestic crisis, he listened attentively to her story. At the first intimation of a seducer having preyed on one of his housemaids, Count Kinsella frowned as a dark thought crossed his mind: he had seen smiling bohemians with artistic pretensions wreak havoc upon women's susceptibilities too often to underestimate the danger they posed; and there was such an individual currently living under his roof. He immediately posed the same question his wife had put to Kitty.

'Who is the father?'

'Martin Farrell.'

The Count's brow cleared. Though reprehensible, that was less scandalous than if one of his house guests – even one employed in a mercenary role – had been responsible. He mentally apologized to Declan for his unjust suspicion.

'Is he prepared to marry her?'

'Very eager to do so, according to Kitty, but they have nothing to make a start in life.'

'I had better speak to him.'

'I've already asked Bridie to fetch him. I shall send him in here to see you as soon as he arrives. You can find out if he means to do right by Kitty, before we let him go anywhere near her.'

'Where is she?'

'In the drawing room, waiting for Bridie.'

'Of course.' He smiled briefly. 'The redoubtable Bridie – she is a tower of strength at times like this.'

'She was so good as to suggest – with many diplomatic preliminaries, of course – I might remind you that old Mrs Halloran's cottage is vacant.'

'So it is. She always had a practical turn of mind, our Bridie.' He started towards the door.

'Where are you going, Bonnie?'

'To telephone Canon Roche. If there is any prospect of a marriage...'

He left the implication hanging in the air and crossed the hall to the telephone. After a brief conversation with the parish priest he hung up and turned to his wife, who was waiting expectantly.

'He's coming here right away. I shall explain things to him when he arrives. You had better stay with Kitty while I talk to young Farrell – here he is now.'

Bridie Byrne ushered – more accurately, propelled – a well-built youth with dark curly hair, handsome features and a deeply apprehensive expression through the front door into the hall. He clawed from his head a weather-beaten tweed cap which he twisted uneasily in his hands while greeting Count and Countess Kinsella with a hoarse, indecipherable utterance.

'Come with me, Farrell,' commanded Count Kinsella.

The door of the morning room closed behind the two men. The Countess and Bridie re-entered the drawing room, where they found Kitty exactly as they had left her; the girl's violent distress had given way to an air of listlessness and a cup of tea stood, neglected and cold, in front of her.

'I'll make some more tea,' said Bridie, picking up the tray. She was on her way back to the drawing room when a crunch of tyres on gravel announced the arrival of Canon Roche. Bridie hastened to forestall his ringing of the bell, which would have brought Corristeen out of his pantry, opened the door to him and took his hat and coat before escorting him to the drawing room. Kitty gave a gasp of dread, as the parish priest entered the room, and clasped a handkerchief to her mouth. She was spared further embarrassment by Countess Kinsella who immediately said:

'My husband would like to see you, Canon. He is next door in the morning room.'

She led the priest back out through the hall, knocked on the morning-room door, ushered him inside and closed it behind him. She heard a murmur of voices, dominated after a minute by an indistinct crescendo from Canon Roche who had evidently just had the situation explained to him. Countess Kinsella shook her head ruefully and rejoined Kitty in the drawing room.

Philip retired from the kitchen, heavy with greedily ingested soda bread, scones and cake, but light in fresh intelligence. He had never known the kitchen community so uncommunicative. To every query the normally gossipy servants had opposed a wall of bland obfuscation. By way of apology for this uncharacteristic refusal to confide in him, they had plied him with more generous amounts of food than he had ever before enjoyed – he had a dim apprehension he might have made himself sick – but he was in no way wiser than before. A rallying kind of humorous evasion had been the response even to leading remarks he had thought cunningly oblique (was Kitty suffering from a cold? – that had provoked an inexplicable explosion of laughter, instantly suppressed), so that he had been denied the slightest glimmer of information. He almost felt, after this rebuff, that he would be justified in listening outside the drawing-room door.

Reluctant to resort to this crude expedient, when he reached the hall he paused, honourably beyond earshot of the drawing room, in front of the painting *Wild Geese Observed at Twilight* and studied it unseeingly, as a potential alibi, while hoping to detect some development. Moments later, the door, not of the drawing room but the morning room, opened to disgorge his father, Canon Roche and – bewilderingly – Martie Farrell who worked in the yard and had never before been seen inside the castle, except occasionally in the kitchen when he was regaled with tea or soup after performing some

242

demanding labour. Before the boy's baffled gaze, this unlikely trio processed to the drawing room and began to file inside. Catching sight of Philip staring across the hall, his father turned and said in a tone of great firmness:

'Philip, go up to the schoolroom.'

He turned obediently up the stairs, revolving in his mind what he had witnessed, to no satisfactory conclusion. The incongruous cast of characters in this drama defeated any attempt at rationalizing the situation. He had almost reached the schoolroom when he decided instead to go to his bedroom; since it was obvious his father simply wanted him out of the way, that would not amount to disobedience and the weight of cake in his stomach made him anxious to lie down. He settled on the bed and gazed at the ceiling while he tried to piece together the mystery. Kitty was obviously at the centre of it; but where did Canon Roche fit in? Or had he just dropped in coincidentally, on a social call? No, there was Martie Farrell to be taken into consideration too… The parish priest had seemed to have business with him, unlikely though that was. Kitty, Bridie, Canon Roche, Martie… His parents, Bridie, Martie, Canon Roche… Kitty… Kitty…

Tired from the exertions of his fencing lesson, heavy with home-baked delicacies and mentally exhausted from trying to solve this puzzle, Philip dozed off.

'That's all settled, then.' Canon Roche closed the conference in the drawing room. 'I'll read your banns for the first time next Sunday. The two of you will tell your parents tonight. How much you tell them is up to you – I suppose it depends on how they react to the news – but when they hear that the Count, like the Christian gentleman he is, has given you a cottage rent-free for the first year and extra work for *you* – ye young spalpeen – I doubt there will be any objections. If there are, I'll go and see them tomorrow.'

'Thank you, Canon,' whispered Kitty in a voice hoarse with relief.

''Tis more than you deserve, the two of you, after besmirching the holy virtue of purity – rutting like swine. Well, there'll be no more of that until this graceless gurrier has made an honest woman of you in front of the altar of God. You are not to see each other again until your wedding day.'

'Will that not look rather strange?' asked Countess Kinsella. 'Might it not provoke gossip?'

'That's a fair point. Very well, you can meet on Sundays, at each other's homes, with family present.'

Martie Farrell, who had mostly remained silent, contributing only laconic answers to questions put to him, was not displeased with his lot. Although the past hour had been the most agonizing of his life, one essential fact had now registered in his mind: he was to marry and set up home with the girl he wanted more than anything in the world. A warm satisfaction was slowly seeping into his soul and, with the telepathy of lovers, he sensed the same reaction in Kitty. He grasped his crumpled cap more firmly and muttered his thanks to the Kinsellas and the parish priest, attempting to take his leave.

'I'll just be gettin' back beyant now, to Diz – to Mr Slattery.'

'Indeed, you'll be doing no such thing, *mo bhuachaill!*' Canon Roche informed him shortly. 'You'll just be going through to the chapel now, to make an examination of conscience – if you have one, which I doubt – and I'll be through in five minutes to hear your confession. While you're waiting you can familiarize yourself with the Stations of the Cross, because you'll be making a few journeys round them after I give you your penance. The same goes for you, miss.' He turned to Kitty. 'I'll see you, too, in the chapel, when I've finished with this fornicator.'

He nodded to Bridie Byrne who, assuming the role of chaperone, led the two penitents off to the chapel.

'Thank you both very much,' the parish priest said feelingly to the Kinsellas when they were alone. ' 'Twas the offer of the cottage saved the day.'

'They were lucky I had anything to offer,' Count Kinsella told him. 'We own practically nothing beyond the demesne. My father took the opportunity of the Wyndham Act to sell off to all our tenants and pocket the government's bonus. I have no doubt that helped us survive the Troubles: not being landlords, we had a better relationship with the people – apart, of course, from one unpleasant episode from which you so providentially saved us, for which I'm eternally grateful. (The parish priest made a deprecatory gesture.) We still have a dozen cottages, but since they are occupied by men who work around the place and the farm is going at full tilt, I had no threats of compulsory purchase from the Land Commission fellow when he called here. You will be scandalized to hear, Canon, that when I noticed he had a Sacred Heart pin in his lapel I immediately took him on a tour of the chapel, just to emphasize our Catholic credentials. If that was some kind of simony, I apologize. Anyway, he was eating out of my hand by the time he left, with no notion of buying up anything at Lissanore. Just as well – I wouldn't want to exchange the little property we have left for a sheaf of worthless government bonds.'

'Well,' said Canon Roche, 'you certainly made a big difference to two young lives today – and to another on the way. By the grace of God, we should get a good Catholic family out of what would otherwise have been a disaster. I shudder to think what might have become of that girl if Farrell had not stood by her – believe me, I've seen some distressing cases.'

Countess Kinsella looked grave at this. It was the thought that had been tormenting her during her interview with Kitty, spurring her to find a solution. Her husband, who had harboured similar forebodings, nodded in acknowledgement of the danger that had been averted.

'Farrell is a good fellow – if a trifle hot-blooded. As for Kitty, one way or another, we should have looked after her, as a member of the household. We have always been close to our servants – for example, we have never adopted the crude English fashion of calling our housemaids by their surnames. I feel a responsibility for what happened – after all, I was *in loco parentis*. The families of the girls who come here put their trust in us. They prefer their daughters to work in a Catholic house, so we have always had the pick of the parish. I doubt if that will remain the case, once the news of this business gets abroad – as it inevitably will.'

'I'm afraid you're right,' said the priest. 'The ould Biddies of both sexes will gossip and destroy the girl's character behind her back; but once she's married and the baby is born, they'll soon forget how it began and, before you know it, Mr and Mrs Farrell will be respected pillars of the parish. I shall have to sit heavily on Prendergast, though,' he added as an afterthought. He took a purple stole from his pocket, kissed it, draped it around his neck and turned towards the door.

'When you have finished in the chapel,' Count Kinsella invited him, 'I hope you will have time to drink a glass of whiskey – to the health of the happy couple, if you like.'

'Count,' said Canon Roche solemnly, 'you are a Christian and a gentleman.'

CHAPTER XV

PHILIP was dismayed when he heard the news that Kitty was to be married. After all his excited speculation about what was going on among the adults, it turned out to be nothing more dramatic than preparations for a wedding; that explained why Canon Roche had been involved. Yet, on further reflection, it seemed to him there were aspects of this development that remained incongruous. Why had Kitty seemed so upset, immediately before the announcement of her engagement? He taxed Bridie Byrne, who had very obviously been closely involved in the affair, with this puzzling contradiction.

'It might be she was worried her fella wouldn't pop the question.' Bridie feigned an ignorance of the matter equal to Philip's.

It was a plausible enough explanation – or would have been, if Philip had not seen her supporting the evidently distressed housemaid across the hall, on their way to the interview with his mother. Perhaps Mummie had told Martie Farrell he must pop the question to Kitty: that would be like her and it would also explain why the tense atmosphere had so quickly given way to celebration. Kitty's demeanour now could only be described as blissful. The same could not be said of Philip. Although he was sufficiently generous-spirited to be glad Kitty had found happiness, in every other respect he found the situation unsatisfactory. Not only was it a disappointing anticlimax to so much mysterious activity but, since Kitty was leaving Lissanore, he was losing his best informant about kitchen politics and most prolific source of contraband cakes and biscuits. Hard on the heels of Conn's death, another familiar face was soon to depart from the household; and Philip hated change.

In search of distraction he wandered towards the tower room, where the armorial mural was at last nearing completion. It crossed his mind that this must presumably mean Declan too would shortly be leaving the house. Yet Philip did not really regard the painter as part of the household; despite his admiration for his work, Declan's long residence at Lissanore and their superficially amicable relations, they had never become close. Philip knew intuitively that Declan's departure, whenever it took place, would not affect him like Kitty's. In the tower room he found the artist stooped in front of one of the larger coats of arms on the mural, watched anxiously by Uncle Dermod. The painter's brush licked delicately at the centre of the shield.

'MacCaffry of Kean More.' Uncle Dermod explained the problem. 'Our kinsmen, the Austrian counts of that name, have completely different arms from those of Maguire, which are commonly assigned to the MacCaffreys as a sept of the princes of Fermanagh. Count MacCaffry of Kean More, in Austria, bears *Azure a chevron gules between three horses courant argent*. It is a considerable challenge to paint three horses on one small shield, especially when the chevron takes up so much space. As you can see, Declan has completed the first horse very successfully.'

'I have, thank God.' Declan paused in his labours to grin over his shoulder at Philip. 'I'm just hoping I can copy the beast another couple of times. I've found, doing these heraldic shields with several identical emblems, it's easier once you've finished one to use it as a model and just repeat the process.'

He spoke with unusual intensity, immersed in the technique of his craft. Philip gazed at the almost completed heraldic family tree, with several dozen brightly coloured coats of arms ornamenting the lush tendrils of realistic ivy (he had been allowed to paint some of the leaves green during the early stages of the work, before the novelty palled, which gave him a proprietorial interest in the project) that now covered the circular walls of the tower room. It was an impressive, almost overwhelming, spectacle.

'With luck,' Uncle Dermod told him, 'we shall complete the three partly painted shields by the end of today. That will leave only one coat of arms to colour in (he pointed to a solitary blank shield outlined in black on the white background of the wall, looking out of place among its multicoloured companions), Talbot of Castle Talbot. Declan wanted to try to finish the whole thing today, but I was afraid his enthusiasm might lead to some last-minute accident, so I have insisted he leave the Talbot arms until tomorrow. It is another rather difficult design since it incorporates a lion rampant, to be executed in gold leaf – a skill in which Declan has become extremely proficient – so it would be best to approach it when fresh.'

'If you say so.' Declan looked up from his task. 'Mind you, the offer to do it today still stands.'

'No, Declan. Tomorrow will be more suitable.'

Although his uncle's reasoning seemed sound, Philip suspected his ulterior motive was to postpone the completion of the project, which had become the chief interest of Dermod's life during the period of more than five months that the artist had worked on it. He stayed to watch until Declan had completed a second horse on the MacCaffry arms, uniform with the first, marvelling at the skill and apparent ease with which the artist achieved his effect. He would have liked to volunteer to paint the red chevron that transected the shield (he had occasionally been allowed to contribute such basic designs), but was intimidated by the splendid appearance of the almost finished mural and dreaded some blunder on his part might destroy its perfection at the last moment. So, he congratulated the painter on his impressive achievement and took his leave.

''Bye, now,' Declan called after him. The young painter was critically contemplating his work. He twisted his head round to treat Philip to the most radiant version of his ever-present smile, which seemed to have the capacity to be turned up, like a gas ring, when required. It was still flared at its full intensity when Philip closed the door of the tower room behind him.

The following day, fixed in Philip's mind as the date when the mural would formally be completed, began in an atmosphere of normality. By mid-morning, however, he became aware of a growing undertone of anxiety infusing the household. Surprisingly, it seemed Uncle Dermod was somehow the source of this unease, whatever the nature of it might be. He wore a worried, distracted air. When Philip approached him with an enquiry about the progress of the mural, he responded almost curtly – an unheard-of rebuff from that pre-eminently kindly and courteous man – and hurried away with a preoccupied expression. That was disturbing; but Philip was too aware of Uncle Dermod's propensity to attach importance to matters that few other people regarded as significant to be persuaded that anything momentous had occurred. He was still smarting from the recent deflation of his expectations, when the grown-ups had acted so mysteriously, only to have the cause of their conspiratorial conduct revealed as Kitty's engagement. In his mood of disillusionment, it seemed likely that whatever was causing a fluttering in the domestic dovecote this morning would turn out to have an equally trivial explanation – especially if it revolved around Uncle Dermod, as seemed to be the case. What would eventually materialize as the reason for this latest agitation – Corristeen's engagement? Philip was so pleased with this private whimsy that he smiled to himself and made a mental note to repeat it to Tom Dixon.

Despite affecting to shrug off the subterranean turmoil among the adults, Philip still entertained a mild curiosity about what might be afoot; but he could not resort to his customary source of information, the servants' hall, since he was closeted in lessons with Father Yves until lunchtime, spent in the schoolroom with his tutor. From the window, he saw his father and Uncle Dermod get into Count Kinsella's motor car and drive off; an hour later he heard them return. One glance then at the faces of his father and uncle alerted him to a crisis. His father had never looked like that at any moment on the day when Kitty had been the object of concern. Something was well and truly up. Philip was now desperate to investigate, but Father Yves, who clearly was unaware of anything untoward in the air, held him rigorously in thrall to *De Bello Gallico*. He was thus excluded from any knowledge of the drama being unfolded in the drawing room where, behind closed doors, his father and Uncle Dermod broke the news to Philip's mother.

'Bolted.' Count Kinsella's expression was grim.

'Bolted? What do you mean?' His wife could not conceal her agitation.

'Just what I say: the two of them have bolted. This morning, at first light. He let himself out before the servants were awake and she picked him up in her car, a few hundred yards along the road from the North Lodge. Feeney heard the car engine, which surprised him at that hour of the morning, looked out and saw the young blackguard getting in. Then it drove off in the direction of Dublin.'

'My God.' Countess Kinsella subsided onto a sofa. 'Did you see her husband?'

'Very briefly. He is in a daze. Deeply shocked and yet, at the same time, not fully aware of what has happened to him.'

'He doted on her. I always thought she treated him rather badly, but she kept it at just a low enough level to make it impossible for anyone to criticize. Poor man – this will destroy him completely.'

'I feel a dreadful responsibility,' Dermod said, his tone anguished. 'I brought that young scoundrel here. If it were not for me, he would never have come anywhere near Lissanore and poor Blackwell would still have his wife.'

'Don't blame yourself, Dermod,' his sister-in-law told him firmly. 'How could you possibly have known what would happen? I might as well take the blame for inviting her so often to the house. Anyway, with a woman of that sort, if it had not been Declan it would have been someone else.'

'I am afraid that's right,' said Count Kinsella. 'I wonder how long it had been going on.'

'Oh, quite a long time, you may be sure. I remember some rather theatrical hostility between them, back in the summer. I should have recognized the signs then: that is often a symptom of something quite different. Then things went quiet; I never saw them together. They must have been incredibly discreet – you know how little privacy there is around here, with everybody knowing everybody else's business. Now I understand why she started going home early from hunting – they must have had a rendezvous.'

'That explains a lot,' said Dermod. 'It surprised me that Declan was such a keen hunt follower, on that dilapidated old bicycle of his. He often took days off from painting, but I didn't feel I could object when he was otherwise making such good progress.'

'Evidently,' said his brother dryly.

'We must be very kind to her husband.' Countess Kinsella sighed gently.

'Yes. Apart from his loss, I'm afraid he will also be an object of ridicule. People are so cruel. A cuckolded Protestant clergyman can expect little sympathy in Ireland.'

'What are we going to tell Philip?'

'I'll take care of Philip,' said Dermod. 'It's the least I can do. I was Declan's patron, so he will probably come to me first for an explanation. I shan't tell him any lies, but I shall try to present things to him in the least squalid light.'

On this constructive note, the conference broke up; but Dermod brought involuntary smiles, which they took pains to conceal, to the faces of his brother and sister-in-law when he remarked ruefully on his way out of the room:

'I should have accepted his offer to paint the Talbot shield yesterday – I see now why he was so keen to finish it… And why he wheedled the payment out of me last night, with the project still incomplete. That blank shield ruins the entire mural. Where am I going to find another artist whose style won't clash with the rest of it? What a selfish young cur.'

Dermod was as good as his word. He waited in the tower room until Philip arrived, as he had predicted, anxious to discover the state of the mural and what was occurring that had so clearly set the household by the heels. In quiet, dispassionate terms he told his nephew what had happened – within the limitations of what could be disclosed to a ten-year-old boy. His task was made easier in that Philip, rather than dwelling on the circumstances of Declan's elopement with Mrs Blackwell, immediately identified this latest crisis as a further depletion of the familiar figures who formed a backcloth to his daily life. First Conn, then Kitty and now the rector's wife whom he had long admired, but who turned out to be, as Bridie Byrne phrased it, a bad lot – all of them had abruptly been removed from his environment. Hitherto, his child's perception of the world had been of a static situation in which the same reassuring faces surrounded him from year to year; now, in a very short space of time, he had been confronted with the constant process of transition that characterizes human existence. Philip recoiled from this revelation. Why could things not stay comfortably the same? His resentment at this change in his circumstances aggravated his newborn dislike of Mrs Blackwell. Yet, despite his clinging to the status quo, he found his reaction to Declan's departure was as detached as he had anticipated. The smiling painter had somehow always remained extraneous to Philip's life.

'All right?' his father asked encouragingly when Philip came downstairs from his conversation with Uncle Dermod.

'Yes, Papa.' He made an effort to sound nonchalant, to assert the normality of his routine, which he was far from feeling. 'I thought I might go out tomorrow, if you are hunting.'

'I'm afraid not, old man. Nobody is hunting tomorrow. All the meets have been cancelled as a mark of respect –'

For a startled instant Philip thought he meant the entire county was in mourning for the betrayal of Mr Blackwell.

'– for Queen Alexandra, whose funeral is being held then.'

Philip knew very little about Queen Alexandra – she did not belong to the Bourbon-Habsburg axis around which Uncle Dermod's dynastic interests revolved – but he recognized that here was another instance of a familiar landmark succumbing to the passage of time and his depression deepened.

As Count Kinsella had forecast, the rector's desertion by his wife made him the butt of bawdy humour throughout the local community. This had little effect on him, since he seemed oblivious to the outside world. To a superficial observer, Mr Blackwell appeared almost to behave normally. He performed his duties as usual, but declined most of the invitations – effectively ministrations – that his parishioners extended to him. He accepted a few that would have been more troublesome to reject and he came as usual to Lissanore for 'Parson's Pleasure', the monthly Sunday luncheon, where association with the two celibate priests, Canon Roche and Father Yves, made the absence of his own spouse least conspicuous. The Kinsellas, though, were troubled by what they saw. Blackwell gave the impression of still being in a state of shock, more baffled than bereft. There was a childlike look of incomprehension in his eyes; whenever someone entered the room, he glanced mechanically towards the door, as if in the expectation it might be his wife, returning to resume their former existence. After seeing him off, his host and hostess exchanged eloquent glances and shook their heads despondently.

Philip woke suddenly from an uneasy sleep, punctuated by strange dreams that involved Declan, Mrs Blackwell, Kitty, Martie Farrell and Conn the wolfhound in a variety of incongruous or fantastic situations. He sat up in bed and rubbed his eyes, fearful he had overslept and would be late to serve Mass for Father Yves. There was no light around the edge of the curtains, but in December he was accustomed to rise in darkness. Then he heard the sound that had penetrated his sleep: a church bell was ringing… faintly… slowly… mournfully. Philip got out of bed, pulled back the curtain and looked out. The pitch-blackness outside revealed nothing; in any case, the tower of Mr Blackwell's church could not be seen from this part of the castle, even in daylight. He opened the window and listened. The bell tolled a few more times, slower and weaker at each stroke, before dwindling into silence. Philip shivered, not entirely from cold, and shut the window. This ghostly bell-ringing in the middle of the night was frighteningly eerie. It struck him that it was the most melancholy sound he had ever heard. What could it mean? At this hour – whatever time it might be – it could not possibly be a summons to a church service. He climbed back into bed. Was Mr Blackwell consoling himself for the loss of his wife, in some unorthodox way, by ringing the bell? Philip revolved the matter in his mind for a few minutes then fell soundly asleep.

He had forgotten the incident by the time he was wakened to get ready for Father Yves' Mass and his preoccupation with his responsibilities kept it banished from his mind. His father, uncharacteristically, came into the chapel very late, when Mass was almost over, and waited there until Philip had finished his sacristan's duties.

'Just come along to my office for a few minutes, old man. I'd like a short chat.'

Philip glanced anxiously at his father and hurriedly examined his conscience for infractions of domestic rules; but Count Kinsella smiled kindly, if a trifle sadly, and laid his hand gently on his son's shoulder as they made their way to the cluttered former boot room that now served as an estate office. His father sat down behind his desk and beckoned Philip to the chair facing him.

'Philip, you are ten now, so I am going to treat you as a little more grown-up than before. We must remember, though, that you are still a child, so there are going to be quite a lot of things in the world you can't quite make sense of yet. Is that fair?'

'Yes, Papa.' He felt excited by this portentous preamble.

'Well, first of all, you must prepare yourself for a bit of a shock. Sad news, I'm afraid. Mr Blackwell is dead.'

'Gosh! What happened, Papa?'

'That is the difficult bit, Philip. Your mother and I debated how much we should tell you. We came to the conclusion you would hear about it, probably in the most lurid way, either from the servants or local people. So I'm going to tell you myself and try to help you understand and be forgiving about Mr Blackwell. Do you know what suicide is?'

'Yes, it's what Judas did – he hanged himself – he –'

In that terrible instant, like a darkened landscape abruptly illuminated by a bolt of lightning, he heard in his inner ear the funereal clang of the church bell in the night and a dreadful image of what had weighted the bell-rope invaded his mind, never to be expelled. He gave an incoherent exclamation of horror that subsided into a choked sob, buried his face in his hands and slumped forward onto the desk.

'Philip!' His father, appalled at this turn of events, sprang up and hurried round the desk to comfort him. He took him in his arms and Philip buried his face in the merciful oblivion of his father's tweed, comforted by the faint, sweet smell of tobacco that he associated with him. It was a moment of intense feeling; never had father and son been so close. After a couple of minutes the boy made an effort to compose himself.

'I heard the bell during the night,' he managed to whisper at last.

'Dear God, I never thought of that,' said his father remorsefully. 'I had no intention of telling you how it happened, but I see you have guessed.' After a pause, he added: 'Well, better here with me than in the kitchen or the village.'

They resumed their seats. His father fumbled for his pipe, then took out his tobacco pouch, but left it neglected on the desk.

'Listen, Philip, I don't have to tell you that taking one's own life is the most awful thing anyone can do. It is the ultimate mortal sin – throwing back the gift of life in God's face. But Mr Blackwell, I am quite sure, didn't know what he was doing. He was unhinged with grief over his wife.'

'She killed him!' Philip shouted with sudden violence. 'It was her fault. I hate her!'

'Hating her won't help,' said his father mildly. 'Certainly she behaved very badly, due to human frailty. You should pray for her and for Mr Blackwell.' He held up his hand to forestall a protest from his son. 'Some time ago, Philip, you asked me what adultery was. I'm afraid I gave you rather an unsatisfactory answer – not dishonest, I would never lie to you, but somewhat on the vague side. That was in deference to your young age. I thought, living within the protection of a Catholic household like ours, there was no danger of your encountering the sordid side of life for a long time yet. Now we have been overtaken by events, thanks to the beastliness of certain people (bitterness at the desecration of his home life momentarily hardened his measured tone), so I shall explain adultery to you more plainly. All right?'

Philip nodded mutely.

'This is adultery – and its consequences: Mrs Blackwell deserting her husband to take up with Declan – a good-looking young man, more entertaining, more lively and high-spirited than Mr Blackwell; doing just what she wanted, for her own selfish gratification, and breaking her husband's heart so that, in his unhappiness, he killed himself. That is adultery: breaking the solemn vows of marriage because someone else seems more handsome or pretty, despising and discarding the love of a husband or wife who is not so handsome or pretty. Of course, the main reason why it is a mortal sin is because God forbids it – "*Thou shalt not commit adultery*" – so it offends against His law and the sacrament of matrimony. At the same time, in ordinary human terms, it tramples on decent people like Blackwell and wrecks their lives. Selfish men and women like Declan and Mrs Blackwell leave a trail of terrible unhappiness behind them. Running away like that is cowardice – running away from responsibilities, from promises made, from real life – chasing after something they call love, when it is no such thing. I'm very sorry that, at your age, you have been exposed to a tragedy like this; but the one way you can gain some benefit from this ghastly experience is to learn a lesson from it for the rest of your life. Do you understand everything I've said?'

'Yes, Papa.'

Relieved to have discharged his parental duty, Count Kinsella set about filling his pipe and kindling it. When he had successfully expelled the first clouds of smoke he smiled at Philip and said:

'Don't let yourself dwell on this awful business. We don't want you to have nightmares. Take my word, the best way of exorcizing this tragedy is to put it out of your mind, except when you pray for the Blackwells – both of them – and Declan, every morning and night. Believe me, old man, it's the only answer. I know it goes against the grain – but that's what being a Catholic is all about.'

The news that the Church of Ireland rector had hanged himself on the bell-rope in his church tower set the county ablaze with excitement, speculation and fabrication. There had not been an event to rival it since the Troubles – if even then. Mrs Skerrett in particular took a prurient interest in the adulterous liaison that had been conducted virtually under her own roof. She was vehement in condemnation of the rector's unfaithful wife.

'To think that strumpet – no, Bridie, I will call her by the name she deserves – moved heaven and earth to lure me into her heretical Church... There were never any soupers in my family and I had no intention of being the first... I always thought she was a flighty piece... Running off with that Dublin jackeen... Bridie Byrne! Will you kindly take care with that hairbrush – you'll have the scalp off me and every hair on my head with it – not to mention bringing on my neuritis...'

Countess Kinsella, while less vociferous, broadly shared her mother's opinion of the conduct of the late rector's wife. Though distinguished among the hard-riding women of the hunting set with whom she associated for the pre-War, convent-bred reticence of her speech, she had expressed herself with uncharacteristic forcefulness to her husband when she first heard of the rector's suicide:

'Myrtle Blackwell is a complete bitch.'

The circumstances surrounding the rector's death provoked many drawn-out formalities. Finally the delicate issue of his interment in consecrated ground was resolved by shipping his body over to England, where some of his family lived. One consequence of the

Blackwell *cause célèbre* was that it totally eclipsed the minor scandal attaching to Kitty the housemaid's precipitate engagement and marriage. So complete was her rehabilitation that the servants' hall laid on the customary farewell party – described by Bridie Byrne as 'a bit of a hooley' – which Philip attended for the first hour, it being understood he must not intrude any longer upon the festivities of the below-stairs community. Having blushingly complied with the company's insistence he should kiss the bride (Kitty, in her happiness, was prettier than ever), Philip said goodnight and withdrew.

Disinclined to go to bed, he paused to study the stars through a window, reflecting on the vastness of the heavens and the complexity of life. Distantly, from the kitchen below, he heard Bridie Byrne's rich contralto break into the inevitable:

'In Mountjoy gaol one Monday morning
High upon the gallows tree,
Kevin Barry gave his young life
For the cause of liberty.'

He had heard this song innumerable times – it was the standard ditty performed at every popular social occasion in Ireland – and it had never touched him with any immediacy. Now, the reference to the gallows, following upon recent events, momentarily cast a pall of gloom over his thoughts. He dispelled it by saying a quick prayer for Mr Blackwell, as his father had recommended, and had recovered his spirits by the time Bridie launched into patriotic reproach.

'Just before he faced the hangman,
In his dreary prison cell,
British soldiers tortured Barry
Just because he would not tell...'

Gazing out at the stars, his thoughts sporadically interrupted by whoops or bursts of laughter from the revellers below, Philip reviewed the occurrences of the past month. It was as if the death of Conn the wolfhound had started a process of dissolution at Lissanore. Kitty would be gone tomorrow. Mrs Blackwell, whom he had once liked so much, had departed like a thief in the night. So had Declan, though he did not regard his leaving as disruptive of the fabric of life, but rather welcomed it in fact. He realized he had always, in some intuitive way, distrusted the permanently smiling painter, probably from the moment he had first glimpsed him in McConkey's trap arriving at Lissanore, and had unconsciously built a protective barrier in his mind against him. More startlingly, he also now recognized that Declan had detected this immunity to his blandishments, had been piqued by it, but had warily resigned himself to maintaining superficial diplomatic relations. In the wake of the havoc wrought by this interloper, Philip drew some consolation and a measure of self-respect from the fact he had not been seduced by Declan's noxious charm.

Soon it would be Christmas, he thought; a more subdued festive season than any he could remember, with some familiar faces missing. Then he felt himself suffused with melancholy, as an unknown but pleasant tenor voice (he later discovered it belonged to the bridegroom, Martie Farrell) from the party in the kitchen began to sing the haunting melody of the *Londonderry Air*. Philip strained to hear the words:

> 'But when ye come, and all the flowers are dying,
> If I am dead, as dead I well may be,
> Ye'll come and find the place where I am lying,
> And kneel and say an Ave there for me.'

It sounded like a dirge for Mr Blackwell who was lying in his grave by now, somewhere in England; but the more important part of him – his soul – had already faced the judgement of God. These were terrible events to have overtaken the mild-mannered clergyman who had been in the house not long ago, talking to Papa, and

261

was now lost in eternity. Philip remembered how Mr Blackwell had surprised him and Tom Dixon by speculating whether the two cannon on the terrace could be fired. His memory presented a sudden image of the rector squinting appraisingly along the cannon barrel, the smoke from his pipe counterfeiting a smouldering fuse; he saw his spare, linen-coated torso leaning out over the battlements of the terrace, poised precariously, in a momentary access of schoolboy enthusiasm, to peer into the mouth of the gun. That genial, good-natured life had been blighted and destroyed because Mrs Blackwell had fallen in love with Declan. It seemed so cruel, so unfair.

Philip felt his eyes brimming with pity and regret. He dashed the backs of his hands against them and turned away from the window, with its vast, enigmatic panorama of the star-studded heavens, and made his way towards his bedroom, where he hoped the nightmares of the daytime would not intrude upon his sleep.

CHAPTER XVI

CHRISTMAS did not fulfil Philip's gloomy forebodings, but passed much as usual, in an atmosphere of good cheer diluted only by the inevitable friction among his siblings, home again for the holidays. His fascination with swashbuckling adventure was reinforced by further immersion in the works of Rafael Sabatini when his father gave him *Captain Blood* as a Christmas present, complemented by Uncle Dermod with a copy of *The Sea Hawk*. The Hunt Ball, held at Lissanore in early January ('We've got Manahan's Band,' Countess Kinsella enticingly informed all her neighbours), with Philip surreptitiously spectating through the staircase bannisters at the throng of people crowding the house, marked the climax of the winter festivities. The new year began on a cheering note, with a report in the local newspaper that Simmie Toal had been sentenced to three years in prison for a catalogue of offences, among which burglary predominated.

One morning at the beginning of March, Philip returned from the stables to find a telegraph boy at the front door, engaged in a heated argument with Grandma Skerrett, heavily wrapped up for one of her rare outdoor expeditions.

'Take it away!' Grandma's voice rose to a shriek. 'No good ever came of one of those horrid things. They've made many a widow – you won't persuade me to open a telegram.'

This impasse was broken by the belated arrival of Corristeen, greeted with relief by the flustered youth.

'Ah, here's the man of the house, praise be! I have a telegram and herself won't take it. There's nothin' in the regulations,' he added desperately, 'to cover a case like this.'

'Give it here,' said Corristeen.

The telegraph boy handed it over with alacrity, observing: 'The ladies is often nervous about telegrams – I always prefer to deal with their husbands.'

Mrs Skerrett, realizing the misunderstanding, jabbed an angry umbrella in the direction of Corristeen.

'*He* is *not* my husband, you – you *fool!*'

'Ah, well, ma'am,' the telegraph boy grinned cheekily, 'that's not for me to judge – your domestic arrangements, like. 'Bye, now.'

He pedalled off, watched in impotent fury by Mrs Skerrett. Then she sallied out to relieve her injured feelings through exercise, repulsing her grandson's attempted greeting with a barked 'Roll on schooldays!'

'Heh, heh.' Corristeen, highly amused, emitted a malicious cackle. '' Tis thankful she should be I'm not demanding me conjugations.'

Philip lurked inquisitively in the hall after Corristeen had delivered the telegram to his parents. He was rewarded within minutes when his mother appeared, holding the flimsy telegraph form, with an animated air.

'Philip, you will never guess. We have a visitor coming – arriving the day after tomorrow.' Her expression indicated it was a very welcome guest. 'Guess who?'

Philip shook his head in mystification.

'Your cousin Nicholas. From Austria – though actually, on this occasion, I gather he is coming from England. You have met him, of course, once before, but you were probably too young to remember.'

In fact, Philip did have a faint recollection of his cousin's previous visit; but this was terrific news. Nicholas had been the last Kinsella to serve the Habsburgs, right up to the dissolution of the Empire less than ten years before, which Uncle Dermod had taught his nephew to regard as the eclipse of civilization and the effectual end of his family's historical purpose. Nicholas would be able to tell him all about life in the Imperial and Royal Army – perhaps even about the Emperor. Philip felt his spirits soar in anticipation. He followed his mother into the drawing room, to which they were both drawn by mutual instinct, and watched her lift the silver-framed photograph from the grand piano and study it. It showed a boy, rather than a man, in the high-collared uniform of a cadet at the Theresian Military Academy of Wiener Neustadt, taken shortly before the War. Philip envied the young man in his Imperial tunic: if the Empire had still existed, he might have gone to Austria, like so many of his forebears, and worn the same uniform.

'There was a terrible row about this photograph, wasn't there, Mummie?' he asked, knowing the answer perfectly well, but eager to savour the retold story.

'There was indeed. During the War, when jingoistic feeling was running very high, several of our neighbours had the impertinence to object to our displaying a photograph of an "enemy officer" in our drawing room. Your father and I told them it was a family photograph that we had no intention of disowning; but if it offended them, the solution was for them to stop frequenting our drawing room. Some of them did, which was no loss. Though I felt some sympathy for the ffreney-Donovan girls, in view of their bereavement; losing their fiancés had made them understandably bitter.'

'I think it was jolly decent of you and Papa to stand up for cousin Nicholas and keep his picture on the piano.'

On the evening when Nicholas was due at Lissanore, Philip extorted permission from his parents to stay up past his bedtime to greet the visitor. When ten o'clock struck and the awaited guest had still not arrived, Count Kinsella declared that his motor car must have broken down and he could no longer be expected that night.

He ordered his son to bed, whither he retired, crestfallen at this disappointment.

Philip surfaced blearily into consciousness. Something had disturbed him, some sound outside his window. Although, to his immense relief, he had not suffered nightmares about Mr Blackwell's death, he often felt apprehensive on waking, in case he might hear again the ghostly tolling of the church bell. Now he listened intently, but heard nothing. The light showing at the edges of his curtains told him it was daytime: he had overslept, but legitimately so, since Father Yves had gone to Dublin for a couple of days and there was no Mass to serve. That was why Papa had allowed him to stay up late to meet his cousin Nicholas – who had failed to arrive, he remembered with dismay. Then he heard again the insidious, muffled sound that had wakened him, which he now recognized as the drumming of horse's hoofs on turf. He jumped out of bed and hurried to the window, just in time to glimpse a horseman in the paddock cantering past. When Philip opened the window and looked out, he heard the stranger's mount snort as his rider gathered him to negotiate the nearest of the practice jumps. He took it with ease, though it was in any case an unchallenging fence. The horseman had his back to Philip as he headed for the next jump; all that could be discerned was black hair, broad tweeded shoulders and an impression of elegance. Suddenly, with a surge of excitement, Philip realized who this stranger must be.

He dressed in record time, ran down the stairs and rushed out of the house. By the time he reached the rail surrounding the paddock the horseman was a distant figure, having abandoned the practice fences to gallop round the grassy expanse that fringed the distant woods. Presently he came cantering back to where Philip stood by the fence and greeted him as he would have done an adult.

'Good morning.' He smiled – not the false smile of the departed Declan, but with real warmth.

'Good morning. Are you my cousin Nicholas?'

'If you are my cousin Philip, yes, undoubtedly.' His voice was a rich baritone, speaking perfect English with no trace of a foreign accent.

'How do you do?' said Philip, his shyness already almost dissolved by his cousin's friendly manner.

'How do you do?' He removed a glove, leaned down from the saddle and shook hands, firmly, but making allowance for the boy's smaller grasp.

Philip studied the visitor. He had grown out of much likeness to his youthful photograph, though there was still some resemblance. His features were even and strong, extremely handsome Philip thought, with just the faintest prominence to the cheekbones to lend a touch of exoticism (Nicholas's mother had been Hungarian, he later learned). The long, straight, well-proportioned nose was the most obvious legacy of his Kinsella heritage. His dominant feature was his eyes: light brown, but with the appearance of changing colour from time to time, almost to dark green; one eye, Philip saw with fascination, held a rimless eyeglass, so highly polished as to be practically invisible except when the light caught the lens. His head was crowned with thick black hair brushed back from his broad forehead. Nicholas lithely dismounted and began to lead his horse – Count Kinsella's second hunter – towards the stable yard. Philip now saw that he was at least six feet tall and bore himself with a combination of military carriage and athletic suppleness. His tweed riding-coat had been cut in Cork Street rather than Vienna, its full skirts matching the flare of his breeches; for his early morning ride he was informally dressed in a shirt open at the neck over a Paisley cravat. Even to a ten-year-old boy, his cousin communicated something of the air of *ton* that had made Captain Count Nicholas Kinsella von Carlow, formerly of the Imperial and Royal Infantry Regiment *Hoch- und Deutschmeister* No. 4, a favourite among the most exclusive society of Europe.

As they walked to the stables, the conventions of introductory small talk could not restrain Philip from raising the questions he burned to ask.

'You were in the Habsburg army, weren't you – like all the other Kinsellas?'

'I had that honour. Nor do I consider myself absolved of that allegiance. I remain as devoted to the service of our rightful Emperor Otto as I was to Karl and to Franz Joseph before him. You see in this demobilized soldier, of a great army that has been disbanded,' he smiled at Philip to soften the bitterness in his voice, 'one who is still defiantly *habsburgstreue*, as we call it – loyal to the Habsburgs. I shall continue so all my days.'

Philip's heart swelled at these sentiments. He wished Uncle Dermod had been present to hear this clarion proclamation of legitimist principles.

'Gosh.' He stared earnestly at his cousin. 'Do you think the Emperor might get his throne back – might be restored? That's what Uncle Dermod wants – he writes letters about it to lots of people.'

'It is perfectly possible. It is less than ten years since the *canaille* in Vienna, Budapest and Prague betrayed the Emperor. What is a decade of misrule, compared to a thousand years of Empire? I tell you, Philip, my friend,' he turned his glance downward to meet the boy's eager gaze, 'it will be my lifetime endeavour to replace the Emperor on his throne. We must not start in Austria, however, but in Hungary. That is where the prospects for a restoration are more favourable. If you are interested in this matter – and I can see you are – we shall talk of it further.'

'Yes, please, cousin Nicholas – I'd like that.'

By now the hunter's hoofs were clattering on the cobbles of the stable yard. A groom came forward and listened, with evident respect, to the visitor's informed appraisal of the horse's qualities. When he had been returned to his stall, Nicholas clapped Philip lightly on the shoulder and said:

'Let's go and have breakfast. The morning air has given me a huge appetite for your delicious Irish bacon.'

At breakfast Uncle Dermod, himself ravenous for any morsel of information about the *ci-devant* Habsburg court, made clear his intention to appropriate their cousin and fillet him of every detail he could supply. To this end he invited Nicholas, with Philip insistently in attendance, to his lair in the tower room that afternoon, ostensibly to admire the armorial pedigree. (Dermod had by now convinced himself that the unfinished shield of Talbot of Castle Talbot, so far from being a blemish on the work, constituted an interesting curiosity and he had abandoned the search for an artist to complete it.) After a perfunctory discussion of the mural, Dermod embarked on his inquisition.

Had Nicholas ever met the old Emperor Franz Joseph? Yes, he had been presented to him once: his memory whimsically retained the detail that the gold lace on his uniform collar had been slightly frayed.

'Only on one side,' he added hastily, as if afraid he might have misrepresented the Emperor and, by extension, the entire Dual Monarchy as down-at-heel.

'Was that when you attended a Ball at Court?'

'No, no. I never went to anything so grand as a Ball at Court – only very senior officers were invited. I once attended a Court Ball, which was open even to junior officers, and it was then I was presented to the Emperor.'

269

There followed more intensive questioning, as Dermod explored every nuance of distinction between a Court Ball and a Ball at Court. This led to the discovery that Nicholas was a Knight of the Teutonic Order, a revelation that delighted Dermod. Himself a Knight of Malta, he wanted to know all about the current circumstances of this symbiotic chivalric brotherhood.

'I was following regimental tradition,' Nicholas told him. 'My unit, the *Hoch- und Deutschmeister*, was founded by the Grand Master of the Teutonic Order in 1696 and each successive Grand Master was the *Inhaber*, the colonel-proprietor of the regiment. The officers, historically, were knights of the Order. During the War, when I was serving on the staff of Field Marshal the Archduke Eugene, Grand Master of the Teutonic Order, I was received as a knight. Unfortunately, three years ago, the Archduke felt obliged to abdicate, to prevent the republican thieves who are now the government in Vienna from confiscating the Order's property, on the pretext it was a Habsburg dependency and so subject to the laws against the dynasty. I have been released from my vows and our Order is in limbo while the Pope decides on our future.'

He fitted a cigarette into a black onyx holder, lit it and began to smoke with a poise and elegance that excited Philip's admiration.

'But you are still a knight?'

'Oh, yes. We retain our honorific status.'

Philip and his uncle breathed sighs of relief that this distinction still attached to a family member. Then Nicholas's conversation turned to the larger upheaval that had disrupted his life: the destruction of the Austro-Hungarian Empire.

'Woodrow Wilson was the instigator, with his hypocritical Fourteen Points and his League of Nations. We had a genuine league of nations in our ancient Empire – but how could an American president be expected to understand Europe? He has left a maelstrom at its heart. France, of course, aided and abetted his folly. My hatred for that low animal Clemenceau, who frustrated our good Emperor Charles in his efforts to make peace, then systematically dismembered Hungary, is second only to my loathing for the traitor Horthy – our so-called Regent who has usurped the Habsburgs' throne.' His eyeglass glinted coldly.

'Do you, then, consider yourself Hungarian?' asked Dermod.

'To a degree – my mother was Hungarian. As a subject of our Dual Monarchy I consider myself to have dual nationality.' He glanced at his watch and rose. 'If you will excuse me, I now have an appointment to call upon Mrs Skerrett, who has been so kind as to invite me to tea.'

He left the room, followed by sympathetic looks from Philip and Dermod. They later heard, however, that Nicholas had been received with unprecedented graciousness by Grandma, on whom he made so favourable an impression that she repeated the invitation two days later and sang his praises for weeks afterwards. Countess Kinsella took her guest to view the Empress's Room, where he gazed reverently at the Imperial double-eagle embroidered on the black-and-gold hangings of the four-poster bed that had never been occupied. Thereafter, Philip appointed himself his cousin's guide, taking him to view the family portraits.

'Ah,' said Nicholas appreciatively. 'Those old generals holding their Khevenhüller hats, wearing the Grand Cross of the Maria Theresia Order – to which I myself belong in a humbler grade – how well they evoke the history of the Empire. We have similar portraits at home – these must be copies made when your great-grandfather, Count Gabriel, returned to Ireland. Count Felix – to whom we have just paid our respects on the staircase – is our common ancestor. He is my great-great-great-great-grandfather and, if I am not mistaken, your great-great-great-grandfather.'

'Yes.' Philip, well schooled in the subject by Uncle Dermod, nodded confirmation. 'He fought at the Battle of Kolín.'

'In which my old regiment, the Deutschmeister, was also engaged,' Nicholas informed him, to his deep satisfaction. 'We were brigaded (he spoke as if he had been present at the action) with two other regiments, under the command of an Irish officer, as it happens: Major General Thomas von Plunket. Military history is my great passion,' he added, with a smile that was almost apologetic.

The bonds between them seemed ever stronger.

'I am one hundred and thirty-seventh in descent from Adam,' said Philip, shyly introducing his genealogical *pièce de résistance*. 'Uncle Dermod worked it out.'

'How fascinating. In that case, since I believe there is a generation between us, I must be one hundred and thirty-eighth.'

Philip then took Nicholas to inspect successively the portrait of his grandfather, who had fought for the Pope and Don Carlos, and, returning to the staircase, the sword of Bonaventure Kinsella, from whom they both descended.

'My six-greats-grandfather,' said Nicholas, with a precision that would have gratified Dermod Kinsella.

'Did you say you were a knight of that Order the generals are wearing in the portraits?' asked Philip, recalling a remark made earlier by Nicholas.

'Yes, the Emperor gave me the Knight's Cross of the Maria Theresia Order – it was more than I deserved.'

'During the War?'

'No. During the restoration attempt in Hungary, in 1921.'

'What? Did you try to put the Emperor back on his throne, cousin Nicholas? Oh, how I wish I had been there. Tell me about it – please.'

Nicholas promised a detailed account of his adventures during the failed attempt by the Emperor Charles to regain his crown, but said it must be postponed until a more suitable occasion. Next day they went for a cross-country hack together when, his narrative disjointed by his repeatedly breaking off to jump enticing fences, Nicholas recounted the wartime exploits of the *K. und K. Infanterie-Regiment Nr. 4 Hoch- und Deutschmeister* on the Isonzo front, with much graphic detail, including the desperate hand-to-hand fighting at the village of Zagora, when the Fourth Battalion of the regiment saved the whole Austrian line by repelling superior Italian forces with repeated bayonet charges, until only two hundred men were left standing, out of eight hundred.

'That was in the Third Battle of the Isonzo; but we saved Gorizia from falling to the Italians.'

'So, there were three battles of the Isonzo?'

'In fact there were twelve – the last was our great victory at the Battle of Karfreit, known to our opponents as Caporetto.'

Encouraged by their growing intimacy, Philip confided to Nicholas the shameful fear he had felt when out hunting and how he hoped he had now conquered it, despite still feeling nervous and being secretly glad that the end of the season was approaching.

'You did very well,' was his cousin's verdict. 'Without fear, there can be no courage. Every soldier learns that.'

Emboldened by this to further confidence, Philip told Nicholas about Constanza and how he was pledged to be her knight and have her always as his lady. By the end of his brief, stumbling account he was conscious of a burning in his cheeks. So, it came as a huge relief when Nicholas, after a moment's reflection, said gravely:

'That was a noble promise and one befitting a Kinsella. You must always honour your lady and hold her in high respect – defend her, too, if ever the need arises.'

'Do you have a lady?' Philip asked timidly.

'I'm afraid not.' His cousin smiled with, for the first time, something wistful in his expression. 'The war I fought, in the freezing snow and ice, was not conducive to romantic encounters; and now – now my life is dedicated to the cause of my Emperor and King.'

Nicholas still insisted, however, on deferring any account of the restoration attempt until a more appropriate moment. He contented himself with initiating Philip into some of the arcana of the Danubian Monarchy, which the boy triumphantly retailed to Uncle Dermod.

'It means "Imperial and Royal" and the abbreviation is pronounced *kah-oont-kah*.'

'Yes, yes, I know.'

'The motto of the military academy at Wiener Neustadt (he pronounced it with great gusto) is "A.E.I.O.U." It stands for *Austriæ est imperare orbi universo –*'

'Of course, the maxim of Emperor Frederick III – not that he could be said to have lived up to it.'

'And the border you see around Austrian flags – all those triangles in red, white, black and yellow – that's called the *Zackenrand*.'

'I didn't know that.' Uncle Dermod made this admission with ill-concealed impatience. 'Did he tell you anything about events in Hungary five years ago?' He was as much agog as Philip to hear about the famous, if doomed, restoration attempt and disappointed by his nephew's negative response.

Nicholas came to spectate at Philip's fencing lesson with his father and ended up joining in. Afterwards he listened sympathetically to his complaints about the humiliation of fighting with bamboo foils. This produced a rewarding outcome. Two days later Nicholas accompanied Dermod on a trip to Dublin, returning just before Philip's bedtime.

'We have a present for you,' Nicholas said, handing him a long, narrow parcel.

Ripping it open, Philip found a matching pair of light, shorter than average, fencing foils with minimal guards.

'Italian.' Nicholas explained their provenance. 'Intended for ladies, I suspect, but adequate for your purposes. I'm afraid they're not in the best of condition.'

'We found them in an antique shop on the Quays,' said Uncle Dermod, smiling at Philip's evident delight.

Philip was inarticulate with gratitude. He knew his father would have no option but to agree to the use of these foils, since they were a present from his cousin. This was more than a kindly gesture: Nicholas was acknowledging his approaching manhood and the right it conferred on him to bear arms. His feeling of comradeship with his cousin was sealed by this symbolic gift.

'Look out for the next crossroads, Millicent.' Major Fenton glanced sidelong at his wife's insubstantial profile in the passenger seat. 'That's where we turn left – there's some kind of monument, covered in Catholic insignia and God knows what.'

'Yes, dear.'

'Can't get the hang of this godforsaken country at all.' The major swerved to avoid a donkey-cart on a blind corner. 'I still can't make out which side of the road they drive on – the middle, mostly, from what I've seen.' He chuckled appreciatively at this sally.

Major Fenton, as he freely confessed, was out of his depth in Ireland. He had come for the purpose of securing a property inherited by his wife and had stayed on to hunt. This transition reflected the restlessness that had afflicted him since the outbreak of peace. The ending of hostilities had left Major Fenton disoriented. In the early months of the War, as a subaltern on the Western Front, he had performed a series of actions which, in a more imaginative man, would have denoted high courage. This had led to a succession of staff postings in which his superiors, even as they planned ever more ambitious carnage, had felt there was something unnerving about his unquestioning acquiescence. On only one issue had he taken a dissident view: he had made no secret of his doubts about the propriety of England fighting alongside a race of perverts and back-stabbers such as the French, whose natural ally was surely the Hun. By the same token, he had regretted that Austria, which he associated with waltzes and excellent pastry, should have been suborned by Germany into entering the War on the wrong side. Recent events had confirmed him in this opinion.

'First-class performance today by that Austrian chap – absolutely first-rate. Blennerhassett couldn't believe his eyes.'

This was a reference to Count Nicholas Kinsella's win in the hunt point-to-point. Nicholas's relationship with the hunt had begun inauspiciously several days before. Going out at the end of a disappointing season that had culminated in a period of remarkably poor scent, Nicholas had reacted to the first successful draw of a covert by jumping every intervening fence until he was running close behind the tail hounds, to the fury of the Master.

'Look at that!' Colonel Blennerhassett blew out his moustache in rage. 'Another damned *hussar!*'

The Master's attitude had changed dramatically, however, during the point-to-point, after witnessing the exhibition of first-class horsemanship with which the visitor had won the cup, earning universal applause.

'My God,' said Miss Malley, '*can that man ride*.' She gazed fixedly at Nicholas Kinsella and drew so heavily on her cigarette that she smoked a third of its length before exhaling.

Philip's father had invited the most prominent members of the hunt to dinner at Lissanore, officially to celebrate the point-to-point, unofficially as a valedictory feast for his cousin at the end of his visit. So, Major Fenton now found himself negotiating the tortuous country roads *en route* to Castle Kinsella, confiding his thoughts on the day's events to his wife.

'Extraordinary thing is, they tell me he served in an infantry regiment – equivalent of our Guards, by the sound of it.'

'He's very distinguished-looking – and terribly handsome.' Mrs Fenton ventured an opinion, echoing the views of the female community of the county.

'Yes, yes. He's well turned-out – good tailor, obviously. No poodle-fakin' antics about him, though, I'm glad to say… Here we are.'

He turned in under the main gatehouse of Castle Kinsella and drove up the avenue to the gravel sweep where several other vehicles were parked, a couple of them in the process of disgorging passengers. Major Fenton caught a glimpse of Father Yves, his black-and-white Dominican habit flowing as he took a hurried shortcut from the chapel to the front door.

'Didn't realize we were dinin' with the Spanish Inquisition,' said the major facetiously. This *bon mot* entertained him so much, it put him in a good mood for the rest of the evening.

From the least frequented corner of the drawing room, Philip surveyed the assembling guests. He was dressed in his gala outfit of Eton suit, manfully ignoring the chafing of his collar and regretting that his short black jacket was so funereal and abbreviated, compared with the scarlet tailcoats worn by his father and other members of the hunt. Even Nicholas, engrossed in equine conversation with the now affable Colonel Blennerhassett, was resplendent in scarlet with the sky blue facings of a famous English hunt. Philip's presence was an exceptional concession, painfully negotiated in exchange for pledges of extra study, the performance of domestic chores and total self-effacement throughout the evening. He fingered his bow tie nervously and took a sip of lemonade. He overheard a young woman nearby confess to Mrs Blennerhassett that when Count Nicholas Kinsella had brought his heels together, bowed over her hand and *almost but not quite* brushed it with his lips, she had gone weak at the knees. Mrs Blennerhassett was less impressionable; but even she allowed that the visitor was extremely charming. She then diverted the conversation to the less emotionally charged topic of the weather, as Corristeen loomed at her elbow, bearing a tray laden with glasses of sherry.

'Sure, we never died a winter yet,' the butler said, genially picking up on the theme (he was at the gregarious stage of intoxication), 'isn't that the truth, ma'am? Can I tempt you ladies to an aperient?'

'Corristeen never disappoints.' Mrs Blennerhassett made this observation to her startled companion, eyeing the butler's retreating back.

Philip's line of vision was now invaded by the smiling faces of Uncle Arthur, flushed from triumphs in the new trout season, and Aunt Clara. By the time he had satisfied the requirements of polite conversation with them, dinner was announced. Miss Malley, who had ascertained that Nicholas Kinsella was committed to take a visibly gratified Mrs Fenton in to dinner, invited Philip to escort her. She had replaced the departed Mrs Blackwell as the lady who conducted a mild flirtation with Philip when no better substitute was on offer. Tonight she looked more feminine than he had ever seen her and she scarcely smelled of the stables at all.

The dining room of Lissanore, with its long table lit by tall candelabra, gleaming with crystal and overlooked from their gilt frames by the powdered or bewhiskered Austrian generals, presented the same spectacle as it must have done under the hospitable regime of its builder, the extravagant Gabriel, Count Kinsella. Corristeen, imbued with a sense of occasion, moved graciously behind the guests, dispensing wine and wisdom impartially. Liam, wearing his footman's livery, nervously seconded his attentions. Countess Kinsella noticed that Maura, the maid who had replaced Kitty, was wearing lipstick – an indulgence strictly reserved for Sundays – in evident tribute to the house guest. She thought that she would have a word with her later; then she recalled the extra five minutes she had spent at her own dressing-table that evening and thought that she would not.

'Why is he wearin' a curtain ring on his lapel?' Major Fenton asked his neighbour, staring at the front of Eanna Kinsella's stained evening-dress coat.

'That's the *fáinne*.'

'The what?'

'The *fáinne*. It means he can speak Irish.'

'And can he?'

'I understand there is some debate about that in Gaelic circles.'

'I see.' After uttering this diplomatic untruth, Major Fenton diluted his bewilderment with a generous intake of Count Kinsella's claret (by George, it was good stuff – not like the anaemic mouthwash served up by Blennerhassett).

The climax of the evening came when an accident at the sideboard wreaked havoc upon the pudding course, provoking an explosion of wrath from Corristeen, before which the two housemaids fled precipitately. With an effort, the butler recovered his composure.

'I'm sorry, ma'am, about that slight congtratomp,' he confided to an embarrassed Mrs Fenton, who happened to be seated nearest to him, 'but I'm that heart-scalded – them gerrills has me nearly compost mentis.'

He made a stately exit, but could be observed by those at the end of the table, when he reached the passage outside, hoisting a bottle of Médoc to his lips and taking a deep draught.

When the last guests had left, Count and Countess Kinsella returned to the drawing room where the surviving members of the party were Nicholas, Dermod and Philip (buried deep and immobile in an armchair, for fear of being noticed and ordered to bed). His father, aware of the situation, suppressed a smile and proffered fresh cigars to Nicholas and Dermod. He took out his pipe and started to kindle it; his wife perched on the arm of a sofa, leafing through a pile of music from the grand piano. Uncle Dermod began to cross-question Nicholas about the War and its aftermath, in the hope of drawing him out about the attempt to restore the monarchy in Hungary. Nicholas sat in an armchair, in a posture at once upright and relaxed, with one leg crossed over the other. During the past week his powerful presence had caused the reanimated atmosphere of the Danubian Monarchy to pervade the house. Now, as if conjuring phantoms out of the cigar smoke, he stared into the middle distance and spoke in the tone of one musing aloud.

'I remember – it seems only yesterday – how the *Hoch- und Deutschmeister* marched out from the Rossauer Barracks to war. The band played our famous regimental march, then the Radetzky, and we sang *"O du mein Österreich!"* The Viennese cheered us to the echo: we were the city's own regiment, besides being the Emperor's élite troops – *die Wiener Edelknaben,* the "Vienna Pages", they used to call the officers because they included so many archdukes and princes. The men, on the other hand, were recruited from the dregs of the populace and the criminal classes, yet you could not find better soldiers; they were comrades to whom one could entrust one's life – as I frequently did. My man Johann, who is downstairs now in your servants' hall, was my orderly during the War; we went through the Isonzo campaign together. We had no idea what lay ahead, though, when we marched through Vienna, with the brightest eyes in the city smiling on us and the men waving their hats.'

Nicholas paused to draw on his cigar then continued.

'A year after the War had ended, I returned to Vienna and found it a drab, impoverished German city: all the colourful soldiers and civilians from the different states of the Empire had gone – departed to their own grey republics. The streets stank of garbage, the citizens looked like beggars. Then I came across real beggars, slumped against the railings of the Volksgarten; starving cripples with limbs missing, begging for small change. Those pathetic scarecrows were my old Deutschmeisters. How many of those who hurried past had cheered them when they marched out four years earlier? I did what I could, for as many as I was able to help, but it was little enough.'

He flicked ash from his cigar with an angry gesture.

Uncle Dermod seized the moment.

'You helped try to repair the situation by bringing the Monarchy back in Hungary five years ago, did you not? Will you please tell us about it?'

Nicholas, who was now in the mood for reminiscence, complied. While Philip sat spellbound and the adults hung on every word, he told the story, displaying a gift for narrative often to be found in soldiers.

'Their Majesties landed secretly in a chartered aeroplane at Dénesfa Castle, the property of Count Cziráky, on the twentieth of October (the year was 1921). Her Majesty was carrying her seventh child, but was determined to be at her husband's side. There had been some confusion and we did not expect them until the following day. The leader of our small royalist army was Colonel Anton Lehár – brother of the composer Franz Lehár whose operettas you must have enjoyed (he smiled at his hostess) and a most loyal and gallant soldier. The King – as I shall call him since we are in Hungary – promoted him to general and gave him command of the enterprise.'

He pursued his tale: the jubilant entry of the royal couple into the city of Sopron in the Burgenland and the formation of a

281

Habsburg government, while Lehár prepared to embark his troops onto trains for an advance by rail on Budapest.

'On the barracks square in Sopron, the Ostenburg battalion and the rest of us roared out our oath of loyalty to King Charles IV: "Through water and fire, on sea, on the land and in the air – for God, King and Country!" I can hear it still.'

Philip, who was very susceptible to such romantic rhetoric, shivered with pleasure. In his imagination he travelled with the royalist convoy along the railway line towards the Hungarian capital, a triumphal progress, as Nicholas described it, with one garrison after another acclaiming the returning King: Győr, Komárom, Bicske…

'Then,' said Nicholas, 'we came to the outskirts of Buda. By this time the traitor Horthy, our forsworn Regent, was in a panic. Yet he still refused to surrender the throne to its rightful King. He secured violent declarations against His Majesty's return from the Entente powers, while that filthy Freemason, Beneš, who had become the Czech prime minister, driven by his hatred of the Habsburgs was orchestrating the pygmies of the Little Entente to threaten intervention. That played into the hands of Gömbös, who commanded Horthy's forces. He raised a band of several hundred students, armed them and placed them on a line of heights called the Türkensprung from which they were able to harass our men, while Gömbös brought up his troops. Our vanguard reached Budaörs, close to the capital, on Saturday night, the twenty-second of October, confident of victory. The following day, everything fell apart.'

Nicholas furrowed his brow, took a sip from the glass of brandy at his elbow and drew again on his cigar before resuming.

'On Sunday morning the Queen ordered Mass to be celebrated. We knelt beside the railway track – I believe I still bear the imprint of the cinders on my knees – and I can assure you it is extremely difficult for the most pious Catholic, if he is a soldier, to concentrate on his prayers while he can hear rifle fire not far away. By the end of Mass we could also hear artillery. Those infernal students had attacked our men, followed shortly by regular troops commanded by Gömbös – the lying traitor had told his soldiers, decent Hungarian patriots, that the King's army was mostly made up of "Austrian and Czech adventurers". To make matters worse, Lehár insisted on handing over command to his superior, General Hegedűs, whom even the King distrusted – and rightly so, since he was in league with Horthy. He asked for an armistice, ordered our forces to occupy vulnerable positions and assigned Horthy's men to the high ground. Then those treacherous hounds broke the armistice three hours early and overran our exhausted men while they slept, before dawn on Monday. Our army was by now split in two: the northern half was attacked on two fronts and gave way; the southern units held out, but no longer with any hope of victory. I had the consolation of sending two traitors to their reward before suffering a trivial wound that prevented my using a rifle. I escaped on board the royal train: His Majesty refused to leave a single wounded man behind – we left only our dead.'

Silence descended on the room. Nicholas expelled cigar smoke and stared sombrely into its blue wreaths.

'What happened then?' asked Dermod Kinsella.

'Their Majesties were effectively the prisoners of Horthy. They retired to Tata, to the castle of Count Esterházy who offered them hospitality. Their train was met by a cortège of carriages with splendidly liveried coachmen and grooms. It was the last day on which the Habsburgs lived in Hungary in royal state. As it happened, they were fortunate to live another day. I was uneasy about Their Majesties' safety, so I settled myself for the night on a sofa outside their apartments. Suddenly, I heard a suspicious noise and detected intruders. Six assassins – it is said they were Czechs and I hope that is true, for I could not bear to think of Hungarians attempting such a crime – had broken into the castle with the intention of murdering the King and Queen. Esterházy's valet heard them at the same time and we raised the alarm while rushing to intercept them. They were armed with pistols and hand grenades. Esterházy ran out in his nightshirt and threw one of the vermin downstairs, while his man hurled another through a window. I charged at a couple carrying grenades – I was fearful they might kill Their Majesties with them – but they had little stomach for a fight and turned tail. I have told you this in such detail, so you may understand how little I did. Nevertheless,' his chest heaved with pride, 'the All-Highest insisted on conferring upon me the Knight's Cross of the Maria Theresia Order. Undeserving though I was of the award, it is my most cherished honour.'

Philip shuddered with emotion. Nicholas refreshed himself with brandy.

'The rest is melancholy history. Their Majesties were once more forced into exile and our Apostolic King died a few months later. I escaped, with some other loyal officers, from the vengeance of the Regent. My greatest ambition is one day to kill Miklós Horthy. At least we satisfied the demands of honour.' For the first time, he looked directly at Philip. 'It is honour that distinguishes man from beast. Honour is everything.'

The boy stared, rapt, at this man who embodied all his ideals, who had just recounted his participation in a real-life adventure as romantic as any Ruritanian novel. Philip's mother seated herself at the piano, set some music on the stand and beckoned to Nicholas. He joined her as she struck up a rousing marching tune.

'Ah,' said Nicholas, laughing. 'Radetzky – how splendid.'

He studied the score attentively, turning the pages for her. Countess Kinsella was an accomplished pianist and it was a rendition to satisfy even a Viennese connoisseur. After the march she played *The Blue Danube* and several other popular waltzes. There followed a muttered consultation with Nicholas, the two of them scanning sheets of music on which the name of Haydn was discernible. Then sounded a stately crash of introductory chords, after which Nicholas stood to attention and began to sing in a thrilling baritone. Instinctively, the other men in the room rose to their feet, as they recognized the anthem of the Habsburg Empire:

> 'Gott erhalte, Gott beschütze
> Unsern Kaiser, unser Land!
> Mächtig durch des Glaubens Stütze,
> Führ' er uns mit weiser Hand!
> Laßt uns seiner Väter Krone
> Schirmen wider jeden Feind:
> Innig bleibt mit Habsburgs Throne
> Österreichs Geschick vereint!'

Nicholas repeated the final phrase with feeling and the last sonorous notes reverberated through the frame of the grand piano, before slowly fading into silence.

'I cannot believe what we have lost,' said Dermod, after a moment, in a brittle voice.

'What has been lost can be regained.' Nicholas spoke with quiet assurance.

Philip noticed how his hazel eyes deepened in colour to dark emerald as he said this.

Down in the kitchen, Bridie Byrne observed to her colleagues: 'The Quality are havin' a bit of a hooley.'

Next morning the whole family assembled to see Nicholas off. Just before getting into his car, he shook hands formally with Philip and asked him a succinct question.

'*Habsburgstreue?*' His eyeglass gleamed interrogatively.

Philip, too overcome with emotion at this parting to answer, nodded vigorously. It was true, he thought, as he waved after the debonair sports car receding from view round the head of the avenue – where he had watched Constanza vanish, months previously – at that moment there was nobody in all Europe who could be described as more fervently *habsburgstreue* than himself. Surely his cousin would not disappear permanently: he was, after all, family. Philip had a keen intuition that Nicholas was someone who would have a significant influence on his future life.

CHAPTER XVII

'GOODBYE now, Philip. Be a good boy and work hard.' His mother hugged him in farewell then called out to her other sons who were already silhouettes inside their father's car, in the darkness of an autumn evening: 'Safe journey.'

Philip turned away, with a pang, and climbed into the car, which was precariously overloaded with trunks and other impedimenta necessary to equip three boys for a term at school. Light from the open front door illuminated the steps and the gravel, reinforced by headlamps as Count Kinsella started the engine. Philip and Dominick waved back at their mother until the turn into the avenue hid the house from view; Edmund sat immobile in front. There was little conversation during the journey to the port. Count Kinsella made occasional observations, usually relating to places they passed. In the back seat, Dominick exchanged sporadic remarks with Philip, while Edmund remained uncommunicative, his thoughts already running on the politics of the new school year and his ambitions to rise in the college hierarchy.

During the two years that had elapsed since the visit of his cousin Nicholas, life had at first continued in its familiar routine for Philip, only to change significantly towards the end. Father Yves had given up his tutelage that summer and returned to France, his volume of apologetics on the *filioque* clause finally completed, to resume the war against his arch-enemy Père Boscher within his own order and the Jesuit *canaille*, as he insistently phrased it, without. It was into the custody of this same Jesuit rabble that Philip was bound – a destination at which Father Yves had shaken his head sadly – now that the time had come for him to join his brothers at their public school in England. A similar fate had overtaken Tom Dixon who had simultaneously been dispatched to Clongowes, much to the approval of Uncle Eanna, an alumnus of that institution, who thought it a more suitable education than the anglicizing influence to which his nephews were being exposed. When he heard that Philip was to follow his elder brothers in undergoing what he regarded as a process of cultural deracination, he had ventured to express his dissatisfaction at breakfast one morning.

'Don't be so insular.' Dermod reproved his brother. 'The boys are being educated at what I regard as the best school in England.'

'What was wrong with Clongowes? I was there for five years.'

'I rest my case.'

During the last stage of the drive Philip found himself nodding off into a light slumber. On his mother's insistence, he had spent the afternoon in bed, to conserve his energy for the overnight journey, but had been too excited to sleep. He awoke with a start when his father said:

'Well, we did that in pretty good time – just coming into Rosslare now.'

A porter loaded their luggage onto a trolley and wheeled it along the lamp-lit quayside, alive with the bustle of departure and dominated by the twin-funnelled steamship moored alongside, with a saint's name painted on its bows and its portholes hospitably ablaze with light. Count Kinsella came aboard with his sons, saw them suitably disposed and chatted briefly, before shaking hands with each in turn.

'Bit of an adventure for you, old man,' he said to Philip, smiling encouragingly.

He waved once from the quay as he walked back to his car; for him, this trip was a routine chore. Edmund ensconced himself in the steamer's small drawing room and signalled his disinclination for the society of his siblings by immersing himself in a book. Philip and Dominick stayed on deck to watch the preparations for departure. After the ship had cast off and moved out into the open sea for the short crossing of St George's Channel, the two boys remained by the rail, enjoying the balmy night air and the smell of the sea. Philip had entertained a secret dread of looking foolish by succumbing to seasickness, but the surface of the water was as smooth as glass inshore and barely ruffled by the time they had left the land far astern. The companionable atmosphere prompted Dominick to a contrite admission.

'You know all that stuff I told you – about ghastly initiation rites for new boys and so on? Well, it was all made up. We don't go in for anything like that at school.'

'I guessed that,' said Philip (though, in fact, he had not been entirely unconcerned).

'It's not at all a bad place and you can have quite a good time if you know the ropes. The rules are pretty strict, of course; but you either go along with them or learn how to get round them without being found out – it's up to you. Just at first, though, I'd advise you to toe the line, at least until you understand how things work. It's actually the best place I can think of to be at school – if we have to go to school. I wouldn't want to go anywhere else.'

This reassured Philip considerably. He spent the rest of the three-hour crossing quizzing Dominick about the college and its customs until the lights of Fishguard drew near. Edmund emerged on deck and approached with an officious, governess-like expression.

'You know how Edmund is always going on about overthrowing the ruling class,' said Dominick, before he came within earshot. 'Well, that's all nonsense. All he thinks about is power.'

On the quay at Fishguard, their eldest brother insisted on monitoring the transfer of their luggage from the ship to the guard's van of the waiting train in its unfamiliar chocolate and cream livery ('like an éclair,' Dominick remarked whimsically), harassing a porter to extract some item he required from the anonymous pile of trunks and suitcases. Dominick listened attentively to the voices of the railway staff, eager to add the Welsh accent to his repertoire of mimicry. His verdict was dismissive.

'The Welsh seem a pretty miserable lot.'

'They have a very strong radical tradition,' said Edmund, almost certainly reinforcing it by the inadequacy of the tip he pressed into the breathless porter's hand with an air of magnanimity.

'Breakfast is served from 5.40, gentlemen,' announced an English attendant as they settled into their compartment, 'after we leave Swansea. We get into Paddington at 9.45.'

'I don't think I shall be feeling much like having breakfast at twenty to six.' Dominick settled himself against the cushions. 'Let's make it half past seven. That gives us four hours to snooze.'

Philip leaned back and shut his eyes. He liked trains and felt relaxed; there were no other travellers in the compartment. Presently he dozed off, woke briefly when the train jolted into motion then slept sporadically for most of the journey. Grey light was creeping around the window blinds when the boys stretched, yawned and rose reluctantly to perform a perfunctory toilet. By the time they arrived in the restaurant car it was filling up with passengers. Dominick belied his own prediction by eating a hearty breakfast, with Philip a close rival, revelling in the holiday atmosphere of this well-appointed restaurant on wheels. Fortified, they returned to their compartment and watched the landscape of the Thames valley, an attractive succession of farmhouses, old churches and inns, flow past the train window until a deterioration in the scenery warned them they were drawing close to the outskirts of London.

When they emerged onto the crowded platform at Paddington and retrieved their luggage, Edmund led the way to another part of the station, where they boarded a local train. At the end of this second, brief journey they followed the trolley carrying their school trunks to where a row of taxis waited. Philip peered out of the cab window, up at the vastness of the royal castle that overlooked the town, its battlements and machicolations resembling a giant version of Lissanore. The taxi chugged its way laboriously out of the town and Philip sat back pensively. Now that they were nearing their destination he felt apprehensive. Dominick's account of life at the college had been reassuring and he clearly enjoyed it, but the disturbing question remained: what would school actually be like? He was roused from his worrisome reverie by Dominick saying jauntily:

'Here we are. Back at the old coll.'

Entrance gates flanked by large stone piers, topped by lamps and a curved balustraded wall, loomed up and they drove through, passing a lodge house on the left. The one thing for which Philip was unprepared was the beauty of the place. The avenue opened onto a vista of grass and trees framing a great white, three-storeyed house dominated by a massive portico of four double columns supporting a pediment. Philip's spirits rose. Whatever kind of Dotheboys Hall he had remotely dreaded, it did not seem possible any sinister institution could be accommodated in such noble premises.

When they had paid off the taxi and stood surrounded by luggage, Edmund made haste to separate himself from his younger brothers, as though afraid of being discovered in their company. His parting from Philip was perfunctory.

'Dominick will show you the ropes.' He turned away, then swung round again for a moment, as though struck by a sudden concern. 'For heaven's sake, don't do anything to embarrass me.'

'What did I tell you?' Dominick gestured at their brother's retreating back with a vindicated air. 'Power mad. He wants to be a captain next year – the whole school knows.'

The ensuing hour passed in a blurred confusion for Philip. Within minutes he sighted his first Jesuit, a tall man in a long black gown with wings, twin lengths of black cloth swinging behind him from each shoulder as he swept past with a preoccupied air, accompanied by a worried-looking senior boy.

'Crisis.' Dominick interpreted the scene.

'What's wrong?'

'Several tea leaves missing from the Js' supplies, I should guess.'

'What are those things hanging down from his cassock?'

'Empty sleeves. The Js used to have four arms each, until they got two of them cut off to make them look like human beings.'

Dominick, despite his teasing, organized his brother's integration into the school community with efficiency. Eventually Philip was interviewed briefly by another Jesuit, who made entries in some kind of register and issued a stream of incomprehensible instructions which clearly made sense to Dominick.

'Thank you, Father,' said Philip politely as they withdrew.

'You don't call him "Father".' Dominick corrected him as they collected Philip's trunk and headed towards a dormitory on the third floor, at the rear of the building.

'Why not? He's a priest, isn't he?'

'No, he's not. He's a scholastic – he won't be a priest for years yet.'

It occurred to Philip that the protocol surrounding the school hierarchy was going to pose rather a challenge. So far, they had encountered very few other boys and the school buildings were practically deserted. Dominick had explained that term did not begin until the following day, but boys travelling from a distance had been given dispensation to arrive early, to help them settle in and recover from their journey. The dormitory, when they entered it, was empty except for one boy of Philip's age unpacking a trunk. He was slightly built, with light brown hair very neatly brushed and an expression of lively intelligence. He looked towards the new arrivals but, in deference to Dominick's seniority, waited to be addressed.

'Hello,' said Dominick. 'Who might you be?'

'Barrington. I've just arrived, a day early, like you.'

'Well, Barrington, this is my kid brother who will be polluting this dormitory for the duration, or until he is sacked. I advise you to count the teaspoons, or whatever valuables you have in that ridiculously large trunk, while he is around. His name, well known in criminal circles, is Kinsella.'

'Hello.' Barrington grinned at Philip, greatly amused by Dominick's banter and flattered to be addressed at such length by an older boy.

'Hello.' Philip smiled back.

'Right, then,' said Dominick, relieved to have found a means of unburdening himself of his fraternal responsibilities. 'I shall leave you two to introduce yourselves and get on with things. *Au revoir, mes enfants.*'

He made a brisk exit.

'I say,' said Barrington, 'your brother is pretty good at ragging – verbally, I mean. He has what I should call a dangerous gift of eloquence.'

Philip stared in speechless astonishment at Barrington.

'Scar – *Scaramouche!*' he managed to stammer at last. 'You must have read *Scaramouche.*'

'Of course,' said Barrington airily. 'I have read most of Sabatini. I didn't realize that was a quotation, though, when I said it. I accumulate so much information it is difficult to remember where it comes from. Reading is my great vice.'

In corroboration, he opened the lid of his trunk to reveal rows of books interspersed with the barest essentials of clothing, his habiliments clearly sacrificed to his acknowledged passion.

'Gosh.' Philip was impressed. 'That's a whole library.'

'Keeping it from the attention of the Js may prove something of a problem,' said Barrington thoughtfully. 'Right now, however, I suggest we repair to the refectory, where they are serving what they are pleased to call a cold collation for today's early arrivals. We can talk about books, if you are interested.'

'I love books – I read them all the time.' Philip was delighted at his good luck in meeting a kindred spirit – and one whose dormitory he would be sharing. Already he began to feel that school life might be rewarding and enjoyable. In the nearly empty refectory where they lunched in comparative solitude, Barrington discussed the personalities in his social circle, which he appeared implicitly to be inviting Philip to join.

'Manley won't be here until tomorrow. He is rather a project of mine. He was a complete shambles, but I put him back on his feet. There is still work to be done, though.'

'What do you mean by "put him back on his feet"? Did he fall over?'

'Manley was born fallen over. There are some men who have to be put on their feet from time to time. My Uncle Guy is like that – my people had to put him on his feet three times. It didn't really work. He lives in Kenya now. Compared to him, Manley is a great success – unless he has wobbled again during the holidays, which is more than likely. I think, Kinsella, you would fit in pretty well with our set. Your appreciation of Sabatini is sufficient recommendation for me. You can judge for yourself tomorrow when Manley turns up – if he remembers the start of term, that is. Then there are Pontifex and Leigh, quite good men. If you aren't going to finish that jam, would you mind if I have the last spoonful?'

When the innumerable distractions at the beginning of term finally allowed, Philip wrote his first letter home:

'A. M. D. G.

Dear Mummie and Papa,

I am settling in well at school. I am in Figures I, my form master is Mr Ellis who is a Jesuit but not a priest. In fact he is a scholastic. My best friends are Barrington and Manley, also Pontifex and Leigh are quite good friends. My house is Heathcote but, as Barrington says, it is not of the least consequence (he talks like that a lot of the time). We only have houses for games, we don't actually live in them the way they do at other schools. Manley and Pontifex are in Heathcote too, but Leigh is in Eccles. We are all in the same dormitory.

'*I am a Roman, but Barrington is a Corinthian so we are opponents. There is a special holiday and a big tea for the winners at the end of the year so we are awfully keen to beat each other.*

'*I do not think I am going to be any good at rugger. I want to row which is very much the thing here, but I shall have to learn to swim properly in the swimming bath which is a bore as the water smells and tastes horrible with antiseptic or something if I am to go on the river. The great thing is I can keep up my fencing, the instructor was quite surprised at how much I knew but he said I had an old-fashioned style, so that is one in the eye for you, Papa. I shall also be able to ride, which is terrific.*

'*I speak better French than my teacher, but Barrington says I must pretend to make mistakes or people will think it is side, which would be fatal, according to Barrington. I am doing Spanish with Mr Flores and I do not have to pretend to make mistakes with him, they are real. The big problem, as we knew it would be, is mathematics. I was sent to see Mr Sinclair and he said he hardly knew where to begin. Then he said at the beginning, he supposed. It is a pity after you spent money on that teacher from the National School to coach me during the summer. I don't really remember much of it and in any case they seem to do it all differently here. I promise I shall try hard.*

'I am joining the altar staff, but just as a torch-bearer sometimes at Benediction. It will be ages before I am allowed to be an acolyte as I was for Canon Roche. Barrington has some very interesting books, he reads them with a torch (that was what reminded me about altar-serving) under the bedclothes after lights out.

'I must go now, so love to both of you and Uncles Dermod, Eanna, Ulick, Arthur and Aunt Clara and a big hug for Dee-Dee. Also Grandma.

Love,

Philip

P.S. When I said Barrington was a Corinthian I made a mistake. He is a Carthaginian.'

Philip's references to the various institutions and customs of the school would have baffled an untutored reader, but his father was himself an old boy and his mother was long used to receiving such epistles from her other sons, so the scene he described was perfectly comprehensible at home. The arrival at school of Manley on the first day of term had been awaited by Philip with keen curiosity, having heard so much about this 'project' of Barrington who constantly required to be put on his feet. He turned out to be an amiable boy with fair hair, rather startling blue eyes and an accommodating disposition. He immediately fell in with any suggestion made by Barrington and smiled tolerantly when his friend offered any criticism of his supposedly too passive demeanour. He accepted Philip incuriously as an established element of school life, behaving as if he had known him for years and only the holidays had temporarily separated them. The other members of the Barrington set, Pontifex and Leigh, similarly accepted Philip on the basis of their leader's approval, though after a few preliminary enquiries such as Manley had not troubled to make.

'Are you a brother of the two Kinsellas we have here already?' asked Pontifex. He wore a judicial air, his brow furrowed below straight black hair, his frame rather heavy-boned, threatening to become thickset in later years.

'Yes.'

'There's a Kinsella, I think, in Grammar II…' said Pontifex, tapping a finger on the palm of his other hand.

'Yes, that's Dominick.'

'He's quite jolly,' said Barrington, 'really pretty decent.'

'…And an older one in Middle Playroom.'

'That's Edmund, he's my eldest brother.'

'Edmund?' Leigh, who had a rather pointed chin, copper-tinged hair and slight freckles, reminding Philip of Tom Dixon, gave a snort of derision. 'What a weedy name.' (The great concern of Leigh's life was to conceal the fact that his own middle name was Fortescue.)

'It could have been much worse,' said Philip, glad to be able to regale his new friends with an entertaining snippet of information he had just recalled. 'My parents nearly called him Hyacinth.'

This revelation provoked raucous and prolonged hilarity. It helpfully sealed the unspoken covenant by which Philip was admitted to the coterie surrounding his sponsor Barrington. The invasion of the school by an increasing number of Kinsellas seemed also to provoke the interest of several members of staff, including Father de la Pole, the acerbic Jesuit who sometimes took Philip's class for catechetical instruction.

'Another Kinsella?' He sat down, laid his biretta at the side of his desk and steepled his fingers enquiringly. 'Are the other two siblings of yours?'

'I – I think so, Father,' said Philip, guessing at the meaning of this term.

'You think so? Such uncertainty suggests a less than close-knit family.' The more sycophantic elements in the class giggled appreciatively; the Barrington set maintained a supportive gravitas.

297

'Well, since you are the third and youngest brother to grace us with your presence, as a means of distinguishing you from the others we must call you Kinsella Minimus.' A moment later, after he had surveyed the boys seated around Philip, a witty refinement suggested itself. Suppressing a thin smile that nearly betrayed itself at the corners of his mouth, the priest added: 'Kinsella Minimus and Pontifex Maximus.'

This typically Jesuit joke, rehearsed before a youthful audience with some familiarity with Latin, provoked genuine amusement; even the Barringtons laughed, a trifle nervously in the case of Pontifex who was startled to find himself suddenly precipitated into the limelight and feared some adverse consequences. These eventually materialized in the form of an attempt to attach to him the nickname 'Max' (not, in any case, particularly offensive) and a more half-hearted effort to christen Philip 'Minnie.' Since the instigator was an unpopular boy named Thomson and the Barrington set refused to give these names any currency, this initiative quickly petered out. The episode impressed upon Philip the protective advantages of belonging to an established and tightly knit group among his classmates. He was the sole newcomer to the Barrington set: their friendship had been established at the preparatory school, which sat on a shelf of the hill behind the college, within easy walking distance beyond its fields and woods, separated by a disused and sunken avenue from the tree-fringed cricket flats and pavilion.

Philip took a keen pleasure in exploring his surroundings; this activity, however, was fraught with hazards – it was difficult to know which areas were out of bounds and which could lawfully be accessed by someone so junior as himself. The stately pillared portico which had provided his first sight of the school belonged to the original building, known as the White House. To the left of it ran the accumulation of structures that had been added: the first block accommodating a study place, theatre (the school had a strong tradition of amateur dramatics) and dormitory; then the chapel, after which a row of buildings ran at right angles towards the rear, including the swimming bath, more classrooms and a dormitory, terminating in the tall, square château-like structure that housed the Jesuit community. Beyond that, further to the rear, stood the Ambulacrum or 'Jubilee Hall'. Outside the sprawl of the main structure was a motley cluster of smaller buildings containing the dairy, stables and garage, carpenter's shop and similar offices. The most striking landmark, behind the college, was the tall War Memorial, where Mass was celebrated annually by the Rector for Old Boys who had fallen in the Great War and earlier conflicts.

What excited Philip's curiosity was the wooded terrain to the rear. The playground was nothing more sophisticated than a large field, the grass much worn from games of rounders and many schoolboy scuffles. Beyond, on rising ground, was the tree-crowned slope known as the Beeches, theoretically out of bounds except to the most senior boys, but regularly invaded by the unentitled. The gracious old beech trees there recalled the demesne at Lissanore. Setting out to explore the woods one afternoon, Philip made a discovery that reminded him even more strongly of home. Taking the path that skirted the far side of the playground he entered the woods, walking up through the Beeches, and had not gone far when he was halted in his tracks by a striking spectacle. This was a breathtaking view over the Thames valley to distant hills, outlined indistinctly in a purplish haze. It was the foreground of this landscape, however, that held him spellbound: the great royal castle rose up, across the fields, its walls and battlements shrouded in autumn mist, like a mirage. The spectacle reminded him of his favourite view at home: Lissanore, as first glimpsed from the field at the top of the boreen. Although the royal residence was much grander, the gothic architecture was similar; there was even a drum tower, though viewed from this angle it stood at the opposite end from the one at Lissanore, like a mirror image. The sudden impression was sufficient to send a spasm of homesickness through him.

He stood for several minutes absorbing this view then walked on for a short distance, savouring the differing perspectives as he progressed. Finally, feeling any further exploration could only prove anticlimactic, he turned and began to retrace his steps. This unexpected view of the castle and its superficial resemblance to Lissanore had filled his mind with thoughts of home more intense than he had entertained since his arrival at school. Moments later, he was given a more acute reminder of domestic connexions.

As he passed the trunk of a large tree, a hand shot out and caught his arm in a vice-like grip that made him cry out in alarm and pain. He found himself gazing up into the enraged face of his brother Edmund.

'You little swine!' Edmund's face was contorted with anger and hate. 'How dare you?'

'Wh-What?' Philip whimpered in fear and bewilderment. He had never seen Edmund looking like this.

'*How dare you?*' His brother snarled with rage. 'How dare you tell lies about me?'

'What lies? I – I haven't told any lies… I don't know what you mean… Ooh, you're hurting me.' Philip began seriously to think that Edmund had gone mad and might be about to murder him.

'Don't play the innocent – you know very well what I'm talking about.'

'I don't! Honestly, I don't.'

'Of course you do. Making up that vicious lie about my being called – being called that ridiculous name.'

'What name? I don't know what you're talking about.'

'You told everybody,' Edmund spoke through gritted teeth, 'that my name was (he hesitated and lowered his voice, glancing around self-consciously as though he feared someone might be within earshot) *Hyacinth*.'

He pronounced the name with loathing, like the hiss of a snake. Understanding dawned on Philip.

'No, no, I didn't say that was your name – I said they nearly called you that… When you were born.'

'You weren't around then – how would *you* know?' Edmund was assailed by the first doubts that there might be some substance to the claim.

'Mummie told me. She said some of our cousins were called that. Honestly, I didn't mean any harm…'

'Harm!' Edmund's fury rose to a crescendo with the knowledge that there actually was some link, however tenuous, between himself and the odious name. 'Have you any idea what I've had to put up with in the Playroom? You little brat, I'll harm *you*. I'm going to thrash you within an inch of your life.'

He bent down to where some broken branches lay on the ground, searching for a suitable punitive switch. In doing so he relaxed his concentration, so that his grip on Philip's arm grew lighter. Seizing the opportunity, Philip wriggled from his grasp and ran frantically down the path towards the school, his heart pounding. Behind him, he heard an angry shout as Edmund started in pursuit. Within a minute the wooded fringe of the path gave way on one side to the open vista of the playground. Here was salvation: not only was it occupied by several groups of boys, but one of them was in conversation with a young scholastic. It would be unthinkable for Edmund to assault him in front of a J. Breathing heavily as he slowed to walking pace, Philip sidled up close to this group and loitered, pretending to adjust a shoelace. Out of the corner of his eye he saw Edmund, his face a mask of frustration, surveying the scene from the edge of the woods. Then, realizing the futility of attempting any further aggression, he set off again down the path, eventually disappearing from sight. Philip waited cautiously for about ten minutes then made his way by the most frequented routes to the Lower Line Playroom, where he found Barrington and his friends.

'I say,' Barrington greeted him, 'you look as if you had seen a ghost.'

'Your brother was looking for you,' Leigh told him, not without a hint of malice. 'He seemed in rather a wax.'

'He *is* in a wax. He attacked me just now in the woods. I thought he was going to kill me.'

'You can't really blame him,' said Pontifex, who prided himself on taking an objective view of things, 'after what you told us about him. He must be getting a terrible ragging about being called Hyacinth.'

'He's *not* called Hyacinth. I only said my parents nearly called him that. I didn't think you were going to tell the whole school,' he added reproachfully.

'I didn't tell anybody,' said Manley, with a shy, placatory smile. The others' silence testified they could not give the same assurance.

'Look here,' Barrington said to Philip, 'you could hardly expect us not to dine out on a gem like that. Frankly, your brother is not exactly the most popular man in the school. In any case, you didn't tell us to keep it quiet. As a general rule, it is always best not to talk about your people.'

'But you did it first – you said an uncle of yours had to be put on his feet three times and went to South Africa.'

'Kenya. Uncles are different – unless they get sent to prison or something awful. If you have a colourful or eccentric uncle there is no harm in regaling the chaps with stories about him.'

It occurred to Philip that, in the matter of eccentric uncles, he was exceptionally well provided; but he refrained from saying so, having resolved that no more family revelations would pass his lips for the duration of his time at school. Edmund made no further attempt to molest him: he was by now leading a beleaguered existence. For years he had painstakingly accumulated, without achieving popularity, a kind of grudging respect. He had meticulously negotiated all the pitfalls of school life, in his single-minded pursuit of status. Now, as a consequence of Philip's unthinking indiscretion, all that progress had been undone. For someone who sought influence over others and prided himself on his political acumen, Edmund handled things very ineptly. A youth with a more relaxed temperament would probably have been able to defuse the crisis with a combination of self-deprecation and reciprocal banter. Edmund, however, took himself extremely seriously and this narcissism aggravated the situation, as his tormentors remorselessly exploited his vulnerability. 'Violet', 'Rosie', 'Pansy' and every other conceivable horticultural allusion were employed by his classmates and their seniors to address him, stimulated by his evident discomfiture. The long-term outcome was that the nickname 'Daisy' was eventually fastened upon him, to endure for the remainder of his schooldays. He never forgave his youngest brother for being the cause of this humiliation.

Edmund's still smouldering resentment created some tension during the journeys between school and home for the Christmas and Easter holidays; but since he had never been particularly communicative towards his brothers and Dominick, always in high spirits on such occasions, more than compensated with his lively conversation, this was a minor inconvenience. By the end of his first year at school, Philip was thoroughly integrated into the college community. He had undergone his baptism of fire at the hands of its severe disciplinary system, having written thousands of lines imposed as punishment and been given ferulae several times for various offences. Ferulae bruised the palms of the hands, which were lashed with a mysterious implement resembling a razor-strop, wielded too quickly to be glimpsed in action before it was once again concealed behind the folds of a Jesuit gown, so that a blueish swelling arose. For some obscure reason, ferulae were awarded in multiples of three strokes, the sentence written on a cheque-like slip for presentation in an office incongruously situated among the music rooms, where the prescribed punishment was meted out with what Philip regarded as unchristian heartiness by a muscular J. He had also been birched, though fairly lightly, by a prefect who was suspected of having been suborned for the purpose by Edmund. The crucial requirement was to endure punishment with the most complete stoicism, displaying no signs of distress; by an effort of will, Philip passed this test.

Gradually, the idiosyncratic customs and routine of the school turned into familiar, ingrained habit. It soon became second nature to Philip to preface every piece of writing with the formula 'A. M. D. G.' – the initial letters of the Jesuit motto 'Ad majorem Dei gloriam'. The emblem of the gilded horseshoe with three ornamental crosses, from the armorial bearings of the family of Saint Stanislaus, patron of the college, acquired a homely familiarity. Uncle Dermod, who wrote to him frequently, sometimes enclosing scrawled messages of goodwill from his brothers Eanna and Ulick, supplied much recondite information on such matters.

'I believe the horseshoe emblem of Kostka, the family of Saint Stanislaus, is what is known in Polish heraldry as a "herb"... With regard to the empty sleeves depending from the Jesuits' soutanes, I understand these are called "zamora" – after a Spanish town, I think, though I cannot now recall where I learned this. I have also heard, however, that they derive from the sixteenth-century costume of students at the Sorbonne in Paris. It might interest you to know that the academic dress of the

304

University of Prague was modelled on the Jesuit gown... The old college custom of calling a holiday a "Blandyke", about which you wondered, refers to a village of that name near St Omer, which the Jesuits acquired in 1649 and where their pupils spent their holidays...'

Philip carefully committed these antiquarian arcana to memory, with a view to employing them to subdue Barrington on occasions when his pedantry became excessive.

'A fairly creditable report, old man,' his father commented when he returned home at the end of his first school year. 'I'm afraid, though, we shall never make a mathematician out of you. On the other hand, a very decent performance in English and History. As for French, thanks to Father Yves it is your second tongue, so your success is hardly surprising. I was concerned you might have found yourself at something of a disadvantage through not having gone to the preparatory school, as Edmund and Dominick did. I even wondered if it had been slightly selfish of me and your mother to have kept you at home for so long; but you seem to have adapted to it all pretty effortlessly. We must have a session in the ballroom and see how your fencing is coming on. Tell me again what that young ass said about the style I taught you...'

One day, late in the holidays, when Philip was entertaining his mother with tales of life at school, she said: 'Your friend Barrington sounds a very bright spark. What is his Christian name?'

'I don't know.' Philip was compelled to make this admission after a moment's baffled consideration.

'How very English.'

CHAPTER XVIII

IN THE Rudiments classroom, where the inmates were undergoing catechetical instruction, contentment reigned. Barrington was surreptitiously reading *Perishable Goods*, by Dornford Yates under his desk. Pontifex and Leigh, under the same clandestine conditions, were playing a game on a travelling chess set that had three pieces missing, using matchsticks as substitutes. Manley was critically inspecting a model of a battleship he was constructing, which he felt was not turning out well. Around the room, other boys scribbled lines they had been given as impositions, struggled to decode Cicero in preparation for a more demanding class to come, or simply luxuriated in the forty-five minutes of leisure afforded by the religious lesson.

In front of this unheeding audience sat the facilitator of their recreation, Father Walton, deeply immersed in his explanation of the contrasting notions of sacramental grace *ex opere operato* and *ex opere operantis*. It was possibly too advanced a topic for a Rudiments class, but he had been expertly lured onto this theme by Todhunter, the class genius (except in Barrington's estimation), whose relentless pursuit of prizes in both the academic and sporting arenas had inevitably provoked the distortion of his name to Pothunter. He had earned immunity from being ragged about his reputation as a 'swot', partly by his parallel successes on the sports field and partly by employing his erudition to distract masters by posing challenging questions. His greatest coup, just before the Christmas holidays, had been to engross the attention of the diminutive Mr Lynch, an earnest young scholastic who was threatening to become importunate about the Rudiments' lack of proficiency in geometry theorems, by asking: 'In Canon Law, is it permissible for a man to marry his widow's sister?'

The baffled cleric had wrestled with this conundrum for seven minutes (as triumphantly recorded by Pontifex on his battered half-hunter) before suddenly pounding the desk and exclaiming: 'Oh, my giddy aunt! If she's the chap's widow – the chap must be dead and in no position to marry anyone!'

This outcome had been greeted with ironic applause, taken in good part by the victim. Today, Potty had successfully diverted Father Walton from investigating his charges' progress in catechism onto a learned disquisition on sacramental grace, having ingenuously queried the meaning of the two contrasting Latin phrases. Not only did this ploy enable the class to pursue its own interests, but when practised upon the more gullible masters it also earned credit for intellectual curiosity. ('Such enquiring minds,' Father Walton observed later to a stony-faced Father de la Pole.) Once the fish had taken the fly, Potty's remaining responsibility was to play him, posing supplementary questions if the monologue showed any sign of petering out. In this instance, no such problem presented itself.

'The first recorded use of the term *ex opere operato* – though I may stand to be corrected – is by Peter of Poitiers in the twelfth century...'

With a grunt of satisfaction, Pontifex took one of Leigh's rooks. Philip watched apathetically; he was not engaged in any occupation, simply enjoying the luxury of daydreaming. The priest's theological exposition reminded him of Father Yves discoursing on the controversy surrounding the *filioque* clause, without actually explaining it. He had only been nine at the time; now he had turned fourteen and would probably have merited a proper explanation. He recalled that Father Yves had been scathingly contemptuous of 'Jesuit *canaille*'; he wondered if he would have contradicted Father Walton's interpretation of *ex opere operato*. It occurred to him that, if Pothunter ever ran out of material, he might gain kudos by asking Father Walton to explain the *filioque* clause. Philip wondered where Father Yves was now and what he was doing. It was strange how people who were very much part of one's daily life eventually departed and were lost to sight.

Philip was well into his second year at school. The passage of time had similarly promoted his brothers in the school hierarchy. Edmund had attained apotheosis as a member of Rhetoric, the senior and uniquely privileged class in the school. This longed-for destination, however, had turned to gall and wormwood for him, since he had failed to fulfil his long-standing ambition of becoming a captain, one of the godlike figures at the apex of authority within the college. This was despite – possibly on account of – his having announced his desire to try his vocation as a Jesuit at the conclusion of his final school year. If he had counted on this to seal his eligibility for a captaincy, he had badly miscalculated. 'Look upon this disappointment as the first of many sacrifices you will make as a Jesuit, in a spirit of abandonment of self and unreserved acceptance of the sometimes inscrutable will of your superiors,' his spiritual director had unctuously counselled him. This characteristic conduct of his Jesuit principals was intended, they claimed, to enhance his spiritual wellbeing. One immediate consequence was that, with more substantial grievances to preoccupy him, Edmund's attitude towards Philip had reverted to his former casual indifference.

Across the aisle, muffled gasps of triumph and dismay signalled that Leigh's remaining bishop had fallen prey to one of Pontifex's knights, represented by a matchstick that Leigh had mistaken for a pawn. The players' muttered recriminations were drowned by the voice of the Jesuit.

'The doctrine of sacramental grace was admirably defined by the Council of Trent, after the Reformers had disseminated the heretical notion that the disposition of the – Come!'

Father Walton called out in a tone that betrayed his irritation at being interrupted, in response to a knock at the classroom door. A prefect entered the room, approached the priest and said something in a low voice.

'Very well.' Father Walton spoke brusquely. He turned to look directly at Philip and called out: 'Kinsella.'

Philip felt the flutter in the pit of his stomach that was always provoked by hearing his name pronounced by those in authority. He rose in his place.

'Yes, Father?'

'You are summoned. Go with Peters, if you please.'

'Yes, Father.'

Followed by curious stares, he accompanied the prefect out of the room. Behind him he heard Father Walton resuming his lecture on the nuances of sacramental grace *ex opere operato*. Peters walked a pace ahead of him, maintaining a lofty silence. Philip's anxiety was mounting. 'You are summoned,' Father Walton had said, but had given no indication as to who had issued the summons. Philip knew better than to question a prefect, so dared not enquire their destination. He examined his conscience for any recent infraction of discipline, but could recall no offence of any significance. That absence of guilt was not completely reassuring: he had learned to beware the capriciousness of Jesuit justice. Gloomily he concluded they must be headed for the office of the Prefect of Studies, who dealt with disciplinary matters; but then, to his mild relief and further bafflement, they digressed from the route that would have taken them there. Finally, Peters deigned to glance over his shoulder and impart disturbing information.

'Father Rector wants to see you.'

Again Philip experienced that fluttering sensation in his stomach. The Rector: this was a more alarming prospect than even the most inauspicious visit to the Prefect of Studies. Philip had never had a conversation with Father Rector, who had only taken up his post at the beginning of that school year, beyond finding himself among groups of boys to whom he had occasionally directed some inconsequential, but genial, remarks while spectating at house matches and on similar occasions. The impression he conveyed was of remote benevolence; but the summoning of a junior boy to his presence was so unusual it could only arouse keen apprehension. As Peters knocked on the door of the Rector's study and ushered him inside, Philip was conscious of the abnormally fast beating of his heart.

Father Rector was not seated behind his desk, but standing in front of it, a tall, austere figure, scion of a famous Recusant family. What startled Philip, however, and set his mind in turmoil was the sight of both his brothers also in the room. Edmund was standing to one side, facing the priest; he barely glanced round at Philip, so his expression could not be discerned. Dominick was sitting in an armchair directly in front of the Rector; the light from the window falling on his face made it look ghostly white. The atmosphere was unbearably tense. Philip was gripped by a feeling of alarm, bordering on panic. Although when the Rector addressed him his tone was kindly, the effect was not reassuring.

'Do please sit down.'

He gestured towards an armchair alongside the one occupied by Dominick. Numbly, Philip obeyed, murmuring in a voice he could not keep from sounding tremulous:

'Thank you, Father.'

The Rector's retiring manner, on this occasion, seemed almost to amount to shyness, or embarrassment of some kind. He spoke in an unexpectedly gentle voice.

'I am afraid you must prepare yourself for some very bad news.

The fact is, there has been an accident – an extremely serious hunting accident – at home. I am very sorry to have to tell you that your mother has been killed.'

In that instant, Philip realized the full horror of what he had just been told. Mummie was dead. This was not a misunderstanding or a bad dream from which he would waken. The person he most loved in the whole world was lost to him. He would never see her again, never hear her voice, never earn her displeasure or approval. He grasped immediately the significance of what had happened, the black tide of misery that had engulfed his life. Moments later, the disbelief and bewilderment with which the mind revolts against unacceptable reality set in; but in that first fraction of a second following the priest's words he fully comprehended the immensity of his loss.

'I am so very, very sorry,' said the Rector, watching Philip anxiously.

The boy gave a strangled gasp that did not quite become a sob then struggled to control himself. He must not give in to an unseemly display of grief. From the adjacent armchair, Dominick reached out and placed a hand on his shoulder, a gesture that both consoled and nearly unmanned him as he fought to hold back tears. The Rector sought refuge in practicalities.

'Of course, you must all return home immediately. Father Meli has looked up the night boat train for Fishguard; it leaves Paddington at 7.55, as you probably know, being regular travellers. There is plenty of time for you to pack the few things you will need and I shall ask the kitchen to give you something to eat before you leave. You have exeats for a week. They can be extended, if your father wishes or there are any problems that detain you at home after the funeral.'

The funeral: the grim finality of the term and the ordeal ahead that it conjured in his imagination filled Philip with despair. After a moment's silence, Father Rector cleared his throat and spoke again, turning his head to include all three brothers in his invitation.

'If you will come with me now to the chapel, we shall pray before the Blessed Sacrament for the repose of your mother's soul.'

In the chapel, instead of entering one of the rows of seats, Father Rector led them to the altar rails, where he knelt down, gesturing to them to kneel alongside him, as though receiving communion. He took out his rosary and began to recite the Five Sorrowful Mysteries; the Kinsella brothers gave the responses in subdued voices. It reminded Philip of family rosary at Lissanore, with Mummie kneeling in her black lace mantilla, and the memory brought a lump to his throat. With an effort he forced himself to concentrate on the prayers. There was still something he could do to help his mother: storm Heaven for the repose of her soul. He gazed imploringly at the tabernacle and prayed in fervent petition. At the conclusion of the rosary, the Rector said the *De Profundis* then stood up, signing to the boys to remain where they were.

'You may as well stay here for a few minutes,' he said in a low voice. 'I am going to make sure the taxi has been ordered and everything is arranged for your journey. When you are ready, just go to the refectory and they will let you have some sandwiches and tea. Please give your father my deepest condolences. God bless you.'

It was not long after dawn, with the light grudgingly revealing a slate-grey winter sky, when they drove in under the gatehouse at the North Lodge of Lissanore. It was still bare of any banner, but when the castle came into view the long-neglected house flag of the Kinsellas was, for the first time in Philip's experience, on display, flapping dismally at half-mast from the highest tower. The same funereal message was proclaimed by the family arms displayed on a lozenge within a large black hatchment ornamented with death's heads and other symbols of mortality, hung above the front door.

Contrary to expectation, their father had met them on the quayside at Rosslare, shaking hands with each of his sons in turn and responding to their stammered expressions of regret by clapping them on the shoulder, before leading the way to the car. His black tie and armband confirmed the grim reality of what had occurred during their absence. He seldom spoke during the journey. When they entered the house he turned to them in the hall and said:

'I imagine you will want a quick wash after your journey. I shall meet you down here in a quarter of an hour and take you to her.'

The chapel was empty except for Uncle Eanna kneeling in prayer. Count Kinsella and his brothers had taken it in turns to keep vigil there throughout the night. Philip walked slowly forward, between Edmund and Dominick, with his father bringing up the rear. Mummie lay in an open coffin between banks of lilies and flanked by yellow, unbleached requiem candles, three on each side. She looked as if she were asleep, apart from the pallor of her features, almost as white as the robe in which she was dressed, making her resemble an alabaster statue, like the effigy of Saint Michael high above the sanctuary. A mother-of-pearl rosary was twined around her clasped hands which were of the same unnaturally pale hue and on her breast there rested a small square of brown cloth with a religious image, attached to two strings of the same colour which passed over her shoulders: the Scapular of Our Lady of Mount Carmel.

Philip had never seen a dead person before and there was nobody he would more have dreaded seeing in this state. He felt his throat working in a sudden spasm of grief. Mummie looked beautiful, even more so than she had done in life, though her features were perhaps a shade more sharply defined. This was the face that belonged to his earliest memories, whose smile had soothed childhood illnesses and terrors; and yet, in a way, he felt that this was not really his mother. That sense almost of alienation was temporarily reinforced by his religious faith: Mummie was in eternity with God – had already seen the face of God, an amazing, terrifying thought – and what lay in the coffin was her discarded body, a vehicle that had carried her through life and was now of no further use. Yet, moments later, as he knelt with his brothers and listened to the opening prayer of the rosary, the Apostles' Creed, he heard his father conclude this profession of faith with '...the resurrection of the body, and life everlasting. Amen'. This reminded him that one day Mummie's soul would be reunited with her body, in a glorified form, which reaffirmed its importance as an essential part of her. That was a doctrine with which he had sometimes struggled (why resurrect the body, which belonged to the tribulations and ailments of life?), but now he found it consoling. It sustained him when, at his father's direction, he followed his brothers' example in kissing his dead mother's forehead and was chilled by its marble-like coldness. The stifling, acrid scent of the lilies that surrounded the coffin, when breathed from close up, mingled with the smell of beeswax from the candles, created a sickly, claustrophobic atmosphere from which he was glad to retreat. He knew that, for the rest of his life, whenever he encountered the scent of lilies it would recall this moment.

On the following two mornings Canon Roche came to say Mass in the chapel (there had been no resident priest at Lissanore since the departure of Father Yves), with the entire household and a good number of people from the village comprising the congregation. Philip also took his turn, partnered by Dominick, to pray beside his mother's body at night, though, in deference to his youth, his vigil was ended at midnight. Even Uncle Ulick overcame his hypochondriac scruples to participate, wearing an overcoat as protection against nocturnal chills. Edmund, in his new character as a candidate for the priesthood, was zealous in attendance in the chapel. Grandma, who was reported to be in a state of shock, remained in her rooms under the ministrations of Bridie Byrne, refusing to see anybody.

Maria Theresia arrived the day after her brothers, recalled from the finishing school that had replaced her convent; with Lissanore deprived of a châtelaine, it was questionable whether the eighteen-year-old daughter of the house could be spared to return abroad. She at once took over responsibility for looking after Dee-Dee, now aged eight and utterly distraught at the loss of her mother. She had rarely stopped weeping since the accident; now, while remaining inconsolable, she clearly found some comfort in her sister's company. Maria Theresia had the happy inspiration of entrusting Countess Kinsella's terrier Balzac, who had been wandering around in a bereft condition since his mistress's death, to Dee-Dee's care; this arrangement provided a distraction and some alleviation of their distress to both the little girl and the dog. Dermod had set himself the task of relieving his grieving brother of the burden of administrative matters relating to the funeral and had made all the arrangements with striking efficiency, though he meticulously submitted every decision to Bonaventure for approval. Eanna loyally seconded his efforts. Corristeen, rheumy-eyed with grief and visibly disoriented, performed his duties like an automaton, while conducting a personal, three-day wake in the privacy of his pantry where he resorted to his usual solace on a heavier scale than usual.

Only once did Count Kinsella allude to the circumstances of his wife's death. Leaving the chapel with his sons on the day before the funeral, he paused as they walked along the passage and said, as though feeling they were owed an explanation:

'It was one of those notorious double ditches – the one down by Clancy's Acre. She had taken it dozens of times before. It was

315

pretty well instantaneous, if that's any kind of consolation.' He was silent for a moment, before adding: 'They had to shoot Chatterbox, I'm afraid.'

That evening Philip stood on the gravel sweep with the rest of the household and many of the men from the village while his mother's coffin was carried out of the chapel and placed in the hearse, drawn by horses crested with black plumes. ('Didn't I see ould Count Dominick, that was father to Himself, in that same jauntin'-car of death,' reminisced an elderly villager.) Canon Roche, wearing a black cope and preceded by an altar boy carrying a processsional cross, walked in front of the hearse, leading it on its journey to the parish church. As the ponderous vehicle, escorted by the black-clad undertaker's men with crepe bows around their high silk hats, moved off down the avenue, followed by a long procession of mourners, the last of the daylight faded. Under the direction of Dizzycourse Slattery the estate workers lighted pitch torches, lending a more intensely hieratic atmosphere to the proceedings: such flambeaux had attended generations of Kinsellas at their obsequies. Arrived in the church, the coffin was placed in front of the sanctuary, draped in a black pall.

'Subvenite, Sancti Dei, occurrite, Angeli Domini…' intoned Canon Roche, adjuring God's saints and angels to conduct the soul of Countess Kinsella into the presence of the Almighty. Presently he began to recite First Vespers from the Office of the Dead. He closed the ceremony of reception of the remains with the ubiquitous Sorrowful Mysteries, in which the congregation joined with a suddenly thunderous response that alerted Philip to how many people had by now crowded into the church.

An even larger congregation assembled for the funeral Mass the following morning, a greater number than the parish church could accommodate. Among the ranks of subfusc suits and black

316

dresses milling around decorously in the church grounds, Philip recognized such disparate mourners as Dempsey the vet, Lord Ardgroom, McConkey the carrier, Colonel Blennerhassett, and Major and Mrs Fenton. The hunt had turned out in force, in tribute to the circumstances of Countess Kinsella's death. Inside, Prendergast the passkeeper presided over the proceedings with monumental self-importance; like a courtier sporting full orders and decorations at a ceremony of state, his lapel was ornamented with an unprecedented number of sodality and confraternity emblems, and he was conducting sporadic warfare with the undertaker's men over issues of precedence.

Prendergast's attempted domination of the occasion was eclipsed by the sensation produced by the arrival of Mrs Skerrett, who had not been seen in the parish church for several years and whose reclusive existence had fuelled much speculation. Grandma's substitution of black for her customary brown vesture, by its novelty, lent her an incongruously festive aspect. Although the hat of pre-War vintage that she wore had a perfunctory, wide-meshed veil suspended over her face, it in no way concealed the hawk-like stare with which she surveyed the congregation as she made her way down the aisle to join the womenfolk of the family – Maria Theresia, Deirdre and Aunt Clara – in the front pew on the epistle side of the church. Across the aisle, beyond the pall-draped and candle-flanked coffin, on the gospel side sat Count Kinsella with his four brothers and three sons. In the row behind, Corristeen, also long a stranger to the parish church, sat with Liam, Dizzycourse Slattery and other members of the outdoor staff from Lissanore. Behind the Kinsella ladies the female contingent consisted of Bridie Byrne, Mrs Ennis the cook, Angela, now the senior housemaid, Maura her colleague and sundry lesser domestics.

The congregation rose as the clergy, including a cadaverous-faced monsignor in violet mantelletta, processed into the sanctuary, Canon Roche as celebrant bringing up the rear with deacon and subdeacon in black vestments trimmed with gold, and the Requiem Mass began. Philip tried to join in the choir's singing of the haunting version of the *Kyrie* peculiar to a Requiem, but his throat was sore as a consequence of three days of determinedly swallowing back grief that had threatened to rise up in the form of a sob, as he struggled to show outward composure. He knelt now in acute misery. He could picture Mummie inside the coffin that stood a few feet away. If only she had not gone out that day, or had taken the treacherous double ditch slightly differently... If only she had given up hunting – he felt a sudden aversion to the sport in which he had lately prided himself on cutting a figure. The irrelevant thought occurred to him that the Rudiments class was at that moment wrestling with mathematics: despite his terror of algebra, he would have given anything to be among them, with Mummie safe and well at home.

Summoning all his resolution, he banished these futile regrets, remembering his impending responsibility to his mother. Philip was determined to make the best Holy Communion of his life and gain a plenary indulgence, applicable to his mother; he had gone to confession to Canon Roche the previous evening, to fulfil all the necessary conditions. If Mummie was still in Purgatory, he wanted it to be his efforts that gained her admission to Heaven. By the time he had finished making his meticulous thanksgiving after communion, Canon Roche was removing his chasuble and draping himself in a black cope to perform the ritual absolution of the dead. As he walked round the coffin, sprinkling it with holy water, Philip silently completed the 'Our Father' begun by the priest. Then Canon Roche took the thurible and incensed the coffin, after which the moment Philip had most dreaded arrived.

As the undertaker's men removed the tall candlesticks from around the coffin, the pallbearers rose and took their positions. Philip and Dominick, the least tall and the only two not wearing morning coats, were on either side at the narrow front end of the coffin, closest to the altar; behind them were Edmund and Uncle Arthur, then Uncles Eanna and Ulick (privately convinced the effort would kill him, but nonetheless resolved to do his duty). Papa and Uncle Dermod brought up the rear. Under the direction of the undertaker, they slowly lifted the coffin. Philip found it was not resting on him at all, his fellow bearers being so much taller; he had to raise one hand above his head to maintain a hold of it, while Dominick linked an arm across his shoulder. The undertaker's assistants deftly withdrew the trestles on which the coffin had rested and the eight pallbearers performed a shuffling motion to turn around and face down the aisle. As they started on their slow progress, the choir began to sing *In paradisum* – 'May angels lead you into Paradise…'

It was the worst moment of his life so far. Every fibre of his being was concentrated on maintaining a stoic demeanour. His throat felt sore every time he swallowed. Despite looking straight ahead, he was aware of individual members of the congregation, as faces swam into his line of vision like a kaleidoscope of his childhood. He glimpsed Dr and Mrs Dixon, both looking grim… Miss Malley sobbing into her handkerchief, bringing the same wholehearted energy to her mourning as to all her other activities. Then he noticed Kitty, the former housemaid, now the mother of three young children, with her husband Martie Farrell – both of them, as Canon Roche had predicted, established pillars of the parish now. Kitty, too, was weeping with abandon: she and her husband were by no means the only people present who owed much to the stealthy good works of Countess Kinsella, including a sprinkling of nuns from various orders she had supported. Petticoats Flaherty was also there, his female attire temporarily replaced by the subfusc suit he reserved exclusively for funerals.

Outside the church, an unexpected sight confirmed the significance of the occasion. After the pallbearers had deposited his mother's coffin once again in the hearse, Philip turned away with a sensation of relief and was startled to see the open carriage of the Misses ffreney-Donovan drawn up opposite the churchyard gate. The two black-clad ladies, whose habitual mourning dress was today wholly appropriate, sat very upright. In appreciation of this gesture of conciliation and respect for his wife, Count Kinsella crossed the road and stood talking for a moment with the occupants of the carriage, silk hat in hand, receiving their condolences. By now the congregation had spilled out of the church and was waiting for the hearse to move off, breath smoking in the winter air as they exchanged muted comments. The scene had particularly affected the women of the parish.

'Them boys carryin' their mother – God love them.'

The cortège made its way back to Lissanore at snail's pace, followed by the male mourners. Eventually the battlemented gatehouse loomed up and Countess Kinsella passed under it, returning home for the last time. A short distance up the avenue, the hearse stopped beside a path that led to the family vault, situated on the edge of the demesne, adjoining the Church of Ireland graveyard. The undertakers carried the coffin along the path to the vault; the gate in the iron railing surrounding it was open, as was the entrance to the mausoleum, prepared by Slattery and his subordinates who stood beside it, heads uncovered. Their presence reminded Philip of the previous occasion he had attended an interment in the demesne: the burial of Conn the wolfhound. It seemed to him that Conn's death had started a train of mortality at Lissanore that had next claimed Mr Blackwell and now the châtelaine herself. He gazed wretchedly at the dank, subterranean chamber that would henceforth be his mother's home, appalled that she, who had always been a creature of warmth and light and gaiety, should be immured out here in the cold. Desperately he reminded himself that her soul was with God, bathed in eternal light, and that was what mattered.

The remaining rites were brief. At their conclusion, Canon Roche sprinkled the coffin with holy water one last time then led the mourners of Countess Kinsella in praying that her soul and the souls of all the faithful departed, through the mercy of God, might rest in peace. There was a chorus of 'Amens' and a flurry of people crossing themselves, then the undertakers carried the coffin down several steps into the vault, accompanied only by Count Kinsella. After a few moments' respectful contemplation the mourners began to walk slowly away.

Up at the house, a buffet had been laid out in the ballroom for all comers; in the drawing room refreshments were served to a more select company. Count Kinsella, welcoming the distraction, performed his duties as host punctiliously, handing a glass of whiskey to the cadaverous monsignor, who was the Bishop's secretary and representative for the occasion, and enquiring solicitously after His Lordship's health. Maria Theresia, who had never lacked social poise, having returned Dee-Dee, who had wept ceaselessly throughout the proceedings, to the care of her governess, now assumed the function of hostess with notable aplomb.

'I am so sorry about your mother,' Mrs Dixon told Philip earnestly, scanning his features with a troubled expression. 'Tom sends his condolences – obviously he couldn't get out of Clongowes when it wasn't a member of his own family. He is writing to you.'

Philip muttered his gratitude. The sight of Mrs Dixon, so kind and understanding, provoked in him a feeling of envy that Tom still had his mother, his life was untroubled; ashamed, Philip banished this unworthy thought. Grandma made an appearance, to receive the sympathy of the company, which she regarded as overdue by many years. Her reaction to her daughter's death had fluctuated erratically, beginning with maternal grief when she first heard the news, followed by resentment that her chief prop and scapegoat had deserted her as a consequence of selfishly indulging a sporting whim, and apprehension regarding her own inevitably reduced status in the household – to all of which contending emotions Bridie Byrne had been cruelly exposed. The mourners breathed a palpable sigh of relief when Mrs Skerrett withdrew. Philip glanced around the drawing room. His mother's music still lay on top of the grand piano, beside the photograph of Nicholas to which the Misses ffreney-Donovan and others had taken exception, causing a rift which only his mother's death had healed, that very morning. His mind conjured the scene when Mummie had played the Imperial anthem while Nicholas sang; it seemed like yesterday. The recollection made the room intolerable to him and he hurried outside.

Wandering around the grounds, he found himself in the vicinity of the walled garden. Philip remembered one day in the scorchingly hot summer of four years ago when he had gone into the garden with his mother. That was the ill-fated occasion when she had told him of the abortive project to give Edmund the name Hyacinth; but that was not why he thought of it now. He recalled instead how she had given a little skip from sheer *joie-de-vivre* and exclaimed, 'Ah! C'est la vie, c'est la vie!' then hugged him in sudden affection and teasingly called him 'My little Phillie-love.' His eyes brimmed at the memory and his throat worked convulsively. Then he was gripped by the extravagant illusion that if he opened the door of the walled garden he would find his mother inside, surrounded by sunlight and flowers, just as he had left her that day. It was an image he knew would constantly recur to him. Perhaps that was what his own death would be like: opening the door in the wall, to meet his mother again, in a haven of brilliant light and fragrant blooms. He turned away, leaving the walled garden behind him, bleak and deserted in winter, the door as fast locked as the vault where his mother now lay.

By the time he returned to the house many of the guests had taken their leave. On the stairs he met his father descending from the nursery.

'I've just been trying to comfort Deirdre, but it was very difficult. She has fallen asleep now, poor lamb, by far the best thing for her.'

Philip looked into his father's eyes and was startled by the desolation he saw there.

'Oh, Papa.' Impulsively, he embraced him. It was like the moment when his father had told him about Mr Blackwell's suicide, with both of them suddenly very close. 'I'm so sorry about Mummie. I miss her dreadfully.'

'So do I,' his father said very gently. 'So do I. All we can do now is pray for her.'

That night, after he had prayed again for his mother, warm tears came at last as a release, in the privacy of his pillow. After that, he knew he would not weep for her again. If grief were not to master him, he must devise a means of controlling it. He would pray for Mummie every morning and night, and at Mass. If the thought of her came unbidden to his mind at other times, he would say a quick prayer and dismiss it; otherwise, the unbearable sadness of her memory would unman him. That was his resolution and he adhered firmly to it – until one unforeseeable circumstance disrupted it.

Philip was glad to return to school: it was a relief to find himself in an environment that held no memories of his mother. He received expressions of sympathy from friends and masters stoically. On the day after his return he was handed an unusually thick bundle of mail – letters of condolence, among them the unmistakable scrawl of Tom Dixon. He took them to the dormitory to read, fanning them out on his bed, grateful that protocol did not require him to reply. Suddenly he froze. The familiar, much-loved handwriting on one envelope swam before his eyes. It was from Mummie.

Slowly, the realization dawned of what had happened. Mummie must have written to him in the morning, before she went out hunting for the last time; or, more likely, the night before. She had always written to her sons in rotation and it had been his turn. Philip sat and stared at this message from beyond the grave. He could not bring himself to open it. He could imagine the everyday events it would chronicle: any domestic incidents or petty disasters that might entertain him, retold by his mother with her customary humour and well-chosen turns of phrase, followed by her affectionate enquiries about his welfare. Yet he could not tear open the envelope to read the contents. So long as this letter remained unread, he still had one last communication to receive from his mother; after that, there would be nothing. He must postpone that final severing of all contact. Even at that moment, his conduct reminded him of the time when he had gone to the summerhouse to look at the lock of hair belonging to the girl Constanza, only to return the box to its hiding place unopened. When he would read his mother's last letter was a decision to be made later; for the time being, he would keep it sealed. He placed it carefully in his inside pocket, threw the other letters into his bedside locker and went down to join his classmates.

CHAPTER XIX

'I SAY, you'll never guess what has happened.'

Barrington was flushed with excitement; there was even a hint of disorder in his immaculately brushed hair. This dramatic preamble provoked the inevitable extravagant suggestions from his friends. He waited impatiently until they had completed this ritual then, lowering his voice, confided his news.

'Parker is *casing Manley.*'

'*Wha-a-at?*' The response was a babble of amazed incredulity, deeply gratifying to Barrington. Philip joined in the chorus of enquiry, a little uncertainly: he had heard occasional whispered references to 'casing', without being entirely sure what it entailed. Pontifex, assuming his air of cross-examining counsel, began to elicit details.

'What did Parker do?' He addressed the question to Barrington rather than to Manley, who sat wearing an unhappy expression at a desk in the empty classroom they had occupied for the purpose of conferring.

'He sent Manley a note. Let me see it again.'

Sheepishly, Manley took a piece of paper from his pocket and handed it over. Barrington studied it critically, his lips pursing in disapproval – not, as it transpired, on account of the content, but with regard to the spelling and grammar. With a shrug of disdain, he passed it round the group. Philip was last to read it. From fear of the consequences of his *billet-doux* being intercepted, Parker had printed it, to disguise his handwriting; he had also expressed himself so elliptically that his meaning was virtually unfathomable, though whether this was due to discretion or to inarticulacy was impossible to gauge. Parker was a morose, ill-favoured youth in Syntax II whose school career had been undistinguished to the point of anonymity; it now appeared that this drab exterior masked at least some spark of romance, since his fancy had fallen upon Manley. Such 'casing' of a younger boy by an older one was a recognized feature of school life, though it was restricted to the surreptitious passing of notes, in a ritual of courtly love that was never, in even the mildest degree, physically consummated – a restraint which reflected the ingrained Catholic morality that permeated the college. Yet even such relatively innocuous correspondence, if detected, would have provoked the heavy wrath of the Jesuits and resulted in automatic expulsion of the culprit, as Leigh now pointed out.

'That's a sacking offence. Nosey Parker had better watch his step.'

'We should burn the note,' said Barrington, who was thoroughly enjoying the drama of this incident. 'On second thoughts, Manley had better eat it, like spies do with secret messages. You can't be too careful.'

'Is ink poisonous?' wondered Philip, anxious to contribute something to a discussion in which he found himself out of his depth. Even as he spoke, he ruefully recognized the hypochondriac influence of his Uncle Ulick implicit in the question.

'Quite possibly.' Barrington spoke with relish.

'What do you think I should say?' asked Manley nervously.

'When?'

'In my answer.'

'You – you mean you are thinking of sending a note back? You – you –' For once, Barrington was rendered speechless.

His companions stared at Manley in consternation.

'It's very rude not to reply to letters,' he said defensively. 'I got a frightful row at home for not writing to my aunt after Christmas.'

'Oh, you prize chump. You perfect ass.' Barrington slapped his forehead in frustration; then, realizing the futility of that exercise, he smacked Manley's head as well.

'What did you do that for?' Manley rubbed his head aggrievedly.

'Listen, you idiot, are you trying to get yourself sacked? Why on earth would you want to write back to Nosey Parker – unless you're as sweet on him as he is on you? Are you completely mad? Besides, it's almost certainly a mortal sin – do you want to have to tell Baldy about it in confession? I suspect it may also constitute a malfeasance under common law – possibly even a tort.'

'What's that?'

'A legal term,' said Barrington evasively.

'I don't think so.' Pontifex, whose father was a barrister, contradicted him, resenting this invasion of what he regarded as his territory. 'A tort has to do with public footpaths and rights of way.' He was gambling on Barrington lacking the knowledge to refute this hasty invention.

'So, what are we going to do?' asked Leigh, whose temperament was the most practical of the five.

'For the moment, nothing at all.' Barrington reasserted his authority. 'Manley must simply ignore Parker's note and that may be enough to discourage him. In the meantime, I've changed my mind about destroying the letter. We had better hold on to it, as it is useful incriminating evidence against Parker if he turns nasty, as men casing chaps sometimes do. I shall take jolly good care of it and hide it away where nobody can possibly find it.'

'I agree with Barrington,' said Manley, for whom inaction was always the most attractive option.

The others nodded assent.

'I strongly suspect, however, that things will not end here. In that case,' Barrington assumed the demeanour of a leader of men, 'we shall take concerted action to defend Manley against these unwanted attentions and repel Parker. All for one and one for all!'

He brandished an imaginary rapier, in a gesture that appealed strongly to Philip.

'All for one and one for all!' chorused the others.

Barrington's policy of ignoring Parker's overtures did not succeed in ending the unsolicited correspondence. After a week, Parker sent a second missive to Manley, slightly more direct in its meaning. Manley, whose reaction to the first message had been one of embarrassment, faintly tinged with a suggestion of his feeling flattered by the attentions of an older boy, now became thoroughly alarmed by the situation and lapsed into a mood of apprehension and depression. Barrington, deciding that no time must be lost in once again putting his protégé back on his feet, confiscated the latest note and, on his own initiative, took retaliatory action. Only afterwards, in a discreet corner of the playground, did he complacently present this *fait accompli* to his dismayed associates.

'You did *what?*'

Pontifex wore a frown of deep concern; beside him, Manley's pallid complexion had blanched to paper whiteness. Philip felt a flutter in his stomach as he listened to Barrington nonchalantly re-counting his coup.

'I pinched a red marking pencil from Unsworth's desk. Then I went through Parker's latest note and underlined all the spelling and grammar mistakes – it was even worse than his first effort – and corrected them, with appropriate comments. At the bottom I put the number of marks he deserved – I gave him four out of ten, which was generous, considering the number of howlers he had managed to cram into a couple of paragraphs. After that, I went to the place in the trees behind the Ambulacrum where he told Manley to leave a reply and put it under the stone he described – under a stone is where Parker belongs. He should have found it by now,' he concluded in a tone of deep satisfaction.

'But he'll think I wrote all that cheek on his letter.' Manley sounded distraught.

'Yes, but that doesn't matter. There is nothing he can do. If the Js found out what he's been up to he would be sacked.'

'It's never wise to annoy men in Middle Playroom,' said Pontifex.

'What can he do? He's not a monitor.' Barrington remained unapologetic.

'Hell hath no fury like a caser scorned.' Leigh cautioned his companions.

'It's all right for the rest of you,' said Manley reproachfully. 'Parker doesn't know you had anything to do with it.'

'*We* didn't.' Pontifex contradicted him indignantly. 'Only Barrington.'

'Yes, but it's me who's in for it, if Parker gets shirty.'

'It's *I*,' Barrington corrected him, with automatic pedantry.

'No – *me*.'

'I was referring to a mistake in your grammar; but it's quite true Parker may try to take it out on you for my little jape. However, if he does try anything, we only have to threaten to let his note be discovered in certain quarters and he will have to desist.'

'But you sent the note back to him.' Philip detected the flaw in this argument.

'Yes, but I still have his first note. Although he doesn't realize it yet, that is the Sword of Damocles hanging over Parker's head. Believe me, he is in no position to bully Manley, provided we stand up to him.'

'I hope you are right,' said Manley gloomily.

'Of course I am. I said I would put you back on your feet again and, as usual, I have.'

'It's Manley's fault,' said Leigh provocatively, 'for looking like Little Lord Fauntleroy.'

He rumpled Manley's blond hair derisively. Manley was a peaceable fellow, but this gibe could not, in honour, be overlooked. He closed with Leigh and the two of them rolled on the grass, pummelling each other with zest. The bellicose spirit was infectious, so that Philip found himself similarly embroiled with Pontifex and Barrington, in a three-cornered combat in which no alignments could be discerned beyond animal high spirits and every man for himself.

Despite Barrington's confidence, Manley's misgivings turned out to be well founded. Retribution struck promptly and in the least expected place – in the chapel during Mass, three mornings later. Philip liked the chapel, with its barrel-vaulted ceiling covered with intricate patterns of painted curlicues, divided into half a dozen bays by pilasters in the walls, between which were medallions depicting eminent saints. The rose window above the altar, with the dove representing the Holy Ghost at its centre, created a kaleidoscope of coloured light on sunny days that dappled the participants in the ceremonies in the sanctuary below. This haven of reverence and peace was now rudely violated.

As the boys knelt in well-ordered devotion, Manley was suddenly and brutally 'slammed' by the senior boy in the row behind him, who punched him in the back with a violence that knocked him over. 'Slamming' was an established custom, a form of discipline exercised over the juniors by senior boys, who sat in the middle of every alternate row and administered this punishment to anybody they suspected of not singing, or of dozing off, or whom they simply disliked. Manley's friends looked round in alarm, to discover the perpetrator was Cardwell, the closest approximation to an intimate that Parker possessed. Clearly he had been suborned, presumably by some tale other than the shameful truth, to execute vengeance on behalf of Parker. Barrington, who had made the mistake of glaring over his shoulder at Cardwell and who was, in any case, already marked down by his seniors as an insubordinate spirit, was next slammed with equal force. Moments later, as Cardwell got into his stride, Pontifex and Leigh were similarly assaulted. Philip was spared, possibly because he was kneeling beyond comfortable range, or perhaps because the small section of the congregation made up of local people that was seated apart, next to the side altars, was becoming scandalized by the sound of blows and gasps of pain reverberating from the college ranks.

'We have to do something about this,' a determined-looking Barrington told the members of his set, at a hastily convened council of war later that day.

'What can we do?' Leigh sounded sceptical.

'Cardwell might not slam us again,' said Manley, with feeble optimism.

'Don't talk rot.' Barrington scornfully dismissed the suggestion. 'Whether he does or not, we can't let Nosey Parker get away with this. Cardwell is an ass, who must have swallowed whatever cock-and-bull story Parker told him to make him rag us like that. It's Parker who must be punished.'

'Who's talking rot now?' Pontifex uttered a snort of incredulity. 'How can we possibly punish a man in Middle Playroom?'

'I have an idea,' said Barrington. 'I haven't thought out all the details yet, but I believe it might work.'

'Then you have to tell us about it now.' Pontifex spoke in firm tones. 'We can't have you going off again and doing something drastic by yourself, and getting the rest of us into trouble.'

'That's right,' said Leigh. 'I have a massive bruise on my back because you wrote all that cheek on Parker's note without even letting us know.'

'How can you see a bruise on your back?' Barrington sought to divert the conversation.

'I can jolly well feel it; it's excruciatingly painful. So, tell us what you are thinking of doing.'

Surrendering to the pressure from his anxious friends, Barrington told them.

'Whew!' Leigh whistled under his breath when their leader had finished outlining his scheme. 'It's dangerous – frightfully risky – but it might just work.'

'A lot depends on chance,' said Pontifex. 'It hinges on how Cardwell reacts: he might just be puzzled by the whole thing and put it out of his mind.'

'I agree,' said Barrington, 'that the great imponderable is Cardwell's monumental stupidity. That's why we have to alter the document slightly, to spell things out clearly even to his primitive intelligence. It's the writing that's the difficult bit.'

'I should like to have a shot at the writing.' Philip volunteered his services. He felt he had not contributed enough to the deliberations and was embarrassed that he alone had been spared a pummelling by Cardwell. If he was to justify his membership of the Barrington set he would have to pull his weight.

'Good man, Kinsella, if you think you can manage it. The tricky thing is you will have to do it in the Study Place. Try it out several times on a separate sheet of paper and remember to have some other piece of writing – an essay or something – to put over it if anybody comes near.' He assumed his inspirational, Henry V at Agincourt air (as Philip privately thought of it). 'Honour demands we avenge the humiliation we have suffered in front of the whole school. All for one and one for all!'

More prosaically Pontifex observed: 'That beast Parker is in for it now.'

Cardwell sauntered up to the board where notices announcing the composition of each XV for forthcoming matches and similar sporting news were regularly posted. He visited it every day, being an avid rugger devotee, though he suffered from a permanent sense of injustice over his failure to be promoted; this he attributed to jealousy of his talents, though the real reason was that the brute strength on which he relied was not complemented by any understanding of tactics or subtlety of play. He had relieved some of his pent-up resentment in the chapel that morning, when he had given those brats in Rudiments a good slamming, for the second time. On the first occasion he had done so at the prompting of Parker, for whom he did not feel particular friendship or esteem; but any pretext for violence was welcome. Having enjoyed giving vent to his feelings, he had repeated the exercise, as a self-indulgence. He thought he might well do so again.

Cardwell had ceased to trouble himself by puzzling over a small, but inexplicable, incident that had befallen him the previous evening when, on retiring to his dormitory cubicle, he had found a rather tired-looking tulip lying on his pillow. He lacked the imagination to surmise how it might have arrived there, though even he recognized there had been something purposeful about its location. Having dismissed the matter as beyond comprehension – along with much of life and most of his academic work – he felt his pulse quicken at the sight of an envelope pinned to the edge of the games notice board and addressed: 'W. Cardwell'.

Convinced this heralded his long-awaited promotion in the football hierarchy, Cardwell snatched the envelope and began to tear it open as he hurried along the dark gallery to where there was adequate light to read. The first sight of the envelope's contents acted like a cold douche on his enthusiasm: this was no official communication, but a crudely printed message whose convoluted meaning would have perplexed a sharper brain than his. So far as he could interpret it, the note seemed friendly, even affectionate, if inscrutable in meaning; until the final sentence, he realized with a shock, as he read: 'Next time I shall leave you a rose, dearest.'

Even so mean an intelligence as Cardwell's was capable of piecing this jigsaw together: the unknown writer promised to leave him a rose 'next time'; ergo, the same individual had deposited the mysterious tulip on his pillow, invading the privacy of his cubicle to do so. With a sensation of rising bile, Cardwell grasped the horror of his situation: despite his mature years and status in Middle Line Playroom, he was being cased by some anonymous invert. No, not entirely anonymous, he now noticed – the note was signed with the initials 'F. X. P.' Displaying a degree of initiative that only so atrocious a provocation could have inspired, he rushed back to the notice board and ran his finger down the various team lists. With a grunt of savage satisfaction, he finally rested it beneath the sole name whose initials corresponded with the signature on the note: 'F. X. Parker.'

Cardwell was notorious for his temper; now rage consumed him. Parker! Parker was the author of the note that insulted his manhood, the anonymous depositor of unwanted horticultural produce in his cubicle, the deviant who risked exposing him to the ridicule of the entire school, if any hint of this bizarre courtship should leak out. He remembered it was Parker who had induced him to slam those little ticks in chapel – very likely they had also been the objects of his unnatural lust. Cardwell now recalled that he had once seen Pontifex score a very creditable try in a house match; he did not know it was the only try of Pontifex's career – an extreme fluke – so it gave him a fellow feeling with the younger sportsman. He would never lay a finger on him or his friends again; but he knew whom he now urgently wanted to slam instead. He knew, too, exactly where he could be found, around this time of day: he had seen Parker setting off on a run by himself an hour and a half earlier, so he would be coming back very soon. Fists clenched with anger, Cardwell rushed outside and made his way to the path through the woods along which Parker must return. He hurried up through the Beeches, anxious to intercept Parker at a discreet distance from the school, ranging through the woods like a wild beast in search of its prey. Like a wild beast, his instinct and timing were sound: within five minutes Parker, breathless from his exertions and hobbling along at walking pace, appeared from around a bend in the path. Cardwell planted himself squarely in his way and waited for him to come up.

'Hello, *dearest.*' He greeted Parker with an allusive sneer.

Parker, still out of breath, gaped uncomprehendingly. Cardwell took the dog-eared note from his pocket and thrust it under his nose.

'Did you write this?'

Parker immediately recognized his own composition, so that the blood rushed ashamedly to his face, a reaction that told Cardwell all he wanted to know.

'N–no...' Parker stammered incoherently. 'I mean – I – I only – what it was about was –'

'You filthy swine.'

A tide of red rage engulfed Cardwell. His first punch threw Parker backwards off his feet. Then Cardwell moved in for the kill.

The Barringtons celebrated their victory with enough ginger beer, buns and cakes to have left the whole of Lower Line Playroom replete. Barrington was intoxicated by the success of his plan. Repeatedly he regaled his companions with the tale of his hazardous incursion into the Syntax dormitory, gaining access when the maids were changing the bed linen, escaping detection by a hair's breadth, being momentarily trapped in a cubicle as he sought out Cardwell's nocturnal lair to deposit the tulip on his pillow, finally making his escape, only to earn six ferulae since his absence from class had been discovered. Philip was the secondary hero of the day, for having undertaken the successful forgery of the additional sentence at the end of Parker's note and the telltale initials.

'It wasn't too difficult,' he said modestly. 'Parker prints his "e"s and "r"s in a funny way it was quite easy to copy. My heart was in my mouth, though, all the time I was writing it in the Study Place – Unsworth nearly caught me.'

Leigh's contribution had been to purloin the tulip from the Marian shrine in the gallery, taking only the most withered bloom, out of respect. Pontifex had pinned the envelope to the notice board, after waiting for a suitable moment when the corridor was deserted. Manley had been excused participation, to avoid compromising him further. The Barrington set had noted with satisfaction the severe contusions on Parker's face, so badly disfigured by Cardwell that the Jesuits had interrogated him about it and received with scepticism his garbled explanation of a fall from his bicycle. Now Barrington raised his glass of lemonade, in the gesture of one proposing a triumphant toast.

' "Next time I shall leave you a rose, dearest." ' He recited the fatal line forged by Philip in a satirical falsetto, to howls of laughter. 'Brilliant, Kinsella. This time we really have put Manley on his feet – and knocked Parker off his. As Edmond Dantès said, in *The Count of Monte-Cristo*: "Now the God of Vengeance yields to me his power to punish the wicked!" '

Though enthused by the reference to his favourite author, Philip thought this a trifle overblown in the circumstances. He clinked glasses with his fellow conspirators and reverted to a more familiar quotation from Dumas.

'All for one and one for all!'

Philip spent much of his time during the Easter holidays at Lissanore cultivating his father's company, in the hope of consoling him in his bereavement. Superficially, Count Kinsella appeared unchanged, diligently transacting his affairs; but Philip detected an underlying apathy towards life. When he pressed his father into joining him in fencing bouts in the ballroom, it was no longer for his own sake, but to provide distraction.

Philip's first act on regaining the by now unaccustomed privacy of his bedroom had been to deposit his mother's last letter, still unopened, in the drawer where he kept the photograph of himself and the Spanish girl Constanza. Gazing at the photograph, he recalled vividly that scorchingly hot day five years before, when they had visited the summerhouse with Conn the wolfhound, now dead, as was Mummie. He felt he would give anything to be back in that happy time. Philip still sometimes thought about Constanza and regarded himself as bound by his pledge to be her knight; but the realism of developing maturity strongly suggested he would never see her again. Nor did he revisit the summerhouse to look at the lock of her hair secreted there: from motives he could not rationalize, it remained in limbo – like his mother's final letter to him. He had no idea when he would be able to bring himself to read it.

Maria Theresia had settled into the role of châtelaine at Lissanore. The novelty of wielding authority had, for the time being, dispelled any resentment over the loss of the frivolous social life being enjoyed by her contemporaries. Count Kinsella, however, recognized that this could only be a temporary arrangement.

'Poor Mattie. She won't find a suitable husband around here and I don't want her taking up with a non-Catholic. Once she has got things running smoothly, we must do something for her.'

Philip had supposed Uncle Dermod would be gratified by the

resolution of the Roman Question the previous year, but this proved to be a mistaken assumption.

'The Lateran Treaty has rewarded those Savoyard bandits,' he said indignantly. 'What have they restored of the Papal States, in return for absolution and international respectability? Not one square yard. I would concede it was probably unrealistic to hope they would give up Umbria and the Legations; but the Pope should have held out for restitution of the Patrimony of Saint Peter, or at the very least the entire Leonine City – Pius IX was offered as much in 1870. What did my father risk his life for, as a Pontifical Zouave?'

In fact, Dermod regretted the ending of the Pope's status as 'The Prisoner in the Vatican' and the intransigent stance it represented; dethroned sovereigns had always engaged his sympathy more than reigning monarchs. Philip's immediate concern was with Grandma, who had assumed a posture similar to that of the Pope before the recent Concordat, immured in her apartments in self-imposed retirement from that world which she had always declared herself to be in, but not of. She received a small number of privileged visitors in her seclusion and had graciously agreed to accord her youngest grandson an audience. This took place during the ceremonious event in Grandma's parlour that Uncle Dermod referred to as Solemn High Tea, a dispiriting occasion made more distasteful since Mrs Skerrett's pendulum mood had swung that day towards the aggrieved conviction that her daughter's demise represented a selfish abandonment of her. Philip fortified himself throughout this ordeal by consuming indecent amounts of cake and thinking about the fishing expedition that Uncle Arthur had planned for him and Tom Dixon, home on holiday from Clongowes, the following day. This turned out to be a triumph for Tom and Philip, but a humiliation for Uncle Arthur. Tom caught three trout and Philip one. Uncle Arthur, however, was experimenting with a fly of his own invention, of so exotic an appearance that even the least cautious fish gave it a wide berth.

'I shall have to make some modifications,' he said ruefully. 'I think I'll put up something more conventional for the evening rise. Anyway, you young chaps have had a good day. Well done, Tom.'

Tom brought Philip up to date on local events and gossip, including the news that their old enemy Simmie Toal had been released from prison at the beginning of the year, but, after a brief reappearance, had vanished from the neighbourhood.

'They say he's with the I.R.A., causing trouble up in the Black North.'

Comparing notes with him about their respective school experiences, Philip concluded that, despite some slight local differences, Jesuit colleges were very similar, regardless of national boundaries. Tom was delighted by the story of how Philip and his friends had turned the tables on their persecutors.

'Jeepers! Your man Barrington sounds great gas. You should bring him over in the summer holidays.'

That struck Philip as an excellent suggestion. His father approved the proposal and, shortly before the end of the summer term, wrote to Barrington's parents, inviting their son to stay at Lissanore during the holidays. His visit was a great success. He arrived with his luggage, as usual, disproportionately comprised of books and spent hours browsing in the library. Philip and Tom took him on expeditions to their favourite haunts; Uncle Arthur initiated him into the arcana of angling; and he had many conversations on historical topics with Uncle Dermod in the tower room. Barrington, however, was most fascinated by Corristeen's dexterity in crafting malapropisms and other whimsical solecisms in a variety of languages, living and dead. He conversed with the butler at every opportunity, retailing his linguistic gems with relish. Barrington's interest in the intricacies of English vocabulary was by this time verging on the obsessive.

When the Barrington set was reunited at the start of the new school year, its members began to be conscious, as never before, of the creeping change that the passage of time effects in human affairs. Even if the nickname had caught on, nobody could now have called Philip 'Kinsella Minimus', since only he and Dominick, now inhabiting the rarefied milieu of the Rhetoric class, remained at the school. Edmund was at Manresa House, the Jesuit novitiate at Roehampton. It seemed strange that Edmund was going to be a priest: he had never given the impression of being very religious – and certainly not saintly; rather worldly, indeed. Yet vocations were mysterious things, with the unlikeliest candidates often the chosen ones. Was it possible, speculated Philip, that he himself had a vocation? He had never thought so, but it would be a sin not to explore the possibility. The question presented itself more forcefully one day when an old boy of the school, recently ordained, came to say Mass and give his First Blessing. Philip confided his thoughts to Barrington.

'The idea just struck me after we had kissed the new priest's hands today. Have you ever wondered if you have a vocation?'

'I have no vocation to be a priest,' said Barrington decisively, 'but I may well have one to become a cardinal – or Pope.'

Other, more secular, vocations preoccupied the boys. Barrington distinguished himself on the river, where Philip showed himself no more than competent. His career on the sports field was mediocre, but when he eventually gravitated to shooting he discovered a talent that, by practice and perseverance, took him into the second IV and nourished his ambition to graduate eventually to the school VIII. This skill usefully complemented his career in the Officers Training Corps. The military life held a strong appeal, so that the Barringtons flocked to the colours *en bloc*. Even Manley joined up and became a spirited side-drummer. Barrington's individualist temperament proved an obstacle to his advancement and he could not conceal his chagrin when Philip was promoted to lance-corporal; while outwardly maintaining a casual demeanour, Philip regarded his single stripe with as much satisfaction as if he had been awarded a field marshal's baton. Both he and Barrington enjoyed friendly relations with their new form master; unusually, that year, this position was held by a layman, Mr Webb, who taught history. He lived in, since he was the only bachelor among the lay masters. Philip and Barrington would sometimes visit his room and listen to his stories about the Great War, when he had served in the Machine Gun Corps.

'What I don't understand,' Barrington said after one of these sessions, 'is why Barney doesn't turn those wartime diaries of his into a book.'

'You think the whole of life should be made into a book.'

'Mostly it is – as you would realize if you read some serious literature, instead of A. E. W. Mason and Stanley J. Weyman all the time.'

Barrington was developing into a literary snob as his tastes grew more sophisticated. He had persuaded Philip to be more adventurous in his reading. Under his tutelage, Philip had read two historical novels by Henryk Sienkiewicz: *Quo Vadis* and *The Teutonic Knights*. While avidly devouring the latter, he had defied the author's Polish nationalist partisanship by mentally siding with the Teutonic Knights, since he was instinctively supportive of a military religious order and, more particularly, because he remembered that his cousin Nicholas, who represented in his eyes the epitome of chivalry, was a Knight of the Teutonic Order and the famous regiment in which he had served – the *Hoch- und Deutschmeister* – had been founded by its Grand Master. Philip was accustomed to resisting the authorial bias of historical fiction, since it so often demonized the Catholic Spaniards or French, with whom he was in sympathy, in favour of the Protestant English. Such issues did not arise in connexion with the novel he was currently reading, at Barrington's suggestion: *War and Peace*. Barrington's saving grace was that, while indulging a precocious taste in reading, he also continued to enjoy lightweight literature. Recently he had converted Philip to the adventure stories of Dornford Yates, though he had met with some initial resistance.

'I don't like stories with motor cars, set in modern times.'

'This is different.' Barrington exuded missionary zeal. 'Start with this one – *Blood Royal* – it's his latest and just like Anthony Hope, in spite of the motor cars.'

Philip received a letter from his father, informing him of a slight change in the Kinsella family fortunes.

'*You may be unsurprised to learn that the Bank has collapsed as a consequence of the American "Crash" last year, which appears to have had worldwide repercussions. There is no need to be unduly concerned: the Bank had become very much a secondary – and rather meagre – source of income in recent times, while the considerable sums it had supplied in the past were mostly unadventurously, but safely, invested. So, there has been no dramatic slump in our fortunes – unlike those of many people we know, I am sorry to say.*

'*On the other hand, any loss of income these days is a blow. I am concerned about how the depression may affect the prices people are willing to pay for horses over the next year or two – not to mention farming income. Therefore I shall be forced to engage in some serious retrenchment, as it would be fatal to dip into capital. I must keep all the indoor servants; they are already at the bare minimum necessary to run the house – indeed, they would be inadequate were it not for the indefatigable Bridie. The outdoor staff are a different matter. I am resolved to let* some of the hangers-on around Slattery go, they seldom do a hand's turn about the place.

'Please don't be concerned about your own situation. There is no problem about you and Dominick continuing at school and going on to university. It is rather a blessing that Edmund is in the novitiate, which saves expense. If he stays the course and becomes a Jesuit, he will not be able to inherit. At some stage, I shall have to have a word with Dominick about that, as he is next in line, but please don't say anything to him just now. It may never happen and I have no idea whether he would regard coming into Lissanore as a privilege or a burden. There is certainly no need to trouble him with such matters at present, so I rely on your discretion, Philip.

'This financial setback makes Mattie's future even more of a headache, but I am determined to do the right thing by her. A cousin of ours in England is bringing out a daughter of her own next season, so I might be able to arrange for her to give a joint dance for Ursula and Mattie, or something like that. It's a pity Bunty Ardgroom brought out Violet several years ago and she won't have another girl on the stocks for a while yet, otherwise I am sure we could have come to an arrangement. Anyway, sorry to burden you with my problems, old man, which I shall now desist from doing any further.

'Very well done about your promotion in the Corps...'

His father's letter provoked conflicting emotions in Philip. Despite the reassuring remarks about the limited nature of the damage caused to the family income, he was confronted for the first time with the possibility of financial insecurity. It would be dreadful to be poor, perhaps even to lose Lissanore – a thought beyond nightmare.

Then there was the question of who would eventually inherit the estate. As soon as Edmund had announced his intention of becoming a Jesuit, Philip had grasped its significance as effectively disinheriting his eldest brother with quiet satisfaction, since the thought of him as master of Lissanore was disquieting. On the other hand, he knew Dominick had a frivolous nature unsuited to the management of an estate; it would be terrible if irresponsible behaviour on his part brought about its ruin, as had happened in many Irish families with unstable heirs. With a pang, Philip acknowledged that he, as the youngest son, had no chance of ever owning the home he loved so much; he thought that was rather a pity, since he would gladly have devoted his life to it and was confident he would have improved its fortunes. He dismissed this envious thought and told himself that, if the situation arose, he would help Dominick to the best of his ability.

More encouragingly, Philip thought he detected a renewed energy in his father's letter, as if the challenge of preserving his heritage and passing on a decent patrimony to his children, in adverse circumstances, had aroused him from the apathy of bereavement. The most gratifying impression this letter left was of the extent to which his father now confided in him, despite his junior position among his siblings. Philip attributed this partly to the bond of sympathy forged between them from the time of his mother's death, partly to his own increasing maturity with the passing of time, a process he now recognized as both insidious and remorseless.

CHAPTER XX

ONE of the distinctions accompanying promotion to Middle Line Playroom was that on Sundays, when weekday dress of tweed coat and grey trousers gave place to formal attire, instead of the juvenile Eton collar and short 'bum-freezer' jacket prescribed for Lower Line classes, a black 'Marlborough' coat, waistcoat and striped trousers were the order of the day. One of the disadvantages was that this new seniority brought the Barringtons into more frequent contact with Father de la Pole, the acidulous Jesuit who now taught them Latin. Father de la Pole regarded the education of the young male animal as a contest for survival between master and pupils: he had seen too many of his less robust colleagues succumb to nervous collapse to entertain any illusions. Insofar as he acknowledged any mentor in educational theory, it was Clausewitz.

He enjoyed subjecting his pupils to a recitation of the banal, nursery-style rhymes set out in their Latin grammar to help them memorize vocabulary and rules of gender. Today he led them ironically in intoning:

'As masculine count *mons*, a mount,
With *pons*, a bridge, and *fons*, a fount...'

What rather defeated this exercise in ritual humiliation was the gusto and self-parody with which the class had embraced the childish routine. Philip acknowledged that some of these rhymes were actually quite useful, as he had discovered when struggling through Latin prose compositions. So long as one understood their context, that was; but if one had forgotten the point being conveyed, they became totally mystifying. One couplet that haunted him, but whose meaning now eluded him, ran:

'He who *panis, piscis* spurneth
Soon to *cinis, pulvis* turneth.'

What on earth was that all about?

Father de la Pole, tiring of this juvenile diversion, produced another textbook and beamed down his beak-like nose at his wary charges, with the air of one announcing a coveted treat.

'Today we embark upon a new adventure. We are about to refresh ourselves with an unfamiliar text by the great Tully.'

He held up a copy of *In Catilinam*, which had been issued to the boys at the start of term.

'Oh no, Cicero again,' Leigh mouthed at Pontifex in dismay.

'Leigh.' Father de la Pole's vigilant eye had detected this exchange. His voice assumed a solicitous tone. 'Is this text not to your taste?'

'No, Father – I mean yes, Father... It's just that I thought you said we were going to read someone else.'

'Tully, do you mean?'

'Yes, Father – that's the name you said.'

'Tully is the demotic nomenclature for Marcus *Tullius* Cicero, Leigh. They are one and the same person.'

'Thank you, Father. I shall remember that in future.'

'Indeed you will, Leigh, since the fact will be indelibly imprinted on your memory by recording it one hundred times.'

'But, Father –'

'Quite right, Leigh.' Father de la Pole's eyes twinkled with paternal benevolence. 'You were about to represent to me that one hundred reiterations of the information might be inadequate to impress it upon your notoriously fragile memory. The point is well taken. You will write it out five hundred times.'

Father de la Pole turned to the first page and began to read aloud theatrically in his fruity voice, the exaggerated diminuendos and crescendoes aggravating the uncompromisingly English pronunciation that had made his countrymen's Latin incomprehensible to their brother prelates at the Vatican Council.

' "*Quo usque tandem abutere, Catilina, patientia nostra?*" '

With a sudden shock of *déjà-vu*, this phrase transported Philip back to the drawing room at Lissanore before Sunday luncheon some years previously, when Mr Blackwell the rector had recited that line of Cicero during a conversation about the Classics with his fellow clerics. A few months later, Mr Blackwell had committed suicide. Another death, much closer to Philip, had occurred since then, blunting the impact of the rector's suicide; but it remained a distressing memory. Automatically, Philip said a quick prayer for the repose of Mr Blackwell's soul, before being brought back to the present by the voice of Father de la Pole.

'Barrington, construe.'

Barrington's technique when confronted with Latin 'unseen' translation was to draw upon his formidable vocabulary to confect English renditions so opaque as to obscure whether or not he had correctly interpreted the text. It had successfully baffled some masters. It did not deceive Father de la Pole.

' "For how much longer, Catiline," ' Barrington began, with well-assumed confidence, ' "will you try our patience?" '

Father de la Pole's patience was that of the hunter who waits for his quarry to falter; he steepled his fingers and listened impassively.

' "How long will that frenzied – er – turbulence yet pertinaciously evade us," ' Barrington continued, ' "by arrogantly casting up affronts for its own meretricious ends…" '

'Beautiful,' said Father de la Pole soulfully. 'For the moment, however, I have a fancy to hear the opening lines of Cicero's *In Catilinam* construed. Pray indulge me, Barrington.'

'Yes, Father – er – "To what end do you cast audacity to the winds?" ' raved Barrington.

'To what end, indeed?' Father de la Pole sighed. 'Barrington, how might you respond to a critic who denounced you as an exponent of the armchair construe – a linguistic *flâneur*?'

Barrington was nettled, but glad that the conversation had taken a turn that relieved him of the necessity to struggle with Latin translation and offered an opportunity to parade his command of English instead. Recently, like an addict progressing to a stronger narcotic, he had taken to supplementing his reading with sessions of browsing through dictionaries. Perversely, the resultant expansion of his vocabulary had diminished his powers of communication. Now he said:

'I should sedulously repudiate any such opprobrious objurgation.'

With a disciplinarian's instinctive reflex, Father de la Pole reached inside his soutane to where the booklet of printed bills for awarding strokes of the ferulae – similar to a chequebook – nestled. He stared penetratingly into Barrington's face; but his practised eye told him that what he encountered there was pedantry, not impertinence, so that his hand emerged empty.

'Do you always employ such sesquipedalian language?' he asked caustically.

'Only sometimes, Father,' said Barrington modestly, his interest aroused by this unfamiliar adjective.

'I withdraw the term "*flâneur*", Barrington.' Father de la Pole's voice had assumed a dangerous silkiness. 'I think I might more appropriately describe you, in the terminology Mr Disraeli applied to Mr Gladstone, as "a sophistical rhetorician, inebriated with the exuberance of his own verbosity".'

This sally reduced the whole class to laughter, at seeing Barrington trumped in rococo vocabulary. Father de la Pole, having scored so palpable a hit, adroitly moved on to a new target.

'Kinsella, construe please.'

This was bad luck: Philip calculated that the class had only five more minutes to run, but that would be long enough for the abrasive Jesuit to demolish his efforts at translation.

'"How much longer, Catiline –"' he began apprehensively.

At that moment, a stifled shriek from the back of the class betrayed that an unknown assailant had stabbed Pontifex in a fleshy part of his anatomy with a mathematical compass. Joyously, Father de la Pole reached for his bill-book. The threat of Cicero receded.

The cycle of the school year, repetitive but incorporating subtle changes in each revolution, continued. For most of the time it seemed to progress at snail's pace; at moments, though – such as the end of each term – it appeared to have passed at lightning speed. Despite its rigorous disciplinary system, which could be accommodated or circumvented depending on individual temperament, the college was a happy school. There were few others in England that could boast such splendid surroundings and this idyllic environment contributed to the atmosphere of wellbeing. There was also a feeling of intimacy, due to the relatively small number on the school roll. Daily Mass, spiritual retreats, wrestling with intractable academic subjects, an eclectic variety of sporting events, Sodality meetings, the frequent plays and entertainments staged by boys of all age groups – such was the kaleidoscope of school life that marked the rotation of the calendar.

Certain occasions stood out. Among these Philip included the Requiem Mass celebrated at the War Memorial and that other *alfresco* liturgical event, the procession to the Corpus Christi oak on the eponymous feast day, which was unfailingly sunny, and the Mass celebrated in its shade. This ancient, gnarled tree (a massive bough had recently collapsed with the resonance of an earthquake) in the school grounds was rumoured to be seven hundred years old. It made Philip think of the cluster of three oaks on a hillock near his home, where the two flanking trees were known respectively as the Good and the Bad Thief. At Benediction in the chapel on the Feast of Corpus Christi the O.T.C. paraded as an honour guard for the Blessed Sacrament, stamping their boots on the church floor with a deafening noise. Even that could not compete with the volume the music master generated from the organ at the end of High Mass and similar ceremonies.

'Ye gods and little fishes!' Leigh voiced his admiration after one such *tour de force.* 'Clayton threw up a real barrage today – I thought the roof would fall in.'

Military metaphor was much in vogue among the Barringtons when they were wearing their khaki uniforms. None of them, however, showed the same dedication as Philip, whose promotion in the Corps now outstripped all his friends. His service in the O.T.C., coupled with his shooting, had become the one non-academic milieu in which he distinguished himself. The highlight of the year for him was Speech Day when, after the parents' luncheon, the Corps paraded for Trooping the Colour – the college was very proud of having a proper colour. Philip was particularly gratified that his father had promised to come to Speech Day that year, to mark Dominick's departure from school (as he had also done previously in tribute to Edmund), and watch him on parade. At the same time, he kept up his fencing and rode whenever he could. Like all his schoolfellows he led a crowded life, his days filled with activity. He made his maiden speech in the Debating Society, as the Hon. Member for Clontarf, in support of the motion that 'In the opinion of this House, science is not the key to true progress'; after which, in the authentic style of the parliament on which the society was modelled, he rarely contributed again to its proceedings. Academically, without gaining particular distinction, he passed the School Certificate and was safely on course for the Elysian Fields of Higher Line and admission to Rhetoric, the privileged senior class in the school which was the prelude to going up to university.

As such adult prospects began to loom, however remotely, Philip and his friends became depressingly conscious of a process of maturation that had crept over them, which they were powerless to reverse. Life had become staid, at least in comparison to their unruly conduct during their time in Third Playroom. Not so very long ago, they had participated in hair-raising battles with powerful air pistols smuggled into school, turning the Beeches into a war zone. Philip had taken part with deep reluctance, as a matter of honour since the other Barringtons were engaged; but he had found himself assailed by the same misgivings that had once inhibited his performance in the hunting field. Why risk the loss of an eye, with all the disadvantages he would suffer for the rest of his life, for no good cause? Yet he felt confident he would have no qualms about risking his life in a real war, with some purpose to it. Philip's training in the O.T.C. had now taught him a proper respect for firearms, which were issued from the armoury in the Ambulacrum with all due precaution, under the supervision of the R.S.M., who was the effective power in the Corps rather than the nominal commanding officer. During the battles in the woods, Philip had taken advantage of his early shooting skills to fend off attackers, while being careful not to inflict injury.

Already such adventures seemed to belong to the distant past. Like pensioned-off Napoleonic *grognards* reliving their campaigns, the Barringtons were reduced to reminiscing about their more youthful indiscretions and, above all – the epic victory to which they always returned – the duping of Parker and Cardwell. Both their victims had by now left school, ignorant to the end of how they had been manipulated.

'Cardwell barred Parker utterly, right up to the day he left.' Barrington recalled this triumph with satisfaction.

'Parker was awfully sick.' Leigh nodded agreement. 'Before that, Cardwell was one of the few men who would have anything to do with him. Parker was a real worm.'

'He really made the most complete ass of himself,' said Pontifex.

'At least he didn't get himself sacked,' Philip put Parker's situation into perspective, 'which he certainly deserved to do.'

'I felt a bit sorry for him,' said Manley.

'Aha,' Leigh saw his chance to bait Manley, 'still feeling the pangs of thwarted passion, are we? Still carrying a torch –'

He was cut short by Manley's attack, as the two of them closed in an old-style mill such as had once been commonplace among them, but was now becoming rare.

'All the same,' Barrington said nostalgically, after order had been restored, 'it was our best rag ever.'

Philip's father was not his only visitor. Uncle Dermod, who was staying in London for a few days, called at the school by appointment one Saturday afternoon and secured permission to take not only Philip out to tea, but also Barrington, whom he regarded as a sympathetic spirit, having enjoyed their conversations during his visit to Lissanore. Uncle Dermod was in a state of some excitement over the recent fall of the monarchy in Spain, which he did not in the least deplore, as Philip had expected, but saw as an opportunity for the Carlists to rise, overthrow the ramshackle Republic and place the rightful king on the throne of Saint Ferdinand. The Carlists, he said, always gained in strength under a republic, since Spanish republics were invariably run by Freemasons and so Catholic Spaniards gravitated in self-defence to the militant traditionalists.

'Did you know,' he told the two boys, 'that the Carlist claimant,

Don Jaime, is an old boy of the college? He was here a bit before my time. There is a Murillo somewhere in the school – *The Espousals of Saint Catherine* – which was presented by his mother, the Duchess of Madrid. She, of course, was the famous Doña Margarita, the consort of Carlos VII. She also gave us a set of vestments, though I could never discover which ones they were; but the very handsome cameoed chalice you may have seen used at Mass was a gift from Don Carlos himself.'

Philip paused in the mastication of a chocolate éclair, startled by this information. It gratified him to know that the son of the prince for whom his grandfather had fought had attended the same school as himself, had sat in the same classrooms and, no doubt, had also endured punishment with ferulae. What puzzled him was why Uncle Dermod had not told him this before. He asked him.

'Er – I'm really not sure. It must have slipped my mind. There were always quite a few Spaniards in the school in my day, usually dukes. At one time there were seven of our old boys in the Spanish cabinet. That's why the school has always taught Spanish; though, come to think of it, that is surely the last language Spanish boys would need to learn. I suppose it worked in reverse for them, having a Spanish master on hand to teach them good English. Are you keeping up your Spanish? You used to be very keen.'

'Oh, yes. I have classes every other day with Señor Flores, though we spend most of the time now just having conversations, to improve my accent and vocabulary.'

'Excellent idea. Who knows – perhaps one day there will be another Carlist war and you will be able to go and fight in it, like your grandfather.'

'I say, sir,' asked Barrington, turning the conversation to a more immediate topic, 'would you mind if I had another of these éclairs? They're absolutely scrumptious.'

'Of course, my boy, that's what they are there for – go ahead.'

The political upheaval in Spain turned out to affect Philip sooner than Uncle Dermod had surmised. A Spanish boy arrived at the school and was immediately enlisted by Señor Flores as a conversational partner for Philip. The rationale was that this would also help the newcomer to improve his English which, though accented, was already impressively fluent. Despite Uncle Dermod's recollection of the college replete with youthful Spanish grandees, that nationality had lately been unrepresented on the school roll until the arrival of Agustín de Portocarrero, who was a year older than Philip but had been relegated to a class slightly below his age group, to compensate for any difficulty he might have in assimilating academic subjects through the medium of English. He explained that his father, a landowner and monarchist, had sent him abroad because he did not wish him to grow up in a republic or to be exposed to the dangers which the inflammatory political situation now threatened.

'Is it really so bad?' asked Philip.

'The Masons and Anarchists are in control now. In Madrid they have burned many churches.'

Philip was shocked to the core at the thought of churches set on fire, especially in Catholic Spain. It sounded depressingly similar to the persecution of the Church in Mexico, which the Jesuits had reported in apocalyptic terms over the past few years, with priests martyred for their faith, including Father Pro, a member of the Society.

'That's dreadful, Agustín.' He and the Spanish boy sometimes used each other's Christian names in private, contrary to the conventions of school life. A sudden, alarmed thought struck Philip.

'Do you know a Spanish lady called the Duquesa de Saladavieja?'

'No, I don't think so.' Agustín shook his head. 'Perhaps my parents would know her, but I have not heard them mention her name. Why do you ask?'

'Oh, it's just that she visited us at home a few years ago and I wondered if she was all right.' It was her daughter Constanza, however, that he was concerned about.

'I think if they had harmed a *duquesa* we should have heard about it.'

'Of course, she may not be in Spain at all. She travels a lot, so I don't think she would stay there, now it is a republic. She always goes somewhere else when she is bored, which I think is quite often.'

'I do not think, whatever its other disadvantages, that she would find Spain boring today,' said Agustín, with the quiet irony that characterized his conversation.

Philip's burgeoning friendship with Agustín de Portocarrero did not conflict with his loyalty to Barrington and his associates, nor were they at all disapproving. The Barrington set, despite its close-knit character, had always been aware of the isolation and eventual unpopularity it would incur if it were seen as an exclusive clique. So, from the outset, the individual members each had friends, or at least close acquaintances, outside the group, to whom they were drawn by shared interests. Philip had become friendly with several men he had met in the Corps, a comradeship strengthened by the communal experience of what was often the shambles of Field Days and by attendance at camp. Neither this nor the parallel intimacies the other Barringtons had formed with outsiders had weakened the bonds that united them in what they confidently assumed would be a lifelong friendship. At the same time, the nature of their association had subtly changed. Although they saw as much of one another as before, they tended now to meet in twos or threes, as divergent timetables and activities made it difficult to convene in the plenary sessions that had been a daily occurrence in their early years at school. Within this looser framework, the Spanish boy soon became acknowledged as an associate member of the Barrington set.

Portocarrero, without resembling a caricature Spaniard, had sleek black hair and a slightly olive complexion. Occasionally he afforded Philip an insight into the problems of assimilation into English language and culture that even someone from his sophisticated background inevitably encountered. One day, Philip was inveighing against the difficulties presented by Greek, which had replaced mathematics as his bugbear subject.

'All those wine-dark seas and cow-eyed goddesses – what a repetitive bore. As for the English cribs, they're almost harder to understand than the Greek and Latin. Why do they call a sword a "brand"? What's the point?'

'You are not the only one to find some English words difficult.' Agustín smiled. 'When I was staying with an English family, before I came here, the lady's brother wrote to her about his farm in Africa and she showed me his letter. He said the soil was quite fertile, but added: "*It is tough to plough, though.*" I tried to speak that sentence out loud several times, but I could not get it right.'

'Why not?' Philip was puzzled. 'It's a very simple sentence.'

'Perhaps if I write it down you will see.'

He wrote it down. Philip saw.

Philip spent the summer holidays preceding his last year at school at Lissanore. Barrington had long since reciprocated his hospitality, having him to stay for two weeks at the sprawling, comfortable house where he lived in Lincolnshire with a relaxed, pipe-smoking father, a placid mother who in temperament reminded Philip of Mrs Dixon, and three sisters – older and younger – who mockingly refused to treat their brother with the deference he believed his genius deserved. This summer the Barrington clan was on holiday in the south of France and Philip's other school friends were similarly dispersed to the four points of the compass. Maria Theresia was also in France, visiting a friend from convent days, and Dominick was in the Dolomites with some cronies from Oxford, where he had miraculously completed his first year without being sent down, though it had been a close-run thing. Edmund, however, was in residence, since his attempt to become a Jesuit had finally proved unsuccessful.

'It was always a rocky relationship with the Society,' Count Kinsella told Philip. 'I don't think I am being disloyal in saying that Edmund has never been the easiest person to get on with and a Jesuit vocation is one of the most demanding in the Church. I was frankly amazed when he completed the two years' novitiate. Then he was sent as a scholastic to Liverpool and, almost immediately, things fell apart. He left, as you know, two weeks ago. He has not abandoned the notion of becoming a priest, though. Again without wishing to be uncharitable, I cannot make out whether he is driven by a genuine vocation or is simply determined to have his own way. He was never a boy who could take "no" for an answer. He has been pestering the Bishop ever since he came home, with a view to entering an Irish seminary. Of course, if he were accepted and became a secular priest, with no vow of poverty, that would not prevent him from inheriting the estate; but it would create a difficult situation.'

Count Kinsella maintained a carefully neutral tone, but Philip suspected he was privately dismayed at the renewed prospect of Edmund succeeding him at Lissanore. His brother's presence in the house did not intrude upon Philip's enjoyment of the holidays, since Edmund appeared only at mealtimes, when he seemed preoccupied, and was frequently absent on visits to influential clergy whom he hoped to enlist in his cause. He knew only too well that the cruel label of 'spoiled priest' already attached to him throughout the county. Philip entertained himself by going for companionable hacks with

Dee-Dee, now eleven years old and a vivacious conversationalist, who had inherited the faithful Pegasus. He spent most of the second half of the holidays in the company of Tom Dixon when he returned from three weeks spent with his family at the seaside. Their activities consisted largely of fishing, since Uncle Arthur's proselytizing zeal had borne fruit and implanted a love of this sport in Tom, whose father was also an 'afishionado', as Count Kinsella, indulging his notorious weakness for puns, termed it.

A few days before Philip was due to return to school a visitor arrived unannounced at Lissanore one afternoon. His conveyance was a lorry stacked high with turf and he beckoned the driver to follow him into the hall of the castle, where he was received by Corristeen with affectionate recognition. The newcomer was of stocky build, with a dark beard already flecked with grey that made him look around fifty years of age, though he was a decade younger. His voice was rich and hearty, exuding a zest for life, as did every aspect of his personality.

'Corristeen, my old friend! How is the arthritis? Ah, I'm sorry to hear that… Count Dermod,' he greeted the figure descending the staircase with a welcoming smile, 'I am glad to see you again, scholar and gentleman that you are. This is my good friend Mr Tobin.' He introduced the driver of the turf lorry, who clasped his hat in his hands and gave a shy smile. 'I met Mr Tobin when we were both restoring our inner man at a hostelry in Kilkenny and he very kindly agreed to drive me here, though it was somewhat out of his way… Eanna, my good friend…' he hailed a second Kinsella brother who appeared, attracted by the commotion.

'I am delighted to see you, Shane,' said Dermod Kinsella, shaking the visitor's hand. 'Philip,' he called to his nephew, who entered the house at that moment, after eyeing in some mystification the lorry laden with turf on the sweep before the front door, 'come and meet our very welcome guest. This is The O'Shaughnessy – my nephew Philip.'

'It is an honour to meet yet another scion of so noble a race.' The O'Shaughnessy pumped Philip's hand vigorously.'I enjoyed your article, Dermod, on the nobility of San Marino. A very good friend of mine is a duke in the peerage of the Republic – not so anomalous a concept as might be thought, considering such ancient republics as Venice and Genoa had distinguished aristocracies. Speaking of dukedoms, however, I took issue with your comments elsewhere on the Duc de Clancarthy-Blarney, since I would dispute that the title is as questionable as you seem to assume...'

Dermod shepherded the guests into the morning room, where Corristeen supervised the serving of tea. Count Kinsella joined them and, while The O'Shaughnessy declaimed at breakneck speed on a bewildering assortment of subjects, made quiet conversation with Tobin, the lorry driver, whose natural good breeding put him at ease in these unaccustomed surroundings. He was more overcome by the personality of O'Shaughnessy, who had commandeered him as transport only two hours previously. When the talk turned to the recent Eucharistic Congress in Dublin, Tobin found himself on common ground with the rest of the company, all of whom, with the exception of Philip (absent at school), had attended the ceremonies.

'That was a very exotic seventeenth-century costume I saw you wearing, in attendance on the Papal Legate,' The O'Shaughnessy said to Dermod Kinsella, not without a hint of envy.

'Sixteenth-century.' Dermod recoiled from the imputation of modernity.'I have the honour to be a Privy Chamberlain Supernumerary of the Sword and Cape to His Holiness.'

This aggravated O'Shaughnessy's disgruntlement, so that his voice betrayed an undertone of asperity.

'"Supernumerary" sounds unfortunately like "superfluous" – to the untutored ear, I mean of course. Did that chain and plaque hung round your neck not make you feel rather like a sommelier?' He gave a slightly forced laugh, to soften the gibe.

'The service of the Holy Father always makes me feel edified.' Dermod deflected the taunt with a baleful smile that indicated retribution would be exacted for this attempt at iconoclasm, whenever the opportunity might present itself.

When they rose from the tea table Count Kinsella escorted the driver to his lorry, shook hands, then watched in some concern while O'Shaughnessy and Corristeen shouted contradictory directions, waving their arms like windmills, as he struggled to turn his heavy vehicle on the gravel sweep. O'Shaughnessy, who had an open invitation to stay at Lissanore whenever he wished, retired to his room and occupied himself in writing letters. When he came downstairs to join Dermod, Eanna and Philip in a short game of croquet before dinner, he placed the results of his labours on the silver salver in the hall where letters were deposited for the outgoing post. Philip covertly inspected the envelopes and discovered that two were directed to obviously humble addresses, one to a professor at Trinity, another to a French nobleman and the last to a cardinal in Rome.

Uncle Ulick joined the party for dinner, during which Corristeen made much of The O'Shaughnessy, who stood high in his esteem. The guest, who had felt a trifle piqued at being defeated at croquet, recovered his spirits as he launched into a discourse on an eclectic variety of topics. Eanna greatly respected him for his wealth of knowledge regarding Celtic history and genealogy. Dermod was similarly engaged by his conversation, though he sometimes detected solecisms among the opinions he expressed with such unbounded confidence. Count Kinsella enjoyed O'Shaughnessy for his entertainment value, though he felt some of his scandalous revelations about the private histories of great families were close to the knuckle for Philip's ears. It was impossible, in any case, to interpose any prudish restraint, faced by the irresistible tide of anecdote and reminiscence that flooded from O'Shaughnessy in full spate.

'...My good friend, the foreign minister of Paraguay, very kindly appointed me Consul for Ireland, though I have never received documentary confirmation, possibly because the appointment was made in a bar in Asunción at an advanced hour of the night. I also suspect he may have been removed from office shortly afterwards.'

'Are you a clan chief?' Philip asked during a momentary lull.

'I have the honour to claim the style and title of The O'Shaughnessy, lord of Kinelee, in Connaught, to which, according to an oral tradition long preserved in my branch of the family, belongs the privilege of bearing the great ceremonial cup of O'Connor Roe at his inauguration as King of Connaught. Some modern scholars have suggested the vessel was in fact a chamber pot, but that is surely incompatible with the ritual of quaffing the contents in one gulp, incumbent on the new ruler – unless it reflects the survival of some extravagant pagan rite. In the last century, the chief of our name exercised the profession of barber in Galway town, but that in no way detracts from our ancient nobility. I am sorry to say, however, I have received no encouragement in establishing my claim from Sir Nevile Wilkinson.'

That struck an immediate chord with Dermod Kinsella, to whom the reigning Ulster King of Arms was a pet aversion. He intervened with some invective of his own relating to Wilkinson's treatment of foreign title-holders in Ireland, but this proved to be only a temporary stemming of the exuberance of O'Shaughnessy's monologue, which grew ever more arcane and wide-ranging.

'Baroness Burdett-Coutts, who was rumoured to harbour self-generated lice...'

Ulick Kinsella, who had been sunk in a lethargy, mesmerized

by the flow of talk, sat bolt upright at this revelation of a hitherto unsuspected health hazard. There was more disturbing information to come.

'One can only marvel at the vagaries of Mother Nature,' observed O'Shaughnessy. 'I recently attended a dining club to which I belong, whimsically named the Select Vestry of Ballymacelligot. It has remote antecedents in a Hell Fire Club of the same name, founded in the eighteenth century by one of the MacElligotts. The death of a family member is signalled by the ghostly apparition of a two-headed dog; but a more rarefied hereditary peculiarity is that the men are frequently born with an irregular number of testes –'

Count Kinsella cast an anxious glance in the direction of the sideboard, but both the housemaids had fortuitously retired to the kitchen to fetch the next course. Corristeen, however, who had just re-entered the dining room, was listening with rapt attention to this instructive conversation.

'– Sometimes exhibiting monorchism, meaning a solitary gonad, in other cases polyorchism, a cluster of three. Nature always compensates, though that might be regarded as scant consolation by the under-endowed –'

'Ah, sir!' Corristeen, who had understood the import of what was said, but not its context, due to his temporary absence from the room, and imagined the speaker was still discoursing on the noble house of O'Shaughnessy, laid a commiserating hand on the guest's shoulder and refilled his glass. 'Sure, there's no stigmata attached to it.'

Count Kinsella dropped his napkin and bent beneath the table to retrieve it, an operation that took longer than might have been thought necessary. Dermod hastily raised his glass to his lips and buried his face in it. O'Shaughnessy, vaguely conscious of some misunderstanding, but more immediately diverted by Corristeen's characteristic malapropism, said dryly:

'I am very relieved to hear it.'

Though momentarily disconcerted, his volubility quickly reasserted itself. Dermod Kinsella's frustration was mounting: he seldom encountered anybody who shared so many of his interests as O'Shaughnessy, albeit in a rather undisciplined style; but what use was that, if he was not permitted to contribute to the conversation on equal terms?

'The credit for restoring O'Neill power over Tyrone in the 1170s,' O'Shaughnessy was now saying, 'belongs to Hugh IX, known as *Toinleasc* – "the Lazy-Arsed Youth" – an ironic nickname reflecting his frantic activity. The Irish language has always been more outspoken than English: the town of Tanderagee in Armagh is *Tóin re Gaoith*, meaning "Arse to the Wind". The root, of course, is Indo-European *"orse"*, meaning buttocks...'

Philip smiled to himself at the involuntary recollection of Pontifex, stabbed in the Indo-European *orse* with a mathematical compass. The verbal tempest rolled on.

'Sir Boyle Roche, father of the Irish "bull", famously asked: "Why should we put ourselves out for posterity, for what has posterity ever done for us?" He, incidentally, though a staunch Protestant and Unionist, was the fourth and last Viscount Cahiravahilla in the Jacobite nobility, created by James II after he had lost the English throne...'

'Yes,' interposed Uncle Dermod insistently, 'the Marquis de Ruvigny records the creation in his *Jacobite Peerage*.'

'The Marquis de Ruvigny,' responded O'Shaughnessy, 'was himself Earl of Galway in the Jacobite peerage, the title bestowed on his ancestor –'

'I think not.' Dermod Kinsella, wearing a wintry smile, halted him in mid-flow. 'So far from being a Jacobite title, the earldom of Galway was conferred on the seventeenth-century Ruvigny by Dutch William, for his military service.'

Dermod's smile broadened in satisfaction: O'Shaughnessy's earlier affront to the dignity of the office of Privy Chamberlain of the Sword and Cape had been suitably punished.

'That's right.' Not for nothing was Philip his uncle's pupil in matters historical and genealogical. Now he came robustly to his support. 'Ruvigny fought against us at Aughrim and later became the Williamite commander in Ireland. I remember reading about it.'

The O'Shaughnessy stared with disfavour at his detractors. He had just recalled that he attributed his defeat at croquet to some suspected sharp practice by his opponents at the fifth hoop; it happened that those opponents had been Dermod and Philip. He took a bitter draught of claret and found himself forced to concede defeat.

'Ye're very well-informed,' he said sourly, and sulked for the remainder of the meal.

CHAPTER XXI

'IT FOLLOWS in *The Practice of Perfection and Christian Virtues*, by Father Alphonsus Rodriguez, of the Society of Jesus...' intoned Philip; then he began, with painstaking care, to read aloud the passage marked in the book on the lectern in front of him. He had taken the precaution of familiarizing himself with the text in advance, to avoid any pitfalls of pronunciation. Reading aloud to the Js during their community luncheon was one of the few relatively menial tasks required of boys who had got their remove to the giddy heights of the Rhetoric class. The passage he had read before the exhortations to Christian perfection of Father Rodriguez had dismayed him, since it used the metaphor of the bridal bed to illustrate some theological point, so that he had felt his ears turning slightly red. The Jesuits, however, had seemed oblivious to any *risqué* implications and, indeed, to his presence; the robust rattle of cutlery betrayed their preoccupation with more material concerns. Philip began to feel that a reversal of roles had taken place, with him struggling to engage the interest of an indifferent audience, just as his Jesuit instructors had so often done with him and his classmates.

The third and final text, chosen to provide lighter subject matter, was the biography of a saint. Philip had not troubled to peruse it in advance, so when its saintly protagonist was recorded as complaining about the smell of the lavatories in his religious house, the ripple of laughter this provoked took him by surprise; it also betrayed that the Js had been paying more attention than he had realized. It was a relief when the Rector signalled an end to the reading. Philip closed the book, bowed to Father Rector and left the refectory, suddenly conscious he had not yet eaten.

'A very competent performance,' Father de la Pole complimented him later, when they met by chance. 'You read fluently and with clear articulation.'

Philip was flattered; lately he had discovered that he liked Father de la Pole, despite his acerbic manner. Now that he was in Rhetoric, a class so privileged that it sometimes breakfasted with the Rector, his relations with the priestly community had subtly grown more relaxed, though never to the point of compromising discipline. Life in Rhetoric was so enjoyable that the school year was going by at breakneck speed. Philip would have liked to slow down the passage of time, to prolong an existence that compared very favourably with the years of Latin prose, incomprehensible algebra, uncongenial games, ferulae and birchings that had gone before. Rhetoric was the antechamber to university, its atmosphere prefiguring academic life. Neither Philip nor any of the Barringtons had been promoted to one of the half-dozen captaincies that comprised the ultimate hierarchy of the school. He did not repine over this lack of preferment as his brother Edmund had done: he had no wish to birch small boys daily in the captains' room as a pre-luncheon apéritif or to burden himself with the other duties of that rank, which he was not confident would have sat easily upon him. Barrington, a stranger to self-doubt, was less reconciled to being passed over.

As things were, the routine of a man in Rhetoric was highly congenial. Classrooms and wooded walks, playrooms and dormitories that had once harboured prohibitions and pitfalls were now the feudal appanage of the seigneurial caste to which Philip and his contemporaries suddenly belonged, saluted with deference and even awe as they went on progress through their domain. On Sundays now, formal dress consisted of tailcoat (passed down from Dominick in Philip's case) and silk hat. Arrayed in this costume, Philip and his friends, setting out for Lord's to attend the annual match against the Oratory, had encountered the Rector. Sporting his idiosyncratic hat, he had stood, smiling tolerantly down from his impressive height, while Barrington subjected him to the courtier-like chaff he thought appropriate to his seniority and the approaching termination of the master-pupil relationship.

'They are rumoured to be turning out a really hot side this year, Father. Kinsella says we are bound to get licked.'

'I didn't say anything of the sort, Father.'

Manley, always so passive and retiring, had attained unexpected status by one of those fortuitous coups in the schoolboy underworld that produce decisive effects. The previous year he had been appointed to the position of thurifer on the altar staff. This had filled him, as most responsibilities did, with foreboding; for it was expected of all holders of this office that, at least once during their tenure, when processing towards the sanctuary they would swing the thurible so energetically as not only to part the hair of the youngest boys in the front row of the congregation, but also to cause the incense-filled vessel to perform a complete revolution. Not only was this a difficult feat to achieve, but since the altar servers preceded the clergy it also required the thurifer to attempt it at the precise moment he turned to enter the sanctuary, the only time when it might escape the notice of the priest bringing up the rear of the procession. Nobody had the slightest confidence that Manley could pull it off. Nevertheless, his friends loyally coached him, using an old thurible liberated from the sacristy. His performance, though gradually improving through endless repetition, was still inept by the time it came to the final Benediction at which he would officiate. It was, as Barrington said, employing a formula hardly calculated to reassure Manley, a case of do or die.

As the stately procession moved slowly from the sacristy to the sanctuary, the congregation watched apathetically, since nobody by then had any expectations that Manley would provide the longed-for entertainment. Suddenly, in one aerobatic loop, the censer soared over the heads of the 'brats' in the front row, who ducked nervously. Then, as Manley turned to face the altar, it made a perfect revolution; beyond that, it repeated the process, so that the chain became shortened as it wrapped around his hand before resuming a vertical position. In fact, Manley had lost control of the thurible, having swung it too energetically in his desperation, but as his back was to the congregation its members could not see the consternation on his face. In the eyes of the spectators it was a flawless performance – a record, too, since no one could recall a double rotation in recent years. If they had dared, they would have liked to applaud. Manley's luck extended still further since Father Sexton, at the tail-end of the procession, remained oblivious to this *coup de théâtre*. So capricious is schoolboy favour that Manley attained a level of popularity as a consequence of this incident that sustained him for the brief remainder of his days at the college.

Such pranks, in an environment where religious ritual was incidental to daily life, did not reflect a climate of irreverence or scepticism. In this final year at school and on the eve of going out into the world, Philip's faith was as strong as it had always been. Benediction was one of the services that moved him most. He loved to kneel and listen while the priest led the congregation in the Litany of Loreto, savouring the poetic fervour of that paean of praise to the Mother of God, its sonorous phrases rising heavenward with the clouds of incense, in a mounting crescendo of devotion:

> *'Mystical rose...*
> *Tower of David...*
> *Tower of ivory...*
> *House of gold...*
> *Ark of the covenant...'*

Then came the moment when the priest, his hands wrapped in the humeral veil, lifted the monstrance and held high the snowy white host at the centre of the golden sunburst glittering with precious stones, and every head bowed in adoration. It was an exaltation that could never pall, no matter how many times he experienced it.

Now he had reached the end of his schooldays and, with it, any vestigial identification with childhood. It was a strange sensation. Philip did not, at heart, feel himself to be fully emancipated: the habit of submission to discipline militated against that. Yet he recognized that, even if he was something slightly less than an adult, the change in him was absolute.

That morning the Bishop had celebrated Solemn High Mass for the Feast of Saint Ignatius, founder of the Society, and had confirmed many of the college boys. Then the sports prizes for that year had been presented in the Study Place. Throughout the proceedings Philip had been oppressed by an awareness that everything was being transacted for the last time, so far as he was concerned. Other boys would assemble here in September and the routine of the school would resume; but he would have no part in it, he would be elsewhere. At the same time he felt excitement, even exhilaration, at the prospect of going to university and discovering new horizons. Nor would he be separated from most of his friends: Barrington was going up to Oxford too, though to a different college; so was Pontifex, who was bound for the most prestigious college in the university, to Barrington's unconcealed chagrin.

'Did you know,' he had asked Philip, 'Pontifex is going up to the House?'

'What house?'

'Christ Church, of course. Dash it all, Kinsella, sometimes you are the bally limit.'

Leigh was destined for Cambridge and Manley for art school,

but they had pledged to keep in touch with the other members of the 'set' that had bound them so closely together throughout their schooldays. Agustín de Portocarrero's future, like that of his troubled country, remained uncertain. Philip had already said his farewells to his friends, at least for the duration of the summer. He found himself prowling around the school buildings and grounds, like a ghost revisiting the scenes of earthly happiness from which he was now excluded. The sensation of being an invisible revenant was reinforced by the fact that the school precincts were invaded all afternoon by the Guild of Catholic Postmen, whose members had come from London, by invitation, with their wives and families. These incongruous visitors penetrated to every part of the college and its environs, cheerfully impressed and loudly expressing Cockney appreciation of the Society of Jesus and all its works and pomps.

In the evening, Philip attended a performance in the school theatre of *The Three Musketeers*, billed as a Grand Opera and produced by some of his classmates in Rhetoric. When he had first seen the title he had thought it singularly appropriate to his final day at school, just before he set out, like his childhood hero D'Artagnan, on the great adventure of life. In the event, he was irritated by the travestied nature of the production. He knew it was absurd to take exception to a piece of light entertainment, but the consciousness of impending departure had put him out of sorts. Philip had always loathed any change in his circumstances; it was intrinsic to his nature. At the close of the performance he joined in the school hymn for the last time. His voice was brittle as he sang:

'*Eia, ergo, pueri*
Deum diligamus;
Ad majorem Domini
Gloriam vivamus...'

Then the curtain came down.

Restlessly he wandered out into the grounds. It was approaching sunset and, even for a grandee in Rhetoric, he was breaking bounds; but he thought it unlikely he would incur any sanction. Almost, it would have gratified him if he had, since it would have testified to his continuing membership of the school community. Instead, his new immunity from discipline was confirmed almost immediately when he met Father Boyle, the Prefect of Studies.

'Good evening, Father.'

'Ah, good evening, Kinsella.' Father Boyle, a classicist, was small and birdlike, with spectacles perched precariously on the end of his nose; nobody had ever seen them fall off, though such an event was eagerly anticipated by the smaller boys. He had a studious demeanour and seemed to live in a world of his own. 'I heard the school hymn coming from the theatre, from which I deduced that the performance had ended.'

'Yes, Father.' Philip spoke in a flat tone. 'The performance is over.'

'There has been frequent debate regarding the cultural respectability of so-called "Silver" Latin,' said Father Boyle. 'I fear that I could only categorize the words of the school hymn – uplifting though they may be in sentiment – as Bronze Latin. Still, there we are. It is believed to have a good influence in promoting college morale… Good night, Kinsella.'

'Good night, Father.'

The Prefect of Studies hurried on towards the school buildings, where lights were now showing in many of the windows, without appearing aware of Philip's infraction of the rules by heading very obviously in the direction of the Beeches, so late in the evening. Philip walked on, up the path where his brother Edmund had confronted him so violently five years before. Other memories crowded upon him. His school life flashed kaleidoscopically through his mind: the early terrors, waiting tremulously outside the office door, in the corridor next to the music rooms, to receive his first ferulae; afternoons on the river, where gaudily striped blazers and caps were sported; the sun shining on white flannels and worn grass, accompanied by the distinctive smack of leather on willow. Where had the time gone? It seemed only yesterday that Dominick had exclaimed, as Philip entered the school gates for the first time: 'Here we are. Back at the old coll.'

In fact, he was not due to sever all links with the school when he left the following morning, since he would be going with the Contingent to O.T.C. camp at Tweseldown. That duty was incumbent on him, in view of the high rank he had attained in the Corps, due to the departure of another boy at Easter which had resulted in Philip's promotion to Under Officer commanding the second Platoon. Earlier, he had passed his Certificate 'A' with flying colours, to his great satisfaction. Although it did not amount to a commission, he had kept re-reading the claret-coloured print which, headed by the Royal Arms, certified that Mr Philip Kinsella of the St Stanislaus' Contingent Junior Division, Officers Training Corps, had fulfilled the necessary conditions as to efficient service, and had qualified in the Infantry syllabus of examinations, as laid down in the Regulations for the Officers Training Corps. He was, therefore, eligible for consideration for a commission in the Supplementary Reserve, Territorial Army, Territorial Army Reserve of Officers or Active Militia of Canada. Philip liked the buccaneering sound of the Active Militia of Canada, whom he pictured in fur caps and fringed buckskins. More seriously, he wondered if he and his friends would ever be called upon to fight in a major war, as had been demanded of his father and his contemporaries.

When he reached the summit of the Beeches, the sun was sinking in a blaze of gold, red, purple and pink. This summer was already being called a 'heat wave', the hottest and sunniest he could remember since that glorious season at Lissanore, eight years before. Lately, he had often found himself thinking about that memorable summer, since it represented the happiest time in his childhood. He had been nine then; in a few months he would turn eighteen, so half of his life had passed since that sun-drenched mirage. Philip remembered his tender meeting with the little Spanish girl who had made him her knight; it was a romantic childhood idyll, yet also a pledge by which he still felt himself bound in some ineluctable way. He wondered where she was and whether she ever thought of him. Then his own thoughts turned to his mother.

He was brought back to the present by the deepened darkness that signalled the final setting of the sun. In the distance, the royal castle was now no more than an anonymous bulk, a looming blackness in the surrounding gloom. Philip turned and began to walk back down the path towards the school, from which the tide of life would bear him away the next morning, on whatever course God might chart for him in His cosmic atlas, the unknown future.

THE KINSELLA CHRONICLES
ARE CONTINUED IN
BOOK II:

THE CROSS OF
BURGUNDY

www.ingramcontent.com/pod-product-compliance
Ingram Content Group UK Ltd.
Pitfield, Milton Keynes, MK11 3LW, UK
UKHW050122070725
460437UK00007B/34/J